This book is dedicated to
Ava Bea Emmery
who is as daring and determined as Cass,
and as stylish as Maman,
with love from Granny.

Acknowledgments

Belmont House, where much of this book is set, is a real place. Our writers' group have had two fantastic weekends there – thank you to Karen of the Belmont Trust for making us so welcome, and to Beth, Claire, Debbie, Doug, June, Marjolein, Nat, Peter, Roger and Vaila for making it such fun.The resulting *Wastside Noir* anthology is for sale on Amazon. Thank you too to Val Turner, for giving me the opportunity to proof-read *Viking Unst* and the papers of the *17ᵗʰ Viking Congress*, and so learn so much more about Viking Shetland. Val assures me that all the sites mentioned in the book have been swept by metal detectors; the treasure hidden there is only in my imagination, so please don't go digging.

Maman wouldn't approve my singing, but I've been involved in drama for many years. The theatrical characters are *of course* not based in any way on Izzy, Barry, Bob, Debbie, Doug, Hilary, James, John, Jonathon, Margaret, Robert, Wendy or anyone else I've shared a stage with! Thank you for all the fun we've had over the years, particularly to Izzy, who encourages me to wear dresses and jewellery Maman would approve.

Thank you also to my amazing agent, Teresa Chris, for all her encouragement. Thank you to Penny Hunter, my editor, and to Rebecca, Bethan, and the design team of

Accent Press for all their hard work.

This is the first of my books to go straight to a mass-market edition. Thank you to all the local museums and shops who have supported me by selling the previous print-on-demand editions, particularly Karen Baxter and her staff at the wonderful Shetland Times Bookshop.

Guddocks is the Shetland name for riddles. Most of these – because I wanted particular answers – have been made up by me, but thank you to Beth for her help in improving them.

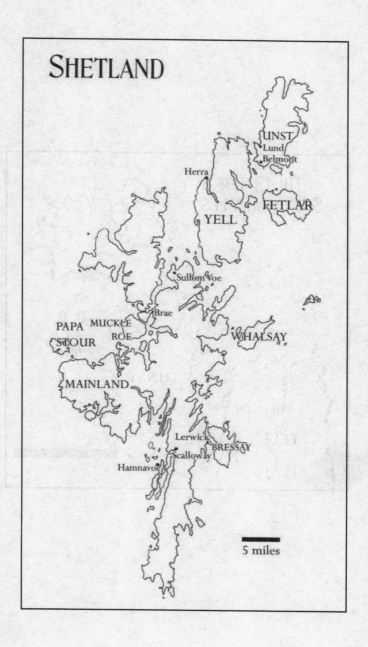

SHETLAND

UNST
Lund
Belmont

Herra

FETLAR

YELL

Sullom Voe

Brae

PAPA
STOUR

MUCKLE
ROE

WHALSAY

MAINLAND

Lerwick
BRESSAY
Scalloway

Hamnavoe

5 miles

THE OUTER
SHETLAND ISLES

Arctic Ocean

• Saxa Vord

Burrafirth
• Valsgarth   • Norwick

Atlantic
Ocean   Haroldswick

• Baliasta
Baltasound •

LUNDA WICK

UNST   North
Sea

CULLIVOE

YELL   • Bellmont

Gutcher •

5 miles

Saturday 21st and Sunday 22nd March

Hotel Château Savigny, near Poitiers

**Nearest tides at La Rochelle, fifty miles away
and not relevant to a woman in an evening gown**

A Shetland Guddock

Deep ida darkest eart' I bide
Set dere by hauns lang turned ta bane
Yet haul me up ta light and fin'
A blaze o' gold and precious stane.

Chapter One

The last clear notes died away. There was a moment's silence in the ballroom, then the applause burst out. On my right hand, Dad was grinning broadly, and you could have heard his clapping back home in Shetland. On my left, Gavin's eyes shone. Before us, Maman led her cast in a bow, twice, a third time, then they filed out. The tumult died away; around us, the ladies in evening gowns and gentlemen in white bow ties rose, murmuring appreciation, and headed for the dining room, where we'd been promised champagne and canapes.

I'd had to borrow one of Maman's dresses for this gala evening, an off-the-shoulder affair in dark green satin with enough skirt to make my *Khalida* a new spinnaker. Luckily my sailor's tan had faded over the winter, but the petticoat kept tangling around my legs, and the low neckline kept my shoulders and back as straight as any sergeant major could want. Gavin gave me an amused look as I stood up, and offered his arm. I took it gratefully, and leant on it while I kicked the layers of skirt away, eased my feet back into the heeled shoes and took an unsteady step. I supposed Victorian ladies had learned to live with this kind of thing.

'You look amazing,' Gavin said consolingly.

'Amazing is as amazing does,' I muttered. 'How

Maman ever managed to sing in this beats me.' I clutched the skirt in both hands to squeeze out between the chairs and gained the wide hall at last. A cool breeze blew in from the open doorway, and I steered Gavin towards it. The crush was heading the other way; we had the terrace to ourselves. I leaned against the wide stone lintel and took a long breath.

The hum of voices was lost behind us, replaced by the silence of the starry night and the splashing of the fountain in the centre of the courtyard. We were in the most romantic of French fairy tale châteaux, a rectangular facade of white stone, encrusted with mouldings around the square doorway and above the lines of windows. The grey roof was adorned with tall, pointed dormer windows and dunce-capped turrets, two from the towers each side of the doorway, and one on each corner. You expected to hear the hum of a spinning wheel. The flight of steps to the terrace was lit with flambeaux, and the sweep of gravel twinkled with pots of bushes entwined with fairy lights. Below the stone balustrade, the lake glinted. It was very beautiful and completely fake; an Edwardian fantasy castle now turned into a luxury hotel, with Maman and her troupe in a semi-staged version of *Hippolyte et Aricie* as the star attractions for its reopening.

For an opera, the plot was simple. Theseus (bass) had just conquered his enemies, and ordered Aricia (soprano, Maman), the last of their royal house, to be a priestess of Diana. Aricia was in love with Theseus' son, Hippolytus (tenor) – cue touching love duet in Diana's temple. As Phaedra, Theseus' second wife, started the ceremony, Aricia protested she was being dedicated against her will – appearance of Diana (soprano), to roll of piano chords, to refuse an unwilling priestess. A messenger (Theseus in a different cloak) then came to announce that

Theseus had been taken down to the Underworld, to rescue his friend (large piece of story cut, to keep it suitable for a five-person touring company). Believing him dead, Phaedra declared her love for Hippolytus, who resisted her – at which point Theseus returned. Hippolytus (being a gentleman) didn't explain what had really happened, but Phaedra's confidante, Oenone (Diana without the headdress) told him that Hippolytus had made advances to Phaedra. Theseus called down Neptune's vengeance (another piece cut). Final act: Hippolytus and Aricia had just sung another love duet in Diana's grove, when a sea monster (accompanist working overtime to make up for missing stage effects) appeared and apparently swallowed him. Aricia swooned. Phaedra reappeared, having confessed all to Theseus, and committed suicide. Theseus learned from Neptune (cut again) that Hippolytus was not really dead, but that he would never see him again, and departed with a last sorrowful aria. Diana reunited Aricia with Hippolytus. It was a happy ending, as Greeks go.

'It was odd having the older couple as the young lovers,' Gavin said. 'But as soon as your mother sang, I forgot all about her age. She even looked seventeen again.'

'Sometime I'll show you a photo of her *really* seventeen. She was gorgeous, with this ripple of hair all down her back.'

'Like yours, right now.'

Maman's dresser had taken one look at my usual plait, muttered French imprecations and brushed it out, then pinned it with little diamanté stars. I didn't dare shake my head, for fear it would all come undone.

'In fact,' Gavin said, stepping back to admire me, 'you look like you've come out of an Edwardian painting. All you need is an ostrich plume fan.'

I'd been offered a fan, and as the ballroom had heated up I'd been sorry I'd refused it. 'You look like a Victorian portrait. The Highland chieftain.'

His scarlet tartan kilt and horsehair sporran had attracted several admiring glances from ladies in the audience. He wore his black jacket, with Bonnie Prince Charlie's silver button sewn firmly opposite the top buttonhole, and the dagger in his stocking had a yellow Cairngorm stone in the handle.

'Victorian chieftains had the bonnet with the eagle's feather. I don't rank one of those. We're youngest sons of youngest sons.' He bowed, and held out his hand. 'A waltz, mademoiselle?'

'We're mad,' I said, but the combination of fairy tale castle and acres of green silk was stirring dramatic instincts I didn't realise I had. We walked down, steps matching, and waltzed round the outside of the terrace, from window-square to shadow, light, darkness, light, steps crunching on the gravel, his arm warm around my waist, my skirt swooshing as it swung. Inside the brightly lit windows, there was applause as the singers came out, and we stopped to look: Maman on Hippolyte's arm; Phaedra with Theseus; and the musical director bringing in Diana/Oenone. 'We'd better go in. Maman will be looking for me.'

His arm tightened around me. We kissed, and I felt my heart racing at the warmth of his body, with only my silk bodice and his cotton shirt between us. His breathing had quickened. 'I was wondering,' he murmured into my hair, 'if I could persuade you to come and visit me in my flat in Inverness before you head for Norway.'

'No parents.' I considered it. 'No mast.'

He held me away to look at me quizzically. 'Flats

don't generally have masts.'

I knew I was blushing. 'They sway as the boat rocks.' It was impossible to have a private sex life in a marina.

It was hard to tell in the moonlight, but I thought his cheeks were colouring too. 'It has a very comfortable rectangular bed.'

Khalida's double berth (such as it was) was in the forepeak, and V-shaped. I tried to sound matter-of-fact. 'Or we could meet up in Norway, between voyages.' In less than two weeks I was heading for the third mate/navigator berth I'd been offered aboard my favourite tall ship, the Norwegian, square-rigged *Sørlandet*. A squiggle of excitement wormed through me at the thought, and Gavin's arm tightened around me.

'You're running away to sea. I can feel you leaving, every time you think of your *Sørlandet*.'

'You wait till you see her. She's beautiful.' But he was right. Already, the land was retreating. In my head, I was standing with my hands on that metre-wide wheel, with the white sails arching, tier after tier, and the shoosh of the waves under her stern, and the shining sea-road before me.

Gavin's voice was serious. 'Don't leave me behind.' I understood what he meant; he wanted me to take him with me inside my head, to text and phone and write letters, and I knew that I wanted to, but I also knew how far away he would be, once there was nothing but the world of the ship, dwarfed by the immensity of sea and sky, once I was back in the rhythm of living aboard.

I lifted my hand to touch his cheek. 'I won't always be able to keep you in my head on board, but you'll be the first person I phone as land comes in sight. Promise.'

We kissed once more, then went back inside to the heat. 'Maman! You were wonderful.'

Maman shrugged the compliment away with one elegant shoulder. Her dark eyes, made huge by the sweep of mascara, were shining. The cast had remained in costume; she wore Aricia's white tunic, floor length, bound criss-cross over her breasts with ribbon, and decorated with a jangle of tiny gold beads: a necklace; earrings; and bracelets. Her hair was piled up above a gold fringe whose ends curved over her brow, and dangled down to her shoulders. There was something familiar about it, a black and white image tugging at my memory.

'It was a good start to our tour, and for Vincent's hotel.' She turned to the man on her other side. 'You remember Vincent Fournier, of course, from Shetland? He worked with your father in the early days at BP.'

I vaguely remembered him from my childhood: those ice-blue eyes set under heavy lids in his tanned face, and the dark hair standing up above his broad brow. He had to be in his early sixties now, a James Dean who'd lived to grow old. It was the charm that I remembered best, coming from him in waves still.

'Cass! What a pleasure to see you again. You've grown up a beauty.' His eyes ignored thebullet scar that bisected my right cheek. 'Look at these cheekbones, and your mother's lovely hair. What are you doing with yourself these days?'

He drew me over to the drinks table and gave me exactly five minutes of intense attention before making his excuses and moving to greet a film-star blonde. Out of interest, I listened.

'Julie! It's been ages. What a pleasure to see you again, and looking like a million dollars. How good of you to make time to come. What are you doing with yourself these days?'

I grimaced wryly into my champagne glass, and wondered if Maman had ever been taken in by his charm. I wasn't quite sure where I'd put him on a ship; he'd be better on shore, charming sponsors and organizing shore receptions. He seemed to be entirely at home in this opera milieu, the rich clientele his hotel was aimed at. I looked around, and was glad I had only a small yacht to maintain. The refurbishment must have cost a packet: the moulded cornice and carved fireplace had been repainted, the ceiling was hung with new-looking chandeliers in the antique style, and the windows were draped with acres of opulent red velvet held back with tasselled gold cords. The nibbles included twists of smoked salmon and dabs of caviare on puff pastry. But, I concluded, listening to him doing his spiel to a suited businessman in mirror shades, he would expect to make a profit. He wouldn't be doing it otherwise.

Gavin echoed my thoughts. 'Is he an opera enthusiast?'

I remembered I was drinking M. Fournier's champagne. 'He's been a friend of Maman's for years, from when I was growing up, so he probably is. He negotiated the Scottish venues.' I looked over at him schmoozing his clients. 'And it's wonderful publicity for his hotel.'

I tried to remember what Maman had said about how he'd organised her tour. He'd gone from Sullom Voe to be business consultant for the National Trust for Scotland – that was it – and so when Maman had talked of a tour, he'd got back to his former colleagues and persuaded them to use her company as advertisement for their stately homes. They'd shared advertising costs, with a photo of the company superimposed on the various baronial piles, and even run a TV trailer with a soundtrack of Maman singing –spending to bring in, and it had worked. The tour was a sell-out, with a waiting list for even the most remote venues, like Castle Fraser and Haddo House, each a forty-minute drive out into the wilds of Aberdeenshire, Cawdor Castle in Inverness-shire, or Broughton House, right down in the bottom left corner of Scotland, looking across the Solway at the English shore.

They'd had a bit of luck too. The promising young mezzo that Maman had suggested for Phaedra two years before, at the planning stage, had suddenly become the latest celeb singer, whose face was so plastered over the newspapers that even I recognised her. Kamilla Lange, she was called, blonde and pretty, with a round, dimpled face, huge blue eyes framed by spiky dark lashes, and a swirl of curls held back by a diamanté clip. She was constantly in motion, like a swarm of tropical fish, facing forward to gaze at the person she was talking to, then turning her head to toss a smile over her bare shoulder. Everything about her glittered like a jewel box under the chandeliers: her hair; her earrings; the sequins on the scarlet tunic that curved across her cleavage and fell in folds on her lower back. I realised now, close up, that it was one of those stage costumes with a net back and front, but from the audience it had looked daringly sexy, as if one pin pulled out would have the whole dress falling at her sandalled feet.

'Austrian,' Maman had said, 'from a village halfway between Vienna and Graz, and determined to become a star.' She'd smiled at me. 'Almost as ambitious as I was, my Cassandre, her career is her whole life.' A shrug. 'It is the way of the world these days. When I was young it was enough to sing very well. Now, these young singers, they must sing very well and be sexy on the cover of the album as well. They must party, and be seen by the papers, and tweet, and Facebook, and all these other things I am very

8

glad I escaped, because nowadays it is fame that sells tickets.' She almost managed to sound convincing. 'I just hope that the fans who have bought tickets realise that *Hippolyte et Aricie* is a serious opera.'

Even as I watched, Kamilla swept an arm through that of the young American who'd sung Theseus, and handed her phone to someone else to snap them together. She pouted up at him, eyes inviting, but his smile was pure professional charm, and his arm didn't go round her waist. A moment uploading, and the shot was whizzed – I presumed – round her followers. Theseus took the chance to slip away, and his place was instantly taken by Hippolytus. It was funny, I reflected, how the young lovers, Hippolytus and Aricia, were played by the older couple, Maman and this Adrien Moreau, with Theseus and Phaedra, the older couple in the story, being played by a pair in their early twenties.

'Schliemann,' Gavin said in my ear. 'Helen of Troy.' I turned to give him a blank look, and he tilted his chin towards Maman, with her dark hair piled up in the gold headdress. The photo I'd half-remembered became clear in my memory: a sepia photo, with Schliemann's wife decked in the jewels he'd found. 'Of course! I was wondering why it looked so familiar. The designer must have copied the real ones.'

'If they were ever real in the first place,' my policeman said. 'He found them during everyone else's lunch break, and smuggled them off the site.'

'Wasn't that because anything he found was the property of the Turkish government?'

'Maybe. But in my experience, archaeologists are keen to get a find verified in every possible way. Do you suppose it's real gold? I don't see your maman wearing cheap imitations.'

'Maybe a museum let them have the originals.'

Gavin snorted. 'Not unless she has very good friends in the Kremlin. They went to Russia after World War II.'

I laughed at him. 'Where do you pick up these bits of information?'

'Quiet night shifts in front of the History channel.'

Maman descended on us once more, sweeping Theseus with her. 'Cassandre, I want you to meet Caleb. Caleb, my daughter, Cassandre.'

She dropped him in front of us and was gone again, leaving him standing in front of me, staring incredulously. Then he gave me an intense, admiring look and bowed over the hand I'd put out for him to shake. '*Mademoiselle Cassandre. Enchanté.*'

Dammit, I was blushing again. I wasn't used to this. I did sailing clothes in practical scarlet Gore-Tex with triple-taped seams and wrist velcro, not shoulders-bare evening dress and hair sparkling with little stars. His voice said American, living in France. I switched the conversation to practical English.

'Pleased to meet you. I'm Cass.' I gestured to Gavin. 'Gavin Macrae.'

The men nodded at each other, then Caleb turned back to me. 'Eugénie's English daughter?'

'*Bilingue,*' I admitted. Part of my embarrassment was because Maman's Theseus was drop-dead gorgeous, with tousled brown hair, designer stubble, green eyes under level brows, and a straight nose above chiselled lips. He was wasted on the classical tunic and breastplate; he should have been in a topcoat and breeches for some torrid Regency bodice-ripper. Alas for opera directors, he was a bass, which meant his romantic looks were wasted on doctors, lawyers and the occasional god. He was heading for six foot tall, and substantial. Singing, his barrel chest had produced a booming voice which would have carried to the topmast against a force ten. His speaking voice had the same quality, and would be trying in a smaller space. 'Where are you from?'

'Canada originally, but my folks moved to Portland when I was a kid. I currently live in Paris – gee, I've only been away a week, rehearsing here, and I'm homesick for it already. You seen Paris in the spring? It's my favourite time.' His eyes flicked across to Maman. 'Your mother showed me round when I arrived. That was spring too, and I'd never seen anything so grand. Right now the whole area round Notre Dame's just filled with cherry blossom. The whole city's dressed up like a candy store getting wed.' He returned his attention to me. 'I never knew Eugénie had a daughter. She doesn't look nearly old enough. You must be twenty, twenty-two, right?'

I'd been thirty last birthday, but I didn't want to spoil Maman's night by giving her age away. 'Thereabouts.'

'But you don't live here in France.'

'I live aboard a yacht. Just now she's moored in Shetland.'

He smiled. 'Ready to meet us during the tour, right?'

I shook my head. 'I'm finishing my college course.'

For some reason that startled him. He took a step backwards from me. 'You live in Shetland?'

'I grew up there.' His eyes had gone blank, but his mouth moved, as if he was calculating something. 'My dad was an oil worker, in the early days of the Sullom Voe terminal.'

'Gee, well ...' He made a desperate recover. 'That's neat. What are you studying?'

'Deck Officer of the Watch. I'm joining my ship in two weeks.'

'You're in the navy?'

11

I shook my head. 'A commercial sailing ship, who takes paying passengers.'

'So you're from Shetland. You'll surely know everyone else on the island.'

'Hardly,' I said, 'in a population of twenty-two thousand. I know most of the folk around Brae.'

His green eyes flashed at that, then narrowed, veiling his expression. His smile returned; he spoke heartily. 'I'm sure looking forward to that part of the tour. I've seen photographs, you know? It sure looks pretty.'

'It's very bonny,' I agreed. 'It's just starting to be spring. By the time you arrive, there will be crocuses everywhere, and the first daffodils.'

He snatched at the opening. 'In Paris, they're out right now, in tubs all along the Seine, and in every little square of grass.' He grimaced. 'In Portland, Oregon, it's warm, but it's still raining. You know Portland?'

'I've never made it to Oregon.'

'City of roses, beer and coffee. Our unofficial slogan is "Keep Portland Weird".'

'Weird in what way?' I asked cautiously. Opera singers were all weird, I reckoned, due to spending too much time in an emotionally overcharged atmosphere, but not in ways a city would normally adopt.

'Voodoo doughnut shop,' Caleb offered. 'A 24-hour church of Elvis.'

'Weird,' I conceded.

'We opted outa the JTTF also. Back when I was in High School.'

I gave him a blank look.

'The Joint Terrorism Task Force. Gives the FBI and the CIA and the police and the government the right to spy on everyone. Our city chambers reckoned it was a threat to civil liberties.'

I began to like the sound of Portland, Oregon. The UK government was currently working on proposals that meant anyone leaving the country had to e-mail their plans and port of arrival beforehand, whereas the whole point of sailing was that you departed 'towards', but the wind meant you didn't necessarily arrive there.

He gave that little bow and admiring look again. 'Forgive me, I need to circulate. All these people are backers, so we artistes got to be nice to them.'

I watched him go, smiling here, bowing there. 'Well now. What do you suppose that was about?'

'A Shetland connection he wants to keep quiet?' Gavin checked a programme left lying on a chair. 'Caleb Portland. You'd need to find out his real name.'

I reverted to Shetlandic 'Boy, he'll be an Anderson, a Georgeson or a Tait. Me pal Magnie'll ken aa about him, right back to the fifteenth generation. You wait and see.'

ᚤ

Sunday, 22nd March.

My cousin Thierry ran Gavin and me to the station the next morning in his ancient Citroën. We'd have liked to stay longer, but Gavin was due back for the start of a trial, and I had my last days of college and final exams. I was wedged in the front with several bags of dog food, which were stored there to stop them being pre-eaten, and Gavin shared the back with two hen-crates stowed ready for impulse buys at the next Lencloître fair.

We were there first, and watched Maman's company arrive. The musical director and accompanist were next. I hadn't met the MD yet, but I knew Charles, who had been Maman's accompanist for all of her solo career. He was short, with large brown eyes like a spaniel, a drooping moustache, and a harassed expression. Caleb Portland was after them, laden with a scarlet backpack that dangled walking boots and a water bottle, then the soprano who'd sung Oenone/Diana.

Fifteen minutes to go. The tenor, Hippolytus, and Kamilla shared a taxi; I gathered she wasn't best pleased about that, for her immaculately lipsticked mouth pouted downwards, until she got out of the car, and saw several reporters and a camera waiting. Suddenly she was all smiles. The tenor produced a cellophane-wrapped bouquet, and she posed with it on the station steps, explaining in prettily accented French that she had adored being here in Poitiers, and hoped to return. Well, well, I thought, and wondered how Maman would counter this upstaging. Meanwhile, Hippolytus had brought her bags in – an enormous pink suitcase and matching flight case – and the moment she'd clocked that they were there, she turned her back on him. He looked around, as if he was too busy for her, spotted us, and came over.

Close to, Adrien Moreau was older than his publicity photos suggested. He'd worn a blond wig for Hippolytus, and his own dark hair was starting to recede at the temples, giving him a Shakespeare forehead. I hadn't quite forgotten, as I had with Maman, that he was approaching fifty. Pretty soon he'd lose the battle to keep his flat stomach, and I suspected that if his beard was allowed to grow, there'd be grey hairs in it, although his eyebrows were still dark above his flashing eyes. He had that air of complacency born of knowing that good tenors are rare, and get the best parts.

'Cassandre! I didn't manage to speak to you at the

party last night,' he said. He kissed me on both cheeks twice, as if we were old friends.'Eugénie's told me all about her sailor daughter.' He shook Gavin's hand and went into perfect English. 'Great to meet you.' He turned back to me, and returned to French. 'How did you enjoy the show?'

As a sulky teenager who'd blamed everything theatrical for having torn me from my Shetland home, I'd refused to play this game, but I was on my best behaviour now. 'It was marvellous.' It was easier to be enthusiastic in French. 'Particularly the love duets – those were exquisite. And your scene with Phaedra, where she declared her love, and you renounced your kingdom, that was so dramatic.'

'Yes, I thought that went well. I was a bit worried about my top notes beforehand.' He touched his throat. 'This season, you know, the last of the winter cold.'

'Oh, no, you sounded perfect. You and Maman together –' I ran out of gush, and compensated with a swirl of both hands.

'And didn't she look magnificent!' He gave me the full wattage of his dark eyes. 'My father created her jewellery, based on Schliemann's finds.'

'It looked wonderful,' I agreed.

'There's a family connection there – my own great-grandfather was a friend of his, and even saw Sophia in them, so we've always taken an interest.'

I nodded, and dodged further info. 'Are you looking forward to the tour?'

'Ah, Scotland!' He turned back to Gavin. 'My people used to have a place up there.' I suddenly realised that in spite of the brooding Russian good looks and French name, he was actually English. 'We'd go up at the end of the summer, round about the time of the Braemar gathering. Magnificent scenery. I'm looking forward to seeing it again.'

'It will be wonderful,' I said. I glanced up at the clock. Ten minutes to. 'Maybe we'd better …?'

He nodded and went back to his luggage. 'I know,' I soothed Gavin. 'Ninety per cent of Scotland in foreign ownership. I didn't realise he was English, did you?'

'Oh yes. Just the cut of his suit says English wealth and privilege.' Gavin looked towards Adrien, eyes resting thoughtfully on his golf bag. 'I've never had much to do with singers. Are they all so insecure?'

'It's a funny world.' I thought about it for a moment. At sea, having made it to the right port was your certificate of success. 'They need to be told how wonderful they were.' I'd done a year of Maman concerts, before I'd got to my sixteenth birthday, and put my long-planned running away to sea into operation. 'Tenors are the worst.'

'I just can't wait to get to Shetland,' the dark girl beside me said. I turned to look at her properly. She was the company 'bit player', the soprano who'd sung the goddess Diana, and Phaedra's confidante Oenone. Bryony Blake, that was her name. She was my age, with a pukka English voice that conjured up childhood pony clubs, ballet lessons and Girl Guide camps. Her face would have been a perfect oval except for the pointed chin. She had cat-narrow eyes under the perfectly plucked brows, and her lipstick was neon-pink against her creamy skin. Her clothes were arty, a bottle-green velvet skirt that swirled round her ankles, and an Edwardian jacket, but they lacked the star panache that made Maman so instantly recognisable. I couldn't have said what was wrong, but the effect was charity shop rather than Chelsea.

'You know Shetland?' I asked.

She shook her head. 'But I loved the Simon King diaries, on the telly, and the detective stories. Too, too thrilling – so dark and sinister.'

'It's spring now. The nights are lightening.' Some days it was even starting to feel warm, though I was still wearing full sailing thermals on board *Khalida*, and Cat was showing no signs of shedding any of his thick winter coat.

'The landscape looked too pretty, in the diaries. Is it true that fishing is still a more important industry than the huge oil terminal?'

I nodded. Between them, the pelagic boats, whitefish boats and salmon and mussel farming brought in three times what Sullom Voe did.

'I just adore seafood. I must try some while we're up there. Are there good restaurants?'

'Several. Where are you eating up in Unst, do you know?'

She shook her head. 'Darling, I just sing when Per points at me. I don't need to know anything else.'

I'd seen Maman's tour folder, with dates, hotels and travel times. It had been issued to all the company, but presumably reading it didn't fit in with Bryony's artistic persona. 'I'm sure they'll offer you local dishes. Our lamb is wonderful too.'

Seven minutes to go. Just as the MD looked at his watch, and Charles made a soothing gesture with his expressive hands, a long-nosed black Bentley slid to a halt outside the station doors and Maman stepped out, entirely unflurried, and with a bouquet twice the size of Kamilla's crooked in one elbow. This was her local press: she greeted some by name, kissed others, and gave the flowers to the cameraman, whose wife, I gathered, had just come out of hospital. She kissed him on both cheeks,

17

then came to do the round of *bonjours* in the station, ignoring the ticking clock. Dad led the procession to the platform; Maman set foot on it just as the *rapide* drew to a halt, and continued her conversation with the tenor as she walked to the exact place on the platform where our carriage had stopped. 'But, Adrien, you do not play golf!'

'My dear Eugénie, you haven't seen me play golf, which is a completely different thing. It isn't possible to go to Scotland and not play golf. We have one gig near St Andrews, remember.' He motioned Maman before him, then hoicked his golf bag up into the train and followed her. 'Now, our seats ...'

Gavin gestured me in before him, and we slid neatly into our places, which gave us a grandstand view of Kamilla realising she was beside Adrien, noticing that put her back-on to the engine, and explaining with a flurry of apologies that she would feel sick facing that way, she must change, if Bryony would be so kind ... Bryony shrugged, and obliged, and Caleb made a face at the window while Kamilla was re-ordering her flowers, water bottle and magazines. Her smiling face filled the cover of the one on top, beneath the headline "*KAMILLA: my beauty secrets*". I noticed Bryony giving it a sour glance, and sympathised. Luck and blonde prettiness had catapulted Kamilla into star status while Bryony, a few years older, was still just one of dozens of good sopranos in bit-roles. Maman gave her white wool coat and black hat to Dad, to put on the rack, and slid into her place without even looking at the seat number or smoothing down her black travelling dress.

'Good style takes work,' Gavin murmured. 'Your mother must have memorized the coach and seat number beforehand, to sweep in so beautifully.' His gaze moved to Adrien, then back to the golf bag. I could see him trying to calculate what clubs were in it.

'But, Gavin,' I murmured, 'you do not play golf.'

'How do you know?'

Fair enough. 'There weren't any clubs lying around in your hallway, at the farm.'

'You're forgetting my Inverness flat. I'm a member of the Inverness Golf Club.' He smiled, and conceded, 'I'm not much good though.' His gaze went back to the bag, then moved thoughtfully to Adrien's dark head.

'Penny for them?'

'At a guess, I'd say the minimum of clubs, as camouflage, and a metal detector.'

My mouth dropped open. 'A ...?'

Gavin nodded. 'Under the dark hood. It's too big to be anything else.'

'But why should he bring one of those on a singing tour?'

We found that out once we reached the airport. "*Viking treasure found in Shetlands!*" screamed the newspapers, above a picture of something gold gleaming through earth. "*Cache worth half a million! Second Viking cache! Finds of huge archaeological significance.*"

ᚼ

Deep ida darkest eart' I bide
Set dere by hauns lang turned ta bane
Yet haul me up ta light and fin'
A blaze o' gold and precious stane

... **a hoard of treasure.**

Monday, 23rd March

Tide Times at Scalloway, UT
Low Water   **04.44, 0.4m;**
High Water   **11.08, 1.7m**
Low Water   **17.10, 0.4m**
High Water   **23.34, 1.6m**

Sunrise   **06.01**
Moonrise   **07.14**
Sunset   **18.22**
Moonset   **23.10**

Crescent moon

What I wis, I amna,
What I am, you ken na,
Dem at loved me, think o' me;
Yet dem at see me shrink fae me.

Chapter Two

Naturally, my friend Magnie knew all about it. 'Two Viking hoards,' he said, as he drove me the five miles from Lerwick, where the airport bus had dropped me, over to Scalloway, on the west of Shetland, where I'd left my *Khalida*.

He was in his late sixties, Magnie, with fair curly hair and rosy cheeks. He'd been a seaman all his life, starting aged fourteen as a deckhand in the last years of the South Atlantic whaling, then in smaller boats around Shetland before he officially retired and took over running the junior sailing at the boating club. He'd put his best gansey on to meet me, knitted by his late mother in alternate bands of blue Fair Isle pattern and blinding white.

'Where?' I asked.

'Unst. It's the first treasure they've found here since the St Ninian hoard, back in 1958, that they took straight to the Edinburgh museum and never gave back.' He snorted. 'Except for kindly "loaning" it to open the new museum here.'

I'd seen the replicas of the St Ninian's Isle treasure, enamelled silver bowls and belt buckles. 'Wasn't the St Ninian treasure Pictish, hidden from the Vikings?'

'That it was, lass. These new finds are Viking, right

enough. There're armbands, rings, brooches, clips, along with silver ingots that they used for money and a purse o' actual coins, gold ones. The museum folk are right excited.'

'They would be.'

His car rattled down the hill past the golf course, over the mile-wide neck of land between the North Sea and the Atlantic, and around the curve. Now the west was spread before us: the grey roofs of Scalloway, dominated by the ruins of Earl Patrick's castle, a red stone Scottish example of the fairy tale château where Maman had sung. Behind it, the sky glimmered blue on the water. The hills were still winter fawn, but the road verges showed the first blue-green haze of new grass, and as we came down into the town and along the main street the gardens were bordered with white and purple crocuses.

'I put your cat to the boat, and left your engine running,' Magnie said, forgetting Vikings for matters of more immediate importance. He'd been looking after Cat over the weekend.

'How did he get on with your Tigger and Siam?'

'There was a war on. I had to keep him in the shed, poor beast, shut in, I was that faerd he would escape and try to walk back to Scalloway. But he's waiting for you on board now, safe and sound.'

The car drew up in front of the marina, handily situated right beside the North Atlantic Fisheries College, where I'd been studying since August. As I got out, I spotted a grey shadow crouched against the gatepost, and called him. 'Cat! I'm home.'

He detached himself from the dimness and trotted towards me, tail held high. I crouched down to make a fuss of him. He was nine months old now, my Cat, and had grown from a scrawny kitten to a beauty: grey fur faintly striped with palest grey; neat white paws; and a great plume of a tail with a pale underside. I opened the gate and motioned Magnie before me. 'Come and get a cup of tea, and tell me all the gossip.'

'Lass, you're only been away a weekend, there's no much happened in that time.'

'There's this treasure.' I opened the washboards of my *Khalida,* paused in the cockpit to enjoy a long breath of salted air, then descended the three steps that fronted the engine. Home.

She was a small yacht for these days, my *Khalida,* only eight metres from bow to stern, but she was a tough little sea boat, and I'd taken her from the Med to Norway, then across to Shetland. Next week, with weather, I'd be sailing her to Kristiansand. I lit the lantern, and the wooden bulkheads and fiddles sprang to life, brown veined with gold warming the white fibreglass of her roof. Her cabin was just over two metres across, with a central aisle. To port were the chart table, two-ring cooker and sink; opposite, the long couch was cushioned in seamanlike navy and bisected by a little prop-legged table that was put away at sea. The hanging locker and heads – a pump-action toilet – were past the first wooden bulkhead, and behind the second was the pointed forepeak, with its vee-berth and anchor chain running up to the hawser pipe on the foredeck.

I put the kettle on and reached for the biscuit tin. 'Come on, then, tell me all about it.'

Magnie settled back into the corner. 'Well, it was Keith Sandison as found the first cache. You'll likely no' ken him, he's a piece older as you, but younger as me. He's a far-oot cousin on me mother's side.' He paused to consider. 'He was starting at the fishing when I left on my third voyage to South Georgia. He'll be just about sixty.'

I set his tea in front of him, a good mahogany colour, the way his late mother had made it, then sat down myself on the warm engine-box cover. Cat jumped into my lap, made a circle, and settled down, purring.

'Thanks to you.' He took a swig, helped himself to a ginger nut, broke it into three pieces using his elbow, and continued. 'So, Keith has a croft just above Underhoull – that's one o' the Viking sites. Someone gave him this metal detector gadget for his Christmas, and he looked round the house and found nothing, then when the weather bettered, he took it a sweep over his parks, and when he came to this particular spot it went crazy. So he got his spade, and began to dig, and not a foot below the grass he found this pot. Well, he kent he shouldna disturb archaeological items, but he was that eager to find out what he'd got that he went on and dug it up, there and then, and wrapped it in a bit o' sacking and carried it home and dumped it on the kitchen table.'

Magnie's weathered face broke into one of his rare grins. 'His wife, Maggie, she had a good deal to say about that. And when he'd shut up her sharging, and cleaned a bit o' the earth off, he opened the pot up, and there was the treasure, all wrapped in cloth. Gold rings, like I said, and silver, and armbands, and a most beautiful worked cross, and brooches.' He glanced around, as if someone might be listening, and lowered his voice. 'His wife keepit the bonniest for herself, but dinna tell the archaeologists that. And this leather purse o' coins, silver and gold.'

'Amazing.'

'So he took photos o' it all, then he phoned the archaeologist, Val Turner, and she came to have a look. They were just dealing wi' it quietly, no publicity. But Maggie mentioned it to her neighbour, and it got known round Unst, then this two young boys decided they'd have a go, so they got out a metal detector, and walked the fields around Belmont, and they found a cache too, not as big, but still wi' a good mix o' armbands and brooches and coins. They went straight to the *Shetland Times*, and they mentioned Keith's find. After that, the archaeologists took it away. He was awful turned about that, but any fool coulda telt him they would.' He took another gulp of tea. 'And no doubt that museum in Edinburgh will find this is o' "national importance" an' aa, and keep it down there, instead of showing it here, where it was found. Keith's fairly rampaging about it.'

'He'll get compensation, though, won't he?'

'He doesna want money. He's a fisherman, and doing fine. He wanted his treasure kept in Shetland. And then, o' course, the papers began talking about a new Gotland – you ken, there's been I dinna ken how many treasure caches found there.' He shook his head. 'Anyway, there's all hell on up in Unst. They're only just discovered all the Viking sites as it was, you mind all the digs twartree summers ago.'

I shook my head. 'I was in Norway.'

'Right enough. Well, back five years ago they had this Viking Unst project, with a big survey of the whole island to see how many sites they could identify.'

'A good few of them are probably under a present-day crofthouse.'

Magnie nodded. His own crofthouse had been built and re-built on Viking foundations using stones from a Pictish broch. 'They found a good number o' possible Viking house sites. Then they picked several different ones to dig. Belmont, and one near the old Lund kirk, Underhoull, and one out on the east, Hamar.'

I recognised that name. 'Beside the Keen o' Hamar, where there's the lunar landscape. We did a trip there from school.'

'Ancient seabed. Yea. I doubt that was the earliest house. I volunteered for Underhoull, because me mother's folk came from there. We dug aa summer, and the next one too, then once they'd had time to think and write up aa their papers, they had this conference, wi' the folk in charge o' the digging presenting their results. I went to the whole weekend o' it, and lass, it was most awful interesting. It seems the Vikings came to Unst first, as early as 730, and they could tell aa sorts o' things about them from the finds – what they'd brought wi' them, and where they'd come from.'

'So,' I said, getting back to the present day, and remembering Adrien's golf bag, 'are all three sites just swarming wi' folk wi' metal detectors now?'

'Metal detectors, spades. Nails give readings, you ken, as well as gold. The sites are scheduled, and they've been searched anyway, but these treasure-seekers're likely doing some awful damage to the archaeology the folk hadn't had time to dig up. So we're decided, a few o' us, to go and patrol a bit, try and dissuade folk from launching in.' He gave me a sideways look from his pebble-green eyes. 'Are you going up to your mother's doo in Unst?'

I nodded. 'The tides are lousy, so I'm heading for Hamnavoe up by Eshaness on Wednesday afternoon, then on to Unst on Thursday. They're performing at Belmont House on Friday, you know, the restored Georgian house. Do you know if I can moor up at the ferry pier, just opposite?'

'Only if you don't mind getting out of the way from six thirty in the morning till ten thirty at night. There's no' room for a yacht and the ferry.'

I made a face. 'Anchoring in the bay?'

Magnie gave a decisive shake of the head. 'Foul and exposed. I'll tell you where there's a better anchorage, Lunda Wick, a bonny sandy bay, with good shelter.'

I reached for my *Clyde Cruising Club Guide to Shetland.* The chart showed a double-beached bay, open to the west, with a clear entrance. 'Looks good.' It was four miles from Belmont House, less over the hills – walking distance.

'Maybe if you were anchored up there, you could keep an eye on that site, in case of treasure-seekers. Not a patrol, just a watching brief from the cockpit. You're well used wi' night watches.'

'I could easy do that,' I agreed, 'and phone you if I spotted anyone suspicious.'

'Yea, lass, do you that. I'm going to bide with an old whaling pal, at Belmont, so we'd only be five minutes away, if there was trouble.' He shook his head. 'Though if what I'm hearing is right, then the sites have better protection than wis. Word is the ghost o' a Viking's been seen walking the hills.'

'Oh, yeah?' I said sceptically.

'There are more things in heaven and earth,' Magnie quoted. 'You're no' going to say you don't believe in ghosts, lass.'

I remembered the night I'd been on watch and seen a ghost ship lit by the moon, her sails tattered by a long, hard voyage. 'No, I'm no' going to say that. It just sounds a bit convenient, that's all, to say nothing of the way that every household in Unst must have a handy Viking costume from the Up Helly Aa.' I considered him. 'So who says they've seen it?'

'Keith, for one. He says that when he began digging, he felt this cold wind round his neck –'

'Not surprising, in March.'

'Wheesht, lass. Then he lookit up and saw this silhouette on the hill, a figure wi' a horned helmet.'

'Then it's definitely not a ghost. The real Vikings didn't have horns. We learned that in school. Not even the Berserkers. She showed us pictures of the Lewis chessmen.'

Magnie shook his head, sighing. 'Teachers this days, they take the romance out o' everything.'

'Anyway,' I said, 'sure I'll help. But I've got these exams to get through first.'

'You'll walk it.' Magnie rose, washed out his cup, and headed for the hatch, then paused. 'What time were you thinking to leave Hamnavoe? I'll maybe hitch a lift wi' you. An extra pair of hands never hurts.'

'That'd be good,' I said. 'Say nine o'clock? And thanks for looking after Cat.'

'No bother.' He raised a hand and headed off into the soft night.

ᚺ

My academic record wasn't good. I'd done well at the Brae school, with my pal Inga and I vying with each other to see who could do best in various tests, but Dad had gone to the Gulf in my Standard Grade year, when I was fifteen, and I'd been sent to France, to Maman, and thrown straight into working for my *bac littéraire*. As I'd run away to sea as soon as I was sixteen, I didn't get it.

I'd done exams since, working my way through the RYA series in evening class and Med sailing schools: Day Skipper; Yachtmaster; Ocean. On top of that, there'd been this year's series of short courses: GMDSS, Diesel

Engine, Navigation, Radar and ARPA, medical care, advanced fire-fighting, and proficiency in survival craft and fast rescue boats. Most of these had ended in exams too, and I now had a sheaf of impressive-looking certificates. All that meant I wasn't panicking, exactly – I just had a cold snake writhing in the pit of my stomach.

I had two written papers to do, both tomorrow. My RYA qualifications, and the time I'd spent at sea since, meant that the navigation part of the Deck Officer of the Watch (Unlimited) syllabus was a doddle. I'd been planning and steering a course on vessels for the last fourteen years, and I could work out tidal curves and secondary ports in my sleep. Exam 2, Stability and Operations, was another matter. I understood bridge watchkeeping procedures and behaviour in the proximity of ice. I was pretty good on safety aboard ship. Pollution prevention was mostly common sense and being able to quote the rules. Then we moved into physics: mass; volume; waterline length; calculating loading weights for a particular freeboard; and statical, longitudinal and transverse stability. I was glad I'd inherited Dad's head for maths and 3D calculations.

I'd also had to pass the medical and prove my time at sea: thirty-six months of qualifying service; at least six months in the last twelve on bridge duties; and testimonials as to my character, behaviour, conduct and ability aboard ship. I'd spent ages on the Internet, looking up every ship I'd ever spent several months on, and sending an e-mail to the master in the hope that he'd remember me, and take the trouble to look up the ship's papers. A good few hadn't answered, but there were enough replies to give me a file of e-mails logging months and voyages.

The written exams were followed by an oral, on

Wednesday morning. That worried me most. I could do everything the questions asked me to, but throughout the course I'd been picked up for not giving a long enough explanation of why.

On that thought, I sighed at my spread-out papers, and looked at my watch. Eleven o'clock. It wasn't too early to phone Maman.

She answered on the second ring. 'Hi, Cassandre! How's your revision going?'

'Good, I think. How's your tour?'

'We have a rehearsal this afternoon, just a walk-through and warm-up, in the venue. Broughton House, Kircudbright. It's an eighteenth-century building which belonged to a young artist, a boy from Glasgow, and we're to sing in the gallery. It looks a nice space, although the pictures show a glass roof, so I hope it doesn't rain during the concert.'

'How about the travelling?'

'Vincent hired a minibus for the mainland part of the tour, so we're travelling in comfort, although the driver is completely unintelligible to everyone else. It's a good thing I'm used to the Shetland accent.'

'A Shetland driver?'

'No, no, he's Scots, with a strong accent, but nothing like as strong as your friend Magnie's, for example. His driving is rather terrifying, but he's cheerful, and obliging with the cases.'

I grinned. 'And has Kamilla succeeded in upstaging you yet?'

'Of course not. I'm too old a hand to play that game. But Bryony is envious, and a little short with her, and Adrien is a former lover, it seems, and he's keen to resume their affair and she is not, so Per and I are easing them apart.' Per, I remembered, was the musical director.

'So, your exam is when?'

I wrinkled my nose. 'Written tomorrow and oral on Wednesday.'

'Then I'll phone to wish you good luck in the morning.'

Chapter Three

Wednesday, 25th March.

Tuesday's exams seemed to have gone fine; the passage planning was easy, and none of the arithmetic came out as strange fractions. My oral slot on Wednesday was a quarter to ten, and it was as bad as I'd feared. I came into the room, looked at the two experienced seamen behind the table, and my tongue froze. After two painful minutes the elder of the two nodded, and leaned across the desk.

'Now, Ms Lynch, I want you to imagine that I'm a new deck cadet on your ship. I just got on board yesterday, and I'm very nervous, particularly of people like you who were obviously born knowing your way round a ship. Don't look at me any more. Imagine the face of this youngster. Blond, blue eyes, trying to grow a moustache.'

I took a deep breath and imagined young Drew from my Brae sailing classes, five years older, and still keen as mustard. The examiner gave me a moment, then passed across a cargo manifesto. His voice went into a nervous stutter. 'I'm supposed to be loading the cargo, but I don't know what to put where.'

I held onto Drew's face and looked at the list. 'Okay, well, you've got heavy mechanical items here, they need to go lowest, amidships.' My cheeks were burning; I gripped the smooth material of my jeans under the table. 'These are perishables – you can't put them anywhere they might get wet ...' I went through it, item by item, and when I'd finished, the other examiner wrote a lengthy note on my paper, and the elder one nodded. Suddenly I was in clear waters, with the wind on the beam, sailing free. We did three more exercises, and then I was free to go.

'You'll get your results in May,' the elder examiner said, shaking my hand, 'but you don't need to worry. I'd welcome you aboard my ship any day.'

'I've got a ship,' I said. I was grinning with relief. 'Third mate, navigation, aboard the Norwegian square rigger *Sørlandet*. I join her in a couple of weeks.'

The other examiner laughed. 'Three whole sentences, unforced. You had us worried at first, Ms Lynch. It's heartbreaking to get an obviously competent candidate who can't make with the words.' He shook my hand too. 'Good luck.'

'Thank you,' I said. They could hear I meant it. I walked out of the classroom as if I was up in the rigging, with the sky below my feet. I'd passed! Cat was waiting by the tideline for me. I picked him up and hugged him, then set him down as he wriggled, and hauled my phone out of my pocket. I texted "*I passed*" to Dad and Maman, and called Gavin.

He answered on the second ring, as if he'd had his phone in his hand, ready. 'How did it go?'

'I passed. I *passed*.'

'Well done. Are you back aboard *Khalida*?'

'Nearly.' I unlocked the marina gate and walked along the pontoon, Cat trotting in front of me, with his plumed tail raised high to show the smoke-grey underside. 'I'll be casting off as soon as I've got my sailing gear on.'

'Well, when you get to Hamnavoe, have a look in the for'ard port locker, under the bag of ropes.'

Naturally I wasn't going to wait until Hamnavoe. I went for'ard in the cabin, burrowed my free hand into the locker and felt the smooth coldness of a bottle. It was real champagne, with a little label saying 'Congratulations, Deck Officer Lynch' in Gavin's spiky handwriting.

I was speechless. 'Found it?' Gavin asked in my ear.

'Yes. When did you plant this?'

'Oh, my last visit. I had faith you'd do it.'

'I nearly didn't,' I said, and told him about the imaginary cadet.

'Our examiners are wonderful. Have a good sail.'

'Speak to you from Hamnavoe, if there's a signal.'

ᚴ

It was a good sail. The spring sunshine was warm in my face as I motored out of the channel leading to Scalloway, the sunlight dancing on the water. The wind was what the forecast had promised, force four gusting five, with the waves curling white, and fleecy cumulus chasing each other in a china-blue sky. I came around the last buoy, slackened speed and went forward to hoist the mainsail, then came back to the cockpit to trim it, and switch off the engine. Silence flowed in, blessed silence after those last intense hours in the classroom, with twenty snuffling, coughing, shuffling young men, and the lecturer's never-stopping voice. The water ran under *Khalida*'s forefoot and broke at her stern; the wind tugged the rigging. I unrolled my new jib and set it in the perfect curve it was designed for, and *Khalida* surged forward. Cat came out to crouch in his usual place in the shelter of the cabin, paws braced against the waves, and I leaned back against the cockpit side, tiller warm under my hand. I was back where I belonged.

We passed below the drying skerry south of the north cardinal, and threaded our way between the scatter of little islands and rocks: Papa; Oxna; the Cheynies to the south; Linga and Hildasay to the north. The Vikings had named them all: Papa was the island of the priests, Linga the island of heather. Now our way was clear ahead, with the crouched headland of Skelda Ness on our starboard bow, and behind it the long run up the west side: green Gruting Voe, the watchtower of Vaila, the red cliffs of Watsness. The swell would bounce off the cliffs, so I kept well off. The three-shelved island of Foula floated to port, its base wreathed in mist. *Khalida* rested her shoulder on the waves and forged steadily forwards, the spray sliding away from her white prow and curling over level with her mast. I heated up a pan of soup and ate a cheese roll at 13.00, and followed them with a mug of tea, then sat back and watched the cliffs roll past. Rugged, spiked walls they were, black with spray below, yellowed with lichen above, and the swell foaming white over the jagged reefs at their base. The seabirds were already pairing off; I got out my spyglasses to look at them, kittiwakes, blackbacks, herring gulls, all paper-white specks two by two on the cliff ledges. Sandness Hill was weathered gold in the sun, but in Dale, where there was a deep geo running down to the sea, the grass was summer-bright.

An hour later, we passed the pale cliffs round the corner from Sandness, on the upper corner of the west, and Papa Sound opened before us, the sea-road in to Swarback's Minn, the sheltered hand-shape of the

Atlantic whose fingers ended in the townships of Brae, Voe and Aith. I couldn't quite see Dad's house, on the sheltering island of Muckle Roe, but the sight of my home waters reminded me. I checked my phone and found two texts: *"Congratulations, Cassie! Knew you could do it. Love Dad"* and *"Felicitations, Officer Lynch xxx"* from Maman.

We sailed steadily northwards. On our port side now was the wild Atlantic, with only the jagged outline of the dangerous Ve Skerries between us and the toe of Greenland. To starboard lay the red cliffs and sea-stacks of Papa Stour, with the smell of the growing grass blowing from the land. In summer fog, in the days of the haaf fishing out in open boats, the Papa men used to know they were approaching home by the smell of the flowers. We were sailing fast, but the current was pushing us back, so that we made only four knots over ground. It was 16.00 as we passed Fogla Skerry, on the upper corner of Papa, and turned towards the smudged hills on the north eastern horizon.

I could just make out the shapes. Those three pillars were the Drongs, then north from them was Dores Holm, a humped island where the sea had broken through to create an arch. The cliffs of Eshaness came next, then, out to sea, the cone shape of Muckle Ossa.

Another mug of tea brought me halfway across St Magnus Bay. 17.30. Now I could see the white and mustard lighthouse (Fl. W.12 secs), and the swell of foam at the cliff bottom. Sunset was at half past six, but there would be light on the water for an hour after that, besides the waxing crescent moon; we'd make it in.

I made a third mug of tea and settled back, my body relaxed, my mind always busy, watching the set of the sail, the movement of the wind across the water, feeling the tiller under my hand. We surged on until the knobbled cliffs were only two cables away, with the sun-green waves pounding at their feet, hurling themselves up the black rock and falling back in milk-white streams. Their tops, way above *Khalida*'s mast, were just touched by the last rays of the sun, the gold spots in the black lava catching the light and making the rock seem afire.

Muckle Ossa was my guide now, the cone-shaped island off Eshaness. You couldn't see it from land, but it was actually two islands. The outer one had an arch in it, and it was this I was watching for. The passageway into Hamnavoe wasn't easy to spot from sea, and there were rocks running out on both sides of the entrance, but I knew that when the arch opened behind me, I could run in with my stern kept square on to that. Nearly ... nearly ... then at last, through the archway, I caught sight of the water, gleaming yellow from the setting sun. I furled the jib and set the engine going, then went forwards to drop the main, and puttered between the skerries, using the pilot book's meid: the prominent rock lined up with the old house on shore.

I tied up at the pier in the last of the light, double checked my ropes, and stowed the mainsail properly. Cat emerged from the cabin, sniffed the outdoors, then jumped ashore for a foray on the pier. I stood on the forehatch for a moment, breathing in the sweet air, filled with the green of grass, the seaweed uncovered by the falling tide, the salt of sea-encrusted rock. This was country Shetland, with one single-track road running down to the stone pier, and another running around the other side of the bay to the cluster of houses tucked in behind the headland, their window-squares shining gold in the dusk. From them, green fields ran down to the shore, grazed by small, sturdy Shetland sheep in shades of black, rust and grey. Above the fields was the scattald, the shared hill grazing, with the heather springing into its summer pine green. The folk here would have been self-sufficient once, between the animals and crops on the land and the harvest of the shore and sea. Now the narrow line of tarmac connected them with the outside world of Tesco home deliveries, and sheep grazed on the rigs their ancestors had fertilised with kishies of seaweed. The half-moon above the hill was the colour of old brass.

Below, the cabin was blissfully warm. I put the washboards up and opened the engine box, then fried up the liver and onions I'd got for tea. Cat slipped through the forward hatch, whiskers twitching. We ate together in the gold lamplight, with blessed silence around us: country silence, made more still by the shushing of a wave against the pier, a sheep coughing up on the hill. It was strange, afterwards, not to have to revise any more. I played a solo game of Scrabble before phoning Gavin. He sounded distant, busy, with the opening salvos of his trial in full swing; or perhaps it was I who was retreating, eight sea hours closer to Norway.

I wanted this to work, for us to be together the way Maman and Dad were now, in a shared life, each keeping the best of their own world ... on the thought, I reached for my phone. Maman would be finished her show now.

'How did it go?'

'Very well. We performed in the Great Hall, a most beautiful panelled room, lit by chandeliers, and the audience was very receptive. But I'm too old for this touring, I think. Artistes are so temperamental.' Maman sighed down the wires, forgetting that she could do a good display of temperament herself. 'Now Kamilla believes herself a sensitive. She is seeing ghosts. This is what comes of bringing people to Scotland, where there is a phantom around every corner.'

The ghost o' a Viking's been seen walking the hills ...

'What sort of ghosts?'

'It is her dead brother.' There was a hint of scorn in Maman's voice. She modulated it to sympathy. 'It seems we are near the anniversary of his death, so I suppose he is much in her mind. He died when they were children, but she believes he is her guardian angel now, and has come to warn her that she is in danger. She found a book open at a page where one character was giving another a warning, and a rose in her room changed from white to red, like blood.'

'Bryony playing tricks?'

'Oh, it could well be. Or Adrien, trying to frighten her back to him – he fancies himself as a mystic – no, as a medium.' Generations of French Catholics resonated distaste in her voice. 'He plays these stupid games with a glass and letters, and believes he has contacted the dead. But I think Bryony is more likely, as they are sharing a room, so I have asked Caleb to take her out to supper, and pay her a bit of attention. That will annoy Kamilla, who also likes him, but we cannot please everyone.'

I tried to remember where she was. The Hill of Tarvit House, near St Andrews; yes, they might be lucky, and find a restaurant still open. 'I was very good,' I said. 'Caleb guessed my age at twenty. I didn't disillusion him.'

Maman sighed. 'Ah, these young men. As if it is likely I would see forty again – but he is very sweet to think me so young.'

'You look it,' I assured her. 'Especially in those Helen of Troy jewels.'

'Ah, yes, gold is very sympathetic to the complexion. Now your father and I are going to take a bottle of champagne to the library in this nice house, and have an after-show drink in peace, without worrying about artistes, and their imaginings.'

'Have fun.' I felt a shudder down my spine as I rang off. *Ghosts* ...

ᚼ

What I wis, I amna,
What I am, you ken na,
Dem at loved me, think o' me;
Yet dem at see me shrink fae me.

... a ghost

Thursday, 26th March

Tide Times at Hillswick, UT and at Dover
| High Water | 00.32, 1.8m; | 02.50 |
| Low Water | 13.05, 0.5m; | 10.17 |

Tide Times at Mid Yell, UT and at Dover
| High Water | 15.00, 2.0m; | 15.18 |
| Low Water | 20.57, 1.1m; | 22.33 |

Sunrise	05:50
Moonrise	09:05
Sunset	18:28
Moonset	01:31

First quarter moon

I dinna eat, yet I grow fat;
I dinna fant, yet I wear awa',
Look up ee day, I amna dere,
Yet twa weeks mair, I'm a silver baa.

Chapter Four

Magnie arrived at half past eight, just in time for breakfast, dropped off by an ancient pick-up truck that sounded like a fifties rocket taking off. I recognised it as belonging to Jeemie, one of the Brae yachties, whose *Starlight* I crewed in, and came out to say hello.

'I'd a come wi' you,' Jeemie said, 'but that I have to take me granddaughter to her driving lesson at half ten. Lerwick.' He gave a dismissive snort. 'Have a good sail, now.'

'Thanks to you,' Magnie said. He sniffed appreciatively. 'Lass, is that you welcoming me wi' bacon?'

'It'll be a long day.' I turned the bacon under the grill, put a couple of slices of bread in the frying pan and lit the burner under the kettle. 'Departure 09.15. We're all set to go, so we have time to fill us up.' I added the eggs to the frying pan, grated some cheese over them, and got the plates out. 'Dip dee doon.'

Magnie sat and reached for the pilot book, which I'd left lying open. 'We'll be going straight nor-east? Outside the Uyea Baas, outside the Ramna Stacks.'

'Outside everything,' I agreed.

It was eyeball navigation: straight out of the bay, then turn right and keep sailing, aiming at a point at the outside of the Ramna Stacks, which stuck out of the water like teeth in a witch's mouth. We took half-hour turns at steering, and kept ourselves warm with cups of tea from the flask, and a tin of stew in rolls at lunchtime, and it wasn't long after four o'clock when we found ourselves looking down through Bluemull Sound, with Yell to port and Unst to starboard. I stowed the sails while Magnie started the engine, and we putted gently into the curving arms of Lunda Wick.

It was a bonny place, with two beaches of golden sand separated by a low headland. On the northernmost side there was the remains of a broch, a massive circular wall overgrown with grass; to the south, a spread-out graveyard with the ruins of a kirk above the pale beach.

'St Olaf's Kirk,' Magnie said. 'It dates back from Viking times, twelfth century. It's fairly ruined now. There's notices on it, warning folk no' to go in, but when I was a bairn there was nothing like that, so we swarmed aa ower.' He waved an arm over the bay. 'Aa this was a Viking settlement. One o' the houses they excavated is up on the hill above the broch, Underhoull. There's another house down by the beach, and up above the kirk, where the House of Lund is, that big ruin there, then they found three mair.'

I checked we were well clear of the rocks extending from the headland, and reduced the engine to a murmur. 'So there could be anything in the ground there.'

'Well, no' in the immediate site, they checked that.' Magnie looked ahead, assessing the bay. 'I'd steer a point more to the right, lass. Maybe the reputation o' the Old House o' Lund has keepit the treasure hunters out so far. The devil's guarding it.'

I slanted him a sceptical look. 'Oh, yea?'

Magnie settled himself back into storytelling mode,

eyes still shifting between the approaching beach and the depth sounder. 'It began wi' the grandson o' the Scott that built it. He got fed up o' folk tethering their ponies on his girse while they were at the kirk, so he persuaded one o' the lads to be tarred and feathered, and a tail put on him, and this lad jumped into the kirk while the minister was preaching, and gluffed him that thoroughly that he would never preach in the kirk again. Well, that's how it came to be disused. Then they said een o' this Scotts had sold his soul to the devil, and to make it clear he'd claimed him, Auld Clootie put his footprint on the doorstep, a clear cloven hoof. It's there to this day, but you canna see it, for the folk were that afraid o' it, the laird had the step turned over.'

'A serious deterrent for modern heathens,' I agreed.

'Five metres depth,' Magnie said, returning to reality. 'Will you take the helm while I rig up the anchor?'

ᚼ

With Magnie on the foredeck, anchoring was easy. We dropped the hook in five metres of water so clear that you could see it lying on the bottom, and in less than half an hour we were rowing ashore, with Cat in his basket. We beached the dinghy on the strip of pale sand and let Cat out, then wandered along the shore towards the Viking sites.

They'd certainly chosen a good place. The beach was two hundred metres long, a smooth curve to a scatter of rocks, then a deeper inlet under the knobbled headland, with a stony ridge to the back of it, and a burn running through the middle of it from a marshy area that was already glinting pale gold with the first patches of celandine. The land around was green with fresh grass, bigger parks enclosed by grey drystane dykes. We walked to the headland, with Cat scampering ahead of us, and climbed up until we could see into the next bay.

'These outcrops, see,' Magnie said, indicating the half-buried rocks at our feet, 'I was aye told they were Viking warrior graves. The archaeology folk scanned them, and thought this een might be one, right enough.'

It just looked like the bones of the land weathering through the grass to me, but tradition was often right. 'Where are the houses?'

Magnie swivelled to face north-east. 'See the broch ruins up there? That's Upper Underhoull, just to the right of it, and the lower house is just above the beach here, just past the fence.'

I looked across. The broch was clearly visible, the two-metre high remains of what had once been a massive, double-walled tower. 'There were little cells inside the walls,' I recalled, from picnics we'd had at Jarlshof when I was peerie. 'And tunnels that Inga and I explored with a torch the custodian had given us.'

Magnie nodded. 'Souterrains,' he said. 'That's a bit older as the broch – Bronze Age. There's een here an' aa. And come you and look at this, lass.'

He led me downwards to the beach, and pointed to the grassy bank overhanging the sand. 'Boat noosts.'

It was the Shetland way of keeping boats safe through the wild weather: a ten-foot V cut into the earth, where the boat would be tied down between sheltering banks. These were more elaborate than I'd seen, faced with stones to stop the earth tumbling over the boat in a downloosing of rain. 'These are really from Norse times?'

Magnie nodded. 'Come up and look at the hooses.'

We strolled on to the lower house: a long, wide depression in the ground, with two layers of grass-covered stone enclosing it. It was bigger than I'd have expected, not far off the size of a crofthouse, some eighteen metres long by five wide. 'They were a poor hand at walls,' I said, looking at the curve.

'The curve proves it's an early een. The first settlers, they just built a couple o' rows o' stone, and used their boats as a roof.' That made sense: protection for both people and boat, and none of the hassle of trying to make a roof in a treeless landscape.'Tenth or eleventh century.' Magnie waved an arm upwards. 'The one above was much the same age. Neighbours, or maybe the same family, with the parents down here, and a son who was doing well for himself built his own house up above, just the same way they do now. See, too, the way the land's been terraced.'

He stomped on upwards. Cat abandoned his investigation of a crack between stones and bounded ahead of us. I paused at the top to admire the view: the two golden beaches, with the rock-topped green of Vinstrick Ness between them, and *Khalida* riding in the centre of the smooth water. Bluemull Sound was racing now the tide had turned; the Vere and the submerged rocks beside it were breaking white. To the north, I could see over the broch headland to a clear sweep of sea. That long-dead Viking had chosen his spot well: a safe anchorage for his boats; a lookout point; running water; green pastures.

The upper house was larger. Magnie led me along a flagged passage between two square rooms. 'Annexes,' he said, indicating them, 'and the main house was divided into three. This wall was drystane dyke, and the annexes were stone an aa, so it woulda looked fairly impressive

51

coming up from the beach.' He gestured at the upper end of the house. 'That was most awful interesting. We found aa kind o' things there. They'd had a turf roof, and stored stuff up in the rafters, just like a modern crofthouse.'

Modern was exaggerating slightly, but I knew what he meant: the rafters of every traditional Shetland byre supported a myriad of washed-up planks, old oars, deflated buoys and other useful gear which the women of the house periodically suggested could go to the bonfire. 'What sort of things?'

'Broken pots, big ones, and loom weights, and line sinkers, from their fishing. Lass, it was that strange to hold one o' them in me hand, and imagine some ancestor o' me own carving it, and threading his line through the hole, just as I'm done many a time, an' andooing oot in his boat to catch a piltick or a mackerel for his tea, same as I'd do now. Then the big excitement – see, there's a picture o' it on the board.' He led me up to the end of the house. 'Here he is.'

The picture showed a roughly carved figure, with a wide mouth, a pudgy nose and knife-point holes for eyes and ears. There was a suggestion of hands clasped across the front. He looked to be about the size of a corn cob.

'A figurine, they called him,' Magnie said, 'and there was talk o' the god Thor, because it might have been a line-sinker it was carved from, or maybe Christian significance, because there was the kirk nearby, but when I got to hold it in my hand, I could see that ancestor wi' a peerie lass at his knee, his grandbairn maybe, carving her a doll to wrap up in an auld piece o' cloth.' He was silent for a moment, then he lifted his head and nodded at a car nosing its way along the road. 'Now, lass, that'll be Peter coming to pick me up. We'll leave you in charge o' these parks.'

The car turned out to be an ancient Volvo in two shades of blue. Magnie's pal looked like a whaling crony; he had a lean, tanned face, a bristle of white whisker, and spoke like a captain.

'Peter,' he said, and shook my hand. 'Jump in, lass, and I'll run you back to your boat.'

I took a firm hold of Cat's harness, and we squeezed together into the back seat. 'Thank you.'

'How's the patrol going?' Magnie asked, once he was into the front seat, and the car moving.

'Well, now, that's getting interesting. We've had a few looking round here, just strolling wi' their instruments, but a walk up to them usually clears them. If they don't go by themselves, we just hang aroond an' watch. But today's ferry brought us birds of another colour.' He turned into the single track road leading down to the pier. 'Are you wont wi' Unst, Cass?'

Did I know it, he meant. I shook my head. 'The last time I was here was for the Baltasound regatta fifteen year ago.'

'Aye, aye.' We drove on, past a couple of ponies dozing in the sun, past a grey standing stone, twice the height of a person, and furred grey-green with lichen. Peter nodded at it. 'Bordastubble Stone. The tallest of Shetland's standing stones.'

He paused to negotiate the single track road leading upwards and stopped at a gate. I took a tighter grip of Cat as Magnie hopped out to open it. Peter nodded his chin at the ruins of the House of Lund, on our left. 'You'll likely have heard about this place. The devil's hoofprint's under that briggistane.' I didn't want to think about devils after that business in Scalloway, which was still inclined to give me nightmares.

'There another two grinds,' Peter said to Magnie, as

we drove on. 'To the left there, now, Cass, that's the remains o' three longhouses. This was a proper Viking community once.'

I could see stones sticking out of the grass in the field, and took his word for it. We stopped for the second gate, the third, then it was a downhill run to the cemetery, a single-track road. I wondered how a shiny modern hearse would cope.

'Birds of another colour,' Magnie prompted, as the car rattled to a halt.

'Yea. Well, I had a phone call from me sister-in-law, she works to the police in Lerwick, that it might be an idea to keep a lookout. Four men came off the North boat this morning, no' exactly criminals, but "known to the police" as being interested in finding treasure.'

'Oh, yea?' Magnie said.

'Well, I got me brother in Lerwick to watch the folk coming off the boat, and he spotted them no bother. They got into a hire car, and headed up here. It's a dark grey Star-rent-a-car saloon. I've got the make an' number in me phone, if you need them.'

I shook my head, and Magnie laughed. 'Cass here couldn't tell a Mini from a Mitsubishi.'

'But I can name my boats,' I retorted. 'A dark grey saloon. Right.'

'All the better for being invisible at night. They're biding in one o' the self-catering chalets at Baltasound Hotel. Now, Shona – that's me sister-in-law, Cass – she said we werna to tackle them ourselves, just to keep an eye on them. There a couple o' Lerwick officers going to come up to the Unst station tomorrow, that's in Baltasound an' aa. It's no illegal to walk over the hills wi' a metal detector, so long as they keep well away from the broch an' the hooses – they're aa scheduled monuments.

It's no even illegal to dig things up, but a policeman watching might make it more likely the items won't just vanish. Anyroad, the men spent the morning settling in, and walking round Baltasound, quiet as you please, then they did a bit of a drive around this afternoon – up Saxavord, out to Hermaness, the usual tourist things. They're back at the hotel now, and they've booked a table for dinner. Me great-niece is the receptionist, so she'll keep us posted.'

Visitors to Shetland didn't realise how closely they could be watched, if the locals felt it necessary. 'What's the mobile coverage like here?'

'What're you on?'

'Vodaphone.'

Peter made a face. 'Fine at Belmont, but not so good in here. You might get a signal up at the broch.'

I felt in my pocket for my phone, and snicked it on. It flickered between one bar and none. 'Not so good, if I need to get hold of you.'

'You've a good torch,' Magnie said, 'and a bosun's whistle. See the house up on the hill there, above the upper longhouse? That's Keith's house. I'll tell him to keep an eye open. If you get in trouble, do three flashes right at the house windows, and blow your pipe for all you're worth.'

'We'll be keeping an eye on them,' Peter said. 'If they head this way, we'll be right ahint them.'

The tide was running out fast now, with three metres of beach between my rubber dinghy and the shooshing waves. The men helped me re-launch the dinghy, then I waved them off and rowed home. I made a mug of tea and drank it sitting in the cockpit, sleeping bag tucked around me, watching over my stretch of Viking world. I imagined the double-pointed boats pulled up at the shore, the ring of hammers echoing from the stone-faced house on the hill, the cattle grazing on the parks, or tethered on the lush grass each side of the cultivated rigs. There would be people moving around those vanished homelands, the men in breeches, tunics, fur hats, the women in those long aprons pinned with oval brooches like the ones Keith Sandison had found, the children playing round the house or on the shore. Maybe an excited little girl was running over the headland to show her friend the baby her grandfather had carved for her ...

I dozed for half an hour and woke refreshed. It was a bonny time, poised between late afternoon and evening. The south wind was soft with the approach of spring, and the half moon glimmered pale above the low hills of Yell. The sun was dipping down behind the headland of Blue Mull, the twilight gathering on the land, but it would be another hour and a half before the light went from the sea. I'd have dinner here in the cockpit, rig up the anchor light, have another sleep then go for a patrol by moonlight. Tucked in by the beach here, *Khalida* was fine and sheltered, and I had a good view of ruined Lund House and the longhouses below it, but Vinstrick Ness, where the Norse warriors had been buried, hid my view of the Underhoull sites.

I waved my phone round the cockpit till I found two bars, and phoned Gavin. 'How's it going?'

'Our way, so far. The witness I was worried about kept her nerve, and the jury believed her. I can relax now.'

'I'm hunting treasure hunters,' I said, and explained. I could hear him being not-happy on the other end of the line, but he didn't tell me to be careful.

'The press is your best ally – you don't know anyone?'

'No.'

'Pity. A journalist with notebook and camera is the

best way of stopping things disappearing. Failing that, you, another witness and a photo. I'm not up in treasure trove laws, because it's a civil matter, not a police one. How about your journey? How's the weather looking?'

'A front coming over, then fair winds behind it. I'll make it with a couple of days to spare.' I had a sudden cold feeling, remembering that I wouldn't see him again before it, then brightened. 'Next time I see you will be in Norway, the fjords. If no police work turns up.'

'I'll do my best to catch all villains before then,' Gavin promised. His voice wavered, as if he'd gone underwater.

'You're breaking up.'

'Good luck with your treasure-seekers.'

'*Beannachd leat.*' I said it into silence, and felt obscurely cheated.

I'd put rice in my wide-necked flask before we'd left that morning, so all I needed to do was re-heat the rest of the onions and chicken livers. Dusk was just after six, although the light would glimmer on the sea for another hour. I left Cat washing his whiskers and headed ashore, tucking the grey dinghy amongst the scatter of rocks below the headland, where only someone looking for her would find her. She'd be safe there for several hours, as the tide ebbed away from her. Here, sheltered from the sea wind, I could hear only the waves washing on the shore and curling round the rocks, and the desolate cry of a whaup from the hill. I came up the side of the hill, boots velvet-soft on the sheep-cropped grass. Now I could see all around, from Lund House to the broch. I found myself a sheltered niche among the out-cropping stones, and snuggled my scarlet sailing jacket around me for warmth.

It was odd to have time just to sit like this. I'd been busy revising for so long that I'd forgotten how to be still. I felt I should be getting out my coloured pens to go over my notes once more, or taking another sheet of paper to make new ones. Now it was all over. I'd achieved my qualification, and soon I'd be joining my ship. *Then what?* asked a voice in my head. *Then ...*

I could feel it already, the deck moving under my feet, the great ship's wheel between my hands. Instead of this solitary life, there'd be other people. I'd have my fellow crew, and the trainees staying for a week: rich Americans; shoe-string backpackers; naval students; teachers on leave; city business folk who dreamed of the endless sea as they sat at their desks. The keen ones who'd be alert at the first touch of your hand on their foot, even if it was three-thirty in the morning, the reluctant ones who objected to hauling on ropes or standing their watch on a cold foredeck, all squeezed together into this little wooden world in an immensity of ocean. I knew how the ship became a universe, with the land world a distant memory of the way you once did things: freshwater showers; a bedroom of your own – though, as I was an officer, Cat and I would enjoy that luxury –; solitary meals at a time of your own choosing. It was too physical, too ever-present a world: the cold spray on your face as you went about your duties; the ropes bar-taut under your hands; and always the ship moving. I knew that I couldn't take Gavin with me.

We could meet, though, as I'd told him. As you came closer to land, as you saw that smudge on the horizon, suddenly you hungered for it: the green of leaves; the gurgling trickle of a stream; meeting your family. I'd want him then. Inverness had flights all over the world, and Aberdeen had loads to Norway, because of oil. Conversely, if we were in port for a while, and the crew wasn't needed, I could fly from there to Inverness. But was it going to be possible to maintain a relationship between two such separate worlds? The voice in my head replied bleakly, *Only if you love each other enough for one of you to give their world up.* We can try it, I told the voice.

I was interrupted in my musings by a flash of light to the south-east, a car turning onto the Lund road. I watched for the headlights coming towards me, but there was only the faint gleam of sidelights as someone drove slowly, cautiously, in the twilight, using the white lines to follow the road. I couldn't see any colour to the car, just the shiny gleam of it catching the moonlight as it crawled along. *Four men*, Peter had said. I watched for another flash of a following car, but there was no sign of the cavalry.

The car crept to a halt just past the upper longhouse. The snick of doors opening and closing carried through the still night, then the car moved on. It was too dark to make out figures from here. I'd have to go closer. I eased my arms out of my too-visible jacket, leaving my dark mid-layer, and began to creep down the side of the hill, torch in hand, thumb on the button, feeling like I was ten again, and playing commandos with Inga and Martin. The important thing was to stay below the skyline and not to run into a flock of sheep, of course. My eyes were well-accustomed to the dark now, and the half-moon cast a silvery light on the ridges, and outlined the tops of the drystane dykes keptup over generations by the crofters whose houses now stood roofless.

I still couldn't see any movement. I stood and listened. For a long moment there was silence, then, unmistakeable, the sound of a foot snicking stone against stone. They were up at the south side of the longhouse. I considered the lie of the land. They might be walking the smooth park between the longhouse and the next abandoned crofthouse, but that was obviously land that had been cultivated, so there was less chance of a find. They were more likely to come seawards, to the terraced hill Magnie and I had walked up. If I stayed below them, on the shore, not only would I be seen against the pale sand, but I'd be out of sightline for flashing my alarm signal. I needed to cross the beach and come up the other side of the broch.

I slipped quickly across the sand by the water, bent double to make me less visible against the gleaming sea, and gained the shelter of the boat noosts. Now I had to go around the lower Viking house and then upwards.

I had an uneasy feeling down my spine as I came to the low grass-mound of walling, as if I was being watched. I didn't think the visitors from the car could have seen me, since I couldn't yet see them, and I was looking for them, while they weren't looking for me. I'd forgotten Magnie's talk of Viking ghosts, but now it returned in full measure, and for a moment I thought I saw something, a tall man in bagged leggings and a tunic, with an axe in his hand, then it was gone again. *Get a grip, Cass.* All the same, I skirted the outside of the house, rather than crossing it, managed to climb over the fence without any of those schrinching noises and headed on hands and feet up the headland to the broch site. It was as tall as me, grassed over too, rock bones covered with velvet sward, sheep-cropped. I leant on it gratefully and set myself to listen.

I could hear the footsteps clearly now, as if they were just on the other side of the broch. There was more than one set, moving quietly but confidently onwards across what ought to be unknown terrain. I risked easing my head over the rim of my wall, and for a moment my heart stopped, for what I saw was goggle-eyed, pig-snouted aliens, with a tiny red light flashing in each forehead.

Then my brain made sense of what I was seeing. They were wearing some kind of infra-red glasses that let them see in the dark. I'd have to be very careful now I was within their range.

There were only three of them, so the fourth man must have remained in the car, ready to drive it with all lights blazing to the nearest getaway point in case of trouble. Each one had a machine he was sweeping in front of him, and, as they moved closer, I could hear the soft bleeps and see the glow of the display on the top of it. They'd begun at the top left corner of the field which enclosed the upper longhouse and bisected the broch, and were walking in line, two metres apart, parallel with the fence: methodical; professional. I watched as they came down to the broch wall, turned, went back up, turned again, until they'd swept the whole field to seaward of the longhouse. Every so often one would stop, a white light flashing from the digital display, and the others would set their machines down and come to confer, then they'd separate again, and continue walking.

Once they'd swept the field they came to the broch itself. Once, it had been a great stone tower, fifteen metres across and fifteen high, with stairs between the thick walls and a lookout post on top, like the surviving complete one on the island of Mousa, down the south end of Shetland. Now it was three circular, grass-covered banks sloping to a narrow path between them, tussocked and rough with stones. The moon flashed on the goggles as the men raised their heads to look at it, then, without a word spoken, they split up. One remained where he was, the others climbed along the line of the fence over the first bank; the second remained in the dip inside the outer bank, and the third climbed the second bank to the inner ring. I slid quietly to well back of the person walking the outermost ring, and watched his lights sweeping left, right, left, right. Every so often his detector would bleep, and he'd stop, re-sweep and either move on or bend and plant a marker tipped with luminous paint that glowed green in the moonlight. He paid particular attention to the old chapel area, but found nothing.

I was getting cold, even in my sailing thermals and warmest socks. My feet were beginning to go numb, and my fingers. I eased my gloves off, lifted my cupped hands to my mouth and yawned into them, then pulled my gloves back on before the warmth could dissipate. I couldn't stamp my feet or 'beat the scarf' with my arms, or any of those seaman's tricks. It was time the cavalry came.

The moon had sailed clear of clouds till now. Suddenly the white radiance of the hill vanished as if a wet cloth had been swirled over a blackboard. It would make no difference to the treasure-seekers, with their goggles, but I was blinded. The only certainty was the rough grass under my hand, and the stone-snick of footsteps from within the broch.

Then I heard, felt, a heavier tread coming up the hill. I waited, and listened, trying to work out where someone could have come from, for there'd been nobody there earlier. The person was moving confidently even in this dark, with a faint clinking sound, like chainmail. He was coming straight towards the broch. A cold shiver ran up my spine, and my breath caught in my throat … *the sites have better protection as wis,* Magnie had said. The glimmer came back to the sea, and I saw a figure outlined against it, not ten metres from me, made taller by the horned helmet, broad shouldered, with a double-headed axe raised in one hand. Then the moon came again, and I felt my scalp tingle. There he was, not the grandfather who carved a doll for his bairn, but a Viking raider, with the moonlight glinting on his chainmail, on the studs of his black belt, the blade of the upraised axe. He gave a roaring shout in a language I'd never heard, although it had the sound of Norwegian or broad Shetland. I stumbled back against the broch, struggling for breath, but it wasn't me he was after. He thrust on past me towards the intruders, axe raised threateningly, and swung it down on the height of the broch wall with a ring of metal on stone.

They were already scattering. One flashed a torch roadwards, and I heard the car's engine whirr into life. Gravel spurted under its wheels as it came towards us, lights blazing. The Viking flung back his head and laughed.

The moon dipped behind the clouds once more. I heard the car stop, the doors slam. The Viking came away from the broch, and I felt, heard, sensed him pause as he passed me. Then he moved on.

When the moonlight shone again, only a breath later, I was alone on the hill.

ᛙ

I dinna eat, yet I grow fat;
I dinna fant, yet I wear awa',
Look up ee day, I amna dere,
Yet twa weeks mair, I'm a silver baa.

... the moon.

Friday, 27th March

Tide Times at Mid Yell, UTand at DoverUT

High Water	03.20, 2.0m;	03.50
Low Water	09.42, 1.0m;	10.55
High Water	16.04, 1.8m;	16.24
Low Water	22.15, 1.2m;	23.19

Sunrise	**05.47**
Moonrise	**09.59**
Sunset	**18.31**
Moonset	**02.23**

First quarter moon

Wirds ir spoken, freend tae freend,
Wi'oot a soond being heard,
Sheeksin, weddings, births and deaths,
Winging dir way across da warld.

Chapter Five

'We had trouble at Belmont,' Magnie explained the next morning, when he and Peter came to see what sort of night I'd had. He sat down on a rock, shaking his head. 'Man, I don't ken what's come o' folk nowadays. There was a whole set of bairns up at the site, racing all over. Een o them had a metal detector he'd been given for his Christmas, and he was showing off for the others, and he kent his laws back to front, and was well ready to quote them to us. Well, you ken the like. There was no point in phoning the parents, they'd just back him to the hilt.'

'Wir bairn has the right to do as he likes and you can't stop him,' Peter agreed. 'So we just held a watching brief, as you might say.'

'Stuck wi' them and put up wi' their cheek.' Magnie grinned. 'They found twartree old nails and a tin can, and that got them fed up enough to mind that it was likely their bedtime, so we let them be then, so they could go without losing face.'

'When are you expecting your folk?' Peter asked. 'Would you like me to run you over to greet them?'

I shook my head. 'I'm fine on duty here for daytime. I'll maybe head over come afternoon teatime, and say hello. The concert's at half past seven, and then there's a meal after that.'

'I can still save you a walk,' Peter insisted. 'If I pick you up about four, then? We'll be out on patrol most of the day, I can easily detour here to get you on me way home.'

'That'd be kind.' If Peter got me, I could take Cat, which would be better; he wasn't keen on being marooned on an anchored boat, and he'd like a Georgian house with a real peat fire. Someone there would have a car to run me back again.

'Well, boy,' Magnie said, 'we'd likely better get back to keeping an eye on these tourists.' They clambered back into the car, and headed off up the road, past the ruined house, leaving Cat and me on the beach. I hadn't been up to the church yet, so I secured the dinghy and headed up the bank towards it.

The cemetery had been enlarged in recent times, with an expanse of grass enclosed by a drystane dyke. At the far side was the old kirkyard, surrounding the roofless chapel. The kirk itself was rectangular in shape, a piece bigger than a crofthouse, with grey-green lichen furring the walls. The front gable looked complete, a curved arch with the shape echoed by the door and an upper window, but the seaward gable's top was level with the walls. The doorway was barred by a grilled gate festooned with yellow and black notices: "Danger: walls unstable – no entry". Naturally I pushed it open and went inside. I didn't see that just walking there would bring the walls down on me, and I had no intention of climbing them.

The interior was almost completely filled with gravestones, proper old-fashioned ones, with a long inscription. Several were set inside a rusty iron railing, and past that was the leper's window Magnie had mentioned. It was funny to think of lepers in Britain – in my head they belonged to the Bible – yet there had been several leper colonies in Shetland. The Lunna Kirk had a leper's squint too. I tried to imagine being banned from all human contact, even the Mass, and having to listen without seeing through this window. They probably hadn't even had leprosy, just a variety of skin diseases which we'd cure today with steroid cream. I stepped gently around the railings. It took me a moment to find the Pictish fish; it was underneath the top lintel, where you'd see it from outside and below. It took a bit of faith to know it was a fish, but perhaps the lepers knew it was so by tradition. I hoped the knowledge that they were in the place their ancestors had also held holy comforted them, a little. A Shetland wren flew out of the stones above my head, and was followed by another, and another, swirling round the old walls like brown velvet butterflies.

I turned my attention to the gravestones. The railed enclosure belonged to the Mouat family, who'd built Belmont House: Thomas and his wife, Elizabeth. I was just bending to look at the other graves, from the 1850s, when Cat sat bolt upright, whiskers forward, then dived back behind Thomas and Elizabeth's headstone. The doorway darkened, and before I knew it, a man was standing in the doorway glowering at me.

I knew he was a Shetlander by the jacket, a navy affair built for weather, not appearance. He was in his sixties, with a close-cut seaman's beard and a good head of hair that had been Viking-red, and was now grizzled. His eyes were shrewd under low-set brows, his mouth set tight under the neatly trimmed moustache. There were more frown marks than laughter ones on his forehead and around his eyes; he'd have auditioned for a grumpy old man no bother.

He spoke roughly in English. 'There's a "Keep Out" sign, did you not see it?'

'I'm no' climming the waas,' I replied, in my broadest Shetland, 'so I didna think I'd be doing ony hairm, joost haeing a skoit inside. Me pal Magnie, you ken him, Magnie o' Strom, fae Brae.'

Everybody knew Magnie. His mouth lost some of its downturn, though he stayed planted in the doorway as if he wanted to stop me escaping.

'He telt me aboot this fish.' I indicated it. 'So I wanted to see it before I began patrolling.' I took a step forward. 'I'm Cass Lynch. That's me boat, anchored in the bay.'

He didn't offer to shake hands. 'Keith Sandison. You're a pal o' Magnie's, then?'

'He came up with me from Brae. He's at Peter's ee noo.'

'I ken that.' The suspicious scowl returned to his brows. 'He didna say he'd brought a lass wi' him.'

I couldn't let that one pass. 'He sailed up wi' me.' I decided to switch topics. 'So you're his cousin that found the treasure?'

The scowl deepened. 'If I'd kent what it would lead to, I'd a left it ida grund, and never said anything more about it to anyeen.'

'Fuss?' I asked sympathetically.

He moved out of the doorway, and motioned me to go before him, back out into the sunlight. I was glad of that; the dank chill of the church was sending shudders down my spine. The warmth outside fell like a blessing. It seemed to soften Keith's mood too. 'Lass, I'm had that much bother wi' it. I'd never a thought o' the like. The government's claiming half o' it, and now the laird's saying he's entitled to it an' aa. I found it, fair and square, on me own land, that's belonged to me family as far back as the records go. It had been buried by someen who's no' coming back to claim it, you're agreed on that?'

70

I nodded. There was no point in interrupting him in full flow.

'So, wha does that treasure belong to? Wha actually owns it? Is it no' the friends of the original owners?' He used 'friends' in the Shetland sense of kinsfolk.

'If they could be traced,' I agreed, cautiously.

'Well, then, who's that most likely to be but the folk still biding on that croft now, that inherited it from their grandfather's grandfather, and so on, back as far as you can go? We're no' like south, where houses change hands every few years or so.' He waved an arm across the sunny hills spread before us. 'You look out there. Nearly every house that still has folk in it, the name or the blood is the same as the first census, in 1841. You're not telling me those folk have no right to what's on their land.' He paused for breath. 'And as for the laird, well, there a piece o' paper says he owns the land, given by a Scottish king five hundred years ago to one o' his ancestors. The Scottish king didna care that there were folk already living on that land when he handed it over. And now he's saying I shoulda asked his permission to metal-detect on me ain land, that I'm wrought on aa' me life.' He turned his head and spat on the ground. 'It's like we're back in the bad old days, where he claimed a third o' the whales folk killed, because they'd walked on his foreshore to get at them. Now, would you no say I have a point?'

I had to concede he did, from one way of looking at it. 'But the other way, I suppose, is that now it belongs to all of us, for finding out more about the Norse folk who lived here a thousand years ago, and the best way of doing that is through the museum, and the experts.' I gestured up at Underhoull, and tried to remember what Magnie had told me. 'They can find out so much from peerie things you wouldn't think mattered, like kenning that the whetstones they brought with them came from a particular Norwegian quarry. Maybe the jewellery can tell us more about who they traded with, or what their important festivals were, or the status of the folk who lived here.'

I'd hit another nerve. 'I wouldna mind so muckle if it was going to wir ain museum. But now they're talking about "nationally important" and that means Edinburgh takes it.' He glared again. 'You ken this, lass, I heard that when the St Ninian's treasure came back, for the opening o' the new museum, een o' the folk there compared the originals to the replicas they so kindly geed us.' His voice dripped sarcasm. 'An' they realised a lock o' the fine detail o' the originals had geen. Someen had been polishing them, to keep them bonny for the visitors. I dinna want my treasure to be ruined like that.'

I thought that a Museum of Scotland curator polishing Pictish silver with Duraglit was unlikely, but there was no arguing with a man with an obsession.

'An' now we're being overrun wi' tourists. I saw you come in here and thought, there's another o' them, taking their detecting into the kirk. I didn't realise you were fae the yacht. I sooda kent. You're the lass that gets mixed up wi' the murders.'

'I didna go looking for them, I promise you.' I tried a smile. 'Murder is even more trouble than treasure.'

He didn't exactly smile back, but his face relaxed. 'So, you're on duty here for the day?'

I nodded. 'This is a fine lookout spot, especially wi' the sun on the wall like this.' I slid down to sit on a dry spot beside it.

He looked round critically. 'You'll no' see the Lower Underhoull site.'

'I can see the road. If a car stops, I can be there as quick as they can.'

He nodded, conceding that. 'Well, hae a fine day, lass. I'll mebbe see you later on, at the concert.'

He didn't look like an opera enthusiast. 'You're going to it?'

'The most o' Unst'll be there. We canna have your mother singing to an empty hall.'

'I hope the Lerwick folk will think the same.' The auditorium in Mareel held six hundred.

'Lerook!' he said, with a countryman's contempt for the town. He raised a hand and headed off. Cat slid out from behind his stone and came to sit beside me on the soft turf, cropped to moss-softness, and scattered with the silvery-yellow celandines. I tilted my face to the sun, and considered.

Keith Sandison was right, of course, about how the lairds had got their land. That was how it was all over Scotland, Gavin had told me, that the king had awarded lands to his nobles without considering that folk already lived there. It was just that in Shetland it was more recent; the Scots hadn't arrived in force until almost 1500. Before then, we'd been Norwegian territory. We'd been pawned to Scotland for two thousand gold pieces as part of a marriage settlement between a James and a daughter of the Norwegian king, and never redeemed – or, to be exact, the Danes – Norway was part of the Danish empire then – had tried to redeem us, and the Scots hadn't played ball. In so far as you could own land, it seemed much fairer that it should belong to the folk who'd lived there all these years.

It was quiet here, just the shooshing of the waves on the beach, and the *ch-ch-ch tzee, tzee, tzee* of the wrens in the stones. I'd hear every car that came down the road. I went back to the dinghy and fetched my flask, binoculars and copy of *Treasure Island* that I'd found in a charity shop. I wasn't totally convinced by the argument that Stevenson's map was Unst – it looked more like a half-forgotten Scotland to me – but it seemed an appropriate read while I was here.

I was deep in Jim-lad's first encounter with Blind Pew when there was an engine hum in the distance. I looked up, and glimpsed a small red car – a Bolt's hired Fiesta, I'd take a bet on it – turning into the Lund road before it disappeared behind the hill and ruined house. It stopped less than a minute later – the driver inspecting the Bordastubble Stone, I reckoned. If he, she, didn't move again soon I'd walk up the road and make myself visible.

I waited, the wrens cheeping above me, and the wind soft on my face. Then there was the snick of a car door, and the distant engine hum again, gradually increasing in volume. The car came into sight, scarlet against the grey walls of the House of Lund, slowed, edged itself into a gateway to leave the road clear for other cars, and stopped again. The driver got out and stretched, as if the Fiesta was too short for him, then walked round to the boot and took something out.

I raised my spyglasses. The house ruins sprang close.The driver was male, tall, dark, and dressed in khaki cargo trousers and a mid-green padded waistcoat over a brown jumper – not quite camouflage gear, but the next best thing without being too conspicuous. His face was too far away to see.

The spyglasses must have flashed as I tilted them, for he turned in my direction, bringing up one hand to shield his eyes against the sun. If he was a treasure-seeker, it was to the good if he knew I was watching him, though it would be most horribly rude if he was just a normal tourist. I stood up, showing my own scarlet jacket against the moss-furred stones of the church, and immediately he turned his back and walked over to the field above the road, where there was a herd of ponies. His elbow went up: photos. Yeah, maybe. I strolled sun-gaits around the church, like a tourist inspecting the sites. The Viking graves were easy to spot, thin slabs of grey rock, as moss-furred as the church, with the cross arms half buried in the soil. I paused by each, slanting an eye landwards each time. The man moved away hastily when the ponies came towards him, no doubt equating photographs with the occasional half sandwich or apple-core, and strolled rather too casually to the lower field, where the three unexcavated longhouses were.

I'd give him plenty of rope. I wandered into the church again, to an indignant *chrrr*ing from the wrens, and, keeping well back, looked out of the window. He'd stopped in the middle of the field. There was some kind of stick in his hand; a surreptitious look with the glasses suggested it had a square metal end to it. Then, as if he was satisfied that I wasn't interested, he began to walk the field, as methodically as the men had done the night before. There was something familiar about the way he moved: not a young man, but not elderly either. That didn't narrow it down much, except to exclude my classmates and Brae sailing cronies. The green waistcoat was laird clothing, or tourists; everyday working Shetlanders wore ganseys or boiler suits, or an all-purpose jacket in serviceable navy, like Keith's, or ex-work gear in high-vis neon yellow.

Besides, no local would have a red hired Fiesta. I sighed. There was only one set of strangers that I might recognise in Unst right now, and whichever of them this was, he'd wasted no time in getting into the treasure hunt. Too old for Caleb, not thin enough for the musical director, too tall for Charles, and if I looked hard I thought

I could distinguish the dark outline of his beard. Of course it was Adrien, who'd brought his metal detector in the bag of golf clubs.

He took half an hour to walk the small field, but seemingly found nothing. He put the detector into the back seat, then the red car bumped down to the turning place in front of the graveyard. I thought it was time to make myself visible again, ready to do the innocent tourist routine of 'What a surprise to see you here!' He was focusing on the road, and didn't seem to notice *Khalida* until he was halfway around in the turning square. I saw him lean forward, staring, then, with a jarring of gears, he glanced up at me, standing by the church in my scarlet sailing jacket. I saw him remembering Maman's sailing daughter. He turned around and set off again, bouncing the car up the road, and juddering impatiently to a halt before each gate. I heard him drive away, but the sound didn't die completely, and less than five minutes later the car appeared again, driving north along the road that led to Underhoull.

It was time I had my mid-morning cuppa. I settled myself in the sun once more, poured myself a mug of tea, and got back to *Treasure Island.* He could spend all the time he liked around Upper Underhoull and the broch; last night's searchers had found nothing there. Time enough to move if he disappeared behind the hill.

It took him a good two hours, with a lot of stops for looking around him, and suspicious glances in my direction. He had binoculars too, for I saw them flash in the sun from time to time, but I was so visibly innocent, with my flask and my book, and Cat stalking dead leaves at my feet, that he lowered them straight away. I had no need to move, I reckoned, for all he had in his hand was the metal detector. Before he could dig, he'd need to go back to his car for a spade, and I'd see him doing that, and be strolling over before he'd got the first square of turf out. Besides, it was lunchtime. My belly was rumbling, and Cat had got tired of chittering at the wrens and was gazing at me with round yellow eyes and the occasional reproachful mew.

'Okay, Cat, lunch,' I said, and we walked down to the dinghy, ignoring the spyglass-flash from the broch. I felt him watching as I rowed out and climbed aboard.

I had the last of my soup, and fed Cat some tinned food, and by the time I'd done that Adrien had disappeared behind Vinstrick Ness. I installed myself in the cockpit, book in hand, waiting. He was gone for so long that I was half thinking I'd better go and check on him, when he reappeared on its crest, and began going over the exposed stones that Magnie had pointed out as Viking graves.

He went back, forwards, back again, round and round on the point of the headland, landwards a bit, a bit more, and then he found something. I could see it just in the way his whole body stiffened. His hand went to his breast pocket for what I saw now was a little monocular, and I lowered my own glasses just in time and bent my head over my book. A long look, then he turned away from me, fumbling in his trouser pocket, and brought out something small and dark – a trowel?

It was time I was interfering. I stretched, closed *Treasure Island* at casual speed and clambered back into the dinghy.

He knew I was coming for him. He did a last small bit of fiddling with his machine – I wondered if it had an inbuilt GPS, to pinpoint a find again – and then turned on his heel and strode off up the hill towards his car. By the time the dinghy's nose touched the beach he was a barely visible moving dot, and just as I set foot on the sand I heard the car engine. I looked up and saw it speeding away, back towards the main road.

I hoped the folk on the other sites were keeping a good lookout.

Chapter Six

I put the VHF radio on for the 13.10 Coastguard forecast. I'd been watching the course of this low as it tracked east across the Atlantic: a great swirl of anti-cyclonic air that would bring storm force winds up Scotland and across the North Sea. Now the Met Office was giving out a gale warning for all areas, and talking of a force nine within twenty-four hours. I could ride out a south-easterly here, even of that force, if I put both anchors out.

I spent the afternoon dozing in the cockpit, preparing the smaller anchor and chain, and reading another section of *Treasure Island*. Cat and I played his favourite game of tossing a ball of silver paper from the cockpit into the cabin: he scudded down the steps after it, played football with it for a bit, then brought it back in his mouth for me to throw again. I set the anchor light, to guide me back in the dark, and was on the beach at four, with Cat muttering darkly in his basket, when Peter's bi-coloured Volvo came over the hill. 'A quiet day?' he asked, once I'd stowed Cat and myself inside, and fastened both our seatbelts.

'Middling,' I said, and described Adrien's antics.

Peter frowned. 'I thought the archaeologists had metal-detected all that section o' hill. Maybe no. They certainly did the geophysics bit. There were several mounds traditionally said to be graves, and they reckoned only one actually was.'

'Magnie said that, and showed me which it was. It looked to me like Adrien was focused on that one.'

Peter grimaced. 'Well, he'll be ower busy tonight to cause any problems, and forewarned is forearmed for tomorrow. You'll keep a good watch tonight.'

'I'll do that,' I agreed.

We came out onto the main road, looking out southwards over Uyeasound, a neat township of grey roofs, surrounded by silver water and guarded by the island of Uyea. Past it, the open sea gleamed – my road to Norway. A curve in the road, and we were enclosed between hills.

Peter nodded up to the right. 'Gallow Hill, up there.'

Gallow Hill had brought me enough trouble in that witches business in Scalloway. I turned my head away from it, towards the long loch on our left, which had several ring cages in it. 'A salmon hatchery?'

'Salmon and trout.'

There were ponies grazing among the first daffodils on the verge, mostly red and white, heavy-bellied and strong-legged, with thick manes blowing in the breeze. They didn't bother to lift their heads as we went by. 'The Belmont stud,' Peter commented, 'and that's the roof o' Belmont House, just behind the farm.'

He turned in past a couple of modern houses. I caught a glimpse of the house from the front as the car came around the last bend: an imposing gateway facing the sea, with two curving walls ending in square pavilions topped by a pyramid roof, then the house itself, pale yellow, with a tall, arched window in the centre. The garden was golden with daffodils, planted in a double cross around a dark cairn. It was just a glimpse, then the drystane walls on each side of the road closed round us again, blotched white, and grey-green with furred lichen. We pulled up at the back of the house, beside a glassy porch. There was no sign of the minibus Maman had mentioned, but Dad's 4x4 was parked there, as well as the red hired Fiesta, a grey hire car, and a black monster I suspected belonged to Fournier, so perhaps between them they'd decided they didn't need it for this weekend.

Peter drew up beside the long shed. 'I'll no' come in ee noo, they'll aa' be busy. See you later.'

Cat shifted in his basket as I clambered out. There was singing drifting out from a window above me, unaccompanied: Aricia's lament at being given to Diana when she loved Hippolytus. Maman practising, I supposed, although it didn't sound quite like her; the muffling window distorted her clear, soaring voice. The pale-blue door opened into a flagged porch, with a pine shelf for putting shoes under and gloves and hats on, and a row of stones and crabby backs on the window sill. I let Cat out of his basket, then gave the barometer a tap. It sank several points: storm.

Another wide door led into a corridor hemmed by grey doors. The first was a toilet and shower, with a mirror above the sink, and a ewer and basin beside it. It was blissfully warm. The next door was the kitchen, with ochre walls and a wooden dresser of willow-pattern plates. After that I came into the hall proper. Maman's wool coat hung beside Bryony's Edwardian jacket on the pegs by the curving staircase. There was a scarf and gloves thrown down on the seaman's chest, and a hint of expensive scent in the air. The front door was framed first by a pillared archway, then by heavy curtains, red flowers on a silvery-white ground. Sun poured in through its glass panes, and brought the outside into the house: the long carriage drive leading straight to the dazzling blue of the sea. I dumped my rucksack on the chest, then eased the door open and stood looking down between the double row of daffodils. Beyond them, the water danced blue, the hills of Yell were summer green. The ferry terminal was down at the other side of the bay, with what looked like an incongruous scarlet double-decker bus sitting in one corner of the parking area. A lark twittered above my head. Cat jumped onto one of the wooden benches by the door, and began washing his paws.

There was a cropped lawn in front of the house, embraced by the curved walls that ended in the pavilions – the servant quarters, I supposed. I strolled over to the nearest one. The blue door opened on a square, bare room, whitewashed and wood-beamed, with a table and four chairs in one corner of the stone-flagged floor. There was a twelve-paned window looking towards the sea, more, I suspected, to match the house than out of any consideration for the servants' eyesight. A wooden door in the corner opened to show the under-stair cupboard. The stairs creaked as I went up them to the wood-lined roofspace. There was a folded bedstead here, and a skylight. It was ice-cold now, but in the summer it would be a lovely place to sleep.

The murmur of voices and the chink of teacups floated on the wind from an open window. I'd need to go and face them soon. I'd brought my one pretty dress for later, but maybe I'd change into it right now. Maman would fit in here, like the lady of the house, while I was acutely conscious of my jeans and navy gansey putting me below the salt. I didn't want to let her down.

Past the pavilion was the wall enclosing the house lawn. I turned to look back at the house, and was reminded of the old rule for boats: 'If she looks right, she

82

is right.' It was a classic house shape, with three windows above, two and a porch below, and a chimney on each side. I knew nothing about proportions, but I could see this was right: the front almost as high as it was broad, the door lintel higher than the top of the downstairs windows, the windows themselves immediately below the roof skylights, the triangle of pediment just taller than the half the roof, the triple, arched window, the niche. I wondered what statue had been in it when the house was new. It was as beautiful and gracious as an Edwardian yacht.

On my left now, as I faced the house, was a maze of wooden fences: four squares, tall as a series of palettes standing in line, with an entry into each, and a grass walk between. At the head of the square was the curved roof of a little summer house, and I was just about to head up there for a moment's peace to square my shoulders before I went to join the company in the drawing room, when a pale flash caught my eye. Someone who'd been sitting there had stood up in one abrupt movement. It was Kamilla, the sun lighting up her fair head. She'd taken a pace back from the summer house, face tilted down as if she was looking at someone sitting on a bench within it. Even as I began to slide backwards, not wanting to interrupt, she spoke in German, a word that hissed like a snake, then changed to English.

'You are mad. *Mad*.' The word echoed across the maze of fences. 'You –' Her hands rose to her breast, clenching, as if she couldn't find the words, then pushed away from her, in a gesture of repudiation. 'I want nothing to do with it, nothing. Nothing to do with *you*.' She spun away and began striding towards me. I had just time to duck out of her way and back into the pavilion as she came around the corner of the fence-maze. I eased the pavilion door to, and held it there as her feet crunched across the gravel at the front door, and clacked on the stone step. The door grinched open, then slammed behind her, glass panes rattling.

Who had she been talking to? I began walking casually into the maze garden, but the summer house was empty. A gate leading to the back of the house swung wide, and angry footsteps crunched across the gravel behind the curved wall linking the pavilion to the house.

I'd been too late to see who she'd called *mad*, but I was pretty sure the footsteps were a man's.

I came slowly back to the front door. A hand waved from the first floor window; there were light footsteps on the stairs, and Maman came out.

'Cassandre!' We kissed. 'I didn't think you would be here so soon. Come in and have a cup of tea.'

I grimaced at my jeans. 'Should I change first?'

Maman waved that away. 'Oh, you will have plenty of time before the performance, while we are all warming up. You could even have a bath – you will love it, an old-fashioned bath, you will see. Hello, Cat. There is no fire for you, it is not permitted, and anyway the chimneys are blocked, but we have two comfortable couches.'

Cat paused in smoothing his spectacular tail, and looked up, then uncurled and stretched his front paws. He associated Maman with saucers of exotic leftovers, worth getting off his bench for.

I gave Maman a thoughtful look. She seemed tired: there were faint blue shadows under her eyes that not even her immaculate foundation could hide, and a line running down each side of her mouth.

'Wearing?' I asked her.

She nodded. 'It's been years since I did a tour. I had forgotten how tiring it was.'

I put an arm round her waist. 'Are they all being very temperamental?' *Mad ... I want nothing to do with you ...*

She shook her head. 'No. It is that which worries me. I would almost prefer a good row. Everyone is being very polite, but there is an atmosphere which feels all wrong. Kamilla – Adrien – Bryony – even Caleb feels on edge.' She sighed. 'And we are only halfway through the tour.' She turned and drew me into the house. 'Come, I must not stand here in this evening air. Come up and have a cup of tea.'

She motioned me up the spacious stairway, fresh with white paint and hushed by a raspberry carpet. The curved banister began with a carved flower on a snail-shell newel post, and was satin-smooth. 'We have ordered the local restaurant, Saxavord, to come and make us a meal after the performance, for us and two of the trustees of the house, and two sponsors, and, oh, I have forgotten who else, but there will be enough for you too, if you wish to stay.'

A meal by the local restaurant sounded good to me. 'Yes, please. So long as I can get a lift back to *Khalida* afterwards.'

Maman waved a hand. 'Oh, your father will do that.'

In the square upstairs hall, the sun flooded in from the triple window. The view was gorgeous: the rows of daffodils; the green turf; the bay of blue water turning to whisky-gold now as the sun began to dip towards the hills of Yell.

'The drawing room,' Maman said. She opened the door on the right and gestured me inside.

85

At first glance it seemed dauntingly full of people: Bryony, on one of the couches, with a tea tray on the coffee table in front of her; Vincent Fournier, slightly aloof in an armchair; Dad, on the other couch, with Adrien leaning over it from behind. The musical director, Per Rolvsson, that was his name, an unexpected Norwegian directing French opera, was standing at the front-facing window, looking out across the water, with his willow-pattern cup and saucer in one hand, still full, as if he'd only just arrived, and Charles was sitting in the corner at the lidded desk, as if he was about to write a letter. I sidled in beside Maman, reached for the teapot, and poured myself a cup of tea.

My first impression was of how bright it was: there were windows front and back, the white wooden shutters reflecting the light into the room, and two more set in the west gable of the house, one on each side of the plastered mantelpiece. Above it, a curved mirror like a ship's porthole reflected the room back to itself: the lidded desk and chair; the row of heads on the couches facing each other in the middle of the room; the half-moon sideboard. The floor was wooden, covered with a ruby Oriental carpet. Cat followed cautiously, willing to put up with all these people for the sake of a fire, then retreated behind the sofa in disgust at the sight of the pristine fireplace, and went back to washing.

There was a pad of feet on the stairs, and Caleb came in behind me. He was wearing boot socks, and had that healthy outdoor glow of someone who'd just been for a ten-mile tramp across the hills. He looked at the teapot, and shook his head. 'I haven't got accustomed to your English tea.' He sat down beside Bryony, and waved a plastic bottle of Diet Coke at her. 'I've brought my own.'

'So,' Per said, as if he was picking up the conversation

at the point where Maman had come down to greet me, 'the usual scales at 17.30, then you will have time to yourselves. If you wish to have more time with Charles, they will be setting out the chairs from 18.45, so it must be before then.'

The heads nodded as if this was all routine. I was interested that he was addressing the company in French. If Kamilla had spoken in French, I'd have known for sure whether the person she'd talked to had been male or female: *fou* or *folle*. I did a quick head-check; she was the only one missing. Then she slid through the door and sat down between Bryony and Caleb. 'Sorry, Per.'

He nodded and repeated the times, then drank his tea. I leaned back to Adrien, whose manly aftershave was giving me breathing problems, and set the cat among the pigeons. 'A lovely morning. Didn't I see you having a walk out at Lund?'

I should have remembered he was an actor. He gazed at me blandly. 'Lund, Cassandre?'

'The old house. The Viking longhouse sites.' I must have overdone the edge to my voice, for Bryony, Kamilla and Caleb all looked up.

'I walked up there just this morning,' Caleb said. 'Up on the hill there.' He waved an arm eastwards. 'Fascinating, even if the flooring's covered over. Presumably they hope to secure the site this season.'

He meant the Belmont site, I supposed, where Magnie and Peter had had trouble with teenagers. I kept my eyes on Adrien, and he took a sip of tea, then responded.

'Oh, yes, the old house above the fantastic beach. Was that your yacht in the bay, then?'

I nodded. 'Wasn't it you?'

'Could well have been. I just drove around a bit. It seems a shame to come to somewhere as special as this

87

and not see a bit more of it.' He smiled at Maman, and slid away from the subject. 'You must miss the sea, Eugénie, when you're in France.'

Maman gave a dismissive flutter of her hands. 'Oh, in summer, yes, when it is blue and smiling. In winter, when it is steel grey and dashes at the beaches as if it would like to eat them, then no.' She touched my arm. 'You can keep it then, Cassandre.'

'You can keep it too,' I said. 'I've just done a winter aboard. My next Christmas will be somewhere warm.'

Per checked his watch. 'But you are going to one of our tall ships now, I think?'

I nodded. '*Sørlandet*.' He had that preoccupied look of someone who's not really listening, but Caleb raised his head from Kamilla.

'One of the Norwegian square-riggers? Gee, that's great. When does your season start?'

'Next weekend.' It was going to be tight timing, but if the storm blew over as it was supposed to I'd make it with a couple of days in hand.

'Another cup of tea, Cassandre?' Bryony leaned forward with the teapot. 'Per?'

He shook his head impatiently, rose, and returned to French. 'Four forty-five. Forty-five minutes, everyone.'

Charles rose too. 'I will change now, unless anyone wants me.' He gave a quick look round.

Bryony reached down for her phone and checked the time. 'I was wanting to dress now. Can I book you for immediately after the rehearsal, just to run through the first Diana aria?'

Charles nodded.

'Our duet, Eugénie, after that?' Adrien said. Maman nodded. My chances of a bath were looking good, if they were all going to be busy singing. Bryony rose and collected cups, then took the tray downstairs. Kamilla slipped away; I heard the further door on the other side of the hall close behind her. Adrien gave me a sideways look, then headed for the door. I hoped he wasn't going back to Lund for a quick bit of digging, while I was safely corralled here. I did a swift calculation. Ten minutes driving twice, a ten minute walk to the headland I'd scared him away from, and back – no, he didn't have time. I could relax.

'Well,' Maman said, rising, 'I must prepare. Do you come, Dermot?' Dad nodded, and rose. 'The bathrooms are upstairs, Cassandre, you will adore the one that has a step, but wait until we are all rehearsing, and then you will bother nobody.'

'Will do,' I said. They went out, and across to what I supposed was the master bedroom, straight across the hall, with the view to the front. I caught a glimpse of a wide bed with a curved wooden headboard, and a fireplace with a tapestry screen. It warmed me inside to be able to imagine them through the closed door, as I'd seen them so often in my childhood. Dad would kick off his shoes and stretch out on the bed with his paper, while Maman did her make-up in her pale apricot silk petticoat, and then he'd zip up her dress and fasten her necklace when she was ready.

Forty-five minutes until their rehearsal. The opera had lasted almost two hours in Savigny, and it wasn't starting until half past seven, which meant we wouldn't eat until ten o'clock – quarter to, at best. I'd be starving by then. I headed back downstairs, leaving Cat to take over the vacated couch. He was used to making himself at home in strange houses; he knew I'd call him when we needed to go. The sun was slipping down, down, but I was met by a dazzle of light as I opened the kitchen door – the last rays were concentrated on the stainless steel of the Aga and flaring back to hit the doorway just at eye level. I paused, flinched, and came in through it. There was bound, I told myself as I checked out various biscuit tins, to be bread somewhere. A sandwich would keep me going.

I was just checking out the fridge in the little pantry at the far end when I heard the kitchen door swing wide, and the tap of heels. I heard the footsteps stop as I had done, and looked out to see Kamilla narrowing her eyes against the dazzle of sunlight. She turned her head and ducked sideways away from it, towards the worktop beside the sink, where a bunch of letters was lying. Per, coming in just behind her, caught the brightness of it as she moved away, and jerked his head backwards. Beside him, Kamilla lifted her head from the letters and stared as if she'd never seen him before. The blood drained from her face; I thought she was going to faint. One hand went outto the top letter.She lifted it with hands that shook. Her scarlet lips opened, moved soundlessly, then she took a step back, still staring at Per as if he was a ghost.

Then she wrenched herself back into reality. She brought the hand holding the letter up to her chest, clutching it to her. Per's eyes fell on it. He gave it a puzzled glance, then brought his eyes back up to her face. She made an inarticulate noise and looked wildly around, as if seeking escape, then dodged past him out of the kitchen door. Her footsteps thudded up the stairs. Per stood for a long half-minute longer, his eyes staring blindly around. I came forward out of the pantry, and he gave a little start. 'Cassandre! I didn't realise you were in there.'

'I was just looking for bread.'

Per turned his face away from the light, frowning, then looked back at me and gestured towards the pile of letters.

'You didn't happen to see what was the letter that upset her so? It was the top one.'

I narrowed my eyes, trying to visualise them, then shook my head. 'I didn't look at them.'

Per sighed. 'It had a French stamp. I'll speak to Bryony, and she can perhaps see what is wrong.' His hand came up in a half-hearted, would-be jaunty dismissal, then he turned as slowly as an old man, and went into the hall. His feet trudged upwards to the first floor, the second, leaving a heavy silence behind them.

ᚻ

Wirds ir spoken, freend tae freend,
Wi'oot a soond being heard,
Sheeksin, weddings, births and deaths,
Winging dir way across da warld.

... **a letter**

N

Friday, 27th March (continued)

Tide Times at Mid Yell, UT and at Dover, UT
High Water   16.04, 1.8m;   16.24
Low Water   22.15, 1.2m;   23.19

Sunset   18.31
Moonset   02.23

First quarter moon

I hae nae hauns, and strike nae blow,
Yet kings and princes bring I low.

Chapter Seven

I found a sliced loaf at the bottom of the fridge, a hunk of cheese in the middle, and made my sandwich, puzzling. I couldn't imagine what could be in Kamilla's letter to make her react so. Blackmail, my mind said helpfully. Murder, incest, child abuse. *A French stamp …*

Thirty-five minutes to hang around before the rehearsal. I took my sandwich up to the drawing room, along with another cup of tea and *Treasure Island*, until Charles began unpacking his keyboard in the far corner, muttering darkly at the sun which was blazing gold in the window behind him, and eventually closing the wooden shutters against it. He started his finger-loosening scales, and I heard feet moving about on the upstairs landing. I dodged into the study and admired the view while they filed past, then headed upwards, in search of the promised bath. *The one with the step*, Maman had said.

The second flight of stairs was as wide as the first, with another leg-height window looking out over the farm, and a square landing with two doors on my left, one straight ahead and a little flight of steps up to the right. A tall mirror stood in one corner – I was surprised Maman hadn't annexed that – and four dinner jackets and white shirts hung on the pegs opposite me, two on each side of the closed door.

The first door on my left was a bathroom with wooden walls painted in warm pink, with a grey fireplace. A skylight let the last rays of the sun shine into a dazzlingly white bath. The shelf above the circular sink was stacked with the men's gear – leather and black washbags, a pair of razors, brushes in the tooth-mug. There was no step, though. I moved on.

The room up the little steps was a bedroom. Caleb's red rucksack was propped against the fireplace, and a French comic-book lay on the nearest bed. Charles, I supposed, the youngest cast member and musician sharing. That meant the room on my left was Per and Adrien. A swift glance sideways showed a Norwegian paperback and Per's jumper on the nearest bed, a bottle of Vittel water on the bedside table.

The last door, then, between the penguin suits, had to be *the one with a step*.

I fell in love straight away. It was the most beautiful bath I'd ever seen: gleamingly white enamel encased in varnished wood, dark with age, and set so high that it really needed the elegantly shaped step to get up into it. There was a shower head with a dangling chrome snake laid across the taps, but I ignored that. I set the hot tap running, skooshed some of the vanilla shower gel in, and let it fill to almost halfway before getting in. Bliss.

The warm-up started on time below me. I floated gently in my beautiful hot bath and listened. I heard Per's voice, then Charles on the keyboard. He played a note, and Caleb and Kamilla, the two lower voices, took it up and sang with it: up the scale for two octaves and down again. A note up, the scale again, another, another, and then Maman, Bryony and Adrien joined in, taking the top notes alone. Then there was a soprano voice, singing an aria alone: Bryony. After that, it was Adrien and Maman.

I could hear that Maman was already Aricia in her head. Kamilla came after them, seeming to have put the letter that had startled her aside, focusing only on the lovely sounds coming from her scarlet mouth. Then the accompaniment stopped, and the sounds died away. It was time I got out, to clear the bathroom for make-up. I towelled, scrunched my hair into its natural curls – where were little stars when you needed them? – and dressed hastily in my one pretty dress, a swirling georgette affair in black with fawn swirls, touched by green and raspberry.

I needn't have hurried. As soon as the bedroom doors had closed behind them, the sounds began again: Maman, in a series of trills, muffled by the floor between us; Caleb next door, thundering out some kind of denunciation, loudly first then softer, with the purity of the notes increasing as the volume diminished. *'The real test of a singer,'* Maman had told me, twenty years ago, *'is to sing beautifully softly.'* It was like sailing, I supposed; any fool could drive a dinghy in a brisk wind, but it took a sailor to keep her moving when the water was glass-calm. Bryony and Kamilla rang out a shared piece. Only Adrien was silent, though I heard him moving about in the other upstairs room.

At twenty to seven, the house suddenly filled with volunteers in turquoise Belmont Trust T-shirts. There were furniture-moving noises from the drawing room, then a march of people carrying plastic chairs. I went to see if I could help. The couches had been moved to the sides of the room, one in the corner below the front window, the other beneath the dropped-paint-pots-style modern art, so that there was a clear space in the middle of the room, with Charles' keyboard to the right of the fireplace. The singers would take up the space in front of the mantelpiece, and the chairs were being set out across the length of the room. I helped hook them together in fours, as required by fire regulations.

'Thanks,' the girl in charge said. She looked across at Gutcher, just ten minutes across the water. 'Okay, guys, that's the ferry moving now. Stations, everyone.'

Footsteps headed for the front door, the back porch, the top of the stairs, the table by the door, ready to take tickets. I produced my ticket and bagged myself a comfy seat on the couch with the best view of the voe. Five minutes later, Dad joined me, in his best black suit with a bow tie. I was glad I'd made the effort to dress up.

'Well, Cassie, are you all set to hear it all again? Not that it's not worth hearing over and over. Now, when do you join your ship?'

Nearly forty years away from Dublin hadn't eased out any of Dad's Irish accent. He'd been a builder's son, and had risen to foreman, then the practical head of the building enterprise in the sudden boom of work when the huge oil terminal of Sullom Voe had been created. He'd also worked on the new opera house in Lille, which was where he'd met Maman, thrilled to have her chance in the chorus. He'd turned on the charm and persuaded her to leave her habitat for domesticity, oil-wife tea parties, and a child toddling behind her. It was a wonder that she'd stayed so long, for she'd fitted like a phoenix trapped in a budgie's cage. Now it seemed they'd worked out a nomadic life together: she would come to Shetland between engagements, and he'd join her at her latest gig. I hoped that Gavin and I could work out something similar.

Apart from that, Dad was tall, energetic and still dark, although he was in his sixties now, with eyes the blue of the Irish Sea. I wouldn't care to cross him in business – at present he was fighting through permission to build a wind farm up the central spine of north Shetland – but we'd got on well in those years when it had been just the two of us, and that companionable relationship seemed to have returned at last.

'As soon as the wind'll let me,' I replied. 'Next week's looking good, once this has blown past.'

'I'll put up a word to St Medard for you.' Dad was a great one for obscure saints with particular duties. 'He's the boy you need to prevent bad weather.' He nodded at Cat, on the couch beside me now, and resolutely ignoring the stamping feet as the audience filed in. 'I see that cat's made himself at home. He's good as a dog, so he is.'

The chairs were filled now, and the audience paused in that expectant hush that said it was half past. The woman on the door set her table to the side, and the company came in: Maman in her Trojan jewellery, on Adrien's arm; Kamilla, scarlet clad, on Caleb's; Bryony walking beside Per. The singers spread themselves in a semicircle, ready to step forward as the story required, and Per sat down beside the keyboard, visible but not obtrusive. A series of notes, and Maman stepped forward and began the lament that I'd heard her singing earlier, notes bell-clear now without the distorting window. Around her, the faces were absorbed, intent only on the music: Kamilla; Bryony; Adrien; Caleb.

You are mad. Mad ...

Who had Kamilla said that to? *Bryony is jealous*, Maman had said, *so we are keeping them apart*. Until now, that was, when it seemed they had to share a room, so that Maman and Dad could be together. Had *Bryony* done something mad? But she was too light-footed to be the steps I'd heard scrunching across the gravel. I looked across at Adrien's dark face, and could envisage him being obsessive ... about Kamilla, perhaps? Maybe he'd believed this tour would get them back together, but if he was keen and she wasn't, why was she meeting him in the garden?

And what had that odd scene in the kitchen meant? Kamilla had been working with Per for two weeks now, so there didn't seem any reason for his presence behind her to startle her so. He'd taken it to be the letter, from France. I couldn't think of anything else. She'd come in, turned her head away from the sun, which meant she was looking towards the sink, the nearest chairs, the Aga. She'd have seen the letters, my sailing jacket slung over the back of the chair ... what sudden terror could come from a worn red Musto jacket?

I qualified that thought. No, it hadn't quite been terror. I saw her face again in my mind's eye, and the nearest I could get was a shock of recognition so intense that it had left her unable to react normally. The handwriting on a letter, or maybe an unexpected visitor by sea.

Whatever it had been, there was no sign of it now. For the moment, Kamilla was Phaedra, in love with her stepson. I thought, as I'd thought at the château, how much this show had been cast against type: the older couple, Maman and Adrien, as the young lovers; and the younger, Caleb and Kamilla, as the parents. Here was another example, with Kamilla, who didn't want Adrien, making passionate love to him. If he still loved her, that had to be pretty hard to take.

Mad, mad ... there was an uneasy feeling trickling down my spine about all this. If I'd been at sea I'd have been lashing down canvas for a brewing storm.

I'd noticed Cat slipping out during the performance, and the reason wasn't hard to guess: the caterers had arrived, and a savoury odour of cullen skink, the Scottish fish and cream soup, was drifting upwards. As Cat knew from Antoine, the college chef, people in kitchens were generally well-disposed towards a handsome cat who kept out of their way while fixing them with a hopeful yellow gaze. I had no doubt that some fish trimmings would be coming his way.

I was hungry myself. It was coming up for half past nine. The opera ended in a final triumphant duet from Maman and Adrien, a swirl of chords from the piano, and a standing ovation from the audience. I'd resigned myself to a round of chat after it, but the company was too professional to stand around in costume. Maman led her troops out, and Dad and I took the compliments on her behalf. One of them, whose face was vaguely familiar, seemed to have been her old singing tutor, here in Shetland. He said he'd been the one to start her off on early music, and gave several highly technical sentences of praise which were totally lost on me, but which I said I'd do my best to pass on. The room emptied at last, and we were free to go down to the dining room, on the right of the front door. The oval table was covered with an immaculately white, ironed tablecloth, laid with silver cutlery, and lit by two candelabras which reflected in the gold-framed mirror and the darkened windows. Crystal glasses stood ready on the mahogany sideboard. There were fifteen places squeezed in. An older woman in waitress black, with a notepad in one hand, stood by the door.

'Do you know,' I asked her, 'if a grey cat's making himself at home in the kitchen?'

She nodded straight off. 'He's been there this last hour.'

'Not being a nuisance?'

'We thought he belonged to the house, so we lured him into the cloakroom with a plate of lamb trimmings.'

'He'll be fine there,' I agreed. 'You could maybe let him out once the serving's over.'

There were place cards beside each setting. The Captain's Table gambit, I reckoned, with the Belmont House trustees and other influential folk beside the lead performers. Maman, at head of the table, was between two of them, with Per and Dad on their other sides, and Vincent Fournier, at the foot, had another two. One was Peter, his beard brushed to Navy smartness, and wearing an eye-dazzling, all-over gansey in shades of brown. He was leaning forward to chat to Fournier about the problems with treasure-seekers. His voice was just loud enough for Adrien to overhear, and he darted the occasional glance at him. The one on Fournier's other side was talking to Adrien about the restoration. Adrien himself seemed distracted, crumbling his roll between his long fingers, and casting sideways glances around the table. Opposite me, Dad had another unknown between him and Kamilla, who was turning on the charm – the Shetland Arts Music Development officer, from the sound of the conversation.

'A Well-Being Choir?' Kamilla cooed, her voice honey-sweet. 'How delightful!'

I had Per on one side of me and Caleb on the other. Per was talking to the unknown between him and Maman, so I complimented Caleb on the performance, and asked how he liked Shetland.

'It's incredible!' He was still in that half-high, after-show state, his green eyes lit up. 'I've never been anywhere that there's so much sea, you know? Everywhere you look.' He took a gulp of the wine the waitress had just poured him and nodded appreciatively. 'And I hadn't expected the islands to be so big. I thought it'd be a half-hour drive from one end to the other, and then it turned out to be a hundred miles, and two ferries. We got off the boat at seven thirty this a.m., and we didn't arrive here until ten o'clock. And this house is real neat. You'd think that the people who built it had just stepped out for a moment.'

The waitress came round to take our orders: a choice of cullen skink or mussels. I went for the mussels; nothing would beat the fish soup I'd had in Bergen last summer, where the chef began with a kilo of prawns, fresh from the market, and a quart of cream. Opposite me, Kamilla frowned and spoke urgently to the waitress, who looked surprised, then nodded soothingly. When our bowls arrived, minutes later, she got a green salad. I wondered if she was vegetarian, or just not keen on mussels. For all they were local products, it seemed dangerous to assume everyone would want fish, without at least checking up on allergies.

Neither Caleb nor Per was having any difficulty. 'I noticed a number of fish farms and mussel buoys as we drove up,' Per said to the bigwig on his right. He waved the mussel on the end of his fork. 'These are excellent quality, a good size.'

'I'm hoping to explore a bit,' Caleb said. He negotiated another mussel, laid his fork down and wiped his fingers. 'I gotta hire car for the weekend. I drove about a piece in Unst here today, up to look at the last of Britain, you know, the lighthouse and the stacks – gee, I wouldn't like to be a keeper there.'

'It's automated,' I said.

'Yeah.' He grinned. 'I'm contradicting myself now, I know that, but it's a kinda pity. It's a romantic thought, a coupla men alone on that rock. What was that poem, where they disappeared?'

'"Flannan Isle",'I said promptly. It was one of the ones nearly every sailor knew by heart. I recited the first verse, and he capped it with the second. 'But,' I added, 'it's usually agreed that the black birds had nothing to do with it. They got washed off by a freak wave.'

'Don't spoil the story! Where's your sense of romance?'

'Sailors are practical people.' I remembered he lived in France, and added quickly, 'Except for Moitissier.'

He frowned for a moment, then his brow cleared. 'Oh, yeah, I saw the movie. He went round the world once then decided he couldn't take civilisation and headed off to go round again, and left Knox-Johnston to be first man home.'

I sopped some wine sauce into a piece of bread and nodded, mouth too full to comment. The sauce was delicious.

'So,' Caleb said, copying me, 'Where should I go?'

'The west side,' I said as soon as my mouth was clear, 'or the north-west. Voes and geos and sea stacks. It's like a little Scottish Highlands. If it's scenery you're after, that is. What're you interested in, apart from work?'

'History, a bit – my grandfather was one for genealogy. Then I'd like to see the oil terminal, and the near by town – Brae, isn't it, where you grew up?'

I nodded.

Caleb glanced away from me and out of the window, suddenly diffident. 'I don't suppose you know of a house called Eastayre?'

Now I was intrigued, for that was where my school pal,

Inga, lived. 'Eastayre? Yes, it's just in the middle, looking out over the voe.'

'I googled it, and it seemed to be a new house.'

'Ah, that was the oil. In the seventies and eighties, the council offered ninety per cent grants to anyone whose house was needing serious repairs, for them to build a new one, so old Charlie – that's the present owner's father – jumped at the chance.'

Caleb glanced around again, and leaned in to me. 'You see, that's where my family came from, three generations back. My great-grandfather ran off from the croft and headed for the States.'

Now his interest in Shetland made better sense. 'So you want to redd up kin.'

He gave me a blank look.

'Get in touch with your Shetland family.'

He flushed. 'Gee, I'm not sure about that. It's a long time ago. They'd never have heard of me.'

'Oh, they'll know you. Charlie did a family tree, one winter, through an evening class with the Shetland Family History Society.' I ate my last mussel, mopped my last piece of bread and lay my fork down. 'That was wonderful. Charlie's the owner of Eastayre now. He's a fisherman, married to my best friend from the school, Inga.'

'Do they have children?'

'Three. Vaila and Dawn, who're heading for their teens, and Peerie Charlie, who's a three-year-old tearaway.'

Caleb didn't reply for a moment, brows drawn together. I turned to Per, and changed to Norwegian.

'I hope Maman and her company have been well-behaved.'

His head went up; he looked at me blankly, as if he

wasn't sure who I was.

'I'm Eugénie's daughter, Cass,' I said helpfully.

He came to life, as if a switch had been touched, but the lines about his mouth, the tiredness in his blue eyes, showed it was an effort, and I felt mean bothering him with idle chit-chat after a performance. He was darker than you'd expect for a Norwegian, with none of my friend Anders' dazzling Norse god looks. Per's face was thin and mobile under his fine, dark-chestnut hair, curved down into a widow's peak. He looked highly-strung, but I suspected he'd be quick-witted in a crisis. 'Of course you are. And you are about to go on a Norwegian ship. Eugénie told me all about it, when you got the offer.'

'*Sørlandet*, from Kristiansand, the smallest of your fleet.' I smiled. 'The oldest square-rigged ship still sailing.'

'And you have your own boat, and live aboard. I took a walk earlier on, along the back of the loch.' He gestured behind us, towards the Loch of Snarravoe. 'Then I went up the hill behind, and I saw a yacht moored in a sandy bay, shaped like a heart. Was that you?'

I nodded. 'A good jumping-off point for Norway, next week.'

His brows rose. 'You're sailing there? She's what, eight metres, nine?'

'Eight, but she's a Van de Stadt.'

'Ah.' He smiled at the name of *Khalida*'s builder. 'Built to go anywhere.'

The waitress came round to clear our plates. 'We'll serve up the lamb, and then your cat can come out. He's a bit indignant at being shut in.'

'I'll come and reassure him. Excuse me,' I said to Per, and slipped into the kitchen. Cat was indeed indignant at being shut out of the warm house; I begged another saucer

106

of lamb scraps from the chef and coaxed him back upstairs. He probably wouldn't stay there, if there were exciting things going on downstairs, but he'd be out from underfoot for the time it took him to eat the lamb and wash his whiskers afterwards.

When I got back, my plate of lamb was waiting for me. Proper local lamb, was a treat, sweet and fat-free, with a delicate taste of heather. I helped myself to roast potatoes, carrots and peas, and tuned back in to Per's conversation with the woman between him and Maman.

'I'd like to know a bit more about the Viking connection here,' Per said. 'Adrien was saying that this was the first place the Norsemen settled in Britain, and apparently there has been a recent investigation of this whole island.'

'Completely,' she assured him. 'The most thorough survey anywhere. They found over thirty definite Norse dwelling sites, and dug three. One's on the east, at Hamar, the second is a few miles north of here, at Lund.' She'd evidently been listening earlier, for she gestured to me. 'Where you're moored, Cass. The third one's just here, up the hill on the other side of the road. It's an old site, used in the Bronze Age, as you can tell by the cup marks on a rock, but continuously occupied by Norse settlers from about the ninth to the thirteenth century, when the climate changed, and it became too exposed.'

'I was thinking I'd go up after breakfast tomorrow, and have a look. I would be interested to see it. We're here all morning, then off on the ferry mid-afternoon for our Lerwick performance in the evening.'

'And how about the treasure?' Caleb asked. He spoke across Charles and Bryony. 'Adrien, didn't you say that one of the hoards had been found not far from here?'

Adrien gestured towards the back of the house. 'In a

field not five hundred metres away.'

I glanced sideways along the table, but he seemed perfectly at ease, with no signs that he was planning his own treasure hunt. Outside, the half-moon had moved round to bathe the front of the house, the pyramid, the gateposts, the two lines of daffodils, in silver. It would be clear as day out on the headland; I'd need to keep good watch.

Caleb shook his head. 'But the Vikings weren't afraid of anyone. Who would they be hiding their treasure from?'

Per smiled at that. 'Each other. All these hoards of silver and coins that have been found in Gotland, for example, were their bank account. You should read the Sagas. There were constant raids – it was their summer pastime, once the crops were planted.'

'To say nothing of strangers visiting,' I added. 'Shetland was the first stop on their trading route to the Faroes, to Iceland, to Greenland, to America.' Once, when all transport had been by water, we'd been the centre of the North Sea world, not just in the Viking days, but in the medieval Hanseatic league, and then again in the days of the Greenland whaling. Now we were a central destination for the sleek, white cruise ships en route from Norway to Iceland, or Scotland to Norway, and on most summer days Lerwick pier was busy with bus tours. Camera-carrying tourists greeted each other in the narrow shopping street, and inspected shop window displays of Fair Isle knitwear, local music CDs, and craft items.

The waitresses removed the dinner plates, and put a selection of desserts on the sideboard for us to help ourselves: a trifle; a cheesecake; a bowl of fruit salad; and a cheese platter. There was a little bustle as everyone took the opportunity to stretch and move about. Adrien slid quietly out, followed by Vincent Fournier and one of the Belmont trustees: smokers, I presumed, hearing the grinch of the front door opening. Per rose and went around Maman to talk to the trustee on her other side, then moved on past Dad, the Shetland Arts bloke and Kamilla, to Peter. I considered the pudding options, and lost a brief argument with my better nature as to whether cream was allowed in Lent. Fruit salad without cream didn't seem worth the bother. I watched Caleb helping himself to toffee cheesecake and turned away, reminding myself that my Christian Aid box was a pound better off for every pudding I resisted. The smokers slid back in, in a nicotine-waft of cold air, and helped themselves to bowls and desserts. Once everyone was seated, Bryony rose. She hadn't taken a pudding either, I'd noticed, though whether it was Lenten conviction or slimming I didn't presume to guess. Now she began serving the teas and coffees, just as she had upstairs. She knew what everyone took, setting the cup down in front of each person without comment, and only asking the guests about milk and sugar. I went over to ask her for a cup of tea, and took it back to the table.

Suddenly, there was the jingle of glass smashing. Opposite me, Kamilla's fair skin was flushed under the powder. She clawed at her throat in a beautifully theatrical gesture, and began to slide sideways off her chair, one hand reaching out for the wall just behind her. Beside her, Peter caught her arm to steady her. Her mouth worked, as if she was trying to swallow, or speak, then she thrust her sequinned clutch bag forward onto the table, eyes fixed on mine. Her lips formed a word I couldn't read, then she toppled in a heap onto the floor.

Chapter Eight

For a moment there was silence, with us all frozen round her like staring waxworks. A long heartbeat, then Maman rose, followed by Bryony and Fournier. *Seafood* ... I shoved my chair back and came around the table in four swift strides, grabbing for Kamilla's bag. One trustee was down on his knees beside her, turning her head to open her airways. Good; an ally who knew what he was doing. If she was seriously allergic she'd have an inhaler or an EpiPen. I yanked the flap open and upended the bag on the floor beside her. Yes, here, two clear tubes. I took the first pen out of its tube, broke off the cap and jammed it against Kamilla's thigh, holding it for ten seconds, then massaging where the needle had been. Kamilla's lips were blue. I picked up her wrist, and felt her pulse racing. I looked at Dad.

'Dad, we need an ambulance. Don't bother with 999, get straight on to the Lerwick hospital. 743000.' He was punching it into his mobile as I spoke. 'Tell them it's suspected anaphylactic shock, caused by seafood.' I turned my head to Peter.'If there's a doctor on Unst, we need him here, fast. Do you have a proper number, not NHS 24?'

Peter nodded. He lifted his phone, checked it, then went outside.

111

Kamilla's face was swelling now. I tilted her head back to open her airway, and felt the puffiness extending to her throat. Our first-aid lecturer's voice echoed in my head: *Twenty per cent of sufferers need a second injection. Don't hesitate. You'll do more harm by not giving it.*

I picked up the second EpiPen, and injected her other thigh. 'Does anyone have an inhaler?'

'I do,' Caleb said, and ran from the room. I heard his feet pounding up the stairs.

Dad had got through to the hospital. 'Possible anapylactic shock. She's been given both EpiPens, but she's still having difficulty breathing. No, she's not conscious.'

Caleb thudded back down the stairs. A tube was pushed into my hands. I put it to Kamilla's mouth, skooshed, felt the cold vapour trickle past my fingers, and felt her pulse again. Nothing. I put two fingers to her neck. Still nothing. 'Dad, I'm going to start CPR. Tell them.'

I heard him relaying it as I cupped my hands for the first heart compressions, ran my hand down her breastbone to find the place and leant forward. Then he must have been passed on to somebody else, for I heard him begin over again, giving the details. I didn't know how much good CPR would do, with so little of my breath going into her through that swollen throat, but it had to be better than nothing. My whole world was focused on the swell of her chest under her scarlet dress. Breathe in, hand firm over her mouth, turn my head and see her chest lift as I exhaled. Lifting meant breath was getting through. Thirty chest compressions, two breaths.

Peter came back in. 'The doctor's coming straight away.'

There wasn't room for the others to crowd around me;

they stood still in their places at the table. The silence of shock had given way to low-voiced murmurs. Bryony was sobbing.

'Can anyone else do CPR?'

The trustee that had been the first to react nodded. 'Will I spell you?'

'Three minutes each.' The whole of Unst was only twelve miles long. If the doctor was in Baltasound, the main town, she could be here in ten minutes. I gave way to the trustee and began giving out instructions. 'Can you all take your coffee up to the drawing room? A crowd will embarrass her when she wakes.' My eyes were on my watch. A minute and a half. 'Dad, could you check the kitchen for another first aider?' Two minutes. Maman put an arm around Bryony and steered her out, followed by the others. I let the trustee work on: two and a half minutes. Three. I knelt down beside Kamilla again. A steady rhythm was what mattered. I sang inside my head, as I'd been taught. A verse and chorus of 'We're all going to the zoo tomorrow', at a steady pace, made thirty compressions. Its cheerfulness jangled. I was afraid that even if help came now, it would be too late.

My arms were aching. I nodded to the trustee and let him take over. Kamilla was horribly inert, but we couldn't give up. Then, during my third spell, there was a bustle at the door, and a middle-aged woman with a medical bag came in. 'Keep going while I get my kit out. Shellfish reaction?'

'Presumably,' the trustee said. 'She had salad for her first course, but only keeled over at the end of the meal. We gave her both EpiPens.' He glanced at his watch, 'Seventeen minutes ago.'

'Response?'

'None.'

'Okay, let me through to her now.' She looked at me. 'Relation?'

'My mother's a member of the opera company.'

'Go up and tell them I've arrived. Reassure them we're doing everything possible. The chopper's on its way.'

But I saw in her face that she wasn't hopeful. I backed to the door, and went upstairs on heavy feet.

The audience chairs had been taken away, the two sofas returned to their place facing the fire, and a tea tray set on a butler's table just inside the door. Maman must have taken Bryony away, for it was only the men there. Peter stepped forward as I came in. 'I'll run you home, lass.'

'Oh, thank you!' I sank down on the couch between Per and Dad. 'Can you give me five minutes?' I looked around at them: Peter, standing by the tea-table, Adrien and Caleb on the other couch, Charles by the desk, Fournier in his armchair. 'The doctor's here, and the chopper's on its way.'

'I will go down,' Per said. He looked at the cup in his hand as if he had forgotten what it was for a moment. 'Would you like tea, Cassandre?'

I nodded, and Peter poured a cup and handed it to Adrien to pass across. Adrien hesitated, the cup in his hand. 'D'you take milk or sugar?'

'Milk, please.' He rose to add it, and passed the cup across. I drank it gratefully.

'She musta been severely allergic.' Caleb said. 'Not to respond to the EpiPens, I mean. How come nobody knew?'

Per shook his head. 'She did not tell me it was so severe. I must go down.'

'She'd only had one attack, years ago,' Adrien said. His face was white, his eyelids red, as if he was with difficulty holding back tears. 'I believe that a second attack can be more severe than the first.' He rose. 'We can do her no good waiting here.' His dark eyes turned to me. 'You'll tell us if there's news? Just knock on my door. I won't be sleeping.'

It would be Dad they'd phone, not me. I looked at him, and he nodded.

'If they are taking her away,' Per said, 'I will go with her.' Adrien half-rose, and Per held out his hand, palm forwards, like a policeman making a 'stop' signal. 'No, the company is my responsibility. I will let you all know how she is doing, and I will see you in Lerwick tomorrow.'

There was an uneasy silence as his steps trailed upstairs. I rose. 'I won't be long, Peter – I just need to fetch Cat.'

The helpful waitress was still in the kitchen, washing up and tidying away. I had an uneasy feeling, as if I should be stopping her. 'I don't suppose you know which glass the girl who collapsed drank from?'

She gave me a sharp look. 'I havena cleared the dining room yet. The doctor's still there, wi' the lass.'

'It's just a feeling,' I said.

'You and me both. It'll do our business no good, even though everyone kens these allergies are nothing you can help. Still, someen's bound to say we shoulda kept the fish sundry from the rest o' the food. She canna have known, poor lass, for I asked most particular when she ordered seafood.'

I felt the jolt of that go down my spine. 'Someone

115

ordered seafood?'

'Just three days ago. I took the call myself. The French lady it was, saying she'd been telling the others how good Shetland seafood was, and they were all eager to try it, so she ordered mussels and the cullen skink for first course, and a choice of lamb or salmon for main. And,' she repeated, 'I asked most particularly if there was anyone with an allergy, and she assured me there was not.'

I stared at her. She was obviously a Shetlander, in her forties, and with a reliable look. I had no reason to doubt that someone from the company had phoned ahead to order seafood, just as she said. I would be surprised if it had been Maman. *You are mad ...*

'Look,' I said, 'I think for your own protection you should keep everything that she ate or drank from separate, in a box, unwashed. Let's gather it up now, and tape it up, labelled.' I picked up two of their catering boxes. 'You keep them. You didn't know her; you'd never met her. And look, for comparison, let's take someone else's place setting. Mine.' I gave her a steady look. 'She carried an EpiPen, so she knew she had the allergy, and anyone who knew that would have warned the people in charge of catering that they couldn't go near seafood.' Our eyes met. Hers were wide with startled, disbelieving horror. 'Especially if it was so severe that she could have a fit like that, without even eating any of it. She'd have said.'

There was a distant thrumming in my ears. We both looked towards the window. A star hung above the pier, blazing brighter even as we looked at it, and the wind swirled the noise of rotor blades towards us, louder, fainter, louder, until the drumming was a presence in the room,. Cat dived under the table. The wind buffeted

116

the house, the helicopter's light tilted and descended, and the drumming rose to a roar as it landed in the field I'd surveyed only this afternoon. It felt a long time ago.

Two men jumped down, heads bowed, collected a stretcher from within and ran for the door. I hurried to fling it open. 'She's in there.' They brought a chill wind in with them. It seemed only seconds before they had bundled Kamilla up on their stretcher and hurried out again, the doctor at their heels. Per came clattering down the stairs, his case in his hand, and ducked after them into the hatch. The rotors whirred, tilted, and the helicopter rose up again, hovered, then set off arrow-straight for Lerwick, leaving a heavy silence behind.

I turned to meet the waitress's eyes. She took the box from me without speaking, and we went together into the dining room. She picked up the larger glass fragments and the dessert plate, while I wrote the name on the box: Kamilla Lange. Then we packaged my own plate and glass. I wrote again: Cass Lynch. We stowed the boxes in the boot of her car, and then, still in silence, I helped her clear the table. Her thoughts, like mine, were with that crazy spinning metal ball in the sky, taking Kamilla to safety.

Two trayfuls had the dishwasher filled. I helped carry boxes to the car, then put Cat in his basket, changed into normal clothes, and went back up to Peter. The men were still there: Dad on one couch, his dark brows drawn together; Caleb on the other, all smiles gone, mouth turned down. Fournier was frowning as if he was calculating. Peter rose as I came in, said a rather awkward goodnight to them all, and ushered me out.

We were silent as the car swooped through the night, throwing its light before it. Peter only spoke as he set me down at the graveyard. 'You'll see all right to row out to the boat?'

I nodded at the anchor light, a burnished star to guide me home. 'I'll just row for that.'

'I'll gie you a hand with the dinghy.'

The tide was almost as far out as it could go. We lugged the dinghy to the water, and Peter shoved me off. Ten hard pulls of the oars and I was at *Khalida*. I tied the dinghy's painter to her stern, fingers clumsy, and clambered aboard. Home, sanctuary. I was so tired that the world was spinning around me, and I staggered as I went down the companion steps. I made my hot water bottle, put down some tinned food for Cat to ignore, and got my sleeping bag out. I was still on duty, but I could doze in the cockpit, where I'd hear any sound, see any lights. Cat waited on the step, looking at me expectantly, but when he saw that I really was going to sleep outside, he padded up too and curled into the crook of my neck, and we dropped into the dizzying dark.

ᚼ

I hae nae hauns, and strike nae blow,
Yet kings and princes bring I low.

... **death**

118

Saturday, 28th March

Tide Times at Mid Yell, UT and at Dover

High Water	04.27, 1.8m;	04.46
Low Water	11.15, 1.0m;	12.07
High Water	17.32,1.7m;	17.53
Low Water	23.49, 1.3m;	00.08
		(Sunday)

Sunrise	05.44
Moonrise	11.00
Sunset	18.33
Moonset	03.04

Waxing quarter moon

Footless and horseless, I gallop abroad,
Mouthless I cry, and handless I destroy.

Chapter Nine

It was light that woke me, just a brief flash of a torch somewhere on land that touched my face and was gone. I raised my head and waited for it to come again. The moon was still high, as if I hadn't slept for long. I listened intently. There was the soft trickle of the water against *Khalida*'s hull, the shoosh of waves on the beach. Then, distinctly, a soft metallic *chink*.

I sat up and looked towards the headland. Yes, on the point of the headland, where Adrien had taken out his trowel, there was some sort of directional lantern, for there was no light shining directly towards me any more, just a diffused glow that was warmer than the bleaching moonlight, with a dark shadow crossing it every so often. I heard the rap of a foot, then the metallic noise again, a trowel on stone. Somebody was digging in the darkness. I wondered if Adrien was really so determined that he'd crept out of the house, in spite of Kamilla's seizure.

I had a powerful lamp at hand, ready plugged in. It was meant for shining into the bridge of large ships that seemed intent on running me down, or onto my own sails to make me visible if I needed rescue, and it lit up the dark shore and headland like a searchlight. I swept it round and thought I caught a dark figure hunched over among the grave rocks. I held it there, but there was no movement, just that darker rounded back among the pointed rocks. I shone it towards the house and gave the signal flashes, twice, then swept it back to the headland. If I wanted to leave it on for long I'd need to put the engine on, and that would take away my ability to listen for these tiny noises that told me where the person was. I held the beam on the headland for another half-minute. When I switched it off, the darkness seemed to smother me. It took a moment before I was able to see that the glow in the darkness was still there, brightening as the moon shadows lengthened. There was a long silence, then the faint chinking began again.

Very well, I'd have to go over there. My arms felt heavy, my head muzzy, as if I was still half-asleep as I swung into the dinghy; not a state to be messing about in a small boat. I shook my head to clear it and slotted the oars into the rowlocks, then rowed quietly shorewards, heading for the headland end of the beach, aware that I'd be visible from above, a plump, black water-beetle on the silver sea. He'd know exactly how long he could keep digging for.

I hadn't thought about personal danger, but it occurred to me now. Whoever this was seemed prepared to keep going for the treasure in spite of my searchlight, and now, my presence. Perhaps he was preparing an unpleasant welcome. Take me out, and he'd have peace to dig all night. I paused at the thought, oars stilled in the water. I was thinking *he*, but there was nothing to say it wasn't *they*. There might be a reception committee on the beach, hiding behind the ridge of stones. Where, I wondered wryly, was a ghost Viking when you needed one?

I had a torch in the dinghy. At ten metres from the shore, I picked it up and flashed the light round. The sand was bare; no sinister figure waiting at the tideline, nor, as far as I could see, peering over the rocky dune. I set the torch in my lap and kept it trained on the beach as I back-watered ashore. Still nothing. I had to turn my back on the beach as I hauled the dinghy's nose onto the sand. The hills seemed to open and close towards me like bellows, and then suddenly blackness rushed over me, and I just had time to put my hands out to break my fall, feel them go limp under me as I rolled on the sand ... then nothing.

ᚼ

I awoke with a start. I was huddled up on *Khalida*'s long couch, fully dressed, with Cat snuggled at my neck, and my sleeping bag over me. The light was bright on the water, though the bay was still in shadow. My head felt thick, as if I'd been drinking, and there was a horrid cotton-wool taste in my mouth. I staggered as I rose to make a cup of tea.

Once I was back in my sleeping bag, with the warm mug clasped in both hands, I tried to make sense of what had happened last night. Peter had driven me back, and I'd curled up in the cockpit, to keep vigil. A light had woken me. I remembered that. I'd heard the sound of digging on the headland, and flashed my lamp at them, but they'd taken no notice. I thought I'd rowed to the beach. I remembered the two headlands, Lund and Vinstrick, swaying towards me and away again as I stood up, then the rough sand under my face. Then nothing, until now, waking up back here.

I put up a hand to explore my head, and found hard grains of sand under my hair. I could trust my memory. I'd got to the beach, and fallen on the sand. I felt round

123

the back of my head, but there was no tenderness or swelling, so I hadn't been hit. I remembered how muzzy I'd felt, clumsy with sleep, and concluded that someone had drugged me. Willpower had got me to the beach, then the drug had taken over. Some nefarious 'someone', who was going to be very sorry indeed once I found out who they were, had manhandled me back into the dinghy, rowed me out here and rearranged me on the couch, with my sleeping bag over me. *Two* nefarious 'someones'; they'd have had to lift me from the dinghy and down into the cabin. One man couldn't have done that alone.

It was only then that I remembered Kamilla. I saw again her face turning blue, her hands clutching at her bag as she'd fallen. The shock hit again; my heart kicked, and I had a sense of something that I'd forgotten, something wrong. Then I remembered the waitress. *The French lady ... she ordered seafood ...* Maman had helped organise the tour, but I'd be very surprised if that included phoning the caterers about the menu. Her accented English would be easy to imitate. Someone who knew about Kamilla's allergy must have done that, but who? Why?

Bryony was jealous, Maman had said, but surely making Kamilla ill would destroy her own chances. Monday's gig, in Edinburgh's Georgian house, was the one the critics would be going to. If Kamilla was so ill that it had to be cancelled, or someone else substituted, Bryony would lose out too; unless ... for a moment I had the brilliant idea that if Kamilla was ill, Bryony could sing her part, be the understudy who stepped in to get the rave reviews from the critics and a starry career ever after, but then I remembered that Bryony was a soprano, like Maman, and Kamilla was a mezzo. Bryony wouldn't be able to sing her role.

Bryony, of course, was the obvious person to imitate Maman, but I wasn't sure the men could be ruled out. Adrien, with his light tenor voice, probably could do a good female imitation. Caleb's normal register was too low, but he could go into falsetto.

Besides, it had seemed to me that Kamilla had collapsed later than I'd have expected if it had been an allergy. The fish plates had been cleared away before she began to have difficulty breathing. Her plate and glass could be analysed, in case it was something more sinister:someone who had organised the seafood, then given her a poison whose effects would be similar.

I shook my head to try and clear the fuzziness from my brain. Drugged. Sleeping pills, I supposed. I didn't see how anyone could have slipped a pill into my meal. The obvious opportunity was when I'd had that cup of tea up in the sitting room at Belmont, just before we'd left. It had been Peter who'd poured my cup of tea from the pot, and Adrien who'd brought my cup over to me. Yes! I could see it clearly in my mind's eye. Adrien had paused, and asked if I took milk or sugar, and turned away for a moment, to add the milk, and stirred the tea. He knew I'd been watching him, and in spite of his distress over Kamilla he'd intended to have another go at his treasure.

I'd wake myself up and listen to the forecast before I tried to phone anyone. I had a basin wash, and re-dressed in a fresh set of thermals under my jeans and jumper. By that time, Shetland Coastguard was crackling in. I changed to Channel 23, and got my pen ready.

It wasn't good news. The south-easterly gale was due to back westerly, and increase to gale nine, then blow right up to storm ten and violent storm eleven 'later' – nautical speak for after twelve hours – with visibility brought down to 'poor' by rain.

Westerly would leave me being blown towards the shore. It was time I was out of here. Cullivoe, on Yell, had a marina. I flipped quickly to the Dover tide tables, and reached for my tidal atlas. HW Dover had been at 04.46. I did the sums; now we were at the start of HW +3. The tide was galloping northwards at six knots in Yell Sound, but the tidal atlas gave Bluemull Sound as okay for this hour. If I went now, I'd make it across.

I hauled my oilskins on and went out on deck. The sky was clear, with rags of grey cloud stretching along the horizon; the sea was ominously still, with that oily gleam on the water. There was no wind at deck level, but when I raised the mainsail, the tell-tale ribbons fluttered at the masthead, and the boom jerked with a heavy clang. I dropped it to put two reefs in, reducing it to half its size; better safe than sorry. I winched the dinghy aboard, noticing that it had been tied with a round turn and two half-hitches instead of my usual bowline, secured it to the cabin roof, and left it to deflate. Three nautical miles, forty minutes. I set the engine clanking away to itself, and used the jib winch to get the anchor up, hauling it into the cockpit. The chain went into a deep bucket, to be hosed later. It was tempting to leave the anchor in the cockpit too, but I knew that I'd regret it if I had any difficulty on the passage, so I took the extra minutes to store it for'ard. I set *Khalida*'s nose for the opening of the bay, hauled the mainsail tight to steady her, pushed the throttle forward and headed towards Bluemull sound.

We'd just cleared the headland, and I was setting *Khalida* on a southerly course, low enough that the northbound stream would push her into Cullivoe, when my phone rang: Dad. Like me, unlike Maman, he was one of the world's early risers.

'Cassie? It's not good news.'

The wind tugged cold at my plait, and there were white horses around me now. It was still a shock, although I'd expected it.

'She didn't make it.They said we'd done everything we could. She had a severe reaction, and that was it.'

'There'll have to be a post-mortem?'

'Yes. Here, your mother wants a word.'

Maman's voice was choked. 'Oh, Cassandre, it's awful. Poor Kamilla.I can hardly believe it. I knew that she had an allergy, but that it could kill her like that … She was so alive.'

I remembered the way she'd glittered in France, like a swarm of tropical fish.

'I wondered if perhaps the shellfish was not good,' Maman continued. 'Bryony was sick, just after we went upstairs last night, and my stomach has been disordered half the night.'

'Did anyone else know she had an allergy?'

'It was not secret. Adrien would have known, if they had been lovers, and she could easily have mentioned it to the others. We have not had fish, so the question has not arisen.'

She sounded so frail that I didn't want to speak of my suspicions. I'd phone Gavin. 'Take care, Maman. When do you leave for Lerwick?'

'Mid-afternoon. I will just check on Bryony, then go back to sleep, if I can. I do not suppose you could come with us to Lerwick?'

'Of course,' I said, alarmed. 'Maman, are you sure you're okay?'

'Just tired. I have been up and down since dawn. But I would be glad of my daughter.'

I hadn't been much of a daughter all the years I'd been knocking round the world in boats. I was touched that she wanted me now. I'd be there. *Khalida* would be fine in Cullivoe overnight, and I could go down with Maman to Lerwick, and come back on the bus tomorrow. I'd planned to go down anyway, to get to Palm Sunday mass; I'd just stay longer.

I was almost halfway across the sound now. 'I'll be with you as soon as I can,' I promised. 'I'm just putting my boat in safety – it's going to blow up. An hour, an hour and a half.'

Our course was looking good for Cullivoe. I nipped below for the Shetland marina guide, and looked it up. Damn. The pontoons were only suitable for 1.2m depth, and *Khalida* drew 1.5m. However, she could lie at the visitors' berth against the pier in reasonable safety, and I'd tie her within an inch of her life.

It was 07.50. I needed to phone Gavin. He'd be at his Inverness flat, preparing to go in to the station. I pressed the buttons, we exchanged 'good morning' in Gaelic and Shetland, then I launched into my story. 'It's probably on the news already,' I finished. 'Tragic death of opera star.'

I heard the sound of his computer switching on. 'I haven't heard anything yet. We may be contacted, in case there's anything suspicious, but from what you say it sounds an accident.'

'Hang on,' I said, and explained about the allergy. 'And Maman knew about it, so she wouldn't have phoned to ask specially for seafood.'

'Your waitress was quite sure about that?'

'Positive. She wasn't just a waitress, she seemed a senior person in the firm. She sent the rest home, and stayed herself to clear up. Anyway, I got her to take what dishes hadn't been washed and keep them, Kamilla's and mine for comparison.'

'And your mother's not well. How about you?'

'Me?' I said, surprised. 'Cast iron stomach. I'm fine.'

I could hear his pen scribbling. 'Bryony was sick, your mother was ill. Anyone else?'

'I don't know. The other thing was, I heard Kamilla having an argument with someone, in the summer house. She hissed something in German, then said, "You're mad. Mad!". I don't know who it was, but the footsteps were heavy, like a man's.' Something tugged at my memory and was lost again, before I had a chance to catch it.

'Adrien, Caleb, Per, Fournier.'

I hadn't thought of Fournier as one of the company, but of course he was. *A charmer* ... I wondered if he, too, might be a former lover of Kamilla's. I made a mental note to ask Maman how the troupe had been assembled.

'And the other odd thing was in the kitchen.' I explained the incident. 'It looked like she recognised something, and it was a shock. There were letters, and she took the top one. It was handwritten, and Per said it had a French stamp. It could have been that, or maybe my oilskin jacket hanging on the chair back, that she thought someone had come by sea, someone she wasn't expecting. Or maybe it just sparked off a memory. Whatever it was, it definitely upset her.'

Gavin was silent for a moment. 'I'll get in touch with Lerwick,' he said eventually. 'The phone call is definitely worth investigating. That could make it actionable, if someone who knew she had an allergy deliberately ordered seafood. I'm not quite sure if you could make a charge of murder, because death wasn't certain to result. Manslaughter, perhaps.'

He fell silent again. I waited.

'What's the tour itinerary?'

'Lerwick this evening, on the boat tomorrow, then the big one in Edinburgh on Monday, in the Georgian House.'

'Charlotte Square. I know it. Then back to France?'

'No, the other half of the tour, stately homes in Scotland. Down to Edinburgh first, the big one in the Georgian House, then one near Loch Earn, then Tayside, the House of Dun, and across to your patch, Cawdor Castle.' I used my fingers again. 'Thursday. Then the last one's Castle Frazer, on Good Friday, and home on the next flight to Paris, on Saturday. Just in time for the bells to bring the chocolate eggs.'

'I'll presume that's an Easter oddity from your French childhood. All over Scotland. I'll get moving on that now. Speak to you later.'

Chapter Ten

The tide was beginning to strengthen now. I set *Khalida*'s nose almost straight into it. We were past halfway now, rocking to the sideways eddies, when, with a shrill whistle in the rigging, the wind arrived. The first gust tilted *Khalida* over to the kind of angle I'd normally associate with full sails in a force five; her lee windows were twenty centimetres from the water, the dish towel hung at a crazy angle against the wooden bulkhead, and up in the mast the halyards thrummed like a didgeridoo. I reached into the cabin for my safety rope and clipped on, then let the mainsail loose. She came slightly more upright, but now the boom was jerking at the traveller, adding to the noise. I sheeted in until it stopped.

Wild wasn't a strong enough word for it. The sea was white with crests and hazy with spindrift. I pushed the throttle forward and felt the engine clank into top speed. The brown-painted ice-plant on the pier showed clearly above the encircling rock wall, the green cone gave me my heading. We jolted through the eddies that created white-capped standing waves at the entrance and into the calmer water behind. The rattle of my rigging made it hard to think, and I'd need to get the mainsail dropped before I could try to berth. I set the engine to ticking over, leaving *Khalida* nose-on to the wind; if I was quick, she wouldn't drift into danger. I clipped my safety rope to the line running from stem to stern, tucked the sail ties into my lifejacket, then took a firm hold of the guard rail with one hand, the wooden handhold on the cabin roof with the other, and crouched my way forward. The wind on my chest was like trying to push against a crowd going the other way. I ducked lower, showed it the top of my head and shuffled forwards until I could grasp the mast, then re-clipped my safety rope around it, and stood upright.

The wind buffeted me against it. I put one arm round the mast's solid metal, and let the mainsail drop, putting the first tie on as it fell, then edging along, one arm around the boom, to fasten the others. I'd laid the bow and stern lines ready in Lunda Wick; now I loosened them, clumsy with haste, the wind freezing my hands even in my sailing gloves. The wind was blowing *Khalida* around, pushing her back towards the eddies. I shoved the throttle forward, then turned her to the visitors' berth. I was just coming alongside when an older man in a navy jacket came to the edge. 'You'd get better shelter over there,' he shouted. He gestured towards the other side of the pier. 'The head of the fishing boat pier.' Another circular gesture, indicating I was to go right in. 'There'll be nobody more coming in this day.'

I always take local advice. I turned *Khalida* around and manoeuvred her into the sheltering arm of rock, with an iron step handily amidships, and the toilet block only a hundred yards away. The tidal rise and fall here was less than a metre. I passed my mooring warps up to the helpful stranger and made a rough moor, then began to prepare her properly: a fenderboard and fenders between her and the pier; double warps on each of her four cleats; and bow and stern springs for good measure.

Halyards next. I might be able to tighten them in the lulls, but equally the wind might snatch them from me and make things worse. It took me a couple of minutes to work out a series of moves to defeat it, and my ears were ringing with cold by the time I'd secured them to my satisfaction. The silence was a relief for a moment, then the other sounds took over: the waves slapping at the pontoon, the wind moaning between the houses and emerging in a roaring, buffeting force that blackened the grey water, and pushed me back against the mast. It was icy on my cheeks as I tied a restrainer round the jib, put the cover on the mainsail and looped a rope along and round it, in case the wind thrust tugging fingers into my furled sails, and set them loose and flogging. I re-checked the mooring warps: all holding, and the fenders were lodged securely between *Khalida*'s hull and the hard dock edges. I lashed the rudder, and stretched, feeling as if I'd just run a marathon.

'You're surely expecting wind,' my helper said, watching approvingly from above me.

'I have to leave her overnight,' I explained.

He shook his head at that. 'I live just up above there.' He gestured to a new-build wooden house five hundred yards up the hill. 'I'll keep an eye on her for you.'

My biggest worry was Cat. I couldn't leave him aboard alone with this forecast. I'd take him to Peter's, and see if he could maybe stay with Magnie overnight.

'Where are you off to?' my helper asked.

I gestured eastwards with my chin. 'Back to Unst. My mother's one of the opera singers, and they've had an upset.'

Of course he knew all about it. 'I heard it on SIBC this morning. A young lass had an allergic reaction, seemingly, and died. You'll be Cass, then. I thought you must be. Give me ten minutes to get the car, and I'll run you to the ferry.' He checked his watch. 'There's one at half past nine.'

Ten minutes. I threw half my wardrobe into an overnight bag, added Cat's tins and biscuits, and put Cat, protesting, into his basket. I hesitated, then added Gavin's bottle of champagne. If I was staying in Lerwick, if he was, if we were staying together ...

I'd secured the washboards, drawn the hatch over them, and was giving a last look around, when Gavin called back. His phone echoed, as if he was in an open space, and just as I answered there was the crackle of an airport tannoy. 'You're on your way already?'

'The boss doesn't like it. She doesn't like the phone call, but she's also wary of coming down heavy on international artists, delaying their tour, all the rest of it. So she said, "Why not head up on the first flight to spend the weekend with your girlfriend, then fly down first thing on Monday morning? If anything develops, you're on the spot, and if it's nothing then we haven't ruffled any feathers."'

'When can you get here?'

'11.45 in Sumburgh, but there's a lunchtime gap in the ferries. I can't get on one until 13.55. I won't be with you until 15.30.'

'We'll be heading for Lerwick by then, you might as well meet us there.'

'We?'

'Maman wanted me to come too. She's shaken by it all. If you have a hired car, I might need you to put me back to the Yell ferry so that I can hitch a lift to Cullivoe, to get back aboard.' I made a face.'Living on an island's so complicated.'

'Keep me posted about what's going on. A watching

brief. What I'd be really interested in is information about Kamilla. People will want to talk about her. Ask how long they've know her, that kind of thing, get them talking.'

'Cass Lynch, girl detective. Will do.'

'And Cass —'He paused. I waited. 'Cass, no sleuthing. At best someone played a nasty trick, and at worst murder was intended. Don't do anything that might make a murderer feel unsafe. Just chat.'

'Just chat,' I promised. 'See you soon.'

It was a ten-minute ferry run back to Belmont, with the dozen-car boat bucking like a playground horse on a spring. From here, the house was a pale yellow toy above its green fields, with the two lines of daffodils running down to the beach. There was a ferry at roughly hourly intervals throughout the day, but how long they'd be able to keep running, with this forecast, was anyone's guess. I had a feeling the inter-island ferries were automatically stopped if the wind rose above a force eight, so the company might need to leave sooner than mid-afternoon. Cat grumped to himself in his basket, as befitted a cat accustomed to travelling by sail. Out in the middle of the voe here, the sea was slashed with white horses, the ragged clouds racing. I hoped Gavin wasn't having too bumpy a flight.

We must have come into a pool of mobile signal, for my phone started bleeping. Inga first: *Whts gng on r u in thick of it?* My Scalloway friend, Reidar, next: *Shet Nws says dth of opra str r u okay?* Then Anders, in Norway: *Have seen death on Shet News. What's hapning should I come over?* I sent one reassuring reply to Reidar and Inga: *Death probably accidental seafood. All well. C.* Anders took a bit longer. Things were awkward, just now, with the growing relationship between Gavin and me; we were friends, Anders and I, but there'd been a time when we could have moved closer. With Gavin coming up, I didn't want Anders jumping on the next fishing boat heading for Shetland. In the end I managed, *Sad accident seafood allergy, otherwise ok. C u soon Norge. Hopng set out Tues.*

The ferry pier was on the other side of the bay from Belmont House. I came ashore into the ferry car park, with its portakabin toilet block, a xylophone boat, and the improbable scarlet double-decker bus labelled "Café". Hefting Cat's basket in one hand, and trying not to shoogle him too much, I strode on up the turf verge of the narrow road towards Peter's lodge. I'd need to stop and tell him about last night's shenanigans, if he was there. A lone man was up on the hill above the road, apparently inspecting the site up there. I looked up and he raised a hand: Magnie. I waved in reply, then continued along the road.

Peter was in, lacing up his walking boots from a comfortable chair by the white enamelled Rayburn. He had a nicely old-fashioned kitchen, like Magnie's, with a scrubbed table in the centre, and a dresser piled with letters and catalogues, held in place by a pair of binoculars.

I saw straight off that he'd heard the news.

'That poor lass. These allergies can be an awful thing.'

I nodded. 'The hospital said we did everything we could.'

'That's good to know.' He left a pause, then changed the subject. 'How got you on last night?'

'*Ah*,' I said, and told him the whole story. 'But because I had to take that tide, I never got the chance to look on the hill, to see if someone really had been digging there.'

His mouth was grim. 'I'll drive over later and look. But, here, lass, are you sure you didn't dream it all? It'd been a hard evening for you.'

I shook my head. 'There was sand in my hair, and the dinghy wasn't tied as I'd have done it. Someone really had drugged me. You didn't notice Adrien doing anything odd with my cup?'

'Lass, I was never even looking at him. I passed it to him, and he passed it on to you, and that was that.'He shook his head. 'You're sure it was this Adrien, the een wi' the high voice, that was sniffing around yesterday?'

'Yes, and in that place too. What's more, he was on his own in the room last night, because he was sharing with Per, and Per went with Kamilla to Lerwick. You know you said the police were up here – can you get a warrant to search his bags on suspicion?'

'Lass, I canna tell you that. I'll gie them a phone. Are you going up to the house now?'

I nodded. 'But Maman wanted me to go down to Lerwick with them, just for the night. I was wondering if I could possibly leave Cat with you, rather than dragging him on a long bus journey to Lerwick?' I nodded my chin at the basket, which was rocking slightly as Cat tried to claw his way out.'He could maybe sleep with Magnie.'

Peter nodded. 'Yea, yea, that would be no bother. Your yacht'll be far safer in Cullivoe, if it blows up anything like the forecast. Just bring your cat down as you go on the ferry. He'll be fine here until you get back to him.'

'Thanks.'

I said goodbye, and headed out, the wind tugging at my plait and buffeting my jacket. The landing at Sumburgh would be fun in this, with a crosswind on the runway. I just hoped Gavin's flight would make it in.

ᚻ

Footless and horseless I gallop abroad,
Mouthless I cry, and handless I destroy.

... the wind

Saturday, 28th March (continued)

Tide Times at Mid Yell, UT
Low Water   11.15, 1.0m
High Water   17.32, 1.7m
Low Water   23.49, 1.3m

Sunrise   05.44
Moonrise   11.00
Sunset   18.33
Moonset   03.04

Waxing quarter moon

I'll come unbidden, and stay as I please,
I'll chain dee in misery, drag dee in mire,
Or make dee dat blyde at du'll walk i da air,
For me du'll clim mountains, or walk into fire …

Chapter Eleven

Belmont House had that stillness of a place in mourning; it should have had drawn blinds, and black crêpe on the door. I went in quietly through the kitchen door. A middle-aged Shetland woman in a pink nylon pinnie, the caretaker, I supposed, was setting out a plate of freshly baked cheese scones in front of Caleb and Adrien. Caleb, in a grey jumper, was eating cornflakes, Adrien was brooding over a cup of coffee. One look at him drove all thoughts of treasure from my mind. His eyelids were red, his face thinned, as if misery had drawn the skin tight against the bones, and he clutched the cup to him like a lifeline. He was formally dressed in a black suit and tie. I gave them a subdued 'good morning', and let Cat out. He miaowed indignantly, and settled on the cushioned window seat to smooth his ruffled fur. I helped myself to a cheesy bannock and spread it with butter.

'Your mother will be glad of you,' Caleb said. He looked as if he was glad of me himself, as if supporting Adrien was hard.

'Has she had any breakfast?'

Caleb shrugged. 'I haven't seen her this morning.' He glanced at the clock, and his face lightened. 'But I wouldn't expect to see Eugénie this early anyway.'

'We were all ill in the night,' Adrien said. 'And my

poor Kamilla –' He stopped, his mouth working, then tipped his head forward so that his dark hair fell over his eyes. A pause, then he spoke, his smooth voice rough. 'What time do we have to be on the ferry?'

Caleb nodded his head at a sheet of paper on the worktop, and Adrien got up to look at it, moving stiffly, as if he had aged overnight. '15.30,' he said. 'Five hours.' They sounded like a long road stretching before him. He looked at the door, as if he was considering going out, then slumped back into his seat. 'Per said he would have to leave her there, in the hospital, in Lerwick.' He shuddered. The feeling of unreality hit me again: lively, sparkling Kamilla, lying stretched and still with a sheet over her. There would have to be a post-mortem, I supposed; and she was young, her parents would still be alive.

'What was her family, Adrien, do you know?' *From a village halfway between Vienna and Graz,* Maman had said, *and determined to become a star* …

'She was an only child. Well, she had a little brother, who died young. Her parents clung to her the more, because of that, and now –' His voice dropped to a near-whisper; he turned away, as if he wanted to hide his emotions. 'I spoke to her father, as soon as Per phoned. He couldn't believe it, that Kamilla, who was so full of life, should be gone, like that.' He turned his face towards mine. His eyes were filled with tears. 'Per said that the doctors said you did everything that could have been done. If what you did failed to save her, it was because she could not be saved.'

It was cold comfort. 'She must have had a serious allergy, to react to shellfish just being in the room.'

'Mebbe there was some in what she did eat,' Caleb said. 'Traces on the hands of the person who prepared the salad, or on the knives.'

I thought it very unlikely. The catering woman had the air of knowing what she was doing, and clean hands, sterilised utensils, and keeping possible allergy causers separate, was second-nature even to me, after three months helping in Reidar's café.

Adrien nodded. 'She gave us a fright, oh, way back, at a seafood restaurant in the West End. Before that, she had no idea she had an allergy. She had prawns, and suddenly her face began swelling up, and we had to rush her to hospital. That was when she was issued with the EpiPens. Ever after that, she avoided any kind of seafood, just in case. She'd never have risked eating it up here, so far from medical help.'

'You've known her a long time then?'

'Oh, years, since she was a promising young debutante. She was in the chorus of my *Carmen*, with the ENO, and I noticed her voice.' He smiled indulgently, as if he saw again the Kamilla she'd been. 'She was straight out of college, with that shaggy student look, you know, jeans and a jumper down to her knees, and hiding behind a fringe. Well, I got to know her, and gave her some advice, took her to a decent stylist, and advised her on dress. She was so young, and shy, and nervous, and glad to have me to look after her. It grew from there.' Tears filled his eyes. 'We were so much in love. She moved into my flat in London, and I gave her some help with decent roles, introduced her to people who would help her get on. We were really happy.' His face darkened; he buried his head in his hands once more with a choked sob.

Caleb rose, with an 'over-to-you' nod, and escaped. *Damn.* Just because I was female..I was lousy at this sort of thing. I abandoned my tea-making, and sat down beside Adrien. Arts people were supposed to be touchy-feely. I put a tentative hand on his shoulder. 'It's an awful shock.'

He nodded, and lifted his head once more. His eyes were wet. 'We were so happy together. Then she got a good offer with an early music group in the States. She'd always wanted to do more early music, and so she didn't want to turn it down. We knew we were strong enough together to cope with the separation, and of course we'd be able to fly back and forward to see each other. Then she was spotted by *The Voice*, and it was the stardom that put pressure on us. She was always here, there, everywhere, they crowded her until she hardly knew who she was. So we talked about it, and agreed to do this tour together and see if we could get back on track. I'd hoped ... we were becoming closer again, just getting this time together ...' He shook his head, covering his eyes with one hand. 'She was so young, so talented ... why is it that people like her have to go?'

My theology wasn't up to answering that one. Besides, I couldn't help my brain noticing, even as I patted his shoulder and murmured soothing platitudes, that it didn't quite ring true. *My Carmen*, he'd said. If there was one thing I did know it was that early music people were specialists. Someone whose normal roles were heroes like Don José wouldn't be asked to sing Hippolyte, just like that. If he'd been introducing Kamilla to people in his classical repetoire world, how had it come about that she'd had an offer from an early music group, and in the States too, when she was working in London? I'd need to run this version past Maman. And hadn't she said that she hadn't known Adrien and Kamilla were an item? The way Adrien had said it, they'd never actually split up.

'But I have a way out,' Adrien said suddenly. 'If I cannot bear it any more, to have her taken from me like that.' He gestured with one hand, then turned it over, spreading the fingers to show me a rather heavy ring, an oval piece of onyx set in silver embossed with Victorian curlicues on the sides.

I looked at him blankly.

'I will not open it.' Adrien rose. 'But it holds my way out of this world, like the heroes of old, who chose glory over unhappiness.' He brought the hand up to his breast and raised his head, in a gesture that I suspected belonged to one of his roles. 'I will not forget her.'

He exited, stage left, leaving me open-mouthed. I'd been wondering about how someone might have got hold of a poison that would have killed Kamilla in the way we'd seen. I had a hazy notion that cyanide would cause that breathlessness and blue skin followed so quickly by unconsciousness And here, it seemed, was a handy little receptacle which everyone might know about if he was given to these dramatic melancholy fits: a ring filled with a quick, deadly poison.

I put two bowls of muesli on a tray, added a cup of herbal tea and headed upstairs. Dad was up and dressed, but Maman was still in bed, looking ready to sing *Traviata*, with her silk and lace nightdress, except that her pallor and the blue circles under her eyes were real, not the work of three make-up artists. I came around the bed to set the tray down on the slender-legged bedside table. 'Poor Maman! I brought you some muesli, and a pot of chamomile tea.'

'Thank you, dear. Chamomile is exactly what I

wanted,' Maman said. 'But not the muesli, for the moment.'

'I'll eat it, Cassie,' Dad said. He gave me a wink. 'I haven't braved the artistes downstairs yet.'

I pulled a sympathetic face, handed him the plate, and looked at Maman. 'Could I bring you something else?'

She shook her head. 'I will have toast, in a while. For food poisoning, it is best to have nothing but water for twenty-four hours.'

Fair enough. I began on my own bowl of muesli.

'Except that I will have to eat something,' Maman said, after a reflective silence, broken only by Dad and me chewing. 'I will have to be ready to sing.'

My spoon froze, mid-air. I gaped at her. The show had to go on, of course, but –

'Per telephoned. He has managed to find a replacement, an Italian mezzo. She is not as celebrated as Kamilla, of course, but she knows the role, and can manage to fit in these two performances.' Maman leant back against her pillows. 'So I must get up soon, to encourage everyone.'

I'd always suspected that singers didn't think like normal people, and here was the proof of it. Come death, come poison, the show had to go on …

'And I'd need to go to that meeting in Cullivoe, now you have Cassie to look after you,' Dad said. He bent over to kiss her cheek. 'You just rest. I'll be back well before time for the ferry, now, so don't you be fretting.'

Maman smiled, and waved him out, then her face clouded over. 'I must get up. I have not yet talked to Adrien – he will be taking it badly.'

'He's not good.' I grimaced. 'He was talking in the kitchen about a poison ring.'

'Oh, that.' Maman made a dismissive face. 'He's

known for his ring. I don't believe for a moment that there really is cyanide in it. Someone would have substituted something harmless long ago. Well, if you hear someone talk of suicide, and flourish the means like that, you would act, of course.'

'Melodramatic,' I said.

'Adrien is melodramatic,' said Maman serenely. She was feeling well enough now to sit up. 'Tenors are very insecure. You noticed that Per had to give him extra encouragement to come in, during the performance.'

I shook my head.

'They have to be supported all the time. I will get up and go to talk to him.'

She was just starting to sweep the covers back when there was a knock on the door. A male voice called, 'Eugénie?'

Maman pulled the duvet back to her chest and answered in French. 'Vincent, is that you? Come in.'

The door eased open, and Vincent Fournier edged in. 'A thousand pardons, Eugénie, to disturb you in bed.'

Maman gestured that away. 'Cassandre is here, as a chaperone.'

He sat down on the chair by the dressing table. He was wearing a leather jacket this morning, heightening the James Dean resemblance, but a James Dean who had grown old, to become the head of a business corporation. There were shadows under his eyes, a greyness beneath the tan, as if he too had been up half the night. 'How is our star?'

Maman made another gesture, grave affliction being bravely borne. 'I am well now.' She smiled. 'Ready to sing this evening.'

'Ah, that's what I have come to tell you. The flights do not suit Gabriella, she can't get here so soon. I've spent all morning on the Internet, then on the phone. She can't arrive before tomorrow, and so I've rescheduled tonight's performance for tomorrow afternoon, before we get on the boat. Fortunately, it's the later ferry, 19.00, so that's perfectly possible. A three p.m. start. Now, what I wished to consult you about is this. We can remain here, in quiet, for tonight, if you feel that is what everyone would prefer, or we can drive down to Lerwick as we'd planned, and spend the night in the Shetland Hotel. Unfortunately our poor Kamilla's death is now headline news.'

Maman made a face. 'Oh, Vincent, no.'

He nodded. 'When I went to where I got a signal, my phone was buzzing with calls. I've agreed to talk to the BBC, but if we go to Lerwick we may find there are others. Here, you are more protected from them. Journalists do not like all these ferry journeys.'

'My vote would be for here. Last night was a dreadful shock, and we could do with a day of peace.'

'You don't think the others would prefer to distract themselves in Lerwick?'

Maman laughed. 'Now, Vincent, you too have lived here. Yes, there is the new cinema, but otherwise, what do you expect? Do you see Adrien or Caleb heading for the Thule Bar, or Bryony living it up in Posers? No, no, we will eat quietly here, and let everyone recover, and take the ferry down to Lerwick tomorrow.'

'Very well, I'll let the others know, and organise catering for tonight. Shall I see if Saxavord is able to come again? Not seafood, of course.' He spread his hand protectively over his stomach and grimaced. 'Adrien was ill, and Per said that he had felt unwell too.'

'Bryony as well,' I said. 'And you too?'

He dodged that one. James Dean didn't get stomach

148

upsets. 'There you are, all the more reason for us all to have a quiet day and a restful evening, and a long lie tomorrow. I'll book us on the 12.05 ferry.' He frowned, thinking. '12.05, the ferry for Toft at 12.45, Lerwick by two o'clock, then the performance at three.'

'A bit tight,' Maman said. 'We will not want to eat much, of course, but it would be better to have some time in Lerwick.'

'Very well, then.There is a 10.45 that will get us on the 11.30 to Toft, Lerwick by 12.40 or so. Is that better?'

'Yes, much better.'

'If they will give us the performers' room at Mareel, you can relax there, and those who wish can go for fast-food.'

Maman cast up her eyes, but made no more comment.

'I was wondering,' I said tentatively, since that seemed to be settled, 'how the cast was chosen.'

Fournier made an over-to-you gesture at Maman. 'Ah, not my province. Per and Eugénie managed that between them. Oh, except for Adrien, when we needed someone to fill in. I know his father – he's a business contact, well, not quite that, but his antiques shop in Paris is right next to my office.'

'He created Aricia's jewellery,' Maman said.

'He said that. Based on Helen of Troy's.'

Fournier laughed. 'The family obsession. Has Adrien told you how his grandfather – no, his great-grandfather – was a friend of Schliemann? He visited the dig at Troy, and then, later, he was there when Sophia was photographed in Helen's gold.' He laughed again. 'I believe Adrien has always hoped some day to find treasure like that to deck his girlfriend in.'

You're mad. Mad ...

'Was that why he brought a metal detector here?'

'Did he?' Fournier shrugged. 'It sounds like him. This treasure found here, just as we were coming, he would see it as fate. But as for Kamilla, and Caleb, and Bryony, I do not know.'

'It was I who was keen on Kamilla and Caleb,' Maman said. 'Per was doubtful about poor Kamilla, he had not heard her, but I knew she would be good, and her voice contrasts – contrasted – well with mine, a dark, smoky style. Gabriella will not be so good, but needs must. I had sung with Caleb in one of the Loire performances.' Her cheeks flushed, becomingly. 'I thought he was a youngster worth encouraging. Bryony was Per's choice, they had worked together before. Then, for Hippolyte, Bernard Latouche was booked, you must have heard of him.'

I hadn't.

'No? He is the best tenor for Rameau, I have sung with him several times. But he was doing a *son-et-lumière*, just two weeks ago, and tripped going off the stage, completely careless, and did something terrible to his ankle, a torn hamstring, I think, and so he is not permitted to walk on it at all for six weeks. The muscle has to be forced back into place. He began with his foot at a strange angle, and slowly it is to be put back.'

'And Adrien called me the moment he heard about it, and offered himself as a replacement,' Fournier finished. 'Well, Eugénie, my dear.' He bent forward to kiss her. 'I'll put that all in hand, and let Per know, then drive down to get him from the Yell ferry. Now, you have a restful day. Try to put all this upset out of your head, and be ready for tomorrow.'

'I must check on how Bryony is too. She was not at all well earlier.'

'I can do that,' I offered. 'You have another sleep.'

Maman held out her hand to squeeze mine. 'Thank you, Cassandre. You are being a great comfort.'

Chapter Twelve

Caleb had returned to the kitchen. He had his jacket on, as if he was going out, but turned to smile at me. 'You heard the good news, Cassandra? Per's managed to find another mezzo. She'll have to sing in Italian, of course. That's the language she's sung Phaedra in before.'

It sounded mad to me. 'She's sung Rameau in Italian?'

'In Italy,' Caleb said. He made it sound quite normal, which I supposed it was, given that Rameau wrote in French for a French audience. 'She doesn't speak French.'

'I thought you learned the different languages you sang in.'

He shook his head. 'Only how to pronounce them. You do a course, during your training, particularly looking at the vowel sounds. But you don't learn the language.'

I filled the kettle, stuck it on and perched on the table while I waited for it to boil. 'So you just sing it, not knowing what you're singing.'

'Hell, no, you get a translation. But it's the music that counts.'

'So,' I said, 'she's going to sing in Italian while the rest of you are singing in French.'

He nodded, laughing at my face. 'It's completely normal, Cassandra. You can't pick up a mezzo who knows Phaedra just like that. We're lucky to have got

153

Gabriella.' Then his face sobered. 'I shouldn't be laughing. Poor Kamilla. I'm getting outa here for the day.'

He was just lacing up his walking boots when there was a tap on the door, and Magnie came in. Naturally, he'd heard all about it.

'Poor lass.' He cocked his head sideways at Caleb. 'How're you this morning, boy? There were a lot of lights on in the night, as if folk were going to the bathroom over often.'

'I had the mussels,' Caleb said, 'and I'm fine. Adrien said he'd been up half the night with stomach cramps and diarrhoea.' He shouldered his bag. 'See you in Lerwick, Cassandra.'

'Oh,' I said surprised, 'you're off on the ferry?' I remembered him asking about Inga and Charlie's house, in Brae. I smiled. 'Redding up kin?'

He gave me a startled look, as if he'd forgotten having told me.

'Last night,' I reminded him. 'You were speaking about relatives in Brae.'

Now he definitely looked shifty. 'Oh, yeah. I'll see. If I'm passing. The connection's a long way back.' He grabbed his case and headed into the corridor before I could say any more, his 'See ya' floating back as the porch door closed.

Magnie raised an eyebrow at me. 'Kin in Brae?'

Magnie was one of the many local geneaology experts. If Caleb really was kin to Charlie, Magnie would know all about him. I tried to remember exactly what Caleb had said. 'I think he said his great-grandfather ran off from Eastayre and went to the States.'

'Eastayre.' Magnie scratched his head, in the classic thinking pose. 'Well, Charlie's great-great-grandfather was Andrew. That would be this man's great-grandfather's father. He's no' an Anderson himself?'

'I don't know. His stage name is Portland, after where he comes from.'

'There were two sons, Andrew, he'd be the oldest, then Charlie, that's this Charlie's great-grandfather, and a lass, Janey. I mind her fine, because she taught at the school, and lived into her nineties. Andrew musta been this boy's relation. Leave it wi' me, lass. There's something knocking at the back o' me memory.' He picked up his jacket. 'Now, Peter was saying you were needing me to take care o' Cat for the night?'

I clapped a hand to my forehead. 'Oh, yes! *Khalida*'s over at Cullivoe. But it's all change now, they're staying here overnight.'

'There plenty o' beds for you. You could take een o' the couches in the sitting room, or there's the peerie pavilion. You're well used wi' the cold.'

I was; and I'd just thought yesterday what a nice bedroom it would make. And what about Gavin? I hoped my face didn't show the warm tingle that went down my back at the thought of having a night together. Then the thrill was blotted out by nerves. Of course one didn't forget, but it was such ages …

'And what's this sickness?' Magnie asked. I tore my thoughts away from baser matters. 'It's no sounding right to me. Peter ate here last night, and he was well enough, and now this boy's saying he's fine too. Off shellfish doesna do that, apart from the likelihood o' it.'

I set the tray out for Bryony. A teapot, with a bag of chamomile in it, and a plate. I stuck a couple of pieces of toast in the toaster. *Up from dawn*, Maman had said, and I'd thought there was something wrong about that, but I hadn't time to really consider it. I tried to remember what I knew about food poisoning. Two hours or two days, that was it. Either you were sick within two hours, as it hit your gut, or it incubated away for two days, and made you ill then.

'Two hours or two days,' I said. 'The time it takes to come on. Isn't that right?'

Magnie nodded. 'Soonds about right.'

'We ate at ten. They should have started to be ill at midnight.' I stared at him. 'Are you thinking it was some kind of poison made them all ill?'

Magnie looked behind him, then rose to kick out the wedge and ease the door shut. 'I'm just saying it doesna seem right. I was up patrolling the site on the hill, and I saw the lights going on. The worst o' them was in the early morning, first light.'

'Seafood can be dodgy.'

Magnie shook his head. 'Naa, lass. Well, look at you. You ate it an aa. Any ill effects?'

'No,' I admitted.

Magnie glanced round again, and lowered his voice. 'Word is someen ordered seafood specially.'

It gave me a cold feeling in the stomach to hear my own fears shared. 'Not Maman. She kent Kamilla was allergic.'

'What did the others eat or drink that you and that youngster didna have?'

It was the question I'd been avoiding. Classic Agatha Christie; poison everyone a little, and one person fatally, with something that would give the same symptoms of breathlessness as an allergy. I poured the boiled water into the teapot, and tried to remember. 'Well, the starter was either mussels or cullen skink. I went for the mussels, and Caleb had the soup. Kamilla had a salad separately, but they made that at the last minute in the kitchen, so I don't see how anyone could have interfered with that.'

'Mind you're thinking of how aabody coulda been given a mild dose.'

'It can't have been the salmon either, that came out on the plates, in portions. Besides, Caleb had that. The lamb came out carved too, and we helped ourselves to the veg.' I shook my head. 'I don't see how it could have been in the main course.'

'What about the puddings?'

I considered. 'They were laid out on a side table, for us to help ourselves while the staff cleared our plates. It was big dishes, a trifle and a cheesecake – oh, there was a fruit salad too, you could have poisoned that if you'd had something prepared to pour in, and you could naturally have stirred it to mix it in.'

'Do you mind who had what?'

I shook my head. 'I didn't have any of it. Caleb had the cheesecake, I remember that.' It had looked temptingly good. 'Maman would have had the fruit salad, she never eats puddings, and probably Bryony doesn't either. They were both ill.' I kept thinking about it. 'The fruit salad was the only one you could have doctored. If you had, say, one of these film canisters, or a tictac packet, something like that, which you could hide easily in one hand, flick open, then just pour in, quick and casual. I suppose it would be possible, but you'd need to be a very cool customer.' I wondered how easily the poison ring opened. Flick open, tilt your hand, close the ring again. What order had they risen in? Maman first, then Adrien, right beside her. I suddenly saw him helping her to fruit salad, stirring it first. He could have done it. But if he loved Kamilla, if he was hoping they'd get back together, why would Adrien poison her?

'Folk who sing in front of total strangers must have nerves o' steel.'

I conceded that one. 'Kamilla had the fruit salad, and we kept her plate.'

'They surely gied you a cup o' tea after it.'

'Yes, they did. Bryony handed those out, as if she usually did it.' In every ship's company, the person who needed tea most became the tea-maker. 'She seemed to know what everyone took without being told.'

'And nobody woulda watched her doing it, because they kent she kent what they wanted. They'd just go on wi' their conversations, and say thanks when she laid it afore them.'

'She could have slipped something into each cup, then pretended to be ill herself. I didn't have time even to taste mine before Kamilla collapsed, and I don't suppose Caleb did either.' I shook my head.'But it doesn't make sense. You're wanting to kill Kamilla, right? So you set up the seafood, she has an allergic reaction, she dies. So why poison everyone else? There's no need for that. It wasn't the seafood being off that killed her.'

'Right enough.' Magnie scratched his head again. 'Leave that for the moment. How about her food, the lass who died? If she was poisoned, wha coulda done that?'

I'd been thinking about this. 'I think it might have been in her wine. Whatever it was acted quickly. It would have been so easy to drop something into her glass, between the main course and the dessert. The smokers got up and went outside, and other folk moved round the table to change the person they were speaking to. It could have been any of us.'

Magnie shook his head, more in thought than negating. 'Well, your policeman will sort it all out.'

I glanced out of the window. Close to shore, the sea had turned from grey to slate-blue; in the sound, waves whitened most of its surface, and there was a pale haze of blown spray over it. I hoped Gavin would make it before the ferries stopped. 15.30 … it would be tight. I turned to Magnie. 'Listen, I don't suppose you know someone with a fast motorboat, who might do a taxi run to Toft?'

He scratched his chin, and considered the waves slashing the sea. 'Keith has one of those Viking cruisers that'll do 28 knots, so he says. When do you need to go?'

'Gavin gets in at 11.45, but there's no ferry from the mainland to Yell until 13.55.'

Magnie glanced out of the window, just as I had done, and drew the same conclusions. 'He'll be lucky to make it before the ferries are called off, wi' this forecast. Leave it wi' me, lass.' He stomped out into the porch. A murmur of conversation, then he came back. 'Yea, lass, no bother, he says. He'll leave in fifteen minutes.' He yawned. 'I'll go and get some shut-eye before more o' this patrolling.'

'Good luck,' I said. I phoned Gavin, and left another voicemail: 'All change here, they're staying another night in Belmont. Head for Toft, the Yell ferry terminal, and wait for a Viking motorboat.'

I'd just got the kettle boiled when there was a roar in the distance, and a motorboat with a navy hull and a high white bridge curved round the ferry pier and headed off down Bluemull Sound, bouncing over the swell. The cavalry was on its way.

4

Bryony was in the room next door to Maman and Dad's. I balanced the tray on my hip, and knocked gently, then pushed it open. The room was the twin of the master bedroom, with the same white-wood panelling and notched cornice. A brass-handled chest of drawers stood in the far corner, with a white lamp on it. The white walls were darkened by a row of dresses hung from the curtain rail: the costumes they'd worn last night.

I slid into the room. 'Hi. How are you feeling? Here's some herbal tea and toast.'

Bryony was in the far bed, curled over as if she'd been trying to sleep. As I came in she turned on her back, dragged herself up the bed and made ineffectual attempts to straighten her pillows. I settled them behind her and put the tray down on the chair by the bed.

She looked awful. There were dark circles under her eyes, and her skin was tinged green, as if she'd spent the night vomiting. Her dark hair bushed out around her head, and she'd dragged a fleece dressing gown over the shoulders of her onesie. If she was just pretending to be ill, I was a landlubber who'd never even been on a rowboat at Brighton.

Her head shook, her mouth opened to refuse, then she changed her mind. 'Thanks. I'd love a cup of tea.'

'Sure.' I poured the mugful, and handed it to her. 'Could you manage dry toast, just to have something inside?'

She shook her head. 'I was sick half the night. I'm not hungry.'

'What you need is a day in bed, with paracetamol and a hot water bottle.' I could sort this one out, at least. 'Look, you lie back. I'll get you a hot water bottle. Then you can just stay put.' I suddenly realised what was awry about Caleb going off. Fournier couldn't have told him yet that there was no performance tonight. 'The replacement can't get here till tomorrow, so you have another night to get really rested. They've changed the performance to tomorrow afternoon.'

'I do feel awful,' she admitted. 'I can't believe it's real.' Her eyes gazed bleakly. 'Kamilla, I mean. Per phoned me. I can't believe someone who was so alive can ...' She paused, searching for another word. 'Can *go*, just like that. She didn't even eat any of it.'

I wasn't going to share our suspicions. 'Sometimes just eating stuff prepared in the same area is enough.'

'I didn't even know she had an allergy.' There was something aggrieved about her voice, as if Kamilla had taken an unfair advantage. 'She never said.'

I felt that same stab of disbelief, and shoved it away in practicality. The room was in as much chaos as if they'd been there for a week, instead of just a night: the costumes hung from the curtain rail, and a tumble of day clothes and Bryony's slightly-too-bright pink evening dress overflowed the chair by her bed. There was a line of potions on top of the dark-blue mantelpiece, below the oval mirror that reflected me standing there in my workaday gansey: day creams; night creams; powder; paint; mascara; paracetamol; and various other tubs of multi-vitamins and capsules. There was a suitcase in the space below them, and another on the washstand tucked in behind the door, both open, with a tumble of clothes within. 'Shall I pack her stuff away, so it doesn't keep reminding you?'

Bryony clutched her mug. 'No, don't worry. I'll sort it later. I feel so awful.' She looked it. Her face was the grey-white of old ropes, the circles under her eyes blue as a bruise. She clasped both hands round the mug of tea and sipped steadily, then paused to clutch the warm mug to her. 'I still can't believe it.' Her voice was anguished. 'I didn't know an allergy could kill someone.' Her eyes were glossy with tears. 'Just like that. She was okay, and then –'

I reached for the paracetamol and sat down on Kamilla's bed to shake two into my hand. There was a photograph case on the bedside table, one of the sort that stands up like a book, with two photos inside. One had two children, a boy and girl, blonde, fair as two young Viking children, and the other was the boy alone, older, in the same pose, but with his hair growing darker, his skin tanned. The girl was Kamilla, I thought, aged about ten. Maman had talked about a brother, but he'd died young, and the second photo showed someone in his twenties. Was he a boyfriend, the classic 'boy next door'? 'Tell me about her,' I said. 'Did you know her quite well?'

She nodded. 'We were really good friends.'

I took that with a pinch of salt, from what I'd seen of them together. Bryony steamed on. 'I had a part in her first show, when she was straight out of college. *Carmen*. She was in the chorus, but you could see she was going to be good. Adrien was playing Don José, and we were all dreamy about him, but he picked her out straight away.' Her voice was steadying. 'Just homed in on her, and before we all knew it they were an item.'

'He must have been a lot older than her.'

'Oh, darling, twenty years.' The colour was coming back to her cheeks, the scratchy note returning to her voice. 'Well, it was cradle-snatching really, but she was starry-eyed, and he was so sweet with her, very protective, and keen she should advance her career with the right parts when she'd have taken anything she was offered, like the rest of us. And of course, knowing him, well …' She shrugged. 'With his influence, what he considered the right parts did come along.'

'What did he consider the right parts?' I asked, curious.

'Darling, the classical stuff. Mozart's breeches parts.

Gluck. Octavian, of course.'

Of course, darling. 'So when did she move to early music?'

Bryony glanced around, as if someone might be listening, and lowered her voice. 'That was because of him. She had to get away.'

'Away from him? Why?'

Bryony grimaced. 'The *Pygmalion* thing. He's very controlling. There she was, young and nervous and over-awed by him, and he took her over completely. You know how it is – at first you're really flattered that they take such an interest in you, want to tell you what to wear, and suggest hairstyles, books to read, all that.'

It was an experience I'd managed to dodge, but I took her word for it.

'She'd enjoyed it for the first couple of years, while she was finding her feet, and he did get her a couple of nice parts –' She flushed. 'Oh, I'm not saying she couldn't sing them. But so could two dozen others. It's all luck in this business, and knowing the right people, and Adrien certainly did. So there they were, the golden couple – until she started feeling like she was in a cage. That's what she said to me. I bumped into her at an after-show party, you know how you do, and I asked her how she was getting on, and we ended up having a heart-to-heart in the loo. She felt there was nothing of her left. Oh, he was really in love with her, she never doubted that, but he just controlled every move she made. He wouldn't even let her go shopping for a dress without taking him – she'd tried it, just two days before, and he'd thrown such a tantrum that it had really frightened her. She'd decided she wanted out, and she was scared he'd stop her. She'd got left without anything of her own, you see – it was his flat, his car, they had a joint bank account, and she just didn't know what to do, how to get away without him knowing.'

We were so happy together, Adrien had said. I wondered if that was self-delusion or whitewashing.

'Well, I'd just had a run in London.' She said it as if she'd been starring in some major production of *Madame Butterfly,* instead of being a bit part or chorus. 'So I was pretty flush. I said to her, "If he frightens you, get out. We'll meet up tomorrow, and I'll book you a flight somewhere, anywhere you want to go. Leave your phone behind in case he's got a tracker on it, take just a change of clothes and post a letter from the airport."'

My mouth dropped open. 'It was really that serious?'

Bryony nodded. 'I said to her, "Every battered wife didn't believe it would happen to them. Just because he's a singer, or a head teacher, or a top policeman, doesn't make you safe. Are you scared?" And she nodded, and I could see by her eyes that she meant it.' Her eyes filled with tears again. She sniffed and brushed them away. 'Poor Kamilla. Well, we arranged to meet in a café the next day, and she arrived with a bag, like I'd suggested, and we used my computer to book her on a flight to Spain, which was where a friend of mine lived. She'd done a *Shirley Valentine,* and I knew she needed a nanny for a bit, so I thought Kamilla could fill in doing that while she decided where to go next. She had to keep her career going, you see. So she was there for two months, while she got all the visas for the States, and then she crossed the pond. And that's when she began doing early music, just to keep well away from what he did.'

She got a good offer with an early music group in the States had been Adrien's version. *We agreed to do this tour together.* That was nonsense, according to Fournier

164

and Maman, who had no reason to spin a yarn. *We were becoming closer again, and it was getting like it used to be ...*

'How long ago was this?'

'Oh ... ages.' Bryony frowned, thinking. 'It was in the autumn she ran away. Not last year, nor the one before. Three and a half years ago. We did the occasional phone call, but you know how it is when you're both busy, and then she got on *The Voice* and suddenly she was a megastar. And now ... now ...'

She broke down then, sobbing gustily into a tissue. I waited, feeling helpless. Behind what I hoped was a suitably sympathetic face, my thoughts were working furiously. I knew all about running away, because I'd done it myself at sixteen, but not out of fear; I'd been young, and daft, and instead of talking my problems through with Maman I'd emptied my bank account to get a berth on a tall ship bound for Scotland, where I was legally of age. I didn't like to think now of the worry I'd caused her, and I was glad it was all behind us. But to cast yourself out like that, afraid of being followed, with virtually only what you stood in, just as you were making a name for yourself, to begin again in a strange country –I gave Kamilla's spirit a mental nod of admiration. *Ambitious*, Maman had said. She'd earned having her face on magazine covers.

Bryony's sobbing had subsided a little. I passed her another tissue. 'It must have been an awful shock to Kamilla when whoever-it-was broke his ankle and Adrien took over.'

'Darling, dreadful. I'm sure she must have thought about backing out, but of course she couldn't let Eugénie down.

'Had she seen him since she'd run away?'

Bryony nodded. 'He came to America. She'd unfriended him on Facebook, of course, but she had a public website, and he was following her on that. She thought about changing her name, but once she'd got away she felt embarrassed about the whole thing, felt she'd made a fuss about nothing. Then when he arrived backstage after a show she nearly fainted, but he was really nice about it – went on about understanding how she needed to pursue her career, and all her stuff was waiting at their flat for her. 'As if I was a wilful child,' she said. Then, when she came back to Europe, they kept meeting up, you know how it is. She didn't like that. He'd kind of behave as if he was with her even though he wasn't – you know, bring her drinks, and stand with her, and check she'd ordered a taxi. Other men would jump to the conclusion they were together. So she thought she'd try getting off with someone else, in front of him, and she began flirting with this guy from the chorus, and then caught Adrien's eye, and she said her heart just turned cold. If looks could have killed, she said – not her, the guy. So she just left.'

'He never tried to get her on her own?'

'He came to her flat once, and she told him straight that if he ever dared to come back there she'd take out an injunction against him for harassment. He went over all smarmy and said she was making far too much of just a friendly visit, but she stuck to her guns and insisted he left.'

'Good for her.'

'And of course they were both working, so most of the time they were in different places, and that kept the lid on it. But when she heard he was coming on this tour – well. Nothing would persuade her he hadn't wangled his way onto it on purpose. He wasn't anywhere near when

Latouche broke his ankle, but she reckoned he'd phoned straight away to offer himself as a substitute.'

'I was wondering about that,' I said. 'You said he was Don José, which is a far cry from the Sun King, even I know that.'

'Well, a good lyric tenor can move between them, but you're right, of course it's not usual. But he started doing early music stuff when Kamilla did, not all the time, but enough to get a name for it. Oozing his way back to her. Well ...' Her eyes peeked at me from under the tousled hair. 'Did your mother tell you about all this ghost stuff? The book being left open, and the rose that changed colour? I bet he was behind that. It fairly spooked Kamilla out.'

Maman had suspected Bryony. I went for a general comment. 'This tour must have been so awkward for everyone.'

Bryony grimaced. 'Well, you know, it was a strain, but they were carrying it off. She clung to me to keep him away, and we were sharing a room, so she knew he wouldn't try anything at night. All the same, she said she'd be glad when we got to the end of it.' She leaned forward. 'The other thing is, she was rather keen on Caleb, and he liked her too. They both talked to me about it.'

My head felt too full. This was so different from what Maman had said, what Adrien had said, from what I'd seen with my own eyes, that I needed space to digest it and sort out the nuggets of truth from the tissue of self-aggrandizement: Bryony as Kamilla's best friend and supporter. I picked up the tray.

'I'll leave you to sleep.'

Bryony held up a hand to stop me. That gossipy spark was in her eyes again. 'They didn't dare do anything about it under Adrien's eye, of course, but Kamilla was intending to visit Caleb in Paris. If Adrien had found out ...'

I'll come unbidden, and stay as I please,
I'll chain dee in misery, drag dee in mire,
Or make dee dat blyde at du'll walk i da air,
For me du'll clim mountains, or walk into fire...

... love.

Saturday, 28th March (continued)

Tide Times at Mid Yell, UT
Low Water   11.15, 1.0m
High Water   17.32, 1.7m
Low Water   23.49, 1.3m

Sunrise05.44
Moonrise   11.00
Sunset   18.33
Moonset   03.04

Waxing quarter moon

A pinchful, a pillful,
Fir spewing, spaigie, pains,
A mouthfu', a cupfu'
For sleep that never ends.

Chapter Thirteen

Toft to Unst had to be a good forty minutes by fast motorboat. I needn't begin watching the clock until two, at least.

I went back up to Maman, and found her standing behind the door, hairbrush in hand, in front of the oval mirror above the mahogany chest of drawers where she'd spread out her make-up. 'If you want to sit,' I offered, 'I could brush your hair for you, the way I used to, when I was peerie.'

'Yes, please.' She handed me the brush. Her hair tumbled in curls down to the middle of her back, as black and glossy as I remembered it from childhood. 'Not a grey hair in sight,' I assured her.

Maman's eyes met mine in the mirror, amused. 'Of course not. One does not have to go grey. It is eccentric.'

'At sea,' I said, 'one's constantly surrounded by grey heads. Grey beards too.'

'Not on your Norwegian ship. Besides, that is a calumny on your friend with the gold head of a young Norse god.'

'Anders?' I smiled. 'He offered to look after *Khalida* for me while I was at sea, but Bergen's a bit far from Kristiansand.'

'When do you leave?'

'There's a weather window after this blows over.' I gestured out of the window at the tumbling waves. 'Tuesday. It's a three-day sail to Kristiansand, so that should give it time to subside on the Norwegian coast.'

Maman sighed. 'By now I should be used to you heading straight off across hair-raising stretches of water, on your own, just like that.'

'You should,' I agreed.

'Your last return, from your Gavin's house, I could hear the wind rising, and there you were still out in it. I think I did not breathe until we saw you going past.'

'See,' I said, 'it's always a mistake to tell parents what you're doing. They just worry.'

'Oh, no,' Maman said, 'keep telling me! What I can imagine is even worse.' She leant forward to do her make-up. I watched with interest: the tinted cream smoothed over her skin, the eyeshadow brushed on and blotted off, the mascara wand wiped with a tissue before she applied it to her dark lashes.

'Maman, what was Kamilla like?'

'Talented, ambitious, attractive.' She began drawing the dark line above her lashes.

'No, I mean, herself. If you were playing her as a character, what would be the traits you would emphasise?'

Maman's face saddened. 'All that brightness and sparkle, and inside, loneliness.'

It wasn't a word I expected.

'Loss. This idea she had that her brother was always with her, like a guardian angel, it is not in the tenets of the church. Her brother is sleeping in our time, and already risen in God's, but the dead do not haunt the living like that.'

She was more certain than I'd dare to be. In that

journey back across the Atlantic, I'd felt Alain at my shoulder so strongly that I expected to turn and see him.

Maman brooded for a moment, then finished, 'I think she believed it because she wanted to cling on to him.'

'What happened to him?'

'Oh, I never heard properly. Some childhood illness, I assumed, but perhaps it was an accident. It was very sudden, and she never got over it. He was younger than she, so I suppose she was the motherly big sister. There is a photo in her room.'

I frowned. 'That's her brother? But –'

Maman's mouth turned down. 'One side is him as he was, the last photo she had of him, and the other side is – what do they call it, computer updating? They do it for missing children, you remember, that little girl who disappeared in Portugal. It is him as he would look now, had he lived to grow up.' She shook her head. 'No, it is not healthy to brood so.' Her smooth, white hand moved to cover mine. I knew she was thinking of my little brother, Patrick, who hadn't lived to be born, and turned my hand to grip hers. 'You must commend their souls to God and move on.'

'He was definitely killed? He didn't disappear?'

'Oh, no, he is certainly dead. She spoke of his spirit watching over her.' She gave a shudder of distaste. 'Leaving her signs. Moving things.'

'A book, and a rose that changed colour.' Bryony had thought Adrien was responsible. It would be easy enough to open a book at an appropriate page, or change a flower in a vase.

Maman nodded. 'Little things that only somebody who was looking for portents would ever notice, especially when she was sharing a room.' Her crimson lips curled. 'I did wonder if it was Bryony doing it, to unsettle her. I had a word with her, oh, not mentioning that, but simply stressing how important it was that we were a company, and had to support each other. It seemed to stop after that.'

'And Kamilla took it as a warning.'

Maman didn't reply. Echoing bleakly in the silence was the knowledge that Kamilla had indeed died.

Gavin was on his way. My job now was to support Maman. 'Well, it's coming up to one o'clock. Do you think your company might be hungry?'

'Not if they have had the night I had,' Maman said, but she let me lead her downstairs. I foraged in the larder and found some tins of soup: creamy mushroom and soothing tomato, just what I'd feed to a crew who were emerging on deck after a gale that had sent them to their bunks with seasickness. I opened three tins of tomato and put them on to heat. Soon the smell brought the survivors into the kitchen: Adrien, in his black suit, and Bryony, still in her onesie, with her hair pulled back in a band. Charles came in behind them, a little pale.

I served up the soup and made a rack of toast. Outside, the hills were hazed over with rain, and the sea was the grey of a herring gull's back, streaked with white crescents of foam that rolled onto the shore. The swell was rising; the ferry's navy hull disappeared between the waves and lurched up again on the crests as it battered its way across to the pier and clung there. The bow clanked down and the cars came off. The third one was white with a neon-green stripe: the police. Now, if Peter had managed to get hold of them before they left, they'd come straight here. Sure enough, the car came round the curve, slowed for the turn and rattled up to the Belmont parking space. I went to the porch door and held it open, waiting.

I recognised the two officers straight away. The driver

had smooth, blonde hair, tied back in a ponytail, and a general air of competence: Sergeant Freya Peterson, a Shetlander headed for higher things. The other one was in his twenties, a half-weaned looking object with sticking out ears and big feet, who'd tried to keep me off my own boat in the Longship case, and thought I needed soothed down from Scalloway castle walls in the witches shenanigans. However, this time they were on the side of the angels, and due all the co-operation I could manage. I tried for a friendly smile.

'Hello.'

'Ms Lynch.' Sergeant Peterson didn't look unduly surprised. 'Living on land now?'

'Sheltering from the storm,' I agreed cordially.

She nodded, conceding the honours even. 'I think you know Constable Buchanan.'

'We've met.' I shook his hand. 'Welcome to Unst. You've missed some of the company, but most of them are still here. Come in.'

I gestured them into the kitchen, like ravens foretelling evil. There was a drawn-breath silence. Bryony put both hands to her cheeks; Maman raised one hand to her throat, as if struggling for breath. Adrien stilled, like a dark-faced heron on the seashore. Only Charles remained unmoved; fifteen years of playing for Maman meant he was impervious to drama.

'Good afternoon,' Sergeant Peterson began. 'We're sorry to disturb you, but we've had a report of a possible removal of archaeological material from a site, and we're doing a house-to-house. Obviously we're focusing more on strangers to Unst. This is entirely voluntary on your part, but we would appreciate it if you would be willing to let us do a quick search of your baggage.'

'Archaeological material?' Maman echoed, and Adrien

breathed, 'A treasure hoard?'

'I'm afraid we can't answer that, sir,' Sergeant Peterson replied. 'We're looking for anything that might have been removed from the earth recently.'

'I was ill all last night.' Bryony sounded like a petulant teenager. 'I couldn't possibly have been out digging at your stupid site.'

Sergeant Peterson gave her mermaid smile, uninterested in what these humans got worked up about. 'Then you have nothing to worry about, madam.' She returned her sea-green gaze to Maman. 'We won't be long, Mrs Lynch.'

I could see the shockwave as she demoted Eugénie Delafauve, international soprano, to Dad's wife. She had, of course, done it on purpose. Maman rose in her most dignified fashion. 'Then you may begin with me.'

Adrien rose too, and Constable Buchanan held his hand up. 'If you don't mind, sir. We'd prefer you just stayed here, while we search one bag at a time.'

To my surprise, Sergeant Peterson turned to me. 'If you'd like to come as an observer, Ms Lynch, I can leave my colleague downstairs.' It seemed that I too was on the side of the angels this time. We tramped up the wooden stairs side by side, two steps behind Maman. 'Do you know what you're looking for?' I murmured to her.

She held up a hand to still me, and waited for the cover-noise of Maman opening her door to murmur, 'Powder, pills, potions.' Her green glance slanted sideways at me. 'DI Macrae phoned me.'

In her room, Maman had already taken Helen's jewellery from her dressing table. 'This is part of my costume, a modern replica. You can see that it was not dug out of the earth.'

In Sergeant Peterson's hands it looked like treasure

from a sunken wreck. There should have been seaweed twined through it, and fish swimming round. She held it to the light, examining the links. 'It certainly doesn't look like it. Is it a replica of something?'

'The headdress of Helen of Troy. It was made in Paris for us, from the Schliemann photographs.'

'Real gold?'

Maman waved one hand dismissively. 'Very thin gold. It was not worth the effort, the jeweller said, to make it in *cuivre jaune,* what is that in English, Cassandre?'

'Brass.'

'Yes, brass. The workmanship was too much bother to make it in brass, so he made it in gold. It is lent for the tour, and of course as publicity for M. Moreau. He is accredited in the programme, with a photograph of the *parure*, the set, but I have to return it. Unless I wish to buy it, of course, but at the moment I do not think I will wish to be reminded of this tour.'

'Very understandable, Mrs Lynch.' I saw Sergeant Peterson stamp down the impulse to try the necklace against her throat. 'It's been an upsetting tour for you, with that poor girl's death.'

Maman's eyes filled with tears. 'The poor child. She was so promising a singer. We are all devastated. It was so sudden.' She shook the tears away, and gestured to the cupboard tucked into the corner. 'I hung my dresses up, of course, so there is only my underwear.' The gesture broadened to the lace-trimmed negligée flung over the embroidered hearth-screen. 'My night clothes.'

Sergeant Peterson looked into the cupboard. 'And Mr Lynch joined you here?'

'But of course. He has gone to Cullivoe, to meet some business associate, since he is here in the isles, but he will be back well soon.' She turned to me. 'It is to do with his

177

wind farm. Now they have permission, there are other groups who wish also to connect to the interconnector south, when it is built.'

Sergeant Peterson was already looking at Maman's row of make-up. 'That's all okay,' I told her. 'I watched Maman use it this morning.'

Maman turned swiftly, her eyes narrowed. Her scarlet lips opened, then closed again. I went over to her, put an arm around her waist, and murmured in French. 'Gavin's on his way up. Unofficial. He'll be here soon.'

I saw her taking that in. 'Then Kamilla ...'

I raised one finger in a shhh gesture. 'Nobody knows anything. It just doesn't feel right. The missing treasure is an excuse to look for other things too.'

She didn't ask what other things, but transferred her gaze to Sergeant Peterson. 'Is there anything else you would like to check, lieutenant?'

Sergeant Peterson swept a last gaze round the room, checked Dad's suit pockets and nodded. 'That's all, thank you, Mrs Lynch.' She came to the door and gestured at the one beside it. 'Whose room is this?'

'Bryony and Kamilla.'

'As head of the group, I presume you have no objection to me examining Ms Lange's baggage? You may, of course, be present if you wish.'

Maman gestured to the room, hand wide open. 'I do not object.'

Sergeant Peterson turned to me. 'Can I ask you, Ms Lynch, to ask Ms Blake to come up and join us.'

'Sure,' I said, and headed downstairs. Bryony was still hunched as I'd left her, soup unfinished, hands tight around the cup of tea. 'Your room and Kamilla's next,' I said. She gripped the mug then thrust it away from her, mouth tense.

'I don't have any hidden treasure.'

'It'll only take five minutes,' I assured her.

'It's so unnecessary!' She glared at the constable. His ears were red, as if she'd been haranguing him while I'd been upstairs. 'I don't want that woman rummaging about in my stuff.'

'Bryony,' Adrien said, 'there's no point in making a fuss, unless you really want to refuse, and make them come back with a warrant.'

'I don't see why I should have to let them search.'

'Why not just get it over with?' I suggested. 'Come on, it won't take long. Besides, Maman's given permission for them to check Kamilla's bags, so we need you to tell us which is which.'

She turned to me, mouth open, as if she'd been struck by a thought. 'But Kamilla wasn't here last night.' Behind the stillness of her face, her eyes were intent, working something out. 'She couldn't have stolen any treasure.'

'No,' I agreed. 'It's maybe something to do with her having ...' What euphemisms did trendy people use? 'Erm, passed so suddenly.'

Bryony wailed into her handkerchief again, but consented to rise and follow me up the stairs, mopping her eyes. 'She didn't even eat any of it.'

'Allergies are funny like that.'

Except that it was supposed to look like food poisoning, if Magnie's suspicions were correct: everyone sick, with one person worse than the others. Had Bryony really poisoned our after-dinner tea? Or had Adrien poisoned the fruit salad?

The room was moving towards some sort of order. Maman had identified Kamilla's suitcase and some of her dresses, and was folding them away on top of a tumble of underwear and T-shirts that looked as if they'd never been taken out. 'The rest are Bryony's, I think.'

Bryony looked around and nodded. 'Yeah, all the rest are mine.'

There seemed to be nothing but clothes in the suitcase. *A letter with a French stamp ...*

I turned around, giving a sweep of the room with my eyes, but couldn't see it anywhere. The bedside table had a drawer, but it was empty. In her handbag sitting temptingly beside her case? I had no helpful excuse for opening that.

'May I look in your case too, Ms Blake?'

Bryony made a grudging face of acquiescence. 'S'pose so.' It was sitting on an upright chair; she gestured towards it. 'The plastic bag is my dirty washing.'

Sergeant Peterson flipped expertly through the clothes, then turned her attention to the mantelpiece. 'How about all this make-up?'

'The red bag is Kamilla's, and that's mine.' She began separating out the jars ranged along the shelf. 'Mine, mine, hers, that one as well – there.' She shoved a shopping bag's worth of little jars and bottles towards the red make-up case. They included several little canisters of vitamin pills, including one labelled in what looked like Finnish, with "*Senna capsules*" in English beside it. I didn't pick it up, in case of fingerprints, though Bryony's would be on it now too, but she saw me looking. The malice sparked in her eyes again. 'That was how she kept her figure.'

'Senna?' I asked. Sergeant Peterson turned round to look.

'Laxatives.'

Laxatives ... suppose there'd been nothing wrong with the seafood. I had no difficulty supposing that. Shetland seafood deserved its high reputation. I could see Sergeant

Peterson watching me figure it out.

'Sooner her than me,' I said casually, and turned away to look out of the window. Allergies were uncertain things, everyone knew that. They could be fatal, or not. Or perhaps the person who'd killed Kamilla didn't know about her allergy. They wanted it to look like an accidental death, in the best Agatha Christie tradition, as Magnie had said: poison everyone and give one person extra. You wanted to make everyone ill. Now, would laxatives given to someone who didn't need them cause sickness and stomach cramps? I didn't know. But Adrien had spoken of 'the runs' too. I wished I had my laptop, to look up how long senna pods would take to work. They'd dissolve in hot liquid: several in the teapot, several in the cafetière. Coffee was bitter stuff, it would cover the taste, whatever it was. I hadn't drunk my tea, and nor had Caleb. It was Bryony who'd served it out, though I had a memory, now I concentrated, of Kamilla lifting up each lid and stirring. Nobody would actually be harmed, just ill for a bit. Then Kamilla was given the dose of whatever had killed her. It would have been easy to drop something into the wine glass that had shattered as she'd fallen. Something that acted fast on the respiratory system ...

Except that these were *Kamilla's* pills. It was too much of a coincidence that she should play a trick with them the day somebody decided to murder her. I wondered how many of the cast knew she had them. Bryony, obviously, and anyone else who'd been in her room: Adrien? Caleb?

I'd been silent too long. 'It's fairly blowing up,' I said, as if the only reason I'd been at the window was to check the weather. On my left, the Loch of Belmont was churned and muddy, choked brown replacing yesterday's sparkling blue; ahead of me, the Loch of Snarravoe was white with crested waves. 'Look at the waves on that loch.'

I turned around again, just in time to see Sergeant Peterson lifting Kamilla's senna pods, oh, so casually, finger and thumb on the rim of the plastic container, and placing them in her suitcase, in a corner, where they would be held still enough not to smudge fingerprints. She made room for the make-up case at the other end, added Kamilla's handbag and closed the zip. 'If you wish, Mrs Lynch, we can take this and return it to Ms Lange's parents. I'll give you a receipt for it.'

Maman made an 'as you like' gesture. 'I will go and see them, of course, when the tour is over, but it would be easier if you took it now.'

'Then I will.' Sergeant Peterson turned to me. 'I'll search the men's rooms next.' She gestured upwards. 'Who is upstairs?'

'Adrien – you met him downstairs – with Per, our director, who went with Kamilla to Lerwick, and has not yet returned. Fournier, our backer, has gone to fetch him – he is in the downstairs room, off the dining room. Then in the other upstairs room are Charles and Caleb.'

'Caleb's gone too,' I said. 'He wanted to explore the mainland.'

'But Charles is here? Very well, we'll start with him.' She turned to me. 'Ms Lynch, you could stay and keep Ms Blake company while she does her make-up.' Her green gaze swept along the pots. My job was to watch Bryony use all of those little jars.

'I'll probably learn a lot,' I said, and sat down on the chair.

'This is *nonsense*,' Bryony said crossly, as they left the room.

I shrugged. 'Police get funny ideas in their heads

sometimes. Maybe what she really wants is for you to keep an eye on me, so that I'm not eavesdropping on them in the men's rooms.'

She stared at me. 'Why on earth would you want to do that?'

'I wouldn't.' Above the sound of the wind buffeting the house, above the sound of the waves crashing on the beach, there was the throb of a distant motorboat. I could imagine it as if I was on it, the bounce as it slammed off one wave and rose into another, the green water spraying over the forepeak and sluicing down the windows. Keith would be standing, braced, the wheel tugging under his hands, with Gavin beside him watching forwards as intently, shoulder against the side of the wheelhouse.

In her reflection, Bryony spread cream over her face from the first tub in the row, and followed it with a skoosh of coloured cream from the mini-dispenser beside it. Then she leaned forward to put powder on her eyes. I didn't see this being of any help; I didn't believe in a cream potent enough to kill from eyeshadow or blusher. If there had been poison in one of these delicately coloured potion pots, it would have to be in the cream spread all over the face, or maybe in hand cream. I had a vague memory of someone Greek dying from poisoned gloves. Bryony finished blackening her curled lashes and stretched out a hand to the bottle of cream, putting a knob in her palm and swirling it around her fingers, working it into her manicured cuticles. No, there was nothing in there. Bryony shot a malicious glance at me from under her mirrored lashes. 'Well, are you learning anything?'

'I'm not a make-up wearer,' I said.

'I can see that.' Her eyes touched my scar. 'You shouldn't be so proud. That could easily be covered, just with cream foundation. Want me to show you?'

I shook my head. 'I'm used to it.'

The throb of the engine became a roar as it curved around into the bay, then cut suddenly as the motorboat edged into the pier. I could imagine Gavin leaning out to catch the rungs of the iron stepladder, bag in the other hand, saying 'thank you', clambering upwards with the wind catching the heavy pleats of his kilt and whisking them backwards as if he was falling. Then he'd be on dry land, head up, alert as one of his own Highland stags, looking around him at the dig of Belmont, up on the hill, and the pale yellow house before him. He'd shoulder his bag and start walking along the road, just as I'd done this morning, past the lodge and round the curved wall to the kitchen door, or he'd make his way through the gate to the front, like a visitor from Scotland for Thomas and Elizabeth Mouat in the days when this house was a home.

Bryony rose. 'Do you think the sergeant wants you to watch me getting dressed too?'

'I'm sure she doesn't,' I said, and escaped. There was a murmur of voices from upstairs, but I didn't try to go there. Instead I went into the writing room, with the three tall windows that looked over the bay. The motorboat was just leaving, and a solitary figure in a kilt was walking briskly up the road, head high, just as I'd imagined. A rush of gladness filled me. Help was at hand.

I caught up my jacket from the curved banister and went out to meet him.

Chapter Fourteen

I wouldn't have flung myself into his arms if they hadn't opened to receive me as soon I got within hugging distance. They were warm and secure around me. Gavin kissed my cheek, then my mouth, and let me go again, tucking my arm under his. 'How's it all going? Has Freya Peterson arrived?'

'She's busy searching right now. I don't suppose you know how long senna pods take to work?'

'No, but I can find out. Has someone got senna pods?'

'Kamilla had. She used them as a diet aid.'

He laughed at the disdain in my voice. 'She should have gone on the Cass Lynch diet, climbing a mast six times a day.'

I remembered Kamilla sparkling in her scarlet frock. 'She didn't need to diet at all. She had a beautiful figure.'

'She was young too,' Gavin said thoughtfully. 'Early twenties?'

'Something like that.' I hugged his arm against me. 'Oh, I'm glad you're here. There's just too much going on – Kamilla, and this skullduggery with the treasure. I can't wait to be out at sea in peace.'

Gavin gave the tumbling white waves a droll look. 'Even in this?'

'Blissfully quiet compared to a day with an opera

company,' I assured him. 'Have you had any lunch?'

'Keith made some soup on board. It was very welcome, even if the mug kept trying to knock my teeth in every time we hit a wave. I'll go and join Freya first, and get a proper look at Moreau's metal detector.'

I remembered Vincent's comments earlier. 'His father runs a jewellery shop, or workshop, specialising in replica antiques. It was him who made Maman's Helen of Troy gold stuff. You don't suppose he's ostensibly selling replicas to cover a trade in the real thing?'

'It's a good theory, but whether someone like Moreau junior, who has a reputation as an opera singer, would involve himself in that kind of trade, is another matter. Why should he? He's getting enough work to keep himself going, unless he's addicted to something expensive, like gambling or drugs.'

'According to Bryony, he's odd. Possessive. Kamilla ran away to the States to get away from him. But according to him, all was roses.' I gave him a brief overview of Maman's, Bryony's and Adrien's own accounts of their affair. 'I'm not sure who to believe. Maman, I suppose, that they'd had an affair four years ago, but after that ...'

'All that's easy to find out.' Gavin made a face. 'Well, when I say *easy*, it will mean a lot of talking to people all over the place, but it can be found out. I'll get on to that one.' He brooded for a moment. 'I don't like the sound of that poison ring at all. I'll get Freya to take it off him.' He stopped and pulled out his mobile. 'What's the signal like here? Oh, four bars.' He sent a text, waited a moment for the reply, then put the phone away. 'What's the skullduggery with the treasure?'

'Of course, I didn't manage to tell you about that this morning. Someone drugged me.' I told him all about it, with a few extra comments on the ancestry and morals of the people who'd humped me back aboard *Khalida.*

'Any interesting bruises?'

'It was too cold to look. But you're right, it would be hard for them not to bump me somewhere.' I was going to add, 'I'll check later' but then I remembered that *later* might be a joint affair. 'I didn't feel anything.'

'Definitely two people, then. Did you get a chance to look at the site where you saw them working?'

I shook my head. 'The tides meant I had to get *Khalida* across while I could. Peter – he lives in that yellow house, there – he was going to go look.'

'Maybe we could get your Dad to run us over later, if he's still with the company.'

'He's at some wind farm meeting in Cullivoe right now, but I'm sure he could. Or would you be okay to drive his car?'

'I'll check insurance with him. I'd like to meet your Viking ghost.'

'To say nothing of the aliens with the fancy headgear?'

'Definitely them, though not without back-up. I've been reading up about them on the police computer. I'll see what Freya has planned.'

We'd come around the bend of the drive now, to where the house was properly in view. Gavin paused to admire it. '1775, according to the brochure, and Britain's most northerly restored Georgian house.'

'It's lovely inside. Well, slightly too grand for the likes of me, but Maman fits in beautifully.'

His fingers twined around mine. 'And if you're not going back over to *Khalida*, where are we going to sleep?'

I knew I was blushing, and didn't mind. 'Can you survive a bit of cold?'

He gave me a quizzical look. 'It's too cold for

camping, if that's what you're suggesting.'

'Not quite.' I nodded towards the further pavilion. 'The little house there. It's not normally used until summer, but there's a blow-up bed we could take over to it.'

'What's the alternative?'

'Separate couches in the sitting room, right opposite Maman and Dad's bedroom.'

'I can survive a bit of cold.'

We walked on in self-conscious silence, into the house, and straight into the middle of a row in the wide hallway.

'You have no right!' Adrien insisted. His cheeks were flushed with anger. 'This isn't school, where the prefect can confiscate a boy's catapult. I am an adult, and this ring is my property.'

'There's no question of confiscation, sir,' Sergeant Peterson said. Her voice didn't even try for soothing. 'We would like to test the substance in it, that's all. It could, for example, be drugs, which I'm sure you'd agree we have every right to take.'

Maman appeared on the stairs. Adrien turned and appealed to her. 'Eugénie, this officer is trying to take my ring. You're the native here. Can you give their CC a bell and sort it out?'

I could see her going for dignity. Her head rose, her shoulders straightened. 'My dear Adrien, I think the easiest thing for you to do is just to let them take it away for whatever tests they wish to do – or, if they would permit, perhaps they could just take the contents, which, I admit, I would be very happy for you not to have access to.' She came down the last steps, took his arm, patted it, and went into best French floweriness. 'Given your great distress at our poor Kamilla's death, I do not think you should have such a thing about you.' She turned to Sergeant Peterson, frowning at this sudden flood of

French, and went into English. 'Would you permit, madame lieutenant, that one gives you only the powder from the ring, and not the ring itself?'

Sergeant Peterson looked across at Gavin, who met her look with the slightly embarrassed stare of someone who'd just arrived in the middle of a row that was nothing to do with him. Her eyes went back to Adrien. 'I think that would be acceptable, sir, so long as you don't dispose of the ring, in case we want to examine it further.'

'But please log that I'm allowing this under protest,' Adrien said. He watched in brooding silence as Sergeant Peterson's henchman produced an evidence envelope. The ring opened as I'd conjectured: a little flick of one finger and the white powder tumbled into the envelope. It would have been easy to spike a bowl of fruit salad. Constable Buchanan sealed it, put it into his briefcase and clicked the locks over.

'Thank you, sir,' Sergeant Peterson said. 'Do you have any more of this powder with you?'

Adrien shook his head. 'Why should I have? What's in this ring is a lethal dose. And, what's more, there's no law in England that says I can't carry it on me.'

'This is Scotland, sir,' Sergeant Peterson said smoothly, but I could see from the hint of uncertainty that crossed her face and was as quickly smoothed away again, that she was longing to be back in the station consulting whatever big book of laws they had to see if he was right. 'Now, you were going to show us your room.'

Adrien gave an annoyed snort, and led the way upstairs. Maman came forward to kiss us. 'Gavin, how nice to see you again.'

She had recovered her poise, although her eyes were still red-rimmed. She gestured upwards. 'You don't really think that the powder is real poison?'

'The labs will tell us,' Gavin said. 'Of course if it isn't, there's the question of when it was changed. It didn't look much, I agree, but very much less than that could be a lethal dose, depending on what it was.'

'Cyanide, I think,' Maman said. 'Was that not what the wartime Resistance carried, cyanide pills?'

Gavin spread his hands. 'If it ever held poison, there'll be traces of it among whatever's been substituted.' He looked around, and went back to visitor mode. 'A beautiful house, this. Will you show me around?'

4

'I haven't tasted it, of course,' Sergeant Peterson said. 'It smells like soda bicarb to me. The lab will know if there's a residue of something more serious.'

We'd taken refuge in the dining room. Gavin turned the evidence bag over in his hands. 'A nice handy source of poison. Did everyone know he had the ring?'

'It sounds like it. And of course he'd take it off to wash, so all our perp had to do was wait for him to go for a shower, and swap it then.'

'Meaning,' Gavin said, 'that the murder, if it was murder, and if this was what was used, was sparked off by something recent. Yes, Moreau said it was poison, but there's no guarantee of that. A murderer who'd planned Lange's death before the start of the tour would have brought his own poison with him.' He echoed Maman. 'If Moreau went on about suicide, and flourished the ring, any sensible friend would have swapped the contents.' He paused, thinking about it, then changed tack. 'Anything interesting in the bags?'

Sergeant Peterson made a disdainful face. 'Pornographic literature in the accompanist's bag.'

'*Really?*' I said, forgetting that I was there on sufferance. I couldn't imagine quiet, homely Charles reading dodgy magazines.

'Hardback comics.'

'Oh, *bandes dessinées*.' They were entirely mainstream in France, but I supposed that Sergeant Peterson hadn't come across them before.

'How about the letter with the French stamp?' Gavin asked.

Sergeant Peterson shook her head. 'Nothing. Not in her case, nor her handbag. No sign of it.'

'Meaning it's probably been taken and destroyed. Easy enough to take it from Lange's room, in the confusion after she collapsed.'

'No,' I said. 'They were all still there, I'm sure of it, until I sent them upstairs. You know the way people stand around, not wanting to just go. Then Maman took Bryony to bed, so the room wouldn't have been empty.'

'Who tidied away her handbag?'

I hadn't thought of that. 'You'd need to ask about that.' Maman, I'd have thought, but I wasn't going to say so to Sergeant Peterson.

'Then there are the three who aren't here.' She consulted her notebook. 'Fournier, though his case is here, we'll get him later. Then Caleb Portland, he went off somewhere, and the musical director, Per Rolvsson, who went with Kamilla. He expected to meet the company in Lerwick.'

'Fournier's bringing him back here, if he can get in before the ferries stop.'

Gavin made a gesture towards me. 'Cass overheard an odd conversation in which Kamilla accused someone of beind "mad".' He nodded at me, and I retold the story.

'Who do you think she might have been talking to?' Sergeant Peterson asked.

'Not Charles,' I said. 'He doesn't speak English. Not Maman; I'd just heard her singing in her bedroom. Probably not Caleb, because he came into the drawing room with that healthy outdoor glow, as if he'd just been for a ten-mile hill tramp.'

'Moreau, Fournier, Ms Blake, Rolvsson.' Gavin's gaze sharpened.'What's Fournier doing here?'

'He's the backer, isn't he?' Sergeant Peterson said. 'Keeping an eye on his investment?'

'He's an empire-builder,' Gavin replied. 'He's just opened a new hotel in France, with a mint of money spent on it, and he's got an office in Paris. He should be keeping an eye on those, instead of hanging about with opera singers.'

'He wasn't with them in the Scotland bit,' I said. 'He just flew over to join them here.'

'Unless he's keen on Kamilla – we need to go into that, check there are no links between them.' Sergeant Peterson made a note. He turned back to me. 'Any preferences, Cass?'

'Probably Adrien or Bryony,' I said slowly. 'Unless there's a link between Kamilla and Fournier that we don't know about. Rolvsson speaks English, of course, but the company language is French, so I'd have thought they'd have spoken in that. Once you've got used to communicating with somebody in one language you wouldn't naturally change.'

'We'll be going into her relationships with all of them.'

Gavin nodded. 'What about the *mad, mad*?'

'Maman spoke about Bryony being jealous of her.

There were some tricks played as if the ghost of her dead brother was haunting her. But,' I said tentatively, conscious of Sergeant Peterson's sceptical gaze, 'there was also a suggestion that it might have been Adrien. He apparently fancies himself as a medium. Maman thought he might have been trying to get her to get him to try to contact her dead brother, you know, as a way to get close to her again. Suppose he tried something like that here, and she'd caught him? Wouldn't that sound *mad* as a ploy to get her to love him again?'

'That strengthens the murder theory,' Sergeant Peterson said. 'He played his trump card, the contact with the brother, and she still turned him down.'

It didn't sound enough to kill someone for.

Gavin nodded, but more in a showing-he-was-listening way than in agreement, and rose. 'Right. I want to keep my cover as Cass's partner.' His head lifted, listening. 'That sounds like Mr Lynch and Fournier have returned. We'll go back out and socialise.'

'I'll talk to Moreau again. See if he admits to being the one she called *mad*.' She rose, and paused. 'Oh, the other interesting thing was the senna pods, in the room shared by Blake and Lange. I've had a look on the Internet, and it seems that a dose of them would give just the symptoms everyone complained of: stomach cramps, the runs. Only Blake claims to have vomited, which makes seafood poisoning unlikely.'

'Get the container fingerprinted. Blake claimed they were Kamilla's?'

Sergeant Peterson nodded.

'It seems unlikely to me. She was young, healthy, active, whereas Blake was thirty, and looks as if she had a sedentary lifestyle.'

'She didn't want to let you search,' I recalled. 'Then

she caved in suddenly when you said she'd need to tell you what was hers and what Kamilla's, as if she'd realised she could disown them that way.'

Gavin nodded. 'Let's see what forensics says about who touched the canister last.'

ᚺ

A pinchful, a pillful,
Fir spewing, spaigie, pains,
A mouthfu', a cupfu'
For sleep that never ends.

... poison

Saturday, 28th March (continued)

Tide Times at Mid Yell, UT
Low Water   11.15, 1.0m
High Water   17.32, 1.7m
Low Water   23.49, 1.3m

Sunrise   05.44
Moonrise   11.00
Sunset   18.33
Moonset   03.04

Waxing quarter moon

Petals o' velvet,
Da colour o' blud,
Proctected bi' thorns,
The symbol o' love.

Chapter Fifteen

Maman came forward to meet us as we emerged into the hall. 'Bryony seems to have gone missing.' Her slim fingers twisted together, and her face was taut with anxiety. 'She got dressed, and sat in the drawing room for a bit, while the caretaker vacuumed the bedrooms, but she was still really upset. Then she went out, and I thought she had gone downstairs to make a cup of tea, but she didn't return.'

'How long's she been gone?'

Maman spread her hands. 'Half an hour, I would think. And it is a cold wind out there. I'm certain she doesn't have suitable clothing to be out in it for this long.'

'Right.' Gavin came into the hall, frowning. 'She's probably perfectly okay, but given the weather conditions, I think we should look for her. Is everyone upstairs in the drawing room?'

Maman nodded. 'Mostly. Charles is in his room, I think, but Adrien is there, and Vincent, and Per have arrived.'

'I don't want to admit to being police unless I have to. Can you send – let me see, yes, your husband and Vincent along the shore, and Adrien and Per in the car to the ferry terminal, in case she's walked there.' He turned to me. 'Another hill walk, Cass?'

'Excelsior.' I zipped my jacket up. 'Where?'

'*I to the hills will lift mine eyes*. It's a natural impulse to go upwards in trouble. We'll look where the dig is, the Belmont longhouse.' He nodded to Maman. 'Don't worry, we'll find her.'

Gavin set a good pace back along the drive, with the wind behind us lending a helping hand. If it hadn't been so serious, I'd have lifted my jacket above my head and used it as a sail, as we used to as bairns, in the school playground. 'If she's up there, if she looks upset, I'll send you in to her first. We've got no reason to think she's dangerous, and she knows you, you looked after her this morning, whereas she doesn't know me at all.'

I didn't have enough breath to say 'Thanks'.

We crossed the road to the marker pointing upwards: Viking Longhouse. The hill was grazed smooth by sheep and ponies, with a clearly marked track leading upwards to a fenced area. I took three steps off the road and found a squelch of bog between us and the start of the path. Gavin sidestepped it neatly, like a sword dancer, kilt swinging, and I took a flying leap over it and just managed to land dry-footed on the one tussock of firm ground projecting out into the bright-green mire. It wouldn't have swallowed me, of course, but I'd have sunk to my knees in stinking peat water. Now I was stranded, with bog all around me. I did two more leaps, soaking one shoe in the process, and landed at last beside Gavin, who was watching with interest from the firm ground. 'Don't tell me,' he said. 'No bogs at sea either.'

'Plenty in my childhood,' I assured him. 'But then I just splosed through.'

From here, the near side of the fence that surrounded the longhouse site was silhouetted against the sky. The grass underfoot was slippery, studded with the first celandines, like pale-gold daisies. We trudged upwards, and gradually the site itself came into view: a gate, an information board, a scatter of waist-high stones, some sort of white canvas.

Gavin paused at the top of the hill. 'Breather,' he said. 'Get your heart rate steady before we go any further.'

The view was worth pausing for, in spite of the freezing, buffeting wind. On our right, the headland was curved like a crouched cat, the cliff at its end highlighted by the sun. The farm was laid out below: two stone byres with the farmhouse in the centre, enclosing a square of farmyard, just like at Gavin's house, and a line of low sheds with red corrugated roofs. Past it, there was a field half-filled with huge black plastic rolls – 'tractor eggs', we used to call them. Belmont was side on, the squares of yellow daffodils bright, and behind it, across Yell Sound, I could make out the ice plant on Cullivoe Pier. If I'd had spyglasses I'd be able to see my *Khalida* … I felt a sudden wrenching of homesickness, that she was there, almost close enough to see, yet barred from me by the tumbling white water. Instead, I'd be in a cold pavilion with a stranger – and at the thought, a curling writhe of panic rose in my throat. He wasn't a stranger, I told myself, he was Gavin, and stamped the panic down in practicality. 'Let's find her.'

'One more minute.' His hand came warm around mine. 'The more upset she is, the more we need to be really calm.' He nodded downwards at the rock beside us. 'Now, that's interesting.'

I looked at it. It was just a flat-topped rock, with a series of indentations in it, holding the water, roughly in a square pattern.

'Those,' Gavin said, dipping one finger into the deepest one. 'Bronze Age cup marks.' He looked around.

'People have been living here for four thousand years.'

I looked at the indentations more closely. 'A board game?' It seemed a lot of work for a game of solitaire.

'Or part of a ceremonial ritual. Nobody knows.' He gave me a quick, keen look. 'Ready now?'

My heart rate had steadied to normal. 'Ready.'

We walked side by side up the last bit of path to the final hill-dyke, and at last we got a view of the far side of the site. Bryony was huddled in the far corner of the longhouse, head sunk into her knees, sheltered from the howling wind by the crazy-paving walls, her green Edwardian jacket pitifully inadequate for this weather. The gate was swinging open over the duckboards underneath it. Past it there was a squared boulder, furred with lime-grey lichen and knobbled moss, and to the right was the interpretation board, with an artist's impression of the longhouse when it was whole: a low house with a thatched roof, and cows kept in the nearer half. The long rectangle of the Viking house was clear to see, but the walls were reduced to waist height, and the floor was spread with agricultural fleece, which the wind had teased to long fibres. Bryony had taken refuge where the people had lived. I pitched my voice low, and called her name. 'Bryony! It's Cass. I've come to help you.'

Her head stayed down; her arms clutched tighter around her knees. I took a deep breath and began walking towards her. Gavin waited by the gate while I stumbled over narrow paths of long grass, and between tumbled boulders. I'd have to cross the longhouse itself. I set a tentative foot on the fleece and found it solid. I picked my way towards her: fleece; the first wall; the soft jumble of peat and gravel core; the inner wall; fleece again, stretched taut over uneven stones so that it gave squashily as I walked, with a crunch like thin ice.

Bryony lifted her head to see me approach, then huddled further into her corner. She was giving out a low moaning, as if she was in pain, and rocking over her doubled legs. The wind made snakes of her dark hair.

I had to go up onto the wall again, and over the corner of the second room. I nearly tripped into a hole under the fleece. Here, it was the dirty colour of dried mud, and it flapped in the wind as I picked my way across to her, and hunkered down beside her. She didn't speak, but her rocking paused for a moment, and the low moaning stopped. 'Bryony,' I said, 'you're getting cold. Let's go back down to the house and get you warm.'

The dark head shook.

'Come on,' I said, in the most encouraging voice I could manage. 'If you stay here much longer you'll never be able to sing tomorrow.'

She began crying, great, gulping sobs that made her breath shudder. I put an arm round her, and waited. At last she lifted her head. Her face was red with crying, her eyes swollen, the lashes dark and gummy with tears. 'It was all my fault. I didn't mean to harm anyone, not like that. I just wanted … she had so much luck, and she wasn't even that good …'

'It was you who phoned to ask for seafood?'

She nodded, and brushed the tears away with one hand. 'But I never meant to kill her. Never, ever!'

'I'm sure they'll understand that,' I said soothingly. 'Come on, now, you can tell us all about it down at the house.'

She shook her head, but I started to draw her upwards. 'You need to get warm. A cup of tea, with brandy in it.'

'I'm cold,' she agreed, surprised.

'All the more reason to get moving. Come on.' I gave a firm, steady pull, and got her to her feet. The wind hit us as we came up above the shelter, slapping our cheeks, probing cold fingers down our necks. I braced myself against her instinctive attempt to sink down again. 'On we go. Let's get out of this wind.'

It was in our faces, so I went first, to shelter her from it, towing her behind me over the jagged boulders that stuck up like teeth into the former doorway, across the second longhouse and onto terra roughly firma. Gavin came up and put his arm round her waist, so that we were walking her between us. She moved like an automaton now, silent, giving the occasional sob, as we manoeuvred her through the gate and on the path down the hill. Gavin must have worked out a dry path, for he steered us to the left, away from the swamp we'd come across, down across heather. As we were coming down, I saw the beach search party look up, spot us, turn, and start walking towards the house, dark dots against the green grass. The pier party was probably back by now. We came over a drier spit of rough grass, and back onto the road at last. Once we were on the flat ground, we linked our arms in hers and fairly marched her up the road. She was beginning to shudder now, as well she might, dressed in her cloth jacket and office pumps, hatless, scarfless, gloveless, in the cold of a March gale. 'Straight to bed with you,' I said cheerfully, 'with a hot water bottle at your feet, and a cup of tea with brandy in it, and nobody bothering you till you feel up to seeing them.'

She gave the ghost of a nod at that. Her feet quickened as we came around the bend in the drive. Gavin went in ahead, and so we found the kitchen door closed on the chinking of mugs, and the hall cleared for us. I took her up to the room she'd shared with Kamilla, and busied myself getting her bed ready, with the covers turned invitingly back, while she took her clothes off and got back into her onesie.

'There,' I said, drawing the covers up over her. 'I'll just go and get the bottle and tea.'

She nodded.

'And don't worry about anything.' I wasn't sure what I should say. Kamilla's things had gone, but the gaps they left shouted her absence. 'They'll understand.'

The kitchen seemed full of people. 'How is she?' Per demanded.

'Cold.' I filled the kettle, and dug my hot water bottle out from my backpack. 'Not hypothermia cold, I'm pretty sure. She just needs rest and peace until she's calmed down.'

'But what in heaven possessed the girl to go charging up the hill like that, without a word to anyone?' Dad asked.

I spread my hands vaguely. 'The shock of Kamilla's death, I think.'

'I will go up and speak to her,' Maman said.

Maman would be better than me at the touchy-feely stuff. I made the bottle and tea, and handed her the mug. 'Bring this.'

We headed upstairs and back into the room. When Maman sat on the chair by the bed, Bryony gave a wail and clung to her. She began crying again, and speaking through the sobs, but the only words I could make out were 'so sorry ...'. I put the hot water bottle at her feet, and sat down on Kamilla's bed.

'I didn't mean to,' Bryony said, surfacing at last from Maman's shoulder. 'I feel so dreadful about it. I just thought ... it wasn't a joke exactly, but I was envious.' Her voice was steady now, her eyes intent, as if she was picking her way through a score that she'd only half-learnt. 'We'd started out together, I'd been singing longer than her, and she'd got everything, just through luck, being blonde and pretty. It wasn't fair ...' She sniffled for a bit, then wiped her eyes again. 'I know, it was horrid of me. I can't believe I did it. I don't know what came over me.'

'But what exactly did you do?' said Per, from behind me. He came around Kamilla's bed to sit on Bryony's bed, beside her. She drew away from Maman, and cuddled up to him instead, face flushing crimson.

'I phoned the restaurant and asked for fish. I knew Kamilla couldn't eat it. I was just being mean. I was fed up of her being so, so *triumphant* all over the place, as if she just had to ask and have.'

I remembered the way Kamilla had cleared her from her seat in the train, without even asking whether Bryony, too, would prefer a forward-facing seat.

'I never expected her to die. I know it was horrid of me, but how could I have thought of that? I knew she wouldn't eat it. I just wanted, just for once, for her not to get everything her own way.'

Per put his arm around her. 'There, now, there. It was a stupid prank to play, but we understand that you did not mean it to have such consequences. You have told us now, you can think no more of it. See, I will stay with you for a bit, and you can drink your tea, and get warm, and rest.'

He nodded a dismissal at Maman, and she rose. I followed, then paused at the door, biting down my curiosity. Were Bryony and Per an item, then? There had been something she'd said earlier ... yes, *Per phoned and told me*, about Kamilla's death. I'd noticed the satisfaction in her voice, as if she was getting special treatment.

It didn't make sense to me. I remembered the aggrieved note in her voice as she'd said *I didn't know she had an allergy*, as if Kamilla had somehow taken an unfair advantage. I was sure she'd been telling the truth then, so why should she lie about it now? Besides, there was everyone being ill; she hadn't confessed to that.

Dad had left his laptop open on the table in the curved-window writing room. I nipped in there now and googled senna pods. Wiki only said it was used as a laxative, which I knew. I tried *senna pods buy*, and found Kamilla's pill bottle. I looked at the reviews. Several people warned of stomach cramps on the first use. Maman had had stomach cramps, and Adrien too had mentioned them. Bryony had been sick, but that could have been distress at Kamilla's death, if she'd really been the person who'd phoned, imitating Maman. I accepted that; she was the most likely person. But why should she have poisoned everyone, and when?

I scrolled up again, and looked for how long the pods took to work. *Effects occur from 8-12 hours after administration,* it said helpfully, *and may last up to 24 hours.* They'd started to be ill in the middle of the night, so the pods had been given sometime between midday and four o'clock. I remembered following Maman up the stairs to find everyone assembled in the drawing room, with Bryony behind the tea and coffee pots, dispensing. It would have been so easy for her to drop a capsule into each cup. Nobody was watching her; why should they? She knew who took what; she'd just pass them their cup, and they'd drink it.

She hadn't poured my cup, though; I'd done that myself. And now I started thinking about it, Caleb had arrived after me, grimaced at the teapot and brought out his own bottle of Diet Coke. Caleb and I, the two who hadn't been ill. I went off downstairs to find Gavin, in the kitchen with Adrien and Fournier. 'Come and see where we'll be sleeping.'

We crossed the grass and went into the pavilion. Gavin looked critically round. 'Lovely in summer.'

'Upstairs is nice too,' I said encouragingly. We clomped up the wooden stairs. I indicated the floor. 'A blow-up mattress, a couple of downies. We'll be fine.'

'Yes, we will,' Gavin agreed. He leaned against the wall, russet head tilted quizzically at me. 'What did you want to tell me?'

'Bryony says she was the person who phoned to ask for seafood.'

'As a trick against Kamilla?'

'That's what she says.' I spread my hands. 'I believe that she phoned. She was the natural person to imitate Maman. I just don't see why. Like she said, Kamilla wouldn't eat the seafood. At worst, she'd just not get a starter. And she didn't mention the senna pods. So if she lied about it, it's likely she used them.' I explained my theory that they were in the afternoon tea. 'Everyone that was there was ill, I think – well, Adrien and Maman were, and Fournier looked as if he'd been up half the night.'

'That could have been digging treasure.'

'True.'

'If Kamilla was ill, could Bryony step into her role?'

I shook my head. 'Wrong voice. She's a soprano, and Kamilla was a mezzo.'

'So she is.' Gavin mused for a moment. 'I agree, it doesn't hold together. On the face of it, the senna pods seem pointless, unless ... you don't suppose they could be connected with your treasure-hunter?' He considered that for a moment, then shook his head. 'All they achieved was keeping everyone awake all night, and so more likely to notice him sneaking out to dig things up. No, it doesn't make sense yet.' He eased himself off the wall. 'But it will. Let's try another tack. Bryony, the perp, goes for the classic Agatha Christie method: poison everyone slightly, and give an extra dose of something lethal to the victim.'

I shook my head. 'Then why go crazy with remorse now? Or rather, if she's crazy with remorse, why not admit to deliberately killing her?'

'Because she's hoping to pass it off as an accident. 'I didn't mean to do it.' A practical joke gone wrong. If all she admits to is phoning the restaurant, that's plausible.'

I made a face. 'I'm certain that she didn't know about the allergy, whatever she says now, and if she didn't know about it, then why phone and ask for seafood?'

'Here's an idea,' Gavin said. 'I'll go with your feeling she didn't know about the allergy. In which case, seafood's ideal for making someone ill. She was all set to make Kamilla ill –' He stopped, shaking his head. 'So she just made everyone ill. No, that doesn't work. It only works if she actually planned to kill Kamilla – in which case, you're right, the remorse doesn't fit, although of course you can never tell. She might not have been prepared for the difference between plotting to kill her and her actually being dead.'

'Suppose someone else overheard her phoning, and decided it was the ideal set-up for murder. In that case, we're assuming Bryony's telling the truth: she knew about the allergy, and decided to play a nasty trick, but she didn't do the senna pods, which were Kamilla's after all.'

'Are you certain nobody else could have doctored the afternoon tea?'

'I wasn't there when it was dished out. She was sitting at the tea tray, but it would have been equally easy for somebody else to pass the cups across. She would know, if somebody did that.' I visualised that. 'It would have been harder for that person to drop a capsule in without either Bryony or the person he was taking it to seeing. People wouldn't look at Bryony making their tea, but they would look at someone passing it to them.'

'No amateur conjurers among the cast?'

'Goodness!' I tried to imagine Adrien, or Caleb, or dignified Per, in tails and a top hat, with yards of knotted handkerchiefs. Suddenly it rang a bell. 'Good grief, yes. Vincent Fournier used to do tricks. I'd forgotten that. He made coins disappear, then found them somewhere else. Maybe that's why I have this vague feeling that he's untrustworthy. I didn't like people who broke the rules of nature, even then.'

'I wish I had the authority to question Bryony,' Gavin said. 'I can't. I'm not officially on the case, I just have a watching brief until we get the cause of Kamilla's death, and that won't be until Monday.' He put an arm around me. 'Come on, let's go and look at this treasure site of yours.'

Chapter Sixteen

Dad was fine about us taking the car. 'Don't go going to Yell, now. You'll maybe get there, but not back again. I had a quick drive to the marina after my meeting, and your boat was fine.'

'Thanks,' I said. I hoped it was true. If I climbed the hill to the west of the house, I might even be able to see her, with the aid of spyglasses. There was bound to be a pair somewhere in the house. We left Cat rattling his marble round the drawing room skirting board, and drove – or rather, Gavin drove, for I'd still not got round to passing my test –around the house, past Peter's yellow house and the two modern ones, then along past the Loch of Snarravoe. Dad's car was too heavy to jump sideways as a gust hit it, but I felt it rock as the wind came at us between the hills.

'You had the clearances here too,' Gavin said, looking up at the long-ruined crofthouses.

'Laird clearances for sheep in the mid-Victorian era,' I said, remembering having read John Graham's *Shadowed Valley* in school, 'and then still more folk emigrated in the days of the herring boom. The merchants in Lerwick made a killing, but the ordinary folk with their sixareens couldn't compete with the Scottish herring drifters.'

'Don't let me miss the turn-off to your bay.'

'A couple of miles yet. Bordastubble, Lund, and it's likely got a 'Viking Trail' sign too.'

'Are you patrolling tonight?'

'Oh ...' I suddenly realised that striding around boggy hills in the freezing dark clashed with being more romantic. 'I did say I would, originally, and then I was supposed to be going to Lerwick for tonight, but I haven't yet told Peter I'm not going ...'

'That sounds like a yes. We'd better walk the land beforehand. I know you know it now, but I'd like to see where I'll be charging around in the dark.'

'You don't need to. I mean, shouldn't you be staying with the suspects?'

'There's no proof they are suspects yet,' he reminded me. 'Here's the turn-off. Lund.'

We came around the corner, and past the Bordastubble Stone, crouched against the bleached heather, with the first green of new grass showing through the brittle stems. Below us, my peaceful, sundrenched bay was slashed with waves, rolling on to the beach in a jigsaw mass of foam, and hurling themselves into the air at the base of Vinstrick Ness. Beyond, Bluemull Sound was purple-grey, hazed over with spindrift, the notched waves rolling down it at a frightening speed. I was glad I wasn't out in it.

We drove past the House of Lund, past the still-buried Viking longhouses and down to the car park in front of the graveyard. Shetland-trained, I let Gavin close the door on his side before I opened my own. Even so, the wind caught it with a force I hadn't expected, and nearly tore it from my hand. I managed to hold it, but I had to lean on it to get it shut again.

It was noisy here: the wind ran steel fingers along the telegraph wires, rattled the twigs of the rugosa bushes, moaned across the empty reaches of the sky. On the beach, the waves pounded and sucked back, knocking pebbles down with them, then crashed on the beach once more. The wind whirled the sand into the air, so that the beach seemed to hover above itself.

Gavin offered me his crooked arm. 'Ready?'

'Ready.'

Our first steps were like walking against a giant hand, heads down, jackets flattened against our chests, each step pushing forwards. Then, as we went along the beach, the wind came sideways on to us, salt-sharp, trying to push us up the beach into the dunes. The waves roared at our ears, the flying sand stung our cheeks. We gained the shadow of Vinstrick Ness at last, and paused for a breather before climbing up the hill.

'Wild,' Gavin said, looking out at the pounding breakers.

'Perfect windsurfing weather.' I'd seen the clear sails whizzing across Tresta or Busta voe in the wildest of winds, with each black-clad figure clinging on below.

Gavin tilted his head back and took a long breath of salt air, then turned his head to smile at me. 'Upwards?'

'Upwards,' I agreed. The wind snatched at us as we came out of the shelter and began scrambling up the side of the headland, hands clutching the tussocks of grass in the steeper places, shoes searching for a foothold on the uneven ground. I pulled my hood up and fastened it with with Velcro, but then had to undo it again to see where I was going. The wind buffeted my windward ear until it hurt, and I tugged my hood back up. We were almost at the top now; a last scramble, and we stood braced against the whirling air.

The view was spectacular: the dark sea whitened with great brush-strokes of foam, which turned close-up into great breakers that smashed on the beaches, or flung themselves halfway up the cliffs. The white streaks of bubbled water streamed away from each headland as if the island itself was moving. Above us, the grey cumulus scurried by, breaking and re-forming against the lighter cloud behind; at our feet, each longer grass stem moved with the ripples of the wind, flattening to show its silver back. You could see the gusts moving across the land as easily as if it was cat's-paws on the water.

It took me a moment to orientate myself among the knobbles of rock on the Ness, but once I found the right place the disturbance was easy to spot. I definitely hadn't been dreaming. Last night's workers had taken a square plug of turf out of the hill, set it to one side – there were crumbs of earth tangled in the heather – and dug beneath. The grass was squashed down where something heavy had rested: a black bag covered with the dug-out earth would be my guess. More earth had been put in, to make up for what was missing, and the turf plug replaced exactly level with the surrounding grass.

'A neat job,' Gavin commented. 'Professional.'

'A couple of days, and there would be no sign that anything had happened,' I agreed.

We were bent over, looking at it, when a shadow loomed over us. For a moment I thought I was seeing my Viking again, the pointed helmet dark against the sky, one arm raised, then I clocked the peak-hooded oilskin jacket, and recognised Keith Sandison.

'I saw the pair of you up here,' he said, 'and thought I'd come and see what you'd found.'

Gavin stood back, gesturing to the just-visible black line. 'Someone's been digging here.'

'They have that,' Keith said. He shot me a sideways look, suddenly mistrustful. 'I thought you were on watch here last night, lass.'

'I was. Someone drugged me, after dinner.'

I got a sceptical look from under the bushy eyebrows. 'Wi' a sleeping pill, something like that?'

'That's what I think it was.' I explained what had happened. 'I'd have thought myself that I'd have dreamt it, if it hadn't been for the sand in my hair – and this.' I nodded at our feet. 'Nobody'd been digging here yesterday, at least, not before four o'clock.'

'Not after, either.' Keith scratched his chin. 'I kept an eye on the place mesel, after you went off to your mam's concert. There was naebody here before seven, I can swear to that.' He seemed to change his mind suddenly. 'It's bitter up here. Come up to the house, and have a cup o' tay, and we'll put our heads together.'

He led us up to the crofthouse above Upper Underhoull, and the field where the pig-snouted aliens had searched. 'Will you tak' tay or coffee?'

'Coffee,' I said. My eyelids were beginning to droop. Gavin nodded in agreement. Keith stomped his rubber boots on the porch floor and gave a shout inside. 'Maggie! Two visitors here.'

Maggie was a little, plump lady with an old-fashioned pinnie in a pink and white print, and a distrustful look to her mouth. I couldn't quite imagine her wearing a Viking brooch. We followed Keith in taking our shoes off, and I was glad we had, for the lino flooring of the hall and kitchen was brand new, and so immaculate you could have eaten your tea off it without risking the smallest germ. Keith waved us into a traditional kitchen, with a couch by the Rayburn, a sheepdog dozing on the rug beside it, a drop-leaf table under the window, and a pair of binoculars on the sill. There was a warm smell of peat smoke. I undid the Velcro under my chin and took my gloves off. Maggie waved us towards the couch. 'Dip dee doon.'

'Coffee, baith,' Keith said, and she nodded, shifted the kettle onto the Rayburn hotplate, and began taking mugs down from the tree on the dresser. 'Milk? Sugar?'

I shook my head. 'Yes, please,' Gavin said. 'Milk.'

Keith sat down on an upright chair by the table, and scratched his chin again. 'I doubt you're right enough. This man you saw, that seemed to find something here in the morning, he's marked it on the metal detector's GPS, and come back when it was quiet.'

'It could have been him who drugged me. He passed me the cup.'

'But in that case,' Gavin said, 'who was the other one? It would have taken two to manhandle you into the cabin.'

I hadn't thought of that. 'Good point.'

'Might it be one of the other singers?' Keith suggested.

I spread my hands. 'Not Per, he went on the helicopter. Bryony wasn't in a fit state this morning.'

'That could be good cover for having been up half the night.'

I shook my head. 'Those nails never saw a spade in their lives. Not Maman, of course. Charles?' I considered Maman's downtrodden accompanist. 'I don't see Charles doing anything so wildly romantic as searching for hidden treasure.'

'Caleb,' Gavin said.

I tried to conjure up his face. 'Maybe ... he has Shetland links, if that's relevant, but to Inga and Charlie, and I'd swear they're not involved in any antique jewellery theft. Besides, he doesn't seem to know them. It's three generations back.'

'Who have we missed?' Gavin totted them up on his fingers. 'Fournier. The businessman who organised the tour.'

I brightened at that idea. 'There's a family link between Adrien and Fournier. He spoke about it this morning. Adrien's father has an antiques shop next door to Fournier's Paris office, and when the role of Hippolytus came up, it was Fournier that Adrien phoned to worm himself into the company.'

Keith Sandison cut into my musings. 'When was that?'

I tried to remember. 'I think it was only a fortnight ago. The other singer broke his ankle – no, his hamstring.'

'My find was a fortnight ago,' Keith said. 'A fortnight and odd days. It only hit the headlines when those young boys found another cache.'

'Was it reported at all?' Gavin asked.

Keith shook his head. 'Oh, it was kent locally, but no' outwith the isles, and I took particular care no' to let Radio Shetland or the paper ken. They only found out because the boys talked about my find as having set them to look.'

'Fournier has links here,' I said. 'He used to work at Sullom Voe, with Dad. He could well know someone who kept him updated with local news.'

Keith nodded to Gavin. 'This Fournier sounds worth keeping an eye on.'

'He went off to the mainland to fetch Per Rolvsson, the musical director, back from the hospital.'

'So his bags won't have been searched. Well, now we have this cause for suspicion, that strengthens our hand. I'll get Freya to talk to him.'

'Except,' I said, 'if Adrien is stealing antiques for his father, why would he need Fournier as a go-between?'

Keith shook his head, and didn't try to answer that one. 'So, are you patrolling here again tonight?'

I nodded, glancing at Gavin.

'Tell you what, lass,' Keith said. 'It'll be a cold night

for the pair of you to be out on the hill. How about I keep an eye open, and phone if I see anything I don't like the look of? That way, you can get the start of a night's sleep, at least.'

'It feels a bit like shutting the stable door after the horse is gone,' I said.

'Not quite that, lass,' Keith said. 'Dinna forget there was that four that came in the car, them as are biding up at Baltasound. They're no' to ken the prize is gone. I'll maybe see you later, then.'

ᚻ

By seven o'clock, the wind was living up to the forecast. I kept reminding myself that I'd tied *Khalida* down within an inch of her life, but I still felt as though I'd abandoned her. On top of that it was years since I'd been ashore in a storm, and I'd forgotten how noisy it was. The wind rummelled down the chimney, rattled the windows, tramped over the roof. The beams creaked as if a giant was walking above our heads.

I was in the kitchen when the catering lady arrived, with several boxes. 'Lamb shanks in an orange and red wine sauce,' she said, and decanted them into two casserole dishes. 'Give them half an hour to heat through. I've done a big plate of starter salad with goat's cheese, and a fruit salad.' She took two tubs of what I took to be ice cream out of one box.

'Craafit,' I read.

'Fetlar Craafit ice cream,' the lady said. 'It's home-made and wonderful. I've brought a tub of strawberry and a tub of salted caramel. I'll put it in the freezer.

Don't forget it now!'

'I won't,' I promised.

I took a deep breath and braced myself mentally for watching everyone else eating it. Lent had felt longer than usual this year. She paused and looked at me sideways.

'I don't suppose you've heard, now, about those plates.'

I shook my head. 'It won't be before Monday, I don't suppose.'

'I heard that the poor lass didn't make it. The man that supplies my seafood, you maybe ken him, Keith Sandison, o' Sandison Seafoods, he was phoning me.'

Keith again. I knew that on a small island like Unst you tended to keep running across the same people, but he felt just a bit too ever-present. 'I met him, yea.'

'Well, Keith'd heard that aabody was up in the night, and he was a bit concerned. He doesna want his seafood to get a bad name. There's been aa this coverage on the TV too.'

I stared at her. 'About her death?' Right enough, Fournier had mentioned that he and Per were going to talk to the BBC.

'Oh, yea. Well, it seems she was een o' the presenters o' *The Voice*, and so there's been a lock about that, an' her career, an' clips o' her singing. I dinna watch the telly much, but I saw it on the news. They interviewed the police, in Lerwick, but he just said "No comment", and "Investigations are ongoing" and that sort o' thing. They had a helicopter shot o' Belmont House too, and an interview wi' Vincent. He said she'd had a severe allergic reaction. He looked right good, no nervous at aa, as if he'd had plenty o' practice. The other man, the Norwegian, he didna say much.'

'We were lucky the ferries stopped running when they

did, or they'd all have been up here.'

'Yea, it's an ill wind ...' She set out a couple of little bowls of salad dressing and washed her hands. 'There, that's me. Enjoy your meal, now.'

I set the table, nipped out to the pavilion to change into my pretty dress, and then came back and rang the brass gong on the mantelpiece. Maman and Dad came down first. Maman was in full dress, with her best pearl drops dangling against her creamy skin, and Dad matched her, in his suit. Charles slipped in behind them, then Fournier, in a charcoal grey affair which had probably cost as much as a new mainsail, with Adrien behind him, red-eyed and silent. Bryony came down on Per's arm, dressed in her pink evening dress, but looking fragile, and jumping when anyone spoke to her. Gavin came in last, in his scarlet kilt, and with his horsehair sporran instead of the leather one.

I'd done my best to space the chairs out, with this smaller party, but even so the place where Kamilla had sparkled shouted her absence. Maman sat at the head of the table again, with Dad on one side and Adrien on the other; Gavin and I were beside Adrien, with me nearest the door, to be handy for waiting. Fournier returned to his seat at the table-foot, and Per, Bryony and Charles were opposite us. Behind them, the dusk had come early, the black clouds veiling the last of the light. The wind slammed at the window. Maman rose, undid the bead circles, and drew the curtains against it. 'There, that is enough of this Shetland weather for tonight. Dermot, will you pour the wine?'

It was an uneasy meal. Gavin and I weren't the only ones watching; it felt like we were all watching each other. Kamilla's ghost presided over us. Dad poured the wine, I brought out the dishes and we passed them to each other, remarking politely on the goat's cheese, the salad; it was all too formal. Per coaxed Bryony to eat, but barely touched his own lamb shank and creamy potato. Adrien finished his impatiently, then crumbled his bread into the gravy. Dad and Fournier talked business, Dad's connection with the projected North Isles wind farm. It felt indecent to be so hungry. I ate my shank as unobtrusively as I could, gave myself a second helping of mash, and resolved to heat up one of the leftover ones for supper.

It was calculating leftovers that reminded me. 'What happened to Caleb?' I looked across at the closed curtains. 'He won't get back now.'

'Oh, he is staying in Lerwick,' Per said. 'He'll take up one of the rooms we had reserved for tonight.' He looked across at Fournier. 'I have warned him not to talk to the press.'

Fournier nodded. 'Good. There are enough rumours flying around. I've already had a call from the seafood bloke, asking me to make a statement exonerating him. I told him I'd already told the BBC that she appeared to have an allergy, and couldn't say more. He'd have to wait for the medical findings.'

'Waiting, waiting!' Adrien shoved his plate away from him. 'We need to do something.' His face suddenly focused, his pupils contracting to pinpoints. 'Where is the picture of Kamilla's brother? I could –'

'No!' Maman cut in, the goddess laying down her orders. 'No, Adrien. We will have none of your spiritualism here. I forbid it.'

Adrien flushed and leaned forward, gesturing with one hand. 'He was trying to contact her.'

'No,' Maman repeated. 'His death was a great shock to Kamilla, she never recovered properly from it. Perhaps someone was playing tricks, I do not know.' Her gaze swept across Bryony, around the table. Her dark eyes sparked with wrath. 'But this I do know. Their souls are together now, reunited, and their earthly bodies sleep in peace.'

Adrien jutted his lip mutinously. 'I may do what I wish, Eugénie.'

Maman straightened her back until she was ten feet tall. 'You will not try to contact the dead in this house.' Her hand slammed down on the table, making the cutlery jangle. 'No.'

For a long moment, their eyes locked: Maman, set and commanding, Adrien angry as a spoiled child. It was his eyes that fell first. He pushed his chair so hard that it fell back against the sideboard behind, and stormed out past us. The door slammed behind him. There was a long silence.

'Anyway,' Bryony said at last, with a touch of petty triumph, 'he can't have the photo, because the police took it, with all Kamilla's other baggage.'

Per looked up quickly. 'The police?' He looked across at Maman. 'I saw, of course, that Kamilla's things had been tidied away, but I thought perhaps you had done it.'

Maman shook her head. 'Of course, that you were not here. No, the police came. They were looking for missing jewellery, taken from the dig over the hill. They looked through everything, and then they offered to return her belongings to her family.'

Per was silent for a moment, frowning. 'That's very helpful of them.' He sounded suspicious, and his eyes looked as if he was calculating something. 'I am not sure our police in Norway would be so obliging, to return suitcases to another country.'

I didn't like the way his suspicions were moving. 'What did happen to Kamilla's brother?' I asked quickly.

'Oh, it was a sad story, but from many years ago, when she was a child,' Maman said. 'It was some kind of accident. I do not remember me what exactly.'

'He was run over,' Bryony said. 'Right in front of her eyes, by a driver who didn't stop.'

I winced away from the picture. 'How awful!'

'It was awful,' Per said. He looked straight across at me, and spoke heavily, as if he too had lost a child to the road. 'She told me of it. It was evening, a beautiful golden evening, and their mother had permitted that they play on the road for that last half hour before bedtime. It was a village they lived in, and there was not much traffic, so they were not looking out, and they were just on the wrong side of a bend that narrowed the road between two old houses – you know the sort, in Austria, with the upper fronts almost touching above the road. Coming into them would have been like a tunnel to the driver, and then he came around the bend at the end of the houses and out into the sun, shining straight into his eyes. I do not know if he was going too fast, or if it was just that, the dark and then the sun, so that he could not see them, but he hit the little boy and flung him clear. He did not stop, but drove straight on. He was never caught.'

He stopped there, looking at me as if he expected an answer, but I couldn't think of anything to say. He'd made me see it: the little girl playing in the sunlight, and the car coming at them suddenly; the girl grabbing for her brother to pull him clear, but too late; seeing him snatched from her hands and flung to the other side of the road by the metal monster that didn't stop. 'Was the little boy killed straight away?'

Bryony took up the story. 'He said her name. She ran across the road and tried to pick him up, and he said her name, then a gush of blood came out of his mouth.' Her eyes filled with tears. 'She was only eleven, and when they took him away from her, she wouldn't believe he was dead, because he'd spoken to her.' She paused and took a sip of wine, then finished, 'She never believed he was dead.'

Loneliness, Maman had said. I imagined the little girl cradling her dead brother, and for a moment I could almost see Kamilla's face opposite me, sparkling in the candlelight. I rose, and began stacking plates to chase her image away. Gavin rose, and opened the door for me. I went past him with the loaded tray, and stopped dead. Behind me, looking over my shoulder, Gavin gave me a gentle nudge forward, so that he could close the door behind us. 'Say nothing,' he breathed in my ear.

Maman had been given a bouquet, one of those bagged arrangements with white roses, carnations, sprays of babies' tears, and curled ferns, which she'd put on the sea-chest in the hall. Now one of the roses in the centre of the arrangement was splashed with crimson, like spots of blood.

ᚻ

Petals o' velvet,
Da colour o' blud,
Proctectd bi' thorns,
The symbol o' love.

... **a rose**

222

Saturday, 28th March (continued)

Tide Times at Mid Yell, UT
Low Water   23.49, 1.3m

Sunset   18.33
Moonset   03.04

Waxing quarter moon

Nae teeth to bite, yet I'll gnaw tae da bane,
Me face ever wi' dee, when du's aa alane,
Plump du up dy pillow, I'll gee dee no rest,
If eence du lats me tak a hold i dy breast.

Chapter Seventeen

Gavin was the first to move. He drew the rose out of the arrangement, and looked at it, sniffed. 'Food colouring, at a guess, and still wet.'

'I saw some in the kitchen, among the assorted stuff other people had obviously left behind.' It had to be Adrien, the only one who'd left the table. 'But why?'

Gavin opened the kitchen door for me. 'Annoyance at being questioned about the changed rose? To get back at your mother? Or simply to cause trouble.' He broke the rose in two and dropped it in the bin. 'Good thing we saw it first.' He lifted the tub of Craafit ice cream, which I'd left softening on the table, and gave me a rueful look. 'Lent.'

'Me too. Shall we just serve it up, and leave them to eat while we make coffee?'

'See how many want it.' He went back to ask, and came back, shaking his head. 'Only three: your father; Per; and Charles.'

'A waste of good ice cream,' I mourned. 'Tomorrow ... can we get to evening Mass?'

He nodded. 'When is it?'

'Six o'clock. We can wave them all onto the ferry, then race for the church.'

'Of course. Then race for the Yell ferry afterwards?

You'll want to come home.'

I hadn't thought as far as *afterwards*. Home to *Khalida* ... with Gavin? The thought made my throat go dry in panic, and I could tell he sensed it, for he didn't press the point, but focused on getting out plates, and helping me hack the ice cream onto them.

After we'd filled the dishwasher, we went together to make up the bed in the pavilion, with Cat trotting beside us. From here, in this dark, Belmont was a magical house, the four tall windows and central arched one lit soft gold from inside: a giant dolls' house, with a family of dolls in eighteenth-century dress, coats with flared skirts and a sword at the hip, high powdered wigs and ribboned stomachers, moving and loving and hating, who would revert to wax and sawdust when the front was opened ... I shook the fantasy away, tightened my arms around my bundle of bedding, and followed Gavin upstairs.

It was like preparing our marriage bed. The pale, new wood was burnished amber by a little corner lamp; the moon winked in the skylight as the clouds scudded across it, and the slates rattled with each gust. We flattened the mattress out on the red and blue patterned rug and contemplated it, too shy to look at one another. Cat put one paw on it, decided it was unstable and went off to sniff round the skirting board.

'Under the skylight, or in a corner?' Gavin asked, his voice determinedly matter-of-fact.

I considered the coombed ceiling. 'In the middle? Otherwise we'll hit our heads when we get up.'

Gavin nodded, and set the foot-pump up. He inflated the mattress, while I coaxed the downie into its cover, then we spread the underblanket, sheet and downie together, and placed the pillows. There was an awkward silence as we looked at it together, the white cover smooth

226

as snow. Gavin's arm came up around me. 'We should be strewing it with lilies, or carnations, or ladies' bedstraw, or whatever else was used in medieval times.'

I smiled at that, and felt less nervous. 'I think I saw a celandine or two in the maze garden.'

'Not quite as romantic.'

I would need to say it. I looked away from him, and felt my cheeks burning hot. 'I'm not on the pill.'

His arm tightened around me. His voice was awkward. 'I didn't think you would be. I bought some condoms on the way up.'

We both gave a huge breath of relief and giggled like teenagers.

'It's going to be cold,' I said.

He smiled. 'You have no idea how icy my room can be in the minus-twenties of a Highland winter.'

I leaned into his warm chest. 'Then we'll thole it together.' All the same, I resolved, I'd go right now, get my hot water bottle back from Bryony's bed, and put it in, to soften the initial shock of getting between ice-cold sheets. I reached into my rucksack, and fished out the bottle of champagne. 'I brought your bubbly too.'

'Then we're sorted.'

We walked back from the pavilion hand in hand. Cat bounded ahead, obviously preferring the warm house; maybe I could leave him in the drawing room overnight, except that he might need out, and I hadn't brought his litter tray. Was it *done* to take a cat on your first night together? Someone was watching us from the drawing-room window, one of the men, silhouetted. I took one last look at the house, then headed for the kitchen to put the kettle on. Somewhere I'd seen a mention of picnic stuff. I searched, found it, and set two Thermos flasks ready to fill. With this wind, the power could go at any minute. I just hoped *Khalida* was okay.

We gathered in the drawing room for the rest of the evening. The wind roared round the house, making the lights flicker, and the power surge and fall, so that Dad swore, put his laptop away in disgust and came to join us. Cat was chasing his marble round the sofa, losing it underneath every so often. I'd found a Scrabble board, so Gavin and I were playing; Charles was reading one of the BDs Sergeant Peterson had disapproved of, and Maman had got out her circular tambour frame, and was adding tiny stitches to a flower design. Fournier was in the armchair, lost in what looked like company accounts. Adrien hadn't reappeared, and Per and Bryony too had gone to ground.

Dad plumped himself down beside me and eyed up my tiles, then the board. 'You've got a good one for a double word score there, so you have.'

I glared at him, and reverted to a teenager. '*Dad.* I was working towards it so neatly, and now I won't be able to use it. Gavin'll think I cheated.'

'I'll take your word that you thought of it first,' Gavin said peaceably. He was twenty-three points ahead, so could afford to be complaisant. I noted Gavin's score, then put my '*l kewise*' around the useful 'i' that I'd created last shot. 'Do you double the bonus too?'

'No,' Dad said, before Gavin could give his version of the rules. 'It's a bonus, not part of the score.'

I rolled my eyes.

'Nice,' Gavin approved, and began to inspect triple-word score opportunities.

One thing I'd loved about Gavin's house, at Christmas, was that both he and his brother, Kenny, were able to amuse themselves. It was something Dad had never learned. He leaned over to inspect Maman's embroidery, got up to pace around the room, rolled Cat's marble a couple of times, and came back to Maman. 'Why don't you come and sing, now, Eugénie. Some of the old songs that you used to sing as a treat for me.'

Instead of braining him, Maman laughed, and put her frame away. 'You mean the Irish songs your grandmother sang to you in your cradle. *Charles, je peux me servir de ton clavier?*'

Charles gave a go-ahead wave of his hand without taking his eyes from his book. I supposed he was used to artistes slumming it with ballads. 'I cannot even remember the words,' Maman protested. She gave a ripple of notes up and down the keyboard, and began picking out 'Danny Boy', then changed to one that I didn't consciously know, although the tune was hauntingly familiar, lifted her head, and sang.

'The water's wide, I can't get o'er, nor have I got
    the wings to fly,
Give me a boat, that will carry two, and we will
    sail, my love and I.'

Gavin stopped sorting his tiles to listen, then raised his head and smiled at me before putting down '*detoxed*' on a space that ended in a triple-word score.

'Neat,' I agreed.

The lights flickered again, the keyboard faltered. Fournier rose from his armchair. 'I know the lease says that there are to be no candles, but it looks like the lights will go out any minute. Sing while you can, Eugénie.' He took the glass candle-jars from the fireplace, and set them on the table beside our board, laid his lighter beside them. 'You see, I haven't forgotten my Shetland.'

I heard the door across the way open. Bryony and Per

came in, as if drawn by the singing. Per sat down in Maman's seat and began scrutinising my Scrabble rack. I remembered I was on my best behaviour, and resisted the natural impulse to hunch my shoulder and turn the rack away from him. Bryony went over to the keyboard. Maman smiled at her.

'Dermot is persuading me to sing his Irish ballads, Bryony, do you know any?'

Bryony shook her head. 'Not the words. I know a few English ones. Do you know "The Ash Grove"?'

'Sing it,' Maman said, and gestured her to the piano. They followed it with the kind of show songs I'd have expected Maman to consider unspeakably vulgar, but I soon realised that she was just encouraging Bryony, because after they'd sung 'Somewhere over the Rainbow', she stepped back to let Bryony take over with bits from *Phantom of the Opera* and *Miss Saigon*.

There was no sign of Adrien. I checked my watch: ten to ten. I was just wondering if I should suggest that Per went up to see how he was when an extra-strong gust shook the house, the power went out, and we were plunged into darkness. For a moment it was intensely black, shocking you into stillness. Bryony gave a wailing gasp, and Maman's voice came, steady and reassuring. 'This happens often in Shetland.' Five seconds more, and the moon's light through the clouds flowed into the room. Now I could see shapes: Maman and Bryony, very still together against the window, Dad leaning by the other one, Fournier's head opposite me.

'I thought so,' Fournier said. There was a snick, and the tiny flame of his lighter broke the darkness. He took out one of the chunky candles from the glass holders, and used it to light the others. The flames winked off the holders and doubled themselves in the windows and the

230

paintings. Now the whole room glowed gold with a dazzle of tiny lights. I saw myself reflected in the window, small and dark against the blue couch, and rose.

'I filled a Thermos earlier. Shall I bring us up a cup of tea?'

'Oh, Cassandre, you are a jewel,' Maman said. 'Yes, if you please.'

'Will the power stay off for long?' Bryony asked.

'Until they get it fixed,' Dad said. Bryony made an alarmed face. 'I'd be surprised if it's back before morning, in this wind. Maybe you should save your hot water for morning tea, Cassie.'

'I filled a Thermos for that too. I'm a native, remember.' I smiled at Bryony. 'And there are candles in hurricane glasses like these in every room. Think how romantic, to go to bed by candlelight.'

She brightened slightly at that, and smiled across at Per, as if she didn't expect to go to bed alone.

'In that case,' Maman said, 'a tisane all around, and an early night for all.'

Gavin came with me downstairs. 'I'm not leaving you to do the classic girl goes for walk in lonely house in the dark with a murderer loose,' he murmured in my ear as we came down the stairs together, cautiously, although the treads were clear enough in the silvery brightness of the halfway window. He lit a candle in the kitchen, and began setting mugs out while I sorted teapot and bags.

We trudged back upwards. As we reached the landing we heard a door slam, and footsteps, then Adrien appeared, flushed still, his movements slow, as if he'd been sleeping. He followed us into the drawing room.

I set the tray on the table, and we all squeezed onto the couches. Gavin's thigh was warm against mine. I thought of the bed waiting in the pavilion and shivered, partly

231

with nerves, partly with anticipation, and his hand came to curl around mine. Adrien leaned forward to look at the Scrabble board. 'Who was winning?'

'Even-steven,' Gavin said. 'All to play for.'

'Someone had a good word here,' Adrien said. His long finger stabbed the board; the dark ring glinted. '*Twist*, in this space.'

Gavin's hand quivered in mine, and I tightened my fingers in agreement. Given that my last score had been sixty-six, and Gavin's had been forty-five, we weren't going to waste letters on a mere eight-pointer, unless nothing better could be devised.

I poured the tea and passed out the mugs. 'Adrien, would you like one?'

He waved it away. 'No, no, I never drink tea at night.' His voice was slowed too, his face smoothed of emotion. I wondered if he'd taken something, a tranquiliser, or maybe smoked a joint, although there was no smell of smoke on him, and surely Sergeant Peterson would have confiscated anything like that.

We drank in silence. Around us, the flames stretched and shrunk, the glow and movement mirrored in their reflections, reflections of reflections from the windows facing each other, a string of flickering lights on the black glass. The wind wailed outside. Charles set his mug down, then rose to unplug his keyboard and put it away, the leads glistening like snakes in his hands. Bryony leaned back against Per with a sigh, cradling the mug in her hands. Maman turned her head to smile at Dad. Only Adrien was restless, moving the tiles on the board to form new words: *sing, drive.* My *likewise* became *skewer*, and Gavin's *detoxed* turned to *toxic*. The silver band around the dark stone glinted as his fingers moved. *House, brother* – then, tiring of it, he swept the tiles together and tipped them back into the bag.

'Bedtime, I think.' Maman folded a white cloth back around her tambour frame, and slid it into the paisley-pattern bag that had belonged to her mother. 'Are you sure, Cass, that you and Gavin will not be too cold?'

'You won't have any heating now either,' I pointed out. She made a face at that, being a child of the sun, and rose.

'In that case, goodnight.' Her dark gaze swept around Adrien, Per and Bryony, Charles. 'Be careful with the candles, please. It said most strictly in the lease that we were not to light any.'

'I think a power cut counts as an exception to the rule,' Dad said.

Bryony reached forward to put the mugs back on the tray. 'I'll take these downstairs and put them in the sink, for tomorrow.' Her face brightened. 'There'll still be hot water. I could have a bath by candlelight.'

I wasn't sure what Gavin would want to do, whether he'd feel we needed to see the others bunkered down before we went to bed, or whether we could just go. I looked at him uncertainly, and he rose. 'Shall we brave the ice-house?'

I stroked Cat. 'Come on, boy. You've got a good coat.' I rose, and he oozed onto the warm space of couch, but when we moved to the door and I called him again, he stretched, jumped down and followed. In the hall, I gestured at the bathroom. 'Must just brush my teeth.'

Gavin was still in the hall when I came out again, two wine glasses in his hand. 'Your escort, mam'selle.'

'Maybe we ought to have slept in the house,' I said, as we came out into the howling night and battled, arms linked, to the pavilion. 'Suppose something happens?'

'If someone was being nefarious, they'd be quiet

enough not to wake us anyway, if we were behind a shut door. We're only a shout away.' He opened the door for me, set the glasses on the table. 'My teeth now. I'll be back in a minute.'

The moonlight glinted into the little room. I'd found my clean clothes for tomorrow by touch, and was just about to go upstairs when I heard footsteps outside; not from the gravel in front of the house, but from behind the curved wall that ran between the house and the pavilion. There was no reason why Gavin should have come that way, and my feet were moving to the door even while my brain was still registering how implausibly quick he'd been. It wasn't his footstep on the briggistane. This was a heavier tread, trying to be silent; there was just one step on the gravel, then nothing, as if he'd moved onto the grass. I waited in the darkness, calculating, heart pounding. If I was quick, I might be able to run to the safety of the house before this person reached the door. I put my hand on the handle, then froze as a dark shadow passed the window: a man, tall, bulky. There was only one place I could hide. I dived for the cupboard under the stairs, praying the snap ball wouldn't click as I opened it, and slid inside. There was no handle on the other side; I pulled it to behind me. Outside, there was a scrape of feet on the low wall that ran from the pavilion to the iron gates, a thud as someone jumped down. Now he was two metres from the door. *Gavin, come soon ...*

The cupboard door opened into a space big enough to house mops, brooms, pails, all the tools the maid who'd once lived here would have needed. Now it was empty, with only the electricity metre on one wall, and a couple of cardboard boxes on the floor. Behind them was the space I'd noticed earlier, running forward under the stair. I swung into it, feet first, curled my legs into the space under the bottom step, and squeezed my body after it. There was dust in my nostrils, and the resin smell of pine. I heard the hand on the door just as I drew the nearest box in behind me. A serious search wouldn't miss me, but I hoped he'd have no time for that, and I knew from Peerie Charlie how hard it could be to drag a reluctant person from a small space. If he found me, I'd hold him off till help came.

The door whispered open. His breathing was only a metre above my head. He stepped in, his shadow falling on the door-crack in the moony dusk of the room, and waited there for what felt like a minute, breath held. I held mine too. My left foot was protesting at the cramped angle it was held in. I flexed my toes in my shoes, and hoped fervently it wouldn't turn to a spasm of cramp. Then, at last, he moved. I felt the floor vibrate as he turned, the pressure of his foot on my knee as he placed it on the first step, silent as a feather falling on water. The second stair creaked, and he took the rest in a rush, thumping past my body, my chest, my head. I heard his feet skid to a halt as he took in the smooth bed, the empty room. Claws scrabbled on the wood as Cat leapt away.

Now was my chance to escape, except that he'd hear every move I made. The hairs were prickling on the back of my neck. I didn't want to wait here to be caught like a lobster in a trap, but if I followed the impulse to come out, I'd be caught even more surely. He'd hear me moving under the wooden stairs and be waiting at the door once I'd uncurled myself. No, I had to sit it out, and prepare to split the night with screams if he found me.

Then, oh praise be, I heard the clunk of the house door shutting, and the click of Gavin's shoes on the stone flags. The man above heard it too. I heard his foot scrape on the floor as he turned, then he thundered down the wooden steps, wrenched the door open and ran into the night. Pulling myself out, I heard the thud as he vaulted over the low wall, the scumble of feet on grass, then the rattle of gravel. I shoved my concealing box aside, hauled myself out from under the stairs and leapt for the door.

Gavin had seen him. Now there were two sets of running feet, one on grass, one retreating on gravel. Gavin was running straight for the pavilion. I waved to show I was fine, and immediately he swerved to give chase. We swung over the low wall together and charged around the house, Gavin overtaking me within a few steps. He was around the corner of the house before I was, but when I arrived at the porch door he was standing and shaking his head. 'Lost him. He probably went into the house.' He looked towards the drive, curving away into the long shadow of the wall, and Peter's yellow house behind it, then up at the farm. 'No sign, but then he'd just have to stand still to be invisible.' He put out one hand to me. 'Are you okay?'

'Fine. I heard him coming and hid under the stairs, preparing to scream like blazes if you didn't get back in time.'

'Did you see who it was?'

I shook my head. 'Tall, bulky. It could have been any of the three of them.'

'Four.' Gavin took a last, long, breath, straightened up, and began to lead the way to the pavilion.

I stared at him. 'You're not thinking Dad had anything to do with this!'

His arm came around me, warm in the cold wind. 'Don't be daft. You're forgetting Caleb. He may have gone to the mainland, but there's nothing preventing him from having come back before the ferries stopped, is there?'

I hadn't thought of Caleb. 'I didn't hear a car, though the wind would have masked the noise of it, or it could be parked at the road end of the drive, behind the modern houses.'

'There's no point in going into the house now. Our perp will be just coming out of one of the bathrooms, meek as a mouse. When you said three ...?'

'Adrien, Per, Fournier. They're all tall, and both Adrien and Fournier are broad-shouldered. Per could look bulky in a jacket blown out by the wind.'

'Worry about it in the morning.' Gavin opened the door for me. 'Our ice-house, Ms Lynch. Shall we see if the champagne helps?'

'I think we should,' I agreed, and turned to kiss him.

Chapter Eighteen

I was woken by my phone ringing. For a moment I didn't know where I was, with the floor firm below me, and no sound of water rippling at my ear, and the warmth of another body against mine. Gavin moved, sleepily reaching out across me, and I recognised him; then I remembered coming to bed together, and smiled. He realised where he was too, and changed the arm movement into a hug. 'It'll be for you,' he murmured.

I reached for the phone and fumbled it silent. 'Hello?'

'Lass, it's Keith Sandison here. The folk wi' the pig-snout masks are come back, to the site by Lund House this time. I'll go and keep an eye on what they're up to, but I thought Gavin might want to call the other police officers, the ones that are biding up at Baltasound.'

'I'll put you onto him.' I passed the phone over, realising as I did so that soon the whole of Unst, and by evening the whole of Shetland, would know that Gavin and I were now sharing a bed. *Damn.* It would be nice to keep some things private. I stretched and curled against his warm back, listening.

'Yes, I'll let her know ... yes ... we'll be with you as quickly as possible.' He switched the phone off, turned over to return it and hug me, then sat up. 'Trouble at t'mill.' His Yorkshire accent was awful. He stretched out a hand for his own phone while I felt for my watch and pressed the button to make the face luminous. Ten to midnight. No wonder I felt as if I'd only just fallen asleep. The wind was still rattling the slates above our head, prising at the skylight. The moon had moved to slant on the wall above our heads, making the room just light enough to see Gavin's outline beside me, the white blur of my T-shirt on the floor. Cat was a warm heavy weight on my feet.

Gavin was explaining the situation to Sergeant Peterson. I didn't move a muscle. She was top of the list of people who didn't need to know about my private life. Then I realised that if I tagged along – which I had every intention of doing – it would be obvious anyway. Tough.

'Ten minutes,' Gavin finished. 'I'll meet you at the main road.' He put the phone down, sighed and began to get up, fumbling for his clothes. I rolled over and slid off the mattress. The floor was freezing, even colder than my *Khalida*'s cabin sole, and naturally my clothes were at the same temperature. I hauled them on as quickly as possible.

'I would say you can't come,' Gavin said, 'except that I don't want to leave you here alone, after last night. I may need to leave you in the car.'

Naturally he knew as well as I did that if anything exciting was going on, the only way he'd keep me in the car was with handcuffs. 'I'll be good,' I promised.

The garden was sinister in the moonlight, the wooden fences of the maze garden casting shadows like prison bars, with the roof of the gazebo as a hump-backed gaol. The wind twisted the shadows of the bushes, and rattled the branches against the wood. We clambered over the wall and crept out through the further garden, then marched briskly along the drive. There was a flash of headlights in the distance, which disappeared behind the shoulder of the hill and reappeared, two yellow stars swooping down the road towards us. The police car stopped, and we clambered in. Sergeant Peterson was driving. 'If they're actually on scheduled land,' she said, 'we can confiscate their equipment. I thought we could suggest they leave Shetland as well. We'll deliver their stuff to the boat when they're on it.' Her voice suggested she knew she was exceeding police authority, and didn't care.

She stopped the car and switched the lights off, waited for a minute, then began driving again, crawling cautiously along. The car turned onto the single-track road leading to Underhoull and Lund. Below us was a landscape drenched in moonlight: the sea glittering silver; the land dark where it touched the sea; headlands outlined sharply, then gradually becoming lighter away from the water dazzle. 'They won't hear our engine in this wind, but they'd see our lights from miles away.'

'They parked their car in the middle of the road last time,' I said, 'ready for a getaway.'

'We can park there too,' Sergeant Peterson said. It was interesting to see her brisk confidence in bending the rules now that she was in charge, with Gavin allowed along only by courtesy. We rolled cautiously down the hill towards Lund, past the silver-bleached bulk of the Bordastubble Stone, and came through the first gate, which had been left open. I slid out to ease it shut; sheep grazing three hills away were liable to be drawn irresistibly to an open gate within seconds of it being left. We rolled gently to a halt ten metres short of Lund House, where the devil had set his footprint on the briggistane.

'Be careful with the doors, in this wind,' Sergeant Peterson warned Constable Buchanan. 'They'll hear a slam.'

We eased ourselves out and began walking down the road. The walls of Lund House towered over us like a fortress, with the moon casting odd shadows through the windows. From this side, in this light, you could almost believe it was still habitable, for the wall seemed smooth and unbroken, and the high gables still held their chimneys up to the sky. Then the front came in sight, a ruin, with the moon shining on a great gap in the wall where an upper window had fallen in. For a moment I thought I saw a head moving in one of the remaining windows, but that was ridiculous, because the walls were an empty shell, with no upper floor. The square porch had a window on each side, and the door to the front was bisected by a 'Do Not Enter' notice that danced and thrummed in the wind. I wouldn't have entered if you paid me. The place had a feel that sent shudders up my spine.

Sergeant Peterson had no such qualms. She slid sideways into the dark shadow in the far angle in the porch, immediately below the window where that shadow head had moved, and beckoned us to follow. I was glad of Gavin's shoulder against mine. From that darkness, we looked out.

The park with the three unexcavated longhouses was just below us, and to the left. There were three men again, walking in line as they'd done before, working towards us. I couldn't hear any sound, but the lights of the metal detectors winked in the darkness. The dark bulk of their car was immediately above the park, and the gate between us had been left open.

The wind still howled around us, but here in the angle of porch and wall it was calm. Sergeant Peterson leaned towards us and breathed her instructions. 'Bob, to the car. Get your card ready to flash at him. The rest of us, spread out around the other three.'

We nodded and followed her out, back to the black shadow of the gable on the moonlit road, sliding across as quickly as possible, and down towards the field. She bent low behind the dyke and we copied her, freezing when she stopped, moving on again. The men were only a hundred metres from us now – fifty. Sergeant Peterson's hand moved to her pocket, then she split the night with a powerful flashlight that slid across the bleached grass to the dark clothes, the pig-snout goggles, frozen by the light. A heartbeat, then her voice roared out. 'Police! Stand still! Police!'

Up on the road, there was an answering shout. The car lights blazed; the engine coughed into life, and revved up. Constable Buchanan yelled a warning. In the field, the men began running towards us, and we fanned out to meet them. Sergeant Peterson shone her torch straight in the eyes of the one heading for her, and he ducked his head away from it, stumbled and fell. One down. Gavin had gone for a rugby tackle. Two. The third one paused, as if trying to assess his opponents, then came straight for me, increasing his speed as he ran the last few yards. He cannoned into me with a thud that sent me sprawling, and ran on towards Lund House.

I picked myself up and ran after him. He didn't even hesitate at the 'Do Not Enter' sign, just ducked under it, as if he'd recce'd the ground beforehand, and knew there was a way straight through to the clear road beyond. On my right, the car was moving now, heading straight for me. I dived towards the dark doorway, and felt the wind of its passing. The brakes squealed as it came nose to nose with the police car. There were running feet behind it: Constable Buchanan. He could deal with the driver. I took a deep breath and stepped into the dark of Lund House.

Instantly the wind stopped. The brightness of the moon on the slanting gables and through the empty windows made the shadowed floor pitch-dark, but I knew what it would be like: a foot-twisting surface of fallen stones, enlivened with splintered wood and the occasional dead sheep. I stood in the doorway and waited. Just thirty seconds would restore my night sight. I heard a foot move ahead of me, confidently; the man I was chasing still had his goggles on. That meant that although I couldn't see him in the darkness, he could see me. There was no sound of anyone coming in after me, and this man was dangerous. Common sense said I should get back out. He couldn't go far without his transport.

I was just starting to slide one foot backwards when the night erupted in a high-pitched keening that echoed round the house, breathy and insistent, and set the hairs standing on the back of my neck, a banshee wail that started low and rose like an air-raid siren to a noise that made you want to duck away from it and cover your ears. I stumbled backwards out of the dark doorway.

Someone was standing on the headland where the Vikings were buried, a tall someone, made taller by the horned helmet that was outlined against the silver, shifting sea. I could see the mid-thigh tunic, the baggy breeches thonged with leather strips below the knee. One hand held his axe; the other was raised in the air, as if he was signalling to us. There was something familiar about the movement, but I couldn't think for the shrieking noise in my head. Then at last it stopped, leaving my ears ringing. He swung away from us in a swirl of cloak, headed down the far side of the hill, and was gone.

I spent the next two hours getting a close-up view of police work in action. The noise had startled the driver enough for Constable Buchanan to get handcuffs on him, and by the time the man I'd been following came out through the back door of Lund House, across the field and onto the road at last, Gavin and Sergeant Peterson were waiting for him. We put two in each car, ignoring the driver's protests that we weren't insured to drive theirs, and headed through the power-cut dark night for the police HQ at Baltasound.

Britain's Most Northerly Police Station turned out to look like a council house with a long extension ending in a blue-doored garage. It was on the road, facing what had once been the RAF houses, in the days when Unst had been an air base of strategic importance in the Cold War – distance to Russia: not far at all, over the top of the globe – Sergeant Peterson parked the police car with its nose to the garage, Constable Buchanan came in behind her, and we invited our captives to join us inside. There would, the Sergeant insisted, be just enough chairs for everyone.

She was wrong. The tiny office had a chair at the desk and two armchairs, and the kitchenette yielded only one more. Still, that gave the visitors one each, while we stood over them in approved jackboot-of-the-state fashion – though when I say *we,* I was banished to the kitchen, for reasons of Data Protection. Still, I heard most of it.

They gave their names and addresses, and proved them by producing drivers' licenses. They insisted they had the landlord's permission, we could phone him to check, and Sergeant Peterson, smiling sweetly, took them at their word. His comments on being woken at that hour for a pack of lies almost blew her across the room. After that they kept quiet when asked if they were looking for buried items, and what they intended to do with any they found. They refused to give their own account of why they were innocently walking the parks of Lund in a gale, at midnight, and they ended the silence by asking to contact their lawyer.

Best of all, the station had its own back-up generator, so I was able to boil kettles and make tea. I envisaged the Hydro men working away on swaying poles in this wind, and wished them luck. It wasn't likely Belmont would get its electricity back before morning.

While Sergeant Peterson was getting silences, Constable Buchanan was filling out forms, one for each item found. It involved finding serial numbers, and each form was seven pages long, so it looked set to take him a fair bit of the night. As well as the night-goggles and the impressively sophisticated metal detectors, there were several pocket items of black metal whose purpose I couldn't even guess. I took one of the night-goggles out into the garden, and was well impressed. Everything was in shades of grey, of course, but it was amazing the detail you could see.

Gavin came out behind me, and slipped his arm around my waist. 'No, I can't lose one pair en route.'

'Pity, they're really good. Have a look.'

Gavin tried them on, and took an experimental walk round the garden. 'Top of the range. A thousand pounds worth, at the least.' He returned them to the table, reluctantly. 'Anyway,I think we're almost finished here. We'll put them to their lodgings, then Freya'll run us back to Belmont.'

I looked at my watch. Nearly half past two. 'It'll be light over the sea in another couple of hours.'

'You can stay awake if you like.' Gavin yawned. 'I won't make any promises.'

The yawn was infectious. We ganted our way back into the station, into the car, and I dozed on his shoulder for the ten-minute run. Sergeant Peterson took us right to the house this time, and we slipped around the back, the way my intruder had come. Glancing up at the house, I stopped, and caught Gavin's arm.

'What?' he breathed, looking up.

I shook my head and began walking again. 'I'm seeing shadows everywhere. I thought I saw someone moving about on the stair, but it's the middle of the night, and there's not a light anywhere.'

'We'd better check,' Gavin said.

We crept into the house and listened. All was still: a house and its occupants sleeping. We slipped out again.

'I'd quite like to know,' Gavin said, as we negotiated round the maze garden, 'who the fellow on the headland was. And how he made that noise.'

'The Viking ghost. Was the noise him?' I opened the pavilion door cautiously, in case someone was waiting to jump out at us. 'I thought it was something horrible in Lund House – apart from the bloke, I mean.'

We clumped up the stairs together. The grey blur that was Cat stood up on the mattress to greet us. 'I'm pretty sure it was coming from the headland,' Gavin said. 'I was imagining something on a string – did you see the way he was moving one arm?'

Now he said it, I knew what the action had reminded me of: a cadet swinging the lead, the circular movement to get a bit of speed on the pendulum before throwing it. 'Of course. And I thought at the time that the noise wound up to full strength, like an air-raid siren, but then it was echoing all around me, and there was no chance to think about anything at all.' I scrambled out of my clothes and dived back into bed. There was a last residual warmth where Cat had been, curled neatly on the hot water bottle. I tucked my feet into it, and cuddled the rest of me into Gavin. 'I don't suppose,' he murmured into the darkness, one hand sliding down my back, 'that dozing in the car has woken you up again?'

4

The wind had subsided to a muffled roar. The sky was creamy-grey, with the first dazzle of light breaking through the clouds: 07.00. Gavin was still asleep, turned on his side away from me, his breathing soft and even. I curled into the curve of his back, one arm round his chest, and his hand came up to clasp mine. I'd forgotten how good this felt, to wake with the warmth of another person beside me. We'd been good together, too, once the first awkwardness was over ... now I felt properly his girlfriend. We could work this out.

I lay for a good half hour curled in his warmth and contemplated yesterday, getting *Khalida* safe from the storm. I must go over to Cullivoe today and check that she was okay. We could maybe have a quick look on our way to Lerwick. Gavin's hired car was at Toft, of course, on the mainland, but if we got a lift with Dad and Maman, they'd maybe do a detour. We'd see them onto the ferry. After that, well, they would still be roughly within Gavin's orbit until the tour ended, which would give time for the results on Kamilla's death to come through. It could still be that her allergy had killed her ... which brought me back to puzzling about Bryony. That aggrieved note in her voice as she'd said, *I didn't know she had an allergy* bothered me. I frowned, snuggled closer to Gavin, and set myself to think it through. Suppose she hadn't known. Suppose she'd set up the seafood and dosed everyone with senna for another purpose altogether … but what? How could putting the company out of action possibly benefit her?

Then it came to me with such dazzling brilliance that I gave a jerk that woke Gavin. He made a sleepy protest. 'Sorry,' I said. 'It's just that I had an idea.' I waited to see if he was an instantly awake person, like me, or one who a needed a cup of tea to function.

He rolled over to face me, grey eyes alert. 'Go on.'

'Bryony,' I said. 'It's Magnie's Agatha Christie idea. Poison everyone mildly, and give one person an extra dose. It's like she said: Kamilla was no better than her, just blonde and luckier.'

'But you said she couldn't sing Kamilla's part.'

'She couldn't. *But*, if she'd practised it, she could sing Maman's.' I left a moment's silence for him to consider this. 'And she did practise it too. I heard her, when I arrived. She was singing Aricia's aria; I heard it through the window. That's what's been vaguely bothering me. Maman and Dad slept at the front. I thought it didn't sound like Maman because of the window muffling it, but it was because it was Bryony. If I hadn't been here, who'd be the obvious fellow-woman to take Maman cups of tea in bed as she was recovering from the effects of the senna pods, which everyone took for the effects of the seafood?' My voice was growing sharp with anger. I wanted to wake Bryony up, and shake her till her teeth rattled. 'These things are uncertain, so nobody would be surprised if Maman took longer to recover. And since Bryony's an item with Per, maybe she counted on persuading him to let her stand in for Maman. The performance at Mareel would have been a try-out for her, and then on Monday she'd have sung Aricia in Edinburgh, in front of all the critics. The bit-parter steps forward as a star.'

Gavin considered this, nodding. 'Except that your mother would have gone on whatever.'

'Not if she'd have sung badly.' I was certain about that. 'Singers aren't like actors, who go on whatever. She'd never have risked her reputation in front of critics. No wonder Bryony didn't want to say anything in front of me! Can Sergeant Peterson give her a very uncomfortable hour of grilling?'

Gavin was following his own line of thought. 'So,' he said, 'with that cleared away, we're left with two possibilities: one, that Kamilla's death really was just due to her allergy, or two, that somebody who knew about her allergy overheard Bryony ordering seafood, and decided to use that as cover for her death.' He frowned. 'Someone who didn't know that any sudden death sparks off a medical investigation for the cause of it.'

'Oh, any opera singer for that one,' I said. 'They live in their own world –you have no idea. I wouldn't bet Maman could tell you who the First Minister was.'

'Your mother knew about it, because Kamilla told her. Adrien did, as her ex-lover. Per did, as leader of the company. I can't see why she should have told Caleb. It might have come up in casual conversation.'

'I thought he was avoiding her, didn't you?'

'I got that impression, but didn't Bryony suggest that was cover, because of Adrien?'

'I'm not taking Bryony's word for anything,' I said waspishly. 'Fournier … I don't suppose it was possible there was something between them? If he knew Adrien, he could have met Kamilla through him.'

'I've got someone investigating that already. Charles?'

'If Maman knew her, so might he, but …' I visualised

quiet, balding Charles at his keyboard in the corner. 'Do you think she'd ever have noticed him?'

'Oh, not as a lover, but she might have confided in him.'

I was just about to reply to that when there was a series of piercing screams from the house. We both leapt up. I grabbed my jeans and a jumper, Gavin swung his kilt around him and buckled it in one smooth movement, and we ran across the cold grass and in through the front door.

ᚴ

Nae teeth to bite, yet I'll gnaw tae da bane,
Me face ever wi' dee, when du's aa alane,
Plump du up dy pillow, I'll gee dee no rest,
If eence du lats me tak a hold i dy breast.

...**envy.**

Sunday, 29th March – Palm Sunday

Tide Times at Mid Yell, BST and at Lerwick

High Water	06.59, 1.8m;	07.20, 1.6m
Low Water	13.31, 1.0m;	14.06, 0.8m
High Water	19.55, 1.7m;	20.18, 1.6m
Low Water	02.00, 1.2m;	02.23, 0.9m

Sunrise	06.41
Moonrise	12.05
Sunset	19.36
Moonset	03.36

Waxing quarter moon

I'm neider maet nor drink
for fantin' man
I'm neider frock nor hat
for bonny lady;
yet yowsed wi' care
I can be aa these things,
an' foolish man and his vain wife
seek me abune aa idder.

Chapter Nineteen

The screams had become choking sobs. We took the steps two at a time, past the upstairs landing, where Dad was coming out of the front bedroom, in trousers and shirt, with Maman in her lace negligée behind him, dark hair loose round her shoulders, and on up to the top floor.

It was Bryony who was sobbing. She was dressed only in a towel, wrapped around her. Her face was hidden in Per's shoulder, but he was staring beyond her into the room he'd shared with Adrien, face stern, brows drawn together. Gavin put out a hand to stop me following, and went forwards to look. His face stilled. He looked round at Per. Suddenly he was inches taller, in spite of the bare chest and feet – DI Macrae of Police Scotland – and he spoke with authority. 'You only found him just now?'

Bryony's dark head nodded.

Per was silent for a moment, considering him, then explained. 'She came up to the lavatory, and then I heard her scream.'

'I'll phone the station,' Gavin said. 'Nobody must go into the room.' He looked around, then lifted the floor-length mirror and stood it in front of the door, a metre forward. 'Don't touch anything. Please go downstairs now. Tell the company not to come up here.'

Per nodded, one man in charge to another, and led Bryony past me, still sobbing.

Gavin turned to Charles, hovering in his doorway up the four steps. He was wearing a surprisingly rakish red silk dressing gown with blue cuffs. 'It probably makes no difference, but I'd be grateful if you, sir, could please cross the landing only once. Pack up and bring your luggage down, and don't go up again.'

'Hang on,' I said, and translated. Charles nodded, and retreated into his room.

'My phone's in the pavilion. Can you stay on guard, make sure nobody comes up?'

I nodded, and he whisked past me. I took a cautious step forward.

The door had been propped open. It was a strange, non-authentic feature of the house that each heavy door swung closed if you didn't hold it open – something to do with fire regulations, no doubt, and a real nuisance when you were carrying dishes between dining room and kitchen – hence the wooden wedge in every room. It seemed odd to me that someone would want to sleep in a house of unknown people with an open door, especially in a room whose door was sandwiched between the two most convenient toilets, but no doubt fingerprints would tell us who'd touched the handle last.

I couldn't see inside the room from where I was, and I didn't want to. I'd seen enough bodies to last me a lifetime. I turned my back on the landing and sat down on the top step. Below, Maman had taken charge of Bryony and was leading her back into her bedroom.

'He was dead!' she wailed. 'His skin was all white and … and still, like a waxwork, and his mouth was open at this horrible angle.'

Maman soothed, and the door shut behind them, cutting the sound off. Dad came up the stairs and stopped halfway. 'He's dead, Cassie?'

'Gavin said not to let anyone go up,' I said.

Dad's eyes went to the open door. 'How?'

I shook my head. 'Don't know. I'm just guarding the stairs.'

'Well ...' – Dad said, as if at a loss, and sat down on the stair beside me.

Gavin was away less than five minutes. He came back dressed and shod, with his notebook at the ready, and sent Dad downstairs, and me back to the pavilion to dress. Five minutes later, as I was rubbing some feeling into my cold feet, I heard a car pulling up, then another. Sergeant Peterson, I surmised, and probably the local doctor. They were going to have fun getting everyone they needed up to Unst, especially if the ferries were still off. I wondered if the police had powers to charter a helicopter.

I put on my shoes and headed downstairs to the window that faced the sea, to check out the ferry situation. The first dazzle of light breaking through the clouds turned the water from the purple-grey of Welsh slate to scoured pewter. Dark cat's-paws still swept across the sound, turning mud brown at the water's edge, where the peaty burns ran. The sea around the ferry pier was smooth, but beyond it was still white with spray; furthermore, there was no sign of the blue and white boat sitting at her pier, although perhaps the 06.30 one only ran on a Sunday if it was pre-booked. I craned my neck around, and spotted the white superstructure over at Gutcher. Half past seven; there should be a ferry. Then I remembered that it was now half past eight; the clocks had changed in the night. An hour less sleep, on top of charging around the hills at midnight, and, well, other activity – I suppressed a smile. No wonder I felt washed out.

The question was, of course, what the policeman's

girlfriend did now. Tea seemed likely, except – I snicked the light switch experimentally. Yes, the power was still out. Good thing I'd prepared that Thermos. I called Cat and headed over to the house. It was only once I got there, and passed the closed door of the little downstairs sitting room, that I realised there had been one person missing this morning. Per and Bryony, Dad and Maman, Charles ... how come Fournier hadn't come out to see what was happening?

The kitchen was deserted. Someone must have thought of tea – Maman, perhaps, for Bryony, for my Thermos was empty. I fed Cat, and was just about to head for Peter's when the porch door opened, there was the shaking noise of someone taking a waterproof off, and the lady in the pink nylon pinnie came in. She had an old-fashioned wicker basket in one hand, loaded down with three Thermos flasks, and a biscuit tin in the other. 'I thought you might be glad of water for tea,' she said, 'and I made a few more bannocks.'

'You're a star,' I said. I ate one bannock while the tea was steeping, buttered another two and headed up to the top landing. Constable Buchanan was on duty; I handed the tray to him. On the way down again I knocked at Maman and Dad's door, but there was no answer. There were still muffled sobs from Bryony's room, so I knocked there, and eased the door open. 'I'm making tea. Will I bring a pot of chamomile up?'

Maman's face lit with hope. 'Is the power back on?'

I shook my head. 'The caretaker wife.'

'Yes, please.' Maman came out into the hall, and closed the door softly behind her. 'The poor child has had a shock. I will stay with her for a little longer, then once she is calmer I'll dress.' She hesitated. 'You did not see what happened?'

I shook my head.

'It seems, from what Bryony says, that he may have committed suicide. Or perhaps she's making that up, or wanting it to be true.' Her hands swirled in the air, pushing it all away from her.

'The police will find out.' I looked around. 'Where's Dad?'

'Oh, he, Per and Vincent are talking ways of salvaging the tour.' The creamy colour was gone from her cheeks, and her mouth was drawn down in a weary line. 'I think it is jinxed. Oh, we have Gabriella to replace Kamilla, and for the performance today we can get John Cormack – do you remember him? Dermot said you were talking to him after the performance on Friday. He was my singing teacher here. It was he who got me interested in early music, because that had been what he specialised in. He still takes pupils, and sings in the Choral Society, so he is well in practice, and he has sung Hippolyte so often he could perform in his sleep. Well, no, the full role would be too much to ask, but this is extracts, and singing with me, as he used to. He could do it. After that, we could get someone for Edinburgh, and the rest of the tour, but, oh, Cassandre, I am too old for this.'

I put my arm round her, alarmed. If my indomitable Maman was losing her nerve, nothing was safe. 'Why don't you go and have a nice, hot shower, if the system will let you? I think it's supplied from the hot tank. I'll make tea for Bryony and take it up, and sit with her till you're ready to face the world again.'

'Cassandre, you are an angel. Thank you.' She kissed me and disappeared into the bedroom.

I made a pot of chamomile tea, and headed up to Bryony. There was a lot I'd have liked to say to her, but I had no proof she'd intended to make Maman keep being

257

ill, and her shock at Kamilla's death had, I presumed, made her abandon the idea. She'd play the bit-parts in Edinburgh, and I hoped a frog sat in her throat throughout.

I felt a bit more sympathetic once I actually saw her. Maman had helped her into her onesie, and she'd put a jumper on top of it, but she was still shivering. She clutched the cup of tea to her. 'It was ghastly. I glanced in, and saw him lying there, with his mouth wide open, as if he was snoring, but there wasn't a sound, and his face was all lit up green from the computer, you know, one of those flickering swirl screensavers. And his eyes were just staring, with the light glinting on them, and the pupils not moving at all.'

It sounded as if she'd gone right into the room. She wouldn't have been able to see his eyes from the doorway.

'Then I saw the bottle. It was lying on the floor, you know, one of those plastic water bottles, with the cap off and a little water still in it. And his hand was hanging down just above it.'

'You went right into the room then?'

She jerked away from me. 'No, I ... why should I do that?'

'You couldn't have seen a bottle on the floor from the door,' I pointed out. 'The bed would have hidden it.'

'No, on this side of his bed.'

'The nearer bed would still have hidden it.' I wasn't certain, but it was worth risking the bluff. 'And you'd never have seen his eyes from the door.'

She changed tack as if the wind had shifted forty degrees. 'I thought at first he'd had a stroke or something. I went in to see. That's when I saw his eyes, and the bottle.'

I remembered what Maman had said. 'Why do you

think he killed himself?'

'He had this ring. Like the Resistance fighters in the war. A suicide ring, a poison ring. He always wore it. It had a big, black stone on it, you must have noticed it. I don't know what poison was in it, but he talked about it being his way out of the world when it got too much for him. Well, he must have used it.'

'He couldn't have.' I didn't think this was classified information. Maman, at least, had heard the row in the hall. 'The police took the powder out of it.'

Her mouth dropped open. 'He must have had more powder, then.'

I shook my head. 'The police searched all your bags, remember. They'd have taken it, if he had.'

'They didn't strip search us. He must have kept it on him.'

I didn't buy that one. 'Why? He didn't know the police were coming, none of us did.' And he wouldn't have seen the police arrive from his room, up in the attic, with the skylight the only window. Even if he had, his guilty knowledge would have focused on treasure, not poison. 'He already had one lot of poison on him, in the ring. Why on earth would he carry another dose?'

'Maybe to stop someone else eating it by mistake.'

I gave her a sceptical look. She flushed, and came clean at last. 'It was the computer, you see. I wondered why he'd left it on, so I touched a key, and there was a note on the screen. It said he'd killed Kamilla, and he couldn't live without her, and so he was taking his own life.'

Huddled in her onesie and patterned jumper, she looked more like a hung-over schoolgirl than someone who'd planned to make the other members of her company ill, just to give herself a chance to impress the critics. Someone who'd let her curiosity overcome her fright at a dead body. She was nearly as old as I was, and in spite of what I'd said to Gavin about opera singers living in their own world, she should have known better than to touch the computer.

Unless, of course, she'd done it on purpose. There may have been a suicide note on the computer, but that didn't prove it had been Adrien who'd typed it.

4

Gavin couldn't interview my parents, of course. Sergeant Peterson took Dad, while Constable Buchanan tackled Maman. Since she'd asked me to stay, he couldn't chuck me out, or at least didn't have enough smeddum to try it, faced with Maman in her most imposing black and white chic, her hair smoothly rolled into its Callas chignon, and her face perfectly made-up.

'It's just routine, madam,' he assured her. 'There are always questions after a sudden death.'

Maman considered him. Since he was obviously terrified she'd go temperamental on him, I saw her deciding to be as down-to-earth as possible. She nodded. 'Of course. I understand.'

His Adam's apple bobbed as he swallowed. 'Did you get up during the night, madam?'

Maman nodded. 'At around one. I went to the lavatory, on the ground floor.'

He noted it. 'And how did you know it was at one, madam?'

'I cannot be certain, of course, but it usually is.' He stared at her, and she explained. 'One has habits, with age.

For me, I usually rise at one, but I did not look at the hour, why should I have? It was dark. I descended, I climbed and went back to sleep, as I always do.'

'And then?'

'Then we were awoken by Bryony screaming. I heard Per running up to her, and pulled on my own wrap. We were just on the way up when Gavin came running past, like a Highlander in the charge for the Bonny Prince, then Cassandre.'

I nodded. 'I can corroborate that. Maman and Dad were just in the doorway as we came up the stairs.'

He wrote that in his notebook as well. 'And Mr Lynch, madam?'

Maman gave him a blank look. 'I do not understand.'

'Did your husband rise in the middle of the night?'

'Oh.' Maman gave an airy wave of her hand. 'Oh, yes, I expect so, he generally does, but you understand I am used to it. I would not it have registered.'

'At what time, madam?'

Maman shook her head. 'I do not know. He does rise, and I expect he did last night, but I would not have awaked me or looked at the time. Why? I continued sleeping.'

It sounded reasonable enough. I saw him shift into detective mode, trying for a Sherlock Holmes steely glare. 'And there's nothing, madam, that you would like to tell us about your relationships with the rest of the singers?'

Maman's make-up was too perfect for her to blush, but to my surprise a tide of colour flooded the base of her neck. 'I don't understand what you mean.'

He'd spotted it too, and was quick to pursue his advantage. 'Something you would prefer your husband didn't know, perhaps?'

Her dark eyes widened. 'Something I am concealing

from Dermot?' she echoed. Her breathing had quickened. She steadied it, and swirled her hand again. 'I do not understand what you are implying. We are a company of singers. I have known Adrien since some years, but we were not particularly close.' She smiled at him, sensible and reasonable. 'He was too dramatic for me.'

She was doing it well. He couldn't see, as I could, that her other hand, lying on her black trousers, was clenched tight. Not Adrien, but there was something with someone else, I could see. Fournier?

Constable Buchanan was thinking along the same lines. 'You've known Mr Fournier for some years, I believe.'

'Oh, Vincent!' Now her tone was entirely natural, but I couldn't tell whether it was genuine. 'For over thirty years now. He worked with Dermot here in Shetland, and we were friends because of his interest in the arts. He encouraged me to continue to sing when I was at home with this small child.' She smiled at me; her slender hand smoothed my hair. 'Then he worked for Scottish Heritage, and I encountered him when I was considering of this tour, oh, two years ago. We talked about it, and he suggested using the Scottish historic houses.'

'Your relations have never been closer, madam?'

'With Vincent? Oh, no.' She brought both hands up to lay elegantly on the table. 'Per, also, I have known for some years. Not as long as I have known Vincent. Twelve years, perhaps. I met him as a young musical director, his first show, I think, for a festival of early music in Vienna. We did not meet properly then, because he had to leave in a hurry, he had an interview in Graz, but we exchanged e-mail addresses. I thought that he was good, so I have recommended him to others. In early music, I do not know if you know, but we are a smaller pool of specialists, so one keeps meeting the same people. We have worked together a number of times, and when Vincent and I were in train of devising this tour, I thought of him to direct.' She gave him a warm smile. 'But no, we have never been lovers. I understand that you have to ask these things. And Caleb, of course, since he is younger than my Cassandre here, is young enough to be my son.'

The smile had charmed him. He blushed to the tips of his ears, but managed to answer, 'You wouldn't think that, madam. Thank you for your help.' Then he gathered up his notebook and got himself out of the room.

'Phew,' Maman said, once the door had swung to behind him. 'Now, I must pack. We are to be on the 10.45 ferry.' Her mouth pursed, uncertain. 'It seems very callous to just go, like that, but Gavin seems to think it would be better, so that the house can be examined properly, and of course they will not let us make arrangements for poor Adrien's body, so we can't remain here, with him in the house, like that.'

I nodded. 'I'll come with you to Lerwick. Gavin's car's at Toft, so if you and Dad can give us a lift, we'll follow you from there.'

'Oh, Cassandre, that would be good.' Her face clouded. 'Poor Adrien. I never believed he would really do it.'

I put an arm round her. 'Try not to think about it. And, Maman, if there *is* something, then tell Gavin. He won't tell Dad.'

She shook her head. 'Perhaps. But it's nothing.' She kissed my cheek. 'Off you go, my Cassandre. I must pack for the ferry.'

I watched her sweep out, and wished I could believe her.

Chapter Twenty

'Timing,' Sergeant Peterson said. It was half past nine. The initial interviews were finished, and now we were sitting around the dining room table: Gavin, Sergeant Peterson, Constable Buchanan, and I. Cat was playing with a shell he'd found in one corner, patting it from paw to paw, then batting it across the floor and scampering after it. Outside, the sea was lavender-grey, slashed with white breakers that pounded the beach. Now the grey cold of the morning sky was clearing to show chinks of blue, bright as summer. 'The doctor's initial estimate of time of death is the early hours of the morning, between one and four. Our own doctor will narrow that down, if we ever manage to get the body to him. The suicide note was typed at 02.37.'

I remembered the shadow I'd seen on the stairs at half past two. Going up, going down? I couldn't be sure.

'Cause: one of the cyanides, in his water bottle.'

'So he did have more poison on him,' I said.

Sergeant Peterson gave me a look that reminded me I shouldn't be there. 'Or someone else had already switched the poison he had for something harmless, and kept what they'd stolen. The lab report will tell us.' She repeated my arguments, 'He didn't see us arrive, and it's not likely he'd have carried more poison when he had the ring.'

'So we're thinking, Freya,' Gavin interposed, 'that someone else doctored his water bottle, then came in and typed the note?'

She nodded. 'SOCO will tell us what prints there are on the laptop.' She glared out at the sea. 'When they get here. The ferrymen say the 10.45 should run.' She flicked through her notes. 'Alibis: well, anyone could have got up in the night. Mr and Mrs Lynch did, but they each said that was earlier, around one o'clock, so unless they're working together, they're out of it. They also both said they went downstairs, so as not to wake anyone else. After that, they say, they heard nothing until Ms Blake started screaming.'

'A husband and wife working together's not impossible,' Gavin said, his voice carefully neutral, 'but I'd need to see a very strong motive.'

I kept quiet.

'Mr Rolvsson, the director, and Ms Blake were together all night. They both said that neither of them got up – but given that the room has twin beds, unless they shared one, it would be possible for one of them to get up without waking the other one. I'll need to ask about exact sleeping arrangements. Mr Fournier, downstairs, said he did get up, around four, he thought, but he stayed downstairs, as would be natural, and Mr Michel, the accompanist, says he didn't get up. No corroboration of the last two. The last one, Mr Portland, well, he checked into the Lerwick hotel all right, just after lunchtime yesterday, but of course there's no proof that he stayed there.'

'Did he have breakfast?'

Sergeant Peterson shook her head. 'But there's coffee in the rooms, so if he's a one-black-coffee-for-breakfast man then he could have taken that and gone. The bed had been lain in, and a mug used.'

'If he went all the way to Lerwick, he'd have had to move fast to get back on Unst before the ferries stopped running. For the moment, I think he's out of it for this one. Let's focus on the others.' Gavin paused for a moment, thinking. 'So, going right back to the first afternoon in Unst. No, earlier, to the phone call to the caterers.' He looked at me. 'Bryony admitted she made it, but her reason didn't make sense. However ...' He explained my putting-Maman-out-of-action theory, and Sergeant Peterson nodded.

'Would she really be naive enough to think it would work?'

'If she thought she'd got the musical director in her pocket. So, the phone call: she couldn't swear nobody overheard her, but she was certain she'd done her best to make sure they wouldn't. That gives us two possibilities. Firstly, that someone did overhear, and used the scheme to poison Kamilla ...' He paused and looked round. 'I'm assuming here that her death was indeed murder, which is still far from being proved. Or, two, that there was someone who knew of the allergy, saw the seafood and took the chance to poison her. I don't think it likely that the allergy was just coincidence. It was too public a way of poisoning her, yet not public enough. By that I mean that there were a number of people around, but too small a number. If you wanted to murder her openly, it would be much easier to get her a glass of poison in a big reception, like the opening night in France.'

'Unless,' I said, 'the murderer had a new and pressing reason to get rid of her, and just hoped we'd put it down to allergy. That fits with using Adrien's poison.' I turned to Sergeant Peterson. 'Did he admit to the "mad" conversation?'

'He denied it most vehemently,' she said. 'I didn't believe him.'

'Maybe he couldn't take her final rejection. If he couldn't have her, nobody would. Operatic. Maybe the poison maybe being soda bicarb was to throw you off the scent, make it possible for somebody else to have killed her. Then he couldn't take it and killed himself. Then there was the letter you didn't find, the one from France.'

I frowned. 'I thought that was odd.'

'Why?' Gavin asked.

I'd been mulling it over while I'd sat in the drawing room, bag at my feet, Cat in my lap. 'Because her French wasn't very good. Kamilla worked in England, then the States, and in that interview she gave in the station she didn't sound very fluent. She'd learned it in school, I'd say, and this was the first time she'd used it since, in the week's rehearsing for the big opening in the château.'

'But she was singing in French,' Gavin said. 'Surely she'd speak it?'

I shook my head, and quoted Caleb at them. 'They get taught how to pronounce the languages they sing in, at music college, emphasising the vowel sounds, but they don't necessarily speak it.'

'Was the handwriting French?' Sergeant Peterson asked.

I shook my head. 'I really didn't look.'

'What became of the letter?' Gavin said. We all looked at him. 'Let's focus on that. It wasn't in her handbag or case, nor in anyone else's that we searched, and I agree with Cass that it's unlikely anyone could have got it before her death. So, unless Fournier, Portland or Rolvsson took it with him, it's been disposed of here. There were no fires to burn it in. So how would you get rid of it?'

'Use a lighter, or a match, in a sheltered corner outside, and stamp the ashes,' Sergeant Peterson said.

'Tear it into tiny pieces and throw them into the sea,' I suggested.

Gavin looked across at Constable Buchanan. 'I'll put you on to investigating that. Think about what you'd do, here, to get rid of an incriminating document.' He made a sympathetic grimace. 'The bin first. You don't know, Cass, if the catering firm took their waste away with them?'

'She took the black bag out, but surely she'd just have taken it to the bin store.'

'When was it stolen?' He considered. 'Kamilla took it away before the performance. There was the rehearsal.' He turned back to me. 'Did Fournier watch that?'

I shook my head. 'But they went back to their rooms afterwards.'

'So it would have been a risk that she'd have seen it was gone, and made a fuss.'

'During the concert,' Sergeant Peterson said.

'They were all at that. Then back to their rooms to get out of costume, and down to dinner.'

'Do you have any idea what order they came down in?'

I shut my eyes and tried to visualise them, but had to shake my head. 'They came in more or less in a bunch. Then, after Kamilla collapsed, they went out in a bunch too. Maman took Bryony straight to her room, so nobody would get a chance to search it after that.'

'Unless she left it,' Sergeant Peterson pointed out. 'Our lives would be so much easier if all these bedrooms were *en suite*. She was being sick, and if she hadn't been, she'd still have needed to clean her teeth, take her make-up off, all that. Someone just needed to wait in the drawing room for her door to open, nip in, get the letter and exit. Plenty of time, when she's going upstairs, and even more if she went downstairs. Furthermore, with these heavy doors, and the handy wedges, she wouldn't have heard the perp, and he would have heard her.'

Gavin nodded. 'Another question. How did the perp know Kamilla had the letter?'

'Maybe she told him,' Constable Buchanan said. 'Just before or just after the rehearsal. It had to be. There was no other time.'

'But they were all dressing,' I protested. 'Two in each room, except for Fournier. She couldn't just march in on them and say, "I've got a letter which …".And what could it have said, to be a motive for murder? Why would it have been sent to her?'

'I tend to agree with that,' Sergeant Peterson said. 'She couldn't have barged in on any of the men then, except for Fournier. Or there was her own room-mate, Bryony.'

Constable Buchanan scribbled frantically.

'Good questions,' Gavin said. 'What could have been in the letter, and why should it have come from France?'

'Something she'd been investigating while she was there. Something she'd noticed and asked about.'

'They all live there,' I said. 'Maybe it was from someone who thought she was falling for one of the others, and wanted to warn her off him because …' My imagination ran out there. 'Because he'd got a wife already, that he'd driven into a psychiatric hospital, or kept shut up in the west wing, like *Jane Eyre*.'

Sergeant Peterson gave me a scornful look. 'You're sure it was from France?'

I shook my head. 'It was certainly a letter, and handwritten. I think it had a foreign stamp, but I never

270

looked any closer.' Aboard a ship, privacy was a matter of delicately balanced etiquette, which included handing over letters without any kind of inspection or comment. 'I assume it was hers, because she took it. It was Per who said it had a French stamp.'

'Can you go back to the way she looked when she saw it? Take us through that again.'

I did my best. 'I was in the kitchen. The sun was coming in the window and hitting the door just at eye height, and as you came in, it dazzled you. She came in and stopped, and turned her head away from it, and that's why her head was turned to the worktop where the letters were. She took a step backwards into the room, and stared. I wasn't sure at first what she'd seen – whether it was the letters, or my sailing jacket across the chair. Whatever it was, it was a shock. Recognition, that's the best I can do. Something she wasn't expecting to see. She grabbed the letter, almost mechanically, as if she didn't really see it, shoved past Per and ran out of the room. Then, half an hour later, at the rehearsal, she was still strange, as if she wasn't quite there.'

'Unexpected recognition,' Gavin repeated. 'She knew the writing, but didn't expect to hear from that person, and hearing from them was a shock.' He shook his head. 'We can investigate the hotel where she stayed in France, and see if she had any visitors during that rehearsal week. Freya, you take that in hand. Get the address from Madame Lynch.' He checked his watch, and stood up. 'So we're agreed – I stick with the company, with Lerwick back-up if need be, and you keep things going here.'

'What about the missing treasure?' I asked. 'Could that have had anything to do with it? Adrien found it that afternoon, and there was the "mad" quarrel he denied.' An idea was stirring deep down in my subconscious.

271

Treasure. 'Maybe the letter's just a red herring.' Something was connecting itself together, and it was just out of sight in my brain. I frowned and repeated 'treasure' to myself. He'd found the treasure that afternoon, before the quarrel.

'She refused to go along with his stealing it, so he killed her?' Gavin said.

'What missing treasure?' Sergeant Peterson asked.

I stared at her. 'But wasn't that what you were looking for? When you were searching?'

She gave me a loftily superior look, the mermaid making allowances for human stupidity. 'That was our excuse. What we were actually looking for, of course, was poisons, something that might have caused Lange's death.'

'But Peter phoned you! After I'd been drugged.'

'Hang on, Cass,' Gavin said. 'Take us through this, slowly.'

I left my train of thought to sort itself out. 'On Friday afternoon, Adrien found something on Vinstrick Ness, the headland where the Viking graves are. I scared him off, but someone drugged me that night, and dug up ... whatever. I told Peter ...' His surname momentarily escaped me; I gestured. 'He lives in the yellow house here, and he said he'd call you. So when you turned up to search, I assumed it was in response to that.'

Sergeant Peterson shook her head. 'I never got that message. We came because Gavin phoned about the suspicions over Kamilla's death.'

'Follow that up, Freya,' Gavin said, 'and let me know as soon as possible.' He glanced up at the shut door between us and Vincent Fournier's sitting room, and lowered his voice. 'Keith Sandison was telling me that he was suspicious that there was someone local selling items on through someone south.' He looked over at me. 'He thought you might be mixed up in that, Cass, until he realised who you were.'

'Fournier wasn't here.' He'd been fetching Per back from Lerwick, I remembered. 'We didn't search his bags.'

'His Paris office is next door to the man who made Maman's jewellery. Adrien's father. *Antiquaire.*'

'Interesting connection. I know he used to live here. Does he visit Shetland often now?'

I shrugged. 'Dad would know.'

Gavin checked his watch again. 'But we wondered why he'd come to join the tour here. Freya, we'll do his bags now. There's just time before the ferry.'

He rapped on the door, and he and Sergeant Peterson went in. The door swung shut behind them. Constable Buchanan went off to search for the missing letter – I presumed – and I was left listening to the swelling noise of voices from the other side of the door. Fournier was at first courteous, but irritated. The irritation grew to annoyance, as they strewed his newly packed belongings over the floor, then a note of real anger came in. I wished I could see what was happening. Gavin's tone, answering him, was even and reasonable, but with an authoritative edge to it. Fournier's anger turned to bluster, then silence. Gavin came out of the room at last with both hands full of a package of bubble wrap. 'There was a false bottom to his case,' he said.

He laid the bubble wrap on the table, and unrolled it. Inside were a dozen plastic bags, each containing objects encrusted in earth. I could make out the shapes of a bead necklace, several of the tortoise brooches, a comb. 'It was a woman's grave,' Gavin said. 'We can take these to the museum, though I'd rather put them back with their owner.'

Suddenly the bead necklace, the words, clicked together in my head. I knew why Kamilla had called Adrien mad. I left the thought safely recovered, and concentrated on the matter in hand. 'So it was Fournier who dug them up?' I shook my head. 'But he didn't get the chance to drug me. He was nowhere near me. It was Adrien who ...' Then I got it. Gavin gave me a questioning look.

'Peter handed my cup to Adrien,' I said slowly. 'It was Peter who poured my tea. He drugged me. I told him about Adrien having found something, and where, and he went straight to Fournier. They knew I'd be on watch, so I had to be put out of action. He said to me that he'd tell the police, and when Sergeant Peterson turned up, I never doubted that was why she'd come. But if Peter didn't phone her after all ...'

'It's a civil offence, not a police one,' Gavin said. 'Sergeant Peterson'll talk to the landlord, and he and Historic Scotland can press charges.'

Sergeant Peterson nodded, and began making notes in her book. Gavin glanced out of the window, then at his watch. Over at Gutcher, the ferry was backing out of its berth.

'I suddenly had an idea.' I leaned forward. 'I know why Kamilla called Adrien mad. See, Adrien apparently had this thing about Schliemann. You know, he dug for Troy and found – or faked – something he said was Helen's jewels. The replicas Maman was wearing.' I remembered them dangling like sunken gold in Sergeant Peterson's hands. 'Adrien's grandfather, or great-grandfather, had seen Schliemann's wife wearing them. I know it was him on the headland.' I spread my hands over the bags. 'Suppose he'd gone to Kamilla and said, "I've found Viking jewellery and I'm going to dress you in it,

the way Schliemann dressed Sophia." Not contact with
her brother, but his real trump card, his ambition. The
reason he brought his metal detector. Wouldn't that sound
mad?'

'And she turned his offer down,' Sergeant Peterson
said. 'Murder and suicide after all? He knew about the
allergy, remember.'

'Let's see what forensics comes up with,' Gavin said.
He lifted the brooch in its bag, turning it over in his hand,
then laid it down. 'We've got this pair, anyway.' He lifted
his rucksack. 'Time for us to go.'

ᚺ

We were just walking towards the metal ramp with our
bags and Cat's basket when a grey Berlingo came racing
down the road, swirled round the car park and skidded to
a halt. Keith Sandison waved at us from the window.
'Magnie phoned me,' he said. 'The police are talking to
Peter o' Belmont.' He scowled. 'And Vincent, that used to
work at Sullom Voe. Is it true you found grave goods on
him?'

Gavin nodded. 'A woman's grave.'

'Well,' Keith said. He nodded to himself several times,
then fished in his pocket, and brought out a piece of wood
attached to a string. He held it out to me. 'Might be
handy, lass, next time you're chasing villains. Just whirl it
abune your head.'

I looked at it, puzzled. It was just a piece of wood with
a couple of holes drilled through it. I unwound the string
and looked at it, then realisation dawned. I caught his
sideways grin at me.

'Don't try it out here, lass.' He jerked his chin at the others, waiting in the cars to be allowed on the ferry. 'Wait for you're on your own.' He glanced down at Cat's basket. 'Really on your own. You'll gluff your cat something terrible.'

He turned to go back into his car.

'Hey,' I said, 'that first night. When you scared the three strangers. Where did you disappear to?' Then I remembered Inga and me playing at Jarlshof, and the moon dipping behind the clouds. 'The *souterrain*.'

He nodded. 'I stood beside the opening and just waited for the moon to go behind the clouds, then ducked into it.'

'I should have thought of that,' I said.

'Na, na, lass. You kept your head very well, what with those pig-snouts, and me appearing wi' me Viking war cry.' He got back into his car. 'Fine to meet you, Gavin. Safe journey south.'

Chapter Twenty-one

My *Khalida* was just as I'd left her. I clambered aboard and felt the familiar smell of wood and polish and lamp oil close around me. *Home.* Cat jumped out of his basket, whiskers twitching, and jumped straight onto my berth.

The storm hadn't done any damage. The only sign of its passing was the logbook having slid down to the fiddled edge of the table, and the little fish horse brass squint on its nail. I straightened it, then set food and water down for Cat. We'd be late back, after Mass; there wasn't a ferry until 20.15. I told him to be good, opened the forehatch so he could slip out, and checked the mooring ropes while Dad turned the car, then ran for it. We had twenty-one miles to go, and twenty-three minutes to do it in. It was lucky that Dad was used to single-track roads, I reflected, as we swung up past the kirk, and along the higher road where Bluemull Sound dazzled below us, then round the curve and down again, past the ferry terminal, past the wooden hut of Wind Dog Café, and onto the main road south. Now we had a double carriageway. Dad put his foot down, and the 4x4 shot forward between the rust-coloured peat hills, past the little industrial estate of Sellafirth, with the grey corrugated hall beside it, and around the long voe, humped with lines of mussel floats. I hoped that Gavin, beside me in the back seat, couldn't see the speedometer.

'Bothwell was captured by the Danish up there,' I said, tilting my chin at the ruined croft on the skyline across the voe. 'He'd been engaged to some Danish woman before he married Mary Queen of Scots, and she was mad about it, so she had him slung in a dungeon. You can still see his mummy.'

Gavin's hand closed around mine. 'Amazing, the stuff you learn in school.

'We did a play about it, for the drama festival.' Inga had been Mary, stately in a red velvet dress, and I'd been one of the Maries.

The small factory where salmon was canned for John West was below us, to the left, and the burn where they raced plastic ducks in hairst. To our right, the neat lodge, and then Windhouse itself, a grey ruin up on its hill, with the castellations standing out against the sky. The windows gaped; I could see a fallen roof timber slanting behind one.

'I remember that house being almost saveable. It's supposed to be horribly haunted.' My friend, Dodie, who worked on the ferries, had several hair-raising tales, which he'd told us at night, after a day's regatta. The car sped on, around the bend above West Sandwick and along the straight above the Wick of Sound, a little island joined to the land by a double beach. Across from us now lay the north mainland with the jagged outline of the Ramna Stacks that Magnie and I had sailed past, only four days ago, and the red cliffs of Fethaland and North Roe, backed by the great silver-pink bulk of Ronas Hill. We came around the last bend and saw the ferry, tight against the pier, with the cars moving forward in line.

'Made it,' Dad said. He stopped at the roundabout and waited for the line to end, then fell in behind a Tesco lorry, painted with tourist slogans: '200,000 sheep – 22,000 people'.

We went up into the lounge to join the company, seated round two tables. Fournier was brooding darkly, and Bryony was still red-eyed, but Per seemed more bouyant, as if they had left the worst of their troubles behind with Adrien's body, in Belmont House, two seas away.

'It won't be the same, of course,' Maman said, sliding into the red-covered seat, 'and we must be prepared for some adverse publicity, but the British also admire the, what is it called, Dermot? Where you carry on regardless.'

'Blitz spirit.' Dad grimaced. 'We need some of that here.'

'The College of Music in Glasgow has two possibles to sing Hippolyte, both fourth-year students,' Per said. 'It's a great opportunity for them. The Principal is going to get back to me today. It means yet another rehearsal, of course, but we'll have time in Edinburgh to listen to them and choose.'

'And Gabriella is meeting us at Mareel,' Dad said. 'Fournier ordered a taxi for her, from the airport.'

Maman rose. 'I need some air. Come with me, Cassandre.'

Beside me, Gavin met her eyes. She gave a little nod, and he rose too. We made our way to the observation deck at the aft end of the cabin and stood together on the little balcony, with the car roofs below us, and the navy tailgate. Behind us, the water churned.

'I was lying,' Maman said.

I nodded. 'I know.'

'I wanted to explain to you.' Her eyes flickered towards Gavin. 'To you both. Constable Buchanan who spoke to me, he might have understood, but the woman

279

with the glass-green eyes, she would not. But I can explain to Gavin.' Her hand flowed towards him, palm up. 'Then you can tell her.'

Gavin shook his head. 'I can't interview you, or take a statement, because of Cass.'

Maman's dark lashes flickered down; her hands gripped together. 'Then I shall tell Cass, and you can listen.' The lashes rose; her dark eyes fixed on him, pleading. 'Will you do that?'

Gavin nodded.

Maman was silent for a moment, then she looked at me. 'You see, Cass, your father and I were not quite separated and not quite together for, oh, so many years. Thirteen years, it was then. We were both too proud. And I was getting older. I would be fifty soon, and I was lonely, and sad.' Her slim hand reached over to mine. 'You have been lonely too.'

I turned my hand to hold hers, and felt how cold it was. 'Yes.'

'Three years ago, I was in a show with Caleb. *Castor et Pollux*, the original version; he sang Pollux, and I was Télaïre. It was his first time in France, and he was love-struck with it. It was spring, and the cherry blossom was out in front of Notre-Dame, and the Seine was patrolled by lovers. And I was all that romance for him. It didn't matter that I was old, and he was young. I was the mystery and the beauty of Paris, and we enjoyed that together.' She flushed a delicate rose. 'Oh, it did not go far – dinners, and walks together, and one kiss, by starlight, on the Pont Saint-Louis. We weren't lovers. I was on a pedestal for him. It was dizzy, and beautiful, and sweet.'

Gavin had been watching her. Now, in this little world between worlds, with the water flowing around us, he cast aside his Scottish taciturn-male heritage. 'If I'd been his age, in Paris, I'd have been honoured to be your squire.' His cheeks went crimson, and he turned his face away. There was silence for a moment.

'And then, you see,' Maman said, 'when the leaves opened, and the blossom began to fall, I knew it was time to get back to real life. You cannot live on starlight.' She smiled at Gavin. 'The squire must not make real love to his lady. I wanted to come home, to Dermot, where I belonged. He would not come to me, so I had to come to him, and hope that somehow being together would bridge the barriers. And so I organised this tour. I knew Vincent Fournier could wangle us the Scottish venues, and I insisted that we must come to Shetland, even if I had to finance that part of the tour myself. I told Dermot the dates. If he still cared, he would be here. It was a gamble, and I do not know if it would have worked – but that does not matter now.' She smiled at me. 'You called me for help, and everything fell into place once more.'

Then she turned to Gavin. 'But this is what is important: there was nothing discreditable about Caleb and I. Oh, I suppose it could be exaggerated to make a story for the papers, but without photos or proof there would be nothing to catch the public's interest. Besides, Dermot is Irish, and romantic, he would believe me and understand. It is not a motive for murder.' She leaned forward, hands eloquent. 'And most important of all, Kamilla was not like that. Your young officer is ferreting here, ferreting there, looking for secrets she could have threatened someone with. I tell you, she was simple and sparkling, like sunshine on a shallow river. She would not have done that. Oh, she had had hard times earlier in her career, we have all struggled, but now she was rising. She was the media's darling, directors were showcasing her.

She was in love with all the world. She would not have been petty, taking a mean way to discredit me.'

Yell Sound slid past us, the waves still choppy from the storm, masking the whirlpools that oiled the surface on a still day. The ferry turned in a churning of reverse-thrust. Maman gripped my hand, let it go, and went back into the cabin.We followed her, clattered down the iron steps and got back into the car. In front of us, the tailgate began to lower.

I leaned towards Gavin. 'Do we have to go straight to Mareel?'

'Why?'

'I'd like to do a detour to Brae.'

'Connected with our business, or because you need a new spanner from the Brae Building Centre?'

'Connected. Maybe.' I wanted to call on Inga and Charlie, to see if they'd heard anything more of Caleb.

ᚴ

'No,' Inga said. when we arrived on her doorstep ten minutes later, via the Brae loop, which involved a grandstand view of Sullom Voe oil terminal, the tugs sitting at their jetty, and a tsunami event from six thousand years ago. 'Come in, the kettle's just boiled. No strange Americans. Why?'

'He said he was related,' I explained. We followed her through the passage and into her spacious kitchen-living room. Peerie Charlie was drawing at his low table, lower lip thrust out in concentration. He looked up. 'Dass! I drawing.' He dropped his crayon and brought it over to show me. 'That Spidey and that Iceman. He's grey.'

Then he noticed Gavin's kilt, and fell silent, dodging behind my leg to peek out. I sat down and pulled him up on the couch beside me. 'Iceman should be white.'

'My Iceman is grey,' Peerie Charlie said. 'He's ice from the sea. It's grey,' he added unanswerably.

'Fair enough,' I agreed. I looked over at Inga, juggling mugs on the other side of the counter. 'He spent all day yesterday on the mainland, and he may just have been checking out ponies and puffins, like a good tourist, but he was asking about you.' I tried to dredge Magnie's recollections out of my memory. 'Something about an Andrew from Eastayre who went to the States around the turn of the century.'

Inga shrugged. 'Charlie's family, Charlie's memory.' She went to the far door and called upwards. 'Charlie!' There was an answering shout and sound of footsteps. 'Tea or coffee?'

'Tea, please.'

'Tea.' Inga set a plate out and reached up for a biscuit tin. 'Cake.'

Big Charlie came in as she was laying out a neat pattern of squares of millionaire's shortbread and the sort of traybake that has Maltesers in it. He was tall, broad, fair, the picture of a Viking descendant; Peerie Charlie had inherited his colouring. 'Now, Cass, fine to see you. Coffee for me, Inga.' He sat down on the couch opposite. 'What's all doing wi' you? I thought Inga said you were heading for a tall ship.'

'Next week, as soon as this gale's blown out. Yourself?'

'Oh, doing away. Working wi' the scallop boat, and a bit of whitefish, not that there's muckle around yet. I got twartree mackerel yesterday, if you want to take one for your cat.'

Cat would love that, but I had doubts about how well a carrier bag of mackerel would go down in Mareel, Shetland's plush new cinema and arts centre. I was just about to turn the offer down, with regret, when there was a diffident knock at the door. Inga and Charlie exchanged one of those couple-glances that mutually said 'I'm not expecting anyone' and Charlie shrugged and went to the door. 'Yes?'

It was Caleb's voice that answered him, formal. 'Mr Anderson? I have a delivery to make. May I come in?'

His stage training stopped him from moving nervously. He clocked me sitting there with Peerie Charlie in my lap, and reddened, then his gaze moved to Gavin, and the embarrassment was replaced by wariness. Inga gestured him to a chair, and he unwound his scarf and sat down.

'Will you take a cup of tea?' Inga asked.

Caleb shook his head. 'I haven't got accustomed to your English tea yet. Do you have coffee?'

Inga nodded, and lifted down another mug.

Caleb fished in his pocket and brought out a leather pouch, shiny with wear, and closed by a drawstring. It chinked as he laid it on the table, exactly in the middle of the square of sun. He loosened the neck, and two coins rolled out, glinting gold.

'This,' Caleb said, 'is for you, from my grandfather's father, Andrew Anderson, your great-great-uncle.'

There was a long silence, as the two coins spun on the table. Peerie Charlie pushed forward from my knee and put out a finger to touch the nearest one. 'Doubloon,' he said. I'd been telling him stories of pirates. 'Pieces of eight.'

I stared at the two gold coins, and the leather purse. I'd never seen a real doubloon. It couldn't be –

'Old Andrew's son,' Charlie said, at last. 'Andrew,

who went off to join the Gold Rush, and never came home.'

'He went to Nome,' Caleb explained. 'The Nome Gold Rush, just a little later than the Klondike one. It's in Alaska, on the Bering Sea, just up from the mouth of the Yukon. As close as Canada gets to Siberia. Now, this is the story as I heard it from my grandfather, when he gave me this. His father was Andrew Anderson, the oldest son. He was expected to stay home on the croft, but when he heard about gold being found in Canada, he was wild to go. There were furious rows about it, with all his kin telling him he was a fool who'd never find anything, and in the end he ran away. That was in 1902, and he was just twenty.' He upended the bag, and the coins flashed and clattered over the table. There must have been thirty, forty of them. 'Well, he didn't strike the big one, but he made enough. He came down into the States, to Portland, and began his own business, got married, had a family of seven, but he never forgot. All his life he meant to come back and tell them he had made good, but there was World War I, and he died at Vimy Ridge. His son, my grandfather, was busy wrestling with the Depression, and then World War II came. He was in the army, and he planned to come up here during his leave, but he found it was a restricted area, nobody allowed in. My father, well, he doesn't leave Portland, he's too busy running it. What do you call it here, the City Council? Whatever you call it, my father's in it. *Is* it. So here I am, only three generations late, and great-grandfather Andrew's purse of gold is on your kitchen table, the way he wanted.'He held out his hand. 'Cousin Charles.'

Charlie shook his hand. 'Boy, you're come a long way. But listen –' He picked up one of the coins. 'This is real gold. We canna take this. It must be worth a fortune, at today's prices.'

Caleb shrugged. 'Forty Edward VII Canadian gold sovereigns, 1908, the first minting. If it had been 1909, they'd only be worth around five hundred pounds apiece. 1908's as rare as gold coins come.' He blushed. 'I've been using this as my overdraft facility in Paris. Last time I pawned one, to see me through a lean patch, it was worth four and a half thousand.'

Inga was in the middle of carrying the plate of fancies through. She stopped dead, and the plate tilted alarmingly. Even though I wasn't going to have any, I put out a hand to steady it. Inga's millionaire shortbread was too good to waste. 'Four and a half thousand.' She set the plate down with hands that trembled, and picked one up. 'Four and a half thousand, each?'

'Pounds?' Charlie said, disbelievingly.

Caleb nodded.'Great-grandfather set it aside. As soon as the sovereigns were minted, he bought them, to bring home.'

'But –' Inga said. 'That's …' She tailed off, her lips moving soundlessly, as she worked it out. 'We can't take that.'

I'd always beaten her at mental arithmetic. After a stunned moment of *It can't possibly be that!* and some re-assessing of zeros, I'd already made it a hundred and eighty grand.

Charlie had worked it out too. Now he reached out to lift one coin wonderingly. He turned it over in his hand. Then, with a decisive movement, he swept them together and tipped them back into the bag. He pulled the string tight and gave it back to Caleb. 'We canna possibly take this.'

'Listen,' Caleb said. He leaned forward, hands

outstretched. 'See, the way my grandfather told it, what his father, old Andrew, minded most about was his sister. Janey, she was called, and she was bright as a button, like this little fellow here.' He made a gesture towards Peerie Charlie, who drew himself up indignantly.

'I not little. I three and a half.'

'That's a good age,' Caleb agreed. 'You'll be four soon.' He turned back to Charlie. 'If Andrew had stayed home, then his sister Janey could have stayed at school, maybe gone for a teacher, instead of having to leave early to help on the croft.'

Charlie's brows drew together. 'Janey ... Inga, where's the folder with all the family tree and that?' He turned back to Caleb. 'I did some research on the Bayanne website. It's something I can do at sea, a bit more interesting than just reading another thriller or watching a film.'

Inga put the plate of fancies in safety, and bent down to rummage in the corner unit. 'This one?' She brandished a beige paper wallet. Then she remembered her duties as a hostess, and passed the plate round. I shook my head at it, comforting myself with the reminder that the two I would have taken made an extra two pounds for Christian Aid. I regretted it; the caretaker's bannocks had been a long time ago, and goodness knew what lunch would be, given that it was Sunday, and most of Lerwick closed.

'That's him,' Charlie agreed. He delved into the folder, and came out with a family tree, which he spread out on the couch beside Caleb. 'Here you are. There's your Andrew, and that's his sister Janey. She was born in 1894, and she lived until she was ninety-five, so I mind her fine. We used to visit her when I was a bairn, for Sunday tea, and then she came to all the family Christmas dinners and the like.'

'Andrew knew he'd ruined her chances by going, and he always regretted that. He meant to bring this back so that she could have her chance.'

Charlie smiled. 'She got her education after all. She took over as a teacher when the men were called up, and qualified properly after the war. She taught English in the Anderson Institute all her days. Hang on.' He delved into the folder and came out with a photograph of what looked like a group of teachers in front of a stone wall. The men had suits and bowler hats, the women were smart in white blouses. The older ones had their heads overshadowed by those cartwheel hats with feathers; the younger ones wore straw boaters. 'This was her on a staff outing to Mousa.' He indicated a young woman at the side of the photo. 'That's Janey.'

Caleb shook his head. His eyes were moist. 'I reckon Great-grandfather would surely have been proud.' He put the bag back on the table. I could hardly believe that little leather purse held more money than I could imagine ever needing. I wondered if Caleb had just brought it here, in his baggage, in his pocket, as if it was nothing at all. 'We inherited the rest of his pile. This was for you.'

'So why are you needing to pawn it?' Inga asked bluntly.

Caleb laughed, and took a piece of millionaire shortbread. He bit into it, and his eyes widened. 'You baked this?' He took another bite, in reverent silence. I didn't blame him; Inga's shortbread was meltingly soft, the toffee layer gooey yet not over sweet, the chocolate crisp. 'You should be exporting this. Yeah, pawning. Because I'm disgracing the family by being a singer. Or maybe I'm lifting it up by being in opera.'

Inga's eyes flicked to me. 'I was wondering where you came in, Cass. So –?' She came to a halt, realising she didn't know his name.

'Caleb. Caleb Portland – well, Caleb Anderson, but there was another one, would you believe it, a ukelele player, so I took the city's name. I didn't figure it would mind.'

'You're part of Eugénie's tour, then?'

He nodded. 'Theseus.'

'One of the parts,' I explained.

The idea of an opera singer in the family had awed Charlie into silence. Caleb looked over at Peerie Charlie. 'And who's this young fellow?'

Peerie Charlie scrambled down off my knee and fixed Caleb with a stern glare. 'I'm Peerie Charlie. Are you a pirate?'

'Not in this production. My grandfather would sure be pleased to meet you.' He looked back at Charlie. 'You take his gold for this little fellow's education.'

'We'll share it between the three of them,' Inga said. She smiled at Caleb. 'Our oldest lass is Vaila Jane, she's twelve, and away playing netball, and then we have Dawn, she's nine and over at her pal's house. That's why the house is so quiet. Normally it's a madhouse.'

'Is your grandfather still living?' Charlie asked.

'We're a long-lived family. He'll be a hundred and two next birthday. He'll be tickled pink that I came. I'll phone him tonight.' He stared straight at them. 'He'd say you should take it too.'

Inga and Charlie exchanged a long look, then Inga nodded. She picked up the purse, weighing it in her hand, then took out one coin and gave it back to Caleb, closing his fingers over it. 'That's your luckpenny. Then you'll still have one to pawn, when the going gets tough.'

A *luckpenny* was a Shetland thing. If you struck a bargain on something, buying a boat, say, then the buyer gave the seller a coin of the purchase price back, for luck.

Caleb gave a little bow. 'Ma'am, thank you.' He put the sovereign away in his pocket. 'I surely believe it will bring me luck.'

I was beginning to feel as if treacle was being poured over me. This was all a bit too touchy-feely. I leaned forward. 'Has anyone from the company managed to get in touch with you?'

Caleb lifted his head. 'We're meeting at Mareel at half past twelve.' Out of the corner of my eye, I saw Gavin clocking that it wasn't quite an answer. 'That's still on, isn't it?' He felt in his pocket for his phone, and made a little business of noticing it wasn't switched on, not quite convincing.

'In that case,' Gavin said, 'I'm afraid we have bad news for you, Mr Portland.'

Inga made a wait gesture, swept Peerie Charlie up and carried him out. Caleb watched them go, face unreadable. Then he turned back to Gavin. Now he was registering concern, with a touch of alarm. 'Bad news, sir?'

'Adrien Moreau is dead.'

Yes, he'd known already. His eyes widened, his mouth opened, but he couldn't counterfeit the shocked whiteness of Bryony, or the blank look in Maman's eyes. He made a wide gesture with his hands. 'Dead?'

Gavin nodded, and gave him rope.

'But how? An accident, like Kamilla?'

'A suicide note was left.'

Caleb nodded. 'I was afraid that might happen. I don't want to sound a heel, but when Kamilla was showing interest, you know, I steered clear because of Adrien. He's – he *was* –' The correction was just too self-conscious. 'He was one of those brooding, intense types, and you could see there would be trouble. I didn't like her enough for that. Well … when did it happen?'

'During the night. Where did you spend the night, sir?'

'I used the hotel room the company had booked in Lerwick. The Lerwick Hotel. I can't prove that, of course. Once I'd got my card, I came and went as I liked. I spent the afternoon exploring, I drove down to the south end and saw that archaeological site, where the people dress up. Old Scatness. And I went up the road to the lighthouse.' He looked at the coin in his hand and reddened. 'I knew it wasn't mine, but it was harder than I expected to hand over a fortune. I was putting off this visit to the last minute. Then I spent the evening in Lerwick. I walked around the little roads running up the hill – gee, your Lerwick folk must be fit – and along the seafront, where the water comes right to the buildings. It would all have been like that when Andrew left. I went into the pub where the music is, and listened for a bit, then I went back to the hotel. I slept until –' There was a sudden pause, then he continued smoothly, '– ten, then I got up, had a cup of coffee, threw my bags in the back of the car, and came here.'

'Did you check out of the hotel, sir?'

'Why, sure, I –' He felt in his pocket again. 'No, I still have their card. I'd need to call in and give it back.' He looked at Gavin's face, which had polite scepticism stamped all over it. 'I had no interest in Kamilla, Inspector. None at all. I certainly wouldn't have killed Adrien over her.'

'And how,' Gavin asked, with polite interest, 'did you know I was an inspector?'

291

I'm neither maet nor drink
for fantin' man
I'm neider frock nor hat
for bonny lady;
yet yowsed wi' care
I can be aa these things,
an' foolish man and his vain wife
seek me abune aa idder.

... **gold.**

Sunday, 29th March (continued)

Tide Times at Lerwick
High Water	07.20, 1.6m
Low Water	14.06, 0.8m
High Water	20.18, 1.6m
Low Water	02.23, 0.9m

Sunrise	06.41
Moonrise	12.05
Sunset	19.36
Moonset	03.36

Waxing quarter moon

Blud shared wi' my blud, bane o' me bane,
Son o' me faider, uncle tae me son.

Chapter Twenty-two

He'd clammed up then, but I had a nasty feeling I knew who'd phoned him: the only one of the company who knew who Gavin really was. I looked out of the car window at the heather hills speeding past us. This, the Lang Kames, the hill ridge that was the central spine of Shetland, was where Dad was going to build his wind farm, now that permission had come through, and the objectors had lost their appeal. It was a jigsaw wilderness of rust heather and soft, brown peat mould, green-hazed pools and olive-orange sphagnum moss. There were Shetland sheep grazing, brown, black, grey, all heavy with lamb, and moorland birds, including the rare whimbrel. I didn't want to think about the destruction of something so beautiful: the heavy machines moving in to tear the peat back to rock, the steam hammers digging down for the tarmac in-fill, to create a heavy-duty road leading to each turbine; then the foundation for the turbine itself, before the heavy lorries brought the 90-metre columns and the three 55-metre blades. Each one would be 145 metres tall – double the height of the Burradale wind farm above Lerwick – and seven times the height of Lerwick's Victorian town hall. When I was sailing with the bairns at Brae I'd see a line of them, marching over the green hills. Inga was one of the objectors, and I had no doubt that now that the legal challenge in the UK had failed – although there was still a chance of taking it to the EU – she'd be sitting in front of the bulldozers when they arrived.

We came past the halfway house – halfway, that is, between Voe and Lerwick, and one of the few places with drink in the times of prohibition – past Sandwater and Girlsta Loch, and into the green pastures of Tingwall. Above the hill, the five Burradale turbines whirled.

'Maman,' I said.

Gavin nodded.

I could understand why Maman had phoned Caleb, to tell him, to warn him, but I was on Gavin's side now. We didn't know whether his knowledge was from her, or for a darker reason, and there would be no chance for further questions, because there would be a rehearsal with the new singers, the performance, and then they'd all be on the boat.

'Are you sure it's safe to let them go? I know you'll be watching, but even so –'

His left hand spread upwards from the wheel. 'We've no reason to detain them. We know where they're going, we've had no lab report to say Kamilla's death was any more than a severe reaction, or Adrien's not suicide. He was known to possess poison. I was hoping to hear by now, but because of the storm, the boats didn't sail, so Kamilla's body will only arrive in Aberdeen tomorrow morning.'

I grimaced. 'She's travelling with them?'

'In an unmarked white van. Don't mention it.'

We came around the last bend, climbed the hill and came into Lerwick. This was the industrial end: two garages; the brown bulk of the power station; the industrial estate; the mustard-coloured block of the

Shetland Hotel opposite the curved red roof of the ferry terminal; and the grey walkway leading to the ferry. It was navy below, white above, with a huge shades-of-blue Viking pointing onwards painted on each side. Past that was the Co-op, a roundabout, then the town proper: a line of fishermen's houses, many still with their net sheds behind, then the first of the Victorian houses on our right, and fifties council ones on our left. Behind them we caught a glimpse of the high brown wings of the new museum, shaped like the sails of the old herring boats.

'Left here,' I reminded Gavin, and he turned at the mini-roundabout, turned again, and parked in Mareel's car park.

There had been huge opposition to it, Inga had told me, at the planning stage. A modern cinema and arts venue, whatever next? It was a waste of money, the critics had screamed. 'Never been to a cinema in me life,' boasted one councillor. Week after week, people had written in to the paper, objecting that nobody would use it, the council would have to bale Shetland Arts out, it would be a white elephant ... Shetland Arts dug their heels in and kept going. Gradually, the structure rose, to more criticism: an 'eyesore' L-shaped glass and wood structure, flat-roofed, sited on the edge of the harbour, 'spoiling the bonny view'. From this side, it was one huge window, showing the foyer to the left, the stair to to upper floor, hung with posters, the white upper corridor and door to the upstairs bar.

'Bankrupt within a month,' the council critics had said, but the Shetland folk ignored them. Audience numbers for the first year had been treble Shetland Arts' most optimistic estimates, and every time Reidar and I had gone to the movies, the foyer and café had been busy with folk: groups of teenagers; families; older people. It had silver screenings and toddler days, art movies and the latest blockbusters, private hirings and worldwide live streamings of ballet and theatre. The huge auditorium hosted choral concerts, visiting writers, jazz artistes, fiddle music, country, rock, and now opera. Maman's face stared out at me from above the stair, twice my height.

We went through the revolving door, Gavin's hand on my back, and into the popcorn-smelling foyer. The stair to the cinema entrances went up to our right; the auditorium door was straight ahead. We eased it open. The singers were all on stage, with, among them,the older man who'd talked to me at Belmont, and a pre-Raphaelite redhead that I took to be Gabriella. I closed the door again.

'In full rehearsal. Lunch?'

We headed for the café, ordered a cheese toastie each and sat down. From here we were looking straight out at the water, towards the little harbour that fronted the Museum, Hay's Dock. Hay and Company had been the main merchants in Shetland for many years, with a finger in every pie: building boats; shipping supplies; fitting out men for the Greenland whaling. The boat sheds were still in use, as part of the museum, and come the summer there would be half a dozen double-ended Shetland sixareens lying on the shingle beach. Now, in winter, only the two larger boats floated by the stone jetty, the historic fishing boats *Pilot Us* and *Nil Desperandum*, and the slip that led from the sheds to the water was green with algae. Five white buoys bobbed gently; the dark head of a seal rose and sank again, until just the tip of its nose was visible.

'Bonny view,' Gavin said.

The tide was almost completely out, and a narrow curve of stony beach showed below the café. Beyond the harbour, the sea was still churned white, with long breakers rolling upwards through the north-south sound between Lerwick and its sheltering island of Bressay. The ferry passengers would feel the movement the minute their boat cleared the jetty. I hoped Maman had her Stugeron to hand. Dad was a good traveller. I leaned back and gave a long sigh, but it didn't dispel the tension I felt building within me. Fournier, Per, Bryony, Caleb. We knew about Caleb now; I cleared him away from the puzzle. Were Kamilla's and Adrien's deaths linked to the Viking treasure, then? I tried to think that one through. Suppose Kamilla's death had been an accident. We hadn't known, that night, that she was already dead. Suppose Adrien had gone out into the dark, headed for Vinstrick Ness, with his GPS marker to guide him, to get the treasure he thought would win her back, and stumbled on Peter and Fournier, digging up the necklace he'd found.

I stuck there. They talked him round ... persuading him that she was going to live – then a day later, Fournier poisoned the water bottle by Adrien's bed. I shook my head.

'What don't you believe?' Gavin's grey eyes smiled at me, and I realised that part of my wound-up feeling was the tension underlying this surface worry. Last night had been good between us, we could work, and we had tonight too, except that I was just about to go back to my real life. With the white waves rolling past not a hundred yards away, and the horizon hazy in the distance, I could feel the sea calling me. The day after tomorrow, if the forecast held, I'd be out there, on my way to Norway, and after that I'd be on the great ocean, with nothing but waves and sky, the creaking of the rig, the wheel kicking under my hands, the ship moving beneath my feet.

I shook the thought away. 'That Fournier killed Adrien because he caught him and Peter digging up the treasure. He wouldn't wait until a day later. And then, if he died round about the time the suicide note was written, Fournier'd have had to stay awake half the night waiting for him to wake and drink the poison. I suppose he could have pretended he was having a bath, but those doors are heavy and practically soundproof, so he'd need to keep looking out, and Adrien would have wondered what he was up to. Charles too. And that solution assumes Kamilla's death really *was* an allergy.'

Gavin nodded. 'I don't like it either. But the same objection applies to all of them: Fournier, Rolvsson, Blake, Portland, Michel. Any of them would have to keep watch so that the note was similar to the time of death. Of all of them, it would be easiest for Michel. All he needed to do was wedge his door open and check every so often.'

I shook my head. 'I can't believe in Charles as an assassin. He's survived years of Maman.'

'What do you know about him?'

I tried to dredge up memories from when I'd lived with Maman, fourteen years ago. 'He lives just outside Poitiers. He's got a wife and two children, a boy my age and a girl a bit older, and a huge vegetable garden. He used to bring us asparagus. *Ordinary*. Not at all the sort of person to have nasty secrets.'

Gavin's face was grave. 'That's just the sort of person who'll kill to protect his ordinary life.'

'I'd rather see Fournier in some sort of skullduggery that Adrien found out about.' I stopped there, because our toasties had arrived, slabs of home-baked bread oozing with hot cheese. I cut mine into quarters and launched in.

It was quarter to three by the time we'd finished the last cheesy crumbs and sprinkling of cress, and drunk the mug of coffee that went with it. I stood up. 'I'd better see if somebody can let me into the backstage area, to wish Maman "break-a-leg".'

'I'll keep you a seat in the auditorium. Back, middle, front?'

'Oh, anywhere. End of a row.' Now I felt awkward; should I kiss him or not? He didn't look as if he was expecting it. 'See you in a minute.'

I found an attendant, and explained who I was. She let me through the pass door at the end of the corridor, beneath the stairs, and I headed straight forward, listening for voices. I was going along the far side of the auditorium, in the heart of the building, with its bare wall to my left, and other doors to my right: studio; dressing rooms; store. I came through another heavy fire door, and past the side audience fire exit, just in front of the stage. A glance in showed me a good crowd, looking expectantly forward, and there was that pre-curtain murmur of voices. The artistes' entrance must be around the other side of the stage. I went past a roll-up door, with a normal one beside it, came around the corner, and saw them all clustered at the far end of the corridor, Charles and Per in their dark suits, the others in costume: Caleb in dark blue; Bryony in grey; with Diana's moon diadem; Maman's former teacher in white,with Adrien's fair wig; Gabriella in Kamilla's scarlet; and Maman in her white robe, the gold headdress shining against her dark hair. I went up and hugged her. 'Break a leg.'

She kissed me. 'Are you watching again?'

'Of course.'

She laughed at that. 'You've seen more opera in one weekend than in the last ten years.'

'Don't worry, the culture'll soon wear off, once I'm on my tall ship.' I gave the rest of them a sketchy wave. 'Have a good one, all of you.'

'Are you going forward to watch?' Per asked. 'I'll come with you.'

We came out into a dazzle of sunlight, slanting between the houses opposite and through the glass wall of the front of the building, low enough to dodge under the stair leading up and come straight to the heavy door to the backstage area. It caught me right in the eyes. I stopped dead, turning my head away from it, and as I flinched and moved, my shadow slid away from Per, and the light struck him full in the face. He winced, and flinched away, as I had done, raising one hand against it.

Suddenly I knew what Kamilla had seen.

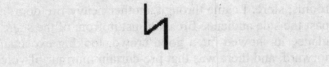

302

Chapter Twenty-three

I wasn't quick enough. Per saw the understanding in my face, and before I'd had time to step through the door to safety, he'd caught my wrist in a vicious grip and forced it up behind my back. 'Struggle or speak and I'll break your arm,' he said, in a conversational tone that frightened me more than menace would have done. I stayed still. 'Take a step backwards. Let the door close.'

I obeyed.

'Turn around.' Now I was facing down the long corridor. I scanned it quickly, wondering where he was taking me. 'Walk forwards.' His grip tightened, sending a spasm of pain up to my shoulder. 'Don't try anything.'

I walked, trying to calculate my options. There was no point in him simply putting me out of the way until the boat had left: the police would just radio the captain, and he'd be arrested the moment she docked in Aberdeen. He needed to do something more final than that. He wouldn't have a gun, why should he? He was a musical director, an early music enthusiast, not a thug. A knife seemed equally unlikely. We passed the first dressing room, the second, and stopped at the heavy corridor fire door.

'Open it. Walk through.'

I obeyed, and kept thinking. No gun, no knife, but a need to finish me off. If he had any cyanide left, he could try to make me drink it. He could find something to hit me with. One of those square stage weights would sort me out no bother. To hit me, though, to poison me, at some point he'd have to let go of my arm. I hoped he wouldn't decide to disable me at that point by breaking it anyway. I'd need two arms aboard *Sørlandet*. If he did, though, I wouldn't be able to keep quiet. I'd be bound to scream. He needed to dispose of me quietly.

We'd almost reached the door into the auditorium. I could shout for help here, but I couldn't bet on it coming quickly enough.

'Stop.'

I stopped, five metres short of the door. He was waiting for something, his breathing coming short and fast. I eyed up the door, wondering how well it was soundproofed. If I shouted and wasn't heard, I'd make matters worse. My heart was pumping uncomfortably, and his fingers gripped like a vice around my wrist. My shoulder and upper arm were racked by pins and needles.

Then my question about the soundproofing was answered, as we heard what he'd been waiting for: the applause as the singers came out onto the stage, loud as rain on a glass roof. They wouldn't hear me if I yelled.

His hand shoved me forwards. 'Walk.'

We were almost at the corner now. He turned me away from the auditorium towards the wide roll-over door that I presumed was for letting in stage scenery, or giant speakers, or an entire orchestra with their instruments. We'd come out beside Mareel, on the continuation of the road to the car park. I hoped Gavin was wondering right now why I'd not joined him. I hoped he'd come and look.

'Open the door and walk out.'

I opened the fire door just enough for me to squeeze through, and got a yank on my arm that brought tears to my eyes. He hauled the door wide with his other hand and shoved me forwards through it. The cold wind hit my face, tugged my hair, went straight through my jumper. I stumbled on the pavement, but the pressure on my arm forced me to right myself.

The street was deserted. We were around the corner from the front of the building, facing the deserted council offices and parking space, with Mareel itself between us and the people visiting the cinema and museum. Per came in close behind me and put his other hand on my shoulder, as if we were lovers going for a stroll. In front of us, as we turned, was the harbour wall, with a little gap in it where steps ran down to the waterfront walk, a three-metre wide footpath going along the water side behind Mareel to join the museum slipway and the near side of Hay's Dock. There would be people there.

'Down the steps.'

I knew then what he planned to do with me. There was no railing between us and the cold, tumbling waves. We were in Shetland, in March, and the water temperature was around six degrees. If I wasn't pounded against the dock by the waves, the cold would kill me in less than three minutes. I looked around, assessing my chances. The pressure on my arm told me how quickly he could damage it if I tried something and got it wrong.

Six steps. Five. If there had been somebody on the far side of Hay's Dock, they'd have seen us, but the tourists were on the landward side, at the museum, and the wall behind us was slanted just enough to hide us from their view. Four. Three. I'd have to risk screaming.

He was an opera director. He knew all about breathing. I was just opening my mouth to fill my lungs when he shoved me down the last step and rushed me forwards, in spite of my thrust-back feet resisting him all the way, in spite of my yell for help, my attempt to hit him with my free hand, in spite of the pain. He pushed me over the edge. I was falling, falling, turning in the air. Then I hit the water, back flat, and the waves grabbed me, sucking me away from safety, and at the same time the cold hit me. For a moment my heart stopped beating. I gasped for air and got a mouthful of greasy salt water, and the cold, the *cold* – if I didn't get ashore soon it would kill me before I could drown. My chest felt like there was an iron band around it, and the waves were pounding against the dock and falling back on me, each one pushing me further from the sea-wall. And all the time Per just stood there and watched me.

The surge of rage that went through me was like a shot of adrenalin. I was going to get out of here and see him locked up where he'd never hear early music again, where – my chilled mind thought savagely – they'd make him listen to non-stop Radio 2. I was going to survive this. I let my arms spread, my legs dangle, and waited to get to the top of the buffeting wave, so that I could see where I'd be taken, once I was free of this wall backlash. The wind had been driving northwards through the sound, and the sheltering outer arm of Hay's Dock was further out than the waterfront walk where Per had thrown me in. If the sea shoved me northwards I might reach it. I couldn't even try to swim in this, but my sea, my love, this ferocious monster that was tossing me like a heap of limp rags, chilling my bones, might put me to safety.

The cold was seeping through me. Had to think while I still could. If the waves swept me out, there was a red can and a green cone, just off the point of North Ness, and the south cardinal mark of Loofa Baa. I could cling to one of these and hope to be seen. Better, much better, if I could get to shore. First of the flooding tide came northwards.

My friend. It would sweep around the curve of the land and push me straight into the dock, where the waves were rolling up the slip, glad not to be bumping against a straight wall that doubled them back on themselves. My wet jumper was heavy, so heavy, or my arms were growing heavy, and Per was still watching. I'd already been swept far enough along that I was visible now from the paving in front of the museum. Another breath. Per wanted to be sure I was dead, but there were people in front of the museum who might see me now if I shouted or waved, and they'd get to me before he did.

I took a deep breath and prayed, then let my legs drop again, and lifted my head and one arm out of the water. 'Help, *help!*'

Lifting my arm put me under. The second shock of cold was no better than the first. But I thought, as I went under, that one of the heads had turned, in the gravel space where the funnel-speakers burbled. I used my legs to bob up to the shifting, oily surface, and yelled again.

I'd been seen. Someone gave an answering shout, and pointed. Per was already walking swiftly towards them. He must have moved the minute he saw me surface. Now he broke into a run, heading straight for the outer dock. Once he'd passed them all, he turned back to yell and gesticulate.

He was going to reach me before they did.

He was twenty metres before them. He grabbed the orange and white buoy from its hold, paused to aim and threw it, quoit fashion, his face dark with concentration. It landed five metres ahead of me, where the waves would carry it further away. Now they couldn't use it to rescue me.

The end of the stone wall of the outer dock was ten metres ahead, coming towards me fast enough to hurt, if the waves hurled me against it. It stood some three metres out of the water, a smooth curve of stone blocks, slippery green with algae, nothing that I could grip, unless I was lucky enough to snatch a trailing rope.

Tyres. The outer wall was hung with tyres.

Five metres. The next wave would bring me to it. I put my hands out, ready to catch at it and found myself being swept past, hands grabbing furiously at the slimy stone, then the next wave swung me inwards and my hands scrabbled at the tyres, and wouldn't hold. I shoved my arm down behind one of the chains that held them in place and felt the snatching waves roll by me, buffeting me, but not taking me.

Above me, Per knelt down. He leaned over, arms extended, as if he was helping me, but I knew that I had to wait here, in spite of the cold that was draining the strength from me, wait where he couldn't quite reach me, until help came. He saw that I wasn't moving, and turned, then took a step down onto the first tyre. I remembered that he'd known the name Van de Stadt. Norwegians were used to scrambling around piers.

One shove, and I'd be back in the water. My hands were no good. I forced my left leg up until I felt my foot find a tyre, at knee height, and stood on it, left arm clamped round the chain, right forearm wedged inside a tyre at shoulder height, to steady myself. They weren't car tyres, but great tractor tyres, almost half my height, and hung in neat rows. No good for someone trying to climb out. Inconsiderate. I heaved myself on my arms, shoved up with my foot, and brought the other one to join it. Now I was secure. I just had to hold on. If I was shouting for help, it would be harder for Per to pretend he was trying to rescue me. I took a lungful of damp salty air and yelled: 'Help, help!'

Per came down one tyre more, and aimed a kick at the side of my head. It missed, but he tried again, and the second one landed. I was too cold for it to hurt much, but I saw stars for a moment. I yelled again. Then he stamped on the arm I'd hooked over the upper chain. I felt a searing pain in my elbow, but I was too tightly tangled to let go. He bent down and began hauling my arm up, and dammit, I was going to be pushed off, I was too cold to fight properly … then there were running feet, and a shout in German, blessedly close.

The hand that was unhooking my arm let go. Per turned, and called, 'She fell in. I can't get her up, she's too heavy.'

A pair of legs swung over the wall, climbing confidently down the tyres. A scarlet sailor's jacket. A dark head turned towards me. 'Hang on. I will come down to you.'

Above me, a head appeared over the top of the dock wall, another, and friendly hands stretched down to me, to Per, pulling him back up, encouraging me upwards. I was going to make it. I wedged my foot in the next row of chains and thrust upwards. The dark-headed German reached down towards me, but my hand couldn't grasp his. He took a firm hold of my wrist and put his arm around my waist, stopping me from falling backwards. I was safe now. Water streamed from me as I rose. I managed to hook my other foot in a chain too, straddling the tyre. Weight on the right foot, bring the left one up, fumbling for the slippery top of the tyre, moving it until I felt it grip level, the German's arm like a bar behind me all the way. Nearly there. He echoed my thought: 'Nearly there. A last effort.'

I gathered my muscles and pushed upwards. Now my chest was level with the walkway, and there were hands grabbing my upper arms from above. My other foot found the tyre top, slithering for a hold, finding it, pushing too. A last shove, and I was swinging clear of the tyres, and rolling over onto the hard stone, blessedly firm under me, with the great grey waves rolling past three metres below.

ᚻ

They hadn't seen anything, of course; just Per running to rescue me. I stumbled along the dock with Per on one side, the German on the other, his scarlet sailing jacket draped round my shoulders. My teeth were chattering now, and the scars on my back where I'd been shot three months ago were hurting. One hand was red with blood, the other blue with cold. I couldn't feel my feet.

'Hypothermia,' Per said. 'We should call an ambulance.'

I shook my head. 'Mareel. Dry clothes.' I looked at the German. 'My boyfriend's there. Clothes in the car.'

It seemed to take an hour to get there. The wind sawed through my wet trousers like glass through rope, and the arriving museum visitors who hadn't seen the drama looked curiously as we passed. We reached the blank brown end of Mareel at last, and stumbled past it to the door. I saw through the glass that Gavin had got the search underway. He was in the middle of the foyer, while black-clad attendants scurried about him. He looked up, saw me there as I saw myself in my reflection, white-faced and dripping, with my hair in crooked rat's tails around my face, and came hurrying forward. The German supported me through the revolving door, with Per in the section behind us. I was so tired I could hardly walk. I made it to Gavin and stood there in front of him, swaying, and holding out my hands to fend off his hug. 'I'm soaking.'

Faintly, through the muffling door, Maman's voice rose up.

'She fell in,' Per said swiftly, from behind me. 'She was feeling faint, and I took her out for some air, then she swayed and overbalanced, and went straight into the sea. I thought for a moment – but she had a lucky escape.' He smiled at Gavin, man to man. 'She is a tough one, your lady.'

'Pushed,' I said, through chattering teeth. Per stepped back from me, as if he was startled, his mouth opening to protest. Gavin's face gave nothing away, but I knew he'd heard. 'I need to get out of these clothes.' The cold was running through me in long shudders. I'd sort Per out later. Already it was all making sense, click, click, in my head. 'Bag. Still in the car.'

A flicker of calculation crossed Per's face, as if he was considering making a run for it should Gavin go himself, then smoothed away again. On an island, there was nowhere to run to. Gavin had seen it too; he gave him a sharp glance, then fished the key from his sporran and gave it to one of the assistants. 'Could you get it, please? The red car, over there, third row, in the middle.A navy rucksack in the back seat.' He put his hand on my shoulder, and gave me a push in the direction of the toilets. 'Go and get your wet clothes off.'

I headed towards the Ladies, turning my head for a quick look just before I went in. He was gesturing Per and the German before him to the café.

I was only half undressed when the assistant came with my bag. I towelled myself briskly all over, and hauled on new clothes, blessedly warm. I had a few interesting bruises, including a beauty on my temple. There was a graze on my hand, and my elbow still hurt where Per had stamped on it, but on the whole I thought I'd come off pretty well, considering. I must have been very close to my time limit in the sea. I gave my dripping hair a hot rinse, towelled it, gave it a good brush, and headed out to see what Per was saying.

A police car was parked outside, and two uniformed officers were waiting in the foyer. I slipped into the café and saw an older woman officer listening with interest as Per leaned forward towards her. They were talking softly, so I couldn't hear what he was saying, but he was using his long, expressive hands to emphasise some point. He turned to the window, and gestured towards the dock wall. Past him, Gavin sat back; this wasn't his case.

Per was the first to leap to his feet as I came in. 'Cassandre! You had a lucky escape. I am so glad I was there.'

'You pushed me in,' I said. I turned to the other officer. 'He frogmarched me out of the building by pushing one arm behind my back, and down the steps, and shoved me in.'

'You felt faint,' Per said. 'Do you not remember? You came backstage to say good luck to your mother, and then you became faint. I opened up the stage scenery door to let you have some air, and you staggered forward, and stumbled down the steps. I was trying to catch you.' He gave me an intense, sympathetic look that reduced me to a fanciful teenager. 'Then I ran to the dock to throw you a lifebelt, and help you out of the water.'

'You've had a knock on the head, Ms Lynch,' the officer said. Her eyes scanned the new bruise. 'Are you sure you're remembering correctly?'

Would I swear to it in court, she meant. 'Positive. He

pushed me in from the back of Mareel, and then he ran round to try and push me back in as I climbed up the side of the dock.' I put a hand up to my face. 'He kicked me on the head.'

'The other people there,' Per said, 'saw me running to help. They saw I'd climbed down to help pull you up. You said nothing to them of me having pushed you.' He gestured to the German, sitting silently, waiting. 'This gentleman was first on the scene. He will bear out what I say.'

'I could not see what you were doing once you climbed over the side of the dock,' the German said. 'But I heard the lady call for help again while you were there with her. Twice, she called. I did not see her go in the water, I only noticed her when she waved and shouted.' He took his scarlet jacket back from me and added, very gently, 'That is why I waited here to speak. Before that you were standing and watching. You only began to run when she shouted the second time, and people heard.'

'Of course, Per said smoothly, 'it is not easy for an onlooker to see what is really happening.' He turned to the senior officer, hands spread. 'I should perhaps not say this, but Cassandre's mother has had many difficulties with her. I am a musical director of good repute, of international reputation, I am proud to say. I think my word would be accepted.'

'You haven't asked me,' I said, gently, 'why you would want to push me in.'

'I did not ask because I did not do it.'

'I realised,' I said to Gavin, 'what Kamilla saw in the kitchen, when the sun dazzled her.'

Per sat back with a dismissive swirl of one hand. 'She saw a letter. What it was, why it should have upset her, I do not know.'

313

I looked straight at him. 'She saw,' I said, 'the face that she had almost forgotten, from twelve years ago. The man who'd come round the corner in his car, and found the sun right in his face. You told us about it, over dinner yesterday. We should have noticed then.' I turned to Gavin. 'He told us from the point of view of the driver, do you remember?' I tried to quote his exact words. 'He spoke about the houses almost touching each other above the road. *Coming into them would have been like a tunnel to the driver*, he said. Then *he came around the bend at the end of the houses and out into the sun, shining straight into his eyes*. Kamilla saw the man who'd killed her brother, just as she'd seen him then, tipping his head away from the sun. She remembered.'

Blud shared wi' my blud, bane o' me bane,
Son o' me faider, uncle tae me son.

…**my brother**.

314

Sunday, 29th March. Palm Sunday (continued)

Tide Times at Mid Yell, BST and at Lerwick
High Water	06.59, 1.8m;	07.20,1.6m
Low Water	13.31, 1.0m;	14.06,0.8m
High Water	19.55, 1.7m;	20.18,1.6m
Low Water	02.00, 1.2m;	02.23,0.9m

Sunrise	06.41
Moonrise	12.05
Sunset	19.36
Moonset	03.36

Waxing quarter moon

I'll come unbidden, and stay as I please,
I'll chain dee in misery, drag dee in mire,
Or make dee dat blyde at du'll walk i da air,
For me du'll clim mountains, or walk into fire ...

Chapter Twenty-four

We spent the rest of the afternoon in the police station, making statements. I was worried I'd miss the end of Maman's concert, but a squad car drove us back, just in time to see the last of the audience filing out, with that excited buzz of talk after a good show. Ten minutes, to let them disperse, then the singers joined us: Caleb first; Bryony, the substitute Hippolytus; and, vying to be last, the substitute Phaedra and Maman. Naturally, Maman achieved the final entrance, timing it to get the doorway to herself.

Dad went up and kissed her. 'Another triumph, Eugénie.'

She waved the compliment away, pleased. 'They were a good audience. Did you enjoy it, Cassandre?' Her eyes went round the foyer. 'Where is Per? We would need to eat quickly, those who want to, then go on the ferry.'

I exchanged a 'Will you tell her, or will I?' glance with Gavin, then, when he nodded, stepped forward. 'Maman, Per's being questioned up at the station.'

She froze, her dark eyes staring at me. 'Per?'

I gestured with my hands. 'It was he who killed Kamilla and Adrien.'

She looked past me at Gavin, seeking confirmation.

He nodded.

I put an arm around her. 'Let's have a coffee in the upstairs place, and I'll tell you all about it.'

Dad took charge. He gestured the others towards the downstairs café. 'If you all go and have a coffee, I'll check up on the transport to the boat.'

Maman let herself be led through the café and upstairs, to the quiet seats on the mezzanine floor, where the chink of mugs and babble of conversation drifted up, muffled, over the balcony. 'Per?' she said again. 'But why? He didn't even know Kamilla. He'd never heard of her when I suggested her, he wasn't keen on having her.'

'He killed her brother. He was the driver who knocked him down and didn't stop. She didn't recognise him until Friday, when she saw him under the same conditions, with his face screwed up against the sun. Then she remembered.'

'It would have been the finish of his career,' Gavin said, 'to be tried and convicted of killing a child. He'd get a prison sentence, at the very least, and when he came out, people would remember.'

'He didn't want her,' Maman repeated. 'I had to persuade him she'd be good.'

'He knew who Kamilla was. He'd have looked in the papers, afterwards, hoping that the child was only injured. He'd have found out the boy's name, and the name of the sister who'd witnessed the accident. He would have known.'

But he'd been lucky; it was only the accident of the sun dazzling his face that had made her recognise him. She wouldn't have expected to find the hit-and-run driver of many years ago in the respected musical director.

'From a practical point of view,' Gavin said, 'he was

the person who could access the poison most quickly. He shared a room with Adrien. He just had to wait until Adrien went off to shower, then empty the poison from the ring into a twist of paper. Circumstantial, of course, but it would be harder for someone else to do that; they'd have to hang around the landing waiting for both Adrien and Per to be out. Charles or Caleb might have done it by wedging the door open, but Fournier would have been too obvious, when his room was on the ground floor.'

Dad came up the stairs with a tray of coffees. I clasped my hands round mine, glad of the warmth.

Maman sipped her espresso, then looked across at Gavin. 'And ... Adrien also?'

Gavin nodded.

'But *why?*' Her hands were shaking on the little cup. She took another sip, then set it down. 'He would not have thought she would tell Adrien, he knew relations between them were strained. If it was such a shock that she had to tell someone, she was more likely to confide in Bryony.'

'Our Scrabble,' Gavin said. He was joining up little incidents too. 'Don't you remember, Cass? He was messing about with the letters, and Per was standing watching him.'

I visualised the board, watching Adrien's hand with the heavy black ring, re-arranging. 'He offered me *twist*, then he began using the tiles on the board to write new words. Sing. Skewer ... *brother*. And Per, standing there watching him, thought that Kamilla had told him.'

'Again, he could most easily have poisoned Adrien's water bottle, and from them sharing a room, he'd know Adrien's habits, like when in the night Adrien drank from it, last thing, mid-night or morning, which meant he'd know when to write the suicide note. Anybody else would have had to hang around and wait. We may get prints from the laptop. His prints or gloved prints, either would be suggestive.'

'Everyone had gloves,' I objected.

'Yes, but they would be left downstairs, with the coats. You can't get your sleeves off easily with gloves on. Whereas Per was likely to have those conductor gloves – wasn't he?'

Reluctantly, Maman dipped her head downwards.

Another conversation came back into my head. 'Didn't you say you met him in Vienna?'

Maman nodded. 'An early music festival. It was in spring – I remember how pretty the tulips were. I could see at once he would be good. We did not speak properly then because he had to rush away, for an interview.' She frowned. 'In Graz, I think.'

'We are about the anniversary of her brother's death,' Maman had said. That phone call seemed a long time ago.

'Twelve years ago?' Gavin asked.

Maman nodded.

'An important interview, that he wouldn't want to be late for,' Gavin said. 'Maybe he'd started out later, or maybe he was taking longer on the road than he'd planned for. Kamilla's home address was Schrauding, a village on what used to be the Vienna-Graz road, before they finished the dual carriageway.'

'Is it too long ago?' I asked. 'Or will there still be evidence?'

Gavin nodded. 'Now we have a name, the Austrian police may be able to get evidence. They will have a description of the car, maybe flakes of paint, to compare against what car he drove twelve years ago. Still circumstantial, but if the case was put together well, it would be enough.'

'And if Per and Bryony were an item, he could have stolen the letter from Kamilla's handbag.' Poor Constable Buchanan, having to turn the bin bags out. 'He was quick-witted, Per. Making the letter sound important, when he saw I'd seen her seeing him.' Making up the stuff about me feeling faint and falling in; but my parents didn't need to know about that.

Maman shook her head, disbelieving still. I knew how she felt. You never wanted to believe that someone you knew, someone you liked, could be a murderer. Dad laid his hand on hers. 'Eugénie, I'll make a few phone calls, then come and take over Per's berth.' He looked across at Gavin. 'I take it he won't be going anywhere?'

'Not tonight,' Gavin agreed.

'Then you're going to have to choose your new tenor. Music students, wasn't it?' He put his arm around her, and gave a little shake. 'Now, girl, there are castles waiting for you, and all the critics in Edinburgh, to say nothing of the hundreds of people who've bought tickets for this tour. You're not going to let them down.'

He'd had three decades of dealing with her. She nodded, and took a sip of her coffee. A little colour returned to her cheeks; her hands were steady on the cup. Dad let her drink up, then rose, holding out his hand to pull her up. 'Let's get these people upstairs to explain to them what's happening.'

We got them to the ferry terminal at last. Like Maman, they hadn't found it easy to accept the news that Per was now in custody for attempted murder and, once the

321

forensic results came in, double murder. Caleb was inclined to be indignant, wanting to rush straight to the station with a lawyer, until Gavin took him to one side and talked evidence. Bryony went into a fit of hysterics at the idea she'd been sleeping with a murderer. I wondered, cynically, how long it would take before she realised that the papers would pay for her story.

It was ten to six now. I'd given Maman and Dad a last hug, waved them through the pale wood door onto the walkway, and waited at the window to wave again each time they appeared in the windows of the metal corridor, until they crossed the opening at the gangplank and disappeared aboard. The company straggled behind: Caleb, with Bryony clinging to his arm, Gabriella, and Charles lugging his keyboard and amplifier. Edinburgh tomorrow.

'We'd better hurry, if we're to make this Mass,' Gavin said. He smiled suddenly, and caught my hand, and we ran together down the stairs and to the car.

We made it with two minutes to spare – ample, given Father Mikhail's habit of allowing another two for latecomers. Kneeling beside Gavin in the pew, I wasn't sure what to pray for. Kamilla, of course, and Adrien, then the company, heading south with this new shock still numbing them, and Maman, who would have to lead them. Per, waiting in the grey police cell. I wondered if he would be angry or relieved that the past he'd spent so long escaping had caught up with him at last. Then the little bell rang, and Mass began: a plain one, this evening mass, with no music, and because it was Passion Sunday we moved from this present-day tragedy back two thousand years, to the older tragedy of God become Man being put to death. It was the long gospel, from St John, read like a play, with Father Mikhail reading Jesus, two parishioners taking the Narrator and the single speakers, and the congregation reading the crowd. Ever since I was little I'd felt a shiver down my spine at taking the part of those who betrayed Him, although I did it day after day, denying him with Peter, adding my failings to the weight of the cross on his shoulders. I thought about my waspishness towards Bryony, my cynicism about Adrien's dramatic grief, and was ashamed. The sky darkened, the veil of the temple was rent, and gospel ended with the quiet of the tomb.

We went to communion together, and knelt side by side afterwards, as if we were asking God's blessing on this new relationship, and suddenly everything felt right. My worry about taking him back to *Khalida* slipped away. It was my home, an extension of who I was, and if he felt at ease with me, as I did with him, he'd feel at home there too. I slipped my hand into his as we stood for the blessing, and his fingers curled round mine.

On the way out, Father Mikhail looked at us, and smiled.

We slid back into the car. Gavin checked his watch. '20.15 for the ferry. We've got twenty-five minutes in hand. Shall we get a Chinese or Indian to re-heat on board, or fish and chips to eat on the ferry?'

'Indian would be a treat, if there's time.' There was an excellent Indian takeaway at Brae, but it was slightly far to walk from the marina. 'The Raba's the same folk as at Brae, and their chicken pasanda's wonderful. Right on the north road.'

We put in our order, and waited, hands linked, fingers meshed. Gavin's tweed jacketed shoulder was warm against mine. 'When do you hope to leave?' he asked.

'Dawn on Tuesday. That'll have me coming up to the Norwegian coast after dark on Thursday, so I'll be able to see the lights and get my bearings, and arriving during Friday.'

'And *Khalida*?'

'One of the crew lives just north of Kristiansand, in Eidebukta, and his house has a pontoon where I can leave her. Ten minutes by bus from *Sørlandet*'s berth, with a ten minute walk at the end.'

'And your trips?'

'Two weekends at sea first of all, just straight out, round the oil rigs and back. A shakedown for the crew. After that we have the two fjord trips, glorious scenery, not much sailing. Are you still thinking you might make one of those?'

His lips curved. 'I've got the time off booked.'

My first rush of gladness was tempered by apprehension. A tall ship was very far from time off. 'You'll have to work, mind, stand your watch.'

He nodded. 'Climbing masts, coiling ropes, helm, safety watch, lookout. Short showers and ship's rations. Can we book into a nice hotel for a couple of nights when we get back to Kristiansand, before your next trip?'

I felt my cheeks colouring. 'Sounds good.'

'And then you have your tall ships race. Belfast, wasn't it?'

I nodded. 'We'll cruise to Belfast, race to Ålesund, cruise in company down to Kristiansand, then race to Aalborg, in Denmark. After that, back to Kristiansand, to shine her up before we become an academy.'

'Our summer holiday dates list will be up soon. Maybe I could try for a fortnight, and come from Belfast with you.'

My fingers tightened on his. 'Oh, that would be good.' I suddenly remembered that he'd have to pay for it, and made a face. 'It's fairly expensive.'

'I'll look it up and see if it can all fit in. I'd like to try being right out at sea like that.' He glanced sideways at me. 'Your habitat.'

Our meal arrived, and we returned to the car, fragrant with the smell of almonds and spices. My stomach rumbled all the way to Toft, and had to be pacified with drinking chocolate from the machine in the ferry lounge, which kept me going for the final half hour to Cullivoe.

The stars blazed above us, and the moon lit the hills with silver. *Khalida* floated high beside the pier, fender board bumping gently. Cat was sitting on guard, a shadow hump on the foredeck. I stepped aboard and reached back for the food. 'Come aboard. Hi, Cat. Sorry we've been so long.'

I made as much of a fuss of him as he'd allow, then set to work lighting the oil lamp and getting out saucepans to re-heat the food.

'I'd offer to help,' Gavin said, 'but I can see the best thing I can do is keep out of the way.'

'You could clear the forecabin,' I said. 'If you lift the sails out on deck, we can stow them in the aft locker for just now, and the storage boxes can sit in the cockpit. I've got all tomorrow to re-stow and re-provision.'

He squeezed past me, pausing for a kiss which threatened to distract us both from the tasks in hand. A blast of cold air rushed in as he lifted the forehatch. There were thumping and dragging noises as he shoved the sail bags out, and followed them with the storage boxes. 'What about the oars and boathook?'

'Them too, unless you want to sleep on them.'

'It's like camping, or playing housies on the shore.' A last clatter, then he swung out of the hatch as neatly as I'd have done myself, and leaned back to say, 'Not that I did that myself, you understand, but I had a girl cousin.' The

325

boat rocked as he humped the two sail bags aft, and came back for the boxes. He put them in the cockpit and ducked his head in. 'Cord to secure the oars and boathook?'

'At your right hand there, the blue stuff.'

He came round to clatter above my head, which gave me time to set up the prop-legged table and lay out two plates. The rice was bubbling; I went out to drain it into the sea, rather than steam up the cabin, and put the kettle on the ring where it had been. 'Ready.' I fished out knives and forks, and divided up the pasanda.

We ate in silence, just smiling at each other from time to time. The cabin had warmed up now, from the gas rings being on; with the washboards and hatch closed, *Khalida* was a little room gleaming with golden light. Over Gavin's shoulder, the forecabin looked surprisingly spacious, with the sail bags removed, and the blue and white checked plastic cushion covers stretching forward to the box. Gavin saw me looking, and twisted his head to look too. 'Plenty of room. Do you fill in the v-gap at the front?'

I nodded. 'Anders made an in-fill, so that there was room for Rat to sleep on his pillow.'

'Bedding?'

Luckily my own sheet, downie and blanket were double, generally doubled over. 'I hope we'll be warm enough.'

His grey eyes danced. 'We'll keep each other warm,' he assured me. 'After all, we survived the ice-palace.' He rose and took my plate. 'Is this kettle for washing up, or for coffee?'

'I don't want coffee this late, but go you. The dishes can sit in cold water overnight, and the rest of the kettle's for a hot water bottle.'

He pumped water on the dishes, and I reached into my

326

berth and hauled out my bedding. I had to wriggle right into the forepeak to tuck the sheet and blanket around the foot of the v-berth, then try not to dislodge it as I wriggled back.

'It's a mad little house,' Gavin said, watching me, 'yet there's a reality about it somehow. I wouldn't have felt we were really together without staying here, on board.' He smiled and put up a hand to smooth my hair. 'All I'd planned for this weekend was going through the last of the apples in the loft, and starting to spread the muck-heap on the vegetable garden ... and instead, here we are.'

I knew what he meant. 'I didn't mean to see quite so much of mad opera singers. I thought I was only in for one performance, then doing some pre-sleeping, ready for the voyage.' I filled the hot water bottle, and tucked it under the downie, impartially central. 'Can you manage with just one pillow?'

'I can manage,' Gavin said. He reached out one arm, turned the lamp down and drew me to him. His cheek was warm on my temple. 'Let's hope nobody's watching the mast.'

ᚼ

I'll come unbidden, and stay as I please,
I'll chain dee in misery, drag dee in mire,
Or make dee dat blyde at du'll walk i da air,
For me du'll clim mountains, or walk into fire,
But if I'm da right een, sic gladness du'll see;
If du'll bide in me, den I'll bide athin dee.

A note on Shetlan

Shetland has its own very distinctive language, *Shetlan* or *Shetlandic*, which derives from old Norse and old Scots. In *Death on a Longship,* Magnie's first words to Cass are, 'Cass, well, for the love of mercy. Norroway, at this season? Yea, yea, we'll find you a berth. Where are you?' Written in west-side Shetlan – each district is slightly different – it would have looked like this: 'Cass, weel, fir da love o mercy. Norroway, at dis saeson? Yea, yea, we'll fin dee a bert. Quaur is du?'

Th becomes a *d* sound in *dis* (this), *da* (the), *dee* and *du* (originally 'thee' and 'thou', now 'you'), *wh* becomes *qu* (*quaur*, where), the vowel sounds are altered (well to *weel*, season to *saeson,* find *to fin*), the verbs are slightly different (quaur is du?) and the whole looks unintelligible to most folk from outwith Shetland, and *twartree* (a few) within it too.

So, rather than writing in the way my characters would speak, I've tried to catch the rhythm and some of the distinctive usages of Shetlan while keeping it intelligible to *soothmoothers*, or people who've come in by boat through the South Mouth of Bressay Sound into Lerwick, and by extension, anyone living south of Fair Isle.

There are also many Shetlan words that my characters would naturally use, and here, to help you, are *some o dem*. No Shetland person would ever use the Scots *wee*; to them, something small would be *peerie*, or, if it was very small, *peerie mootie*. They'd *caa* sheep in a *park*, that is, herd them up in a field – *moorit* sheep, coloured black, brown, fawn.They'd take a *skiff* (a small rowing boat) out along the *banks* (cliffs) or on the *voe* (sea inlet), with the *tirricks* (Arctic terns) crying above them, and the *selkies* (seals) watching.Hungry folk are *black fanted* (because they've forgotten their *faerdie maet*, the snack that would have kept them going) and upset folk *greet* (cry). An older housewife would have her *makkin*, (knitting) *belt* buckled around her waist, and her *reestit* (smoke-dried) *mutton* hanging above the Rayburn. And finally … my favourite Shetland verb, which I didn't manage to work into this novel, but which is too good not to share: *to kettle* – as in, *Wir cat's just kettled. Four ketlings, twa strippet and twa black and quite.* I'll leave you to work that one out on your own … or, of course, you could consult Joanie Graham's *Shetland Dictionary*, if your local bookshop hasn't *just selt* their last copy *dastreen*.

The diminutive Magnie (Magnus) may also seem strange to non-Shetland ears. In a traditional country family (I can't speak for *toonie* Lerwick habits) the oldest son would often be called after his father or grandfather, and be distinguished from that father and grandfather and perhaps a cousin or two as well, by his own version of their shared name. Or, of course, by a *Peerie* in front of it, which would stick for life, like the *eart kyent* (well-known) guitarist Peerie Willie Johnson, who recently celebrated his 80th birthday. There was also a patronymic system, which meant that a Peter's four sons, Peter, Andrew, John and Matthew, would all have the surname Peterson, and so would his son Peter's children. Andrew's children, however, would have the surname Anderson, John's would be Johnson, and Matthew's would be Matthewson. The Scots ministers stamped this out in the nineteenth century, but in one district you can have a lot of *folk* with the same surname, and so they're distinguished by their house name: *Magnie o' Strom, Peter o' da Knowe.*

Glossary

For those who like to look up unfamiliar words as they go, here's a glossary of Scots and Shetlan words.

aa: all
an aa: as well
aabody: everybody
aawye: everywhere
ahint: behind
ain: own
amang: among
anyroad: anyway
ashet: large serving dish
auld: old
aye: always
bairn: child
ball (verb): throw out
banks: sea cliffs, or peatbanks, the slice of moor where peats are cast
bannock: flat triangular scone
birl, birling: paired spinning round in a dance
blinkie: torch
blootered: very drunk
blyde: pleased
boanie: pretty, good looking
breeks: trousers
brigstanes: flagged stones at the door of a crofthouse
bruck: rubbish
caa: round up
canna: can't
clarted: thickly covered
cludgie: toilet
cowp: capsize

cratur: creature

crofthouse: the long, low traditional house set in its own land

daander: to traveluncertainly or in a leisurely fashion

darrow: a hand fishing line

dastreen: yesterday evening

de-crofted: land that has been taken out of agricultural use, eg for a house site

dee: you – du is also you, depending on the grammar of the sentence – they're equivalent to thee and thou. Like French, you would only use dee or du to one friend; for several people, or an adult if you're a younger person, it would be 'you'

denner: midday meal

didna: didn't

dinna: don't

dip dee doon: sit yourself down

dis: this

doesna: doesn't

doon: down

drewie lines:a type of seaweed made of long strands

duke: duck

dukey-hole: pond for ducks

du kens: you know

dyck, dyke: a wall, generally drystane, i.e. built without cement

eart: direction, *the eart o wind*

ee now: right now

eela: fishing, generally these days a competition

everywye: everywhere

faersome: frightening

faither, usually faider: father

fanted: hungry, often black fanted, absolutely starving

folk: people

frae: from
gansey: a knitted jumper
gant: to yawn
geen: gone
girse: grass
gluff: fright
greff: the area in front of a peat bank
gret: cried
grind: gate
guid: good
guid kens: God knows
hae: have
hadna: hadn't
hairst: autumn, harvest time
harled: exterior plaster using small stones
heid: head
hoosie: little house, usually for bairns
howk: to search among e.g. I *howked* ida box o auld claes.
isna: isn't
just: just
ken, kent: know, knew
keek: peep at
kirk: church
kirkyard: graveyard
kishie: wicker basket carried on the back, supported by a *kishie baand* around the forehead
knowe: hillock
Lerook: Lerwick
lem: china
likit: liked
lintie: skylark
lipper: a cheeky or harum-scarum child, generally affectionate
mad: annoyed

mair: more

makkin belt: a knitting belt with a padded oval, perforated for holding the 'wires' or knitting needles.

mam: mum

mareel: sea phosphorescence, caused by plankton, which makes every wave break in a curl of gold sparks

meids: shore features to line up against each other to pinpoint a spot on the water

midder: mother

mind: remember

moorit: coloured brown or black, usually used of sheep

mooritoog: earwig

muckle: big – as in Muckle Roe, the big red island. Vikings were very literal in their names, and almost all Shetland names come from the Norse.

muckle biscuit: large water biscuit, for putting cheese on

myrd: a good number and variety – a *myrd* o peerie things

na: no, or more emphatically, nall

needna: needn't

Norroway: the old Shetland pronunciation of Norway

o: of

oot: out

ower: over

park: fenced field

peat: brick-like lump of dried peat earth, used as fuel

peerie: small

peerie biscuit: small sweet biscuit

Peeriebreeks: affectionate name for a small thing, person or animal

piltick: a sea fish common in Shetland waters

pinnie: apron

postie: postman

quen: when

redding up: tidying

redd up kin: get in touch with family – for example, a five-generations New Zealander might come to meet Shetland cousins still staying in the house his or her forebears had left

reestit mutton: wind-dried shanks of mutton

riggit: dressed, sometimes with the sense dressed up

roadymen: men working on the roads

roog: a pile of peats

rummle: untidy scattering

Santy: Santa Claus

scaddy man's heids:sea urchins

scattald: common grazing land

scuppered: put paid to, done for

selkie: seal, or seal person who came ashore at night, cast his/her skin and became human

Setturday: Saturday

shalder: oystercatcher

sheeksing: chatting

sho: she

shoulda: should have

shouldna: shouldn't have

SIBC: Shetland Islands Broadcasting Company, the independent radio station

skafe: squint

skerry: a rock in the sea

skoit: a good hard look

smeddum: (Scots) determination of character, a spirit not easily daunted

smoorikins: kisses

snicked: move a switch that makes a clicking noise

snyirked: made a squeaking or rattling noise

solan: gannet

somewye: somewhere

sooking up: sucking up

soothified: behaving like someone from outwith Shetland

spew: be sick

spewings: piles of sick

splatched: walked in a splashy way with wet feet, or in water

steekit mist: thick mist

sundry: apart

sun-gaits: with the sun (i.e. clockwise) – it's bad luck to go against the sun, particularlywalking around a church

swack: smart, fine

swee: to sting (of injury)

tak: take

tatties: potatoes

tay: tea, or meal eaten in the evening

thole: (Scots) to put up with

tink: think

tirricks: Arctic terns

trows: trolls

tushker: L-shaped spade for cutting peat

twa: two

twartree: a small number, several

tulley: pocket knife

unken: unknown

vexed: sorry or sympathetic "I was that vexed to hear that"

vee-lined: lined with wood planking

voe: sea inlet

voehead: the landwards end of a sea inlet

waander: wander

waar: seaweed

whatna: what

wasna: wasn't

wha's: who is

whaup: curlew

whit: what

whitteret: weasel

wi: with

wir: we've – in Shetlan grammar, 'we are' is sometimes 'we have'

wir: our

wife: woman, not necessarily married

wouldna: would not

yaird: enclosed area around or near the crofthouse

yoal: a traditional clinker-built six-oared rowing boat

For more information about **Marsali Taylor**
and other **Accent Press** titles
please visit

www.accentpress.co.uk